# JOHN CLIVE

# Broken Wings

D1189070

LIBRARY
WITHDRAWN

**PANTHER**
Granada Publishing

740.5472/R 218244

Panther Books
Granada Publishing Ltd
8 Grafton Street, London W1X 3LA

Published by Panther Books 1984

First published in Great Britain by
Granada Publishing Ltd 1983

Copyright © John Clive 1983

ISBN 0 586 05582 7

Printed and bound in Great Britain by
Collins, Glasgow

Set in Plantin

All rights reserved. No part of this publication may
be reproduced, stored in a retrieval system, or
transmitted, in any form, or by any means, electronic,
mechanical, photocopying, recording or otherwise,
without the prior permission of the publishers.

This book is sold subject to the condition that it
shall not, by way of trade or otherwise, be lent,
re-sold, hired out or otherwise circulated
without the publisher's prior consent in any
form of binding or cover other than that in
which it is published and without a similar
condition including this condition being imposed
on the subsequent purchaser.

This book is dedicated to the Wall's Ice Cream lady who pedalled her delicious three-wheeled cycle around the streets of North Finchley. My brother and I were the only kids who never had to pay.

For Mum.

Blackbird singing in the dead of night,
Take these broken wings and learn to fly.
All your life,
You were only waiting for this moment to arise.
Blackbird singing in the dead of night,
Take these sunken eyes and learn to see.
All your life,
You were only waiting for this moment to be free.
Blackbird fly . . .
Blackbird fly . . .
Into the light of a dark black night . . .

'Blackbird' by Lennon & McCartney
Copyright © Northern Songs Ltd

# Acknowledgements

I am grateful to many people for their generous and interested response and I should like to thank:
Aubrey Brabazon; Lt-Commander Niall Brunicardi; Lt-Colonel John Buchan; George Buller; Gay Byrne; Dr Coffey; Mrs Corrigan; Anthony Dillan; Agnes and Bridie Dobbyn; Ryle Dwyer; James Foley; Kitty Guiney; John Holgate (RAF); Brian and Ann Kenny; Commandant Hugh Lalor; Colonel Ferdinand E. Lee; Patrick Lehane; J. C. Masterson (RAF); William Murphy; Pat O'Donnel; Michael O'Niell; Terry O'Sullivan; James Plunkett; Sheamus Smith; Jacqueline Tyson; Arthur Voigt (Luftwaffe); Declan, Red, Niall and Mrs Whelan Snr.

And many, many more.

From September 1939, until March 1940, and as long as Germany retained military superiority on the Continent, Ireland offered Hitler a great potential for espionage.

Information from: Germany, Auswartiges Amt., Records of the German Foreign Office received by the Department of State, Washington DC (microfilm): T-120, Reel 89, frame 100408, Document of 3 October 1940.

The Führer had envisioned some kind of military role for Ireland, as the maps and plans of transportation facilities, power installations, roads and bridges discovered in Belgium indicate.

Information from: Clement R. Attlee, *As It Happened*, Heinemann, 1954.

# Prologue

# LONDON: 1940

'I know that Churchill had drawn up plans for an invasion of Southern Ireland if necessary . . .'

*Malcolm MacDonald, former Dominion Secretary, in an interview with Robert Kee for the BBC television series* Ireland: A Television History

He opened his eyes and blinked. He felt stiff, his mouth was dry. God, he'd give anything for a cup of tea right now, but the train was jammed with people and he was lucky to even have a seat. The first-class compartment was crowded, but he doubted that anybody else had a first-class ticket. Class barriers seemed to have disappeared with the exigencies of war. He glanced out of the window; the sky was becoming grey outside and the familiar red of a tube train slowly overtook them as it clicked alongside.

He felt relief. They were into the suburbs of London at last and his long journey was nearly over. He looked at his watch, six-thirty A.M. The boat-train from Holyhead had taken almost nine hours to reach London, and the crossing from Dun Laoghaire over the Irish Sea, another six. Luckily that had been without incident; the U-boats were getting bolder and inflicting heavy losses on British shipping almost everywhere. The Irish Sea was no longer a preserve of the Royal Navy. It was one of the reasons his mission had been so important.

The familiar twin towers of Wembley Stadium rose off to his left, then the train pulled slowly through the wide empty spaces of Willesden Goods Yard, and finally into the short tunnel under the bridges into Euston Station.

Mackay waited until the people in the corridor began to move, then slipped outside as quickly as he could, running past the crowds of disembarking passengers towards the exit. He was carrying only an overnight case so he was able to make swift progress, and nobody else appeared to be in a hurry. He handed his ticket to the collector at the barrier and glanced around to see if there was anyone there to meet him. No one. It wasn't surprising; it was almost impossible to know when or where a train would arrive these days.

He ran out through the colonnades at the front entrance to the cab rank. It was early and he was in luck – a solitary cab pulled up beside him and the cabbie leaned out to take his case. Mackay shook his head.

'It's all right. I'll hold on to it.'

The driver slid his side window shut and waited for him to get into his seat. He slipped the gear into first and pulled away, half-turning his head towards him.

'Where to, sir?'

'Downing Street,' Mackay said. 'Be as quick as you can.'

The cabbie glanced in his mirror, staring at Mackay curiously.

'You in the Government, sir?'

'Sort of,' Mackay replied. He didn't want to be drawn into a debate on the war effort. He could smell burning. It was acrid, stale and familiar. He knew there had been more raids the night before. The driver had turned left out of Euston instead of heading directly south. Mackay guessed it was a deliberate diversion.

'Was it bad last night?'

The driver turned into Grays Inn Road.

'Yeah, pretty bad. They got the West End for a change. I hear one of the theatres copped it.'

Mackay didn't ask which one; he preferred not to know. The driver made his way down past the Clerkenwell Road and turned right at Holborn. The smell of burning was

12

stronger here and Mackay could see the blackened windows and hollowed buildings still smouldering from the raid.

The taxi slowed down and Mackay heard the driver swear. He leaned forward and peered out over his shoulder. There was a huge crater in the middle of the road and, sticking up from it, the red remains of a London bus. The front was crumpled in, resting at the base of the bomb crater, and his driver swore again.

'Poor sod – no way he was going to see that in the blackout. Probably never even knew what hit him.'

Mackay stared at it as they crawled carefully by. It was incredible, a bizarre, tragic sight, and somehow deeply depressing even to someone who had lived in London since the blitz began. The familiar, secure double-decker bus had been tossed aside and crumpled like a children's toy. It was horrible and curiously upsetting. It pulled the rug from beneath one's feet, and for a moment Mackay could almost see, in his mind's eye, the arrogant goose-stepping soldiers of the *Wehrmacht* marching down the London street; then they were into Kingsway, which was relatively unscathed, and the moment passed.

They drove down the Strand, through Trafalgar Square. Sandbags seemed to be everywhere, piled up around doorways, windows crisscrossed with tape against the blast. The cabbie half-turned in his seat again. 'Whereabouts in Downing Street, sir?'

'Number Ten,' Mackay said. He could see the disbelief in the stillness of the cabbie's reaction.

'You going to see Churchill, sir?'

'I hope so,' Mackay said.

'Jesus Christ,' the driver muttered under his breath.

Mackay pulled a pound out of his pocket.

'No, not quite as high as that,' he replied.

The taxi turned right off Whitehall into Downing Street and pulled up in front of the solitary policeman standing by the front door. Mackay stepped out and offered the cabbie the note. The driver shook his head.

'No, you keep it, sir, just tell him to get on with it and see those bastards off, all right?'

Mackay nodded. 'I'll pass it on. Look out for holes in the road. It's hard to get a good cabbie these days.'

The driver grinned and did a smart U-turn out of the street. Mackay watched him turn into the traffic of Whitehall and disappear, then he faced the door of Number Ten and squared his shoulders.

'You look tired, Mackay, sit down. Would you like a brandy?'

Mackay nodded gratefully and sank into the leather chair.

'I came straight here from the station as you asked me to, Prime Minister. It was an uncomfortable journey, but uneventful.'

Churchill was slumped in his huge chair behind the desk, but he was still a formidable figure. Mackay was not the first to feel as though he were sitting next to a volcano that could erupt at any moment. A personal aide appeared beside Mackay and proffered the brandy. Churchill grunted and Mackay had a feeling he would have liked a snifter himself.

'You don't want anything in that, do you, Mackay?'

He shook his head. He wouldn't have dared admit it even if he had.

Churchill dismissed the aide with a peremptory wave of his hand. 'Pity to spoil a good brandy.'

Mackay sipped it; it was good. Churchill waited for him to swallow, then broached the subject.

'How did our Irish friends respond to our proposals?'

Mackay thought he detected a faint irony in the question, but he ignored it. 'Well, I don't think there is any doubt, Prime Minister, that De Valera and his Ministers trusted our sincerity regarding the proposals . . .'

14

Churchill cut him short. 'But they rejected them,' he said flatly.

Mackay nodded. 'I'm afraid so, Prime Minister. De Valera listened carefully to the points I raised regarding the necessity of an Irish participation – even on a limited basis – in the war against Hitler but in the end he would have none of it.'

Churchill considered this for a moment. 'What were our final proposals regarding Irish unity?'

Mackay took another sip of the brandy. 'I put it to him directly that we, that is, the British Government, would issue a statement that would indicate the firm belief that a United Ireland would soon be in existence. I made that as clear as possible.'

Churchill stirred for the first time, reaching for the cigar box. 'And you think he accepted that we were quite sincere on this?'

'Absolutely, Prime Minister. The proposals foundered on their suspicions about the Northern Ireland reaction.'

Churchill rolled the Havana delicately, then removed the end before lighting up. 'How did he react to the proposals for a Joint Committee to work out the Constitution for a United Ireland?'

The aroma from the cigar was delicious, and Mackay tried not to look disappointed at not being offered one.

'That was the nub of it, sir. De Valera was convinced that the Northern Ireland Ministers would never reach any agreement on the Constitution and that the whole thing would break down.'

Churchill sat back in his chair and blew some smoke at the ceiling. 'He's probably quite right. I don't suppose their attitudes have changed since Carson's time.'

Mackay made no comment, but sipped gratefully at the brandy. He felt tired, and the warmth of the room was making him sleepy. A silence fell between the two men and

15

faintly through the window Mackay heard the traffic in Whitehall. He remembered the taxi driver and the bus sticking up from the bomb crater in the road. He heard Churchill speak, and focused his attention upon him.

'You realize how vulnerable that makes our convoys? Any shipping using the Western Approaches . . .' He slammed his fist hard down on the desk. 'Damn it, Mackay, we need those ports in Southern Ireland.' He stared balefully at Mackay. 'You were Dominion Secretary in thirty-eight. Why did Chamberlain give up the Garrison Rights to the ports? If we had them now, we wouldn't need Irish participation in the war.'

Mackay shifted uneasily. He thought Churchill knew the answer anyway. He was being tested.

'I recommended it to the Cabinet, Prime Minister.'

Churchill blew out a cloud of smoke and Mackay could not see his reaction. He gritted his teeth and ploughed on.

'It seemed to me at the time, that if we retained those Garrison Rights for Cork and other strategic sites, and if war between us and Germany did break out and we made use of those rights from a neutral Ireland, then Irish public opinion would blow up against us and they would ally themselves with Germany. This in turn would give Hitler the perfect excuse to invade Ireland in order to free the ports. This view was also taken by the Chiefs of Staff,' he added.

Churchill grunted, but made no comment. He didn't have to, his silence was disapproval enough. He leaned forward in his chair and took a sheet of paper from the file in front of him, scanning it briefly before placing it face down on the desk in front of him.

'I get these figures every month, Mackay. They are the tonnage losses of our Merchant Fleet, mainly from attacks by U-boats. They've never been higher. They're taking a

16

terrible beating, and the loss of life . . .' He stopped and shook his head, unable to continue.

Mackay felt uncomfortable, yet deeply sympathetic. For a moment the mask had slipped, and he had glimpsed inside, seen the burden of ultimate responsibility.

'We still have Northern Ireland, sir. Belfast can offer some protection for any shipping out of Liverpool.'

Churchill glanced at him from beneath his heavy eyebrows. 'Yes,' he said softly. 'Yes, we still have Northern Ireland, thank God.' He shook his head irritably. 'You did point out to them that all their imports from us come via those convoys from America. How do I explain to my seamen that it's all right for them to lose their lives bringing vital supplies in, some of which ultimately go to Ireland, but it's not all right for them to seek protection in her ports.'

Mackay didn't answer. He knew the question was rhetorical. He felt enormous understanding for this man who was now wrestling with a decision that would have far-reaching effects on Ireland's future. Like most people in Britain he found the answer to the Irish question impossible to determine. He could not understand what he saw as their intransigence. He became aware that Churchill was staring at him.

'When did you last talk with the Chiefs of Staff, Mackay?'

'Shortly before I left for Dublin, Prime Minister.'

'They were fully aware of these proposals?'

'Yes, Prime Minister. Further, they pressed me to seek Irish participation as strongly as I could.'

Churchill nodded. 'Yes, the Admiralty have been pressing me hard, too.'

Mackay sensed the irony. Churchill himself had done more than his fair share of pressing when he had been First Secretary to the Admiralty.

Churchill straightened himself up in his chair. 'Well,

17

Mackay, thank you for your efforts. I know that if anybody could have changed their minds, it was you. Would you like another brandy before you go?'

He'd passed the test. Without comment the matter had been opened and closed. Mackay shook his head and stood up.

'No thank you, Prime Minister. Is there anything else you would like me to do? I feel that I have a good relationship with Mr De Valera. Perhaps there is some inducement . . .?'

Churchill raised himself slowly from his chair and walked around his desk towards him. 'If a United Ireland could not persuade him, Mackay, nothing will. I fear I have to make other plans for Mr De Valera. We may be forced to close quarters over those damned ports – I am not prepared to sacrifice my seamen unnecessarily.'

He walked with Mackay to the door. 'Have you got transport?'

Mackay shook his head. 'No, but I can get a cab.'

'Nonsense, I'll get something laid on. Taxis are not for you.'

Mackay smiled to himself and decided not to pass on his cabbie's message. There'd be a better time, a better place.

## BOOK ONE
# Beginnings

# HARRISON

The pines rose ghostly around him, like dripping sentinels materializing through the mist shrouding the forest. The horse made no sound on the soft matting of coarse grass. Harrison felt suspended, floating between the trees, but he ducked instinctively beneath the branches when he had to. They were hard and real and would sweep him from the saddle however unearthly they appeared to be. Harrison pulled the wide-brimmed hat down over his face and tightened the oilskin round his neck. The moisture had an uncanny knack of finding the gap and trickling down under his chin, then inside the neckband of his shirt. The weather had been cold and wet ever since he left the cabin early yesterday morning, and the night in the open miserable. Although he was used to sleeping out it didn't get any easier. He'd known the weather was closing in, but he'd left anyway, there was nothing to keep him any longer. He'd made his arrangements, the livestock had gone and the place already seemed deserted and lifeless, full of ghosts and memories. He'd been glad to get away.

His horse padded silently on, sliding between the trees, making his way slowly down the gradient. The mountains were behind them now; already they were on the lower slopes and soon they'd reach the valley floor. He'd miss his horse, he was quick and intuitive and learnt fast. They had a good working relationship, but he'd broken him in from the wild and the animal would return to it just as quickly. He patted the back of his neck with his gloved hand. The steam rose gently from his mane and flanks, mingling almost immediately into the mist. The trees disappeared and the horse stopped, waiting for him to decide. They'd reached the edge of the treeline and the valley bottomed out somewhere beneath him, still swathed in foggy tendrils, seething now like a river as the morning breeze caught the upper layers. It was beginning to clear above him. He could see patches of blue sky and the diffused glow of the sun through the vapour. He prodded the flank of his horse and they moved off down the slope into the deeper layers of mist shrouding the valley, continuing their descent.

He heard a deep throaty growl getting closer. It seemed to envelop him, distorted by the conditions, coming at him from all sides. The horse pricked up his ears, his head high, curious, not recognizing the unfamiliar sound of a truck engine. It roared below them on the unseen road, the tyres swishing on the wet macadam. Slowly the sound receded up the valley and silence wrapped itself protectively around them once again. He rode on for some distance, straining his eyes, peering at the ground ahead of them, trying to see the road. His horse stopped, lifting his head again, scenting something unfamiliar. The rider caught a whiff of it too. He recognized it. Exhaust fumes. He dismounted and led the horse forward until he reached the hard shoulder of the road crossing his path from left to right.

Now he could see it, gleaming wetly, the white line down the centre disappearing into the mist. He stood there for a moment listening, but it was deserted, empty. Little or no traffic this early in the day. He glanced at his wrist watch, it was nearly time, though it would probably be late because of the weather. He led the horse back from the road a short distance and began to unbuckle the cinch on the saddle. His horse turned and peered at him, surprised by this unusual break in their routine. He pulled the saddle free, dumping it on the ground, then grabbed some clumps of the rough grass

22

and began to brush the steaming flanks of the animal. Carefully he wiped away the sweat, talking to him all the time. He continued to work on him until his coat was gleaming.

The sun had broken through to the valley floor now and he could see the road winding back down between the high wooded slopes that gradually merged into the mountains he'd crossed the day before. Something glinted in the distance, reflecting the sun. He shaded his eyes, gazing down the road and the line of telegraph poles to the speck drawing closer. It was coming. He turned back towards his horse and began to remove the bridle and bit from his mouth. He talked to him, his voice quiet, reassuring. The horse nuzzled the man, sensing the sadness in the man's voice, aware somehow of its significance.

The man could hear the engine now; he knew the time had come. He stood back from the animal and pointed towards the mountains. 'Go . . .' The horse stood frozen for a moment, disbelieving the command. The man took off his hat and thwacked it across his hindquarters, repeating the instruction. The horse, startled, turned and galloped off towards the hills leading back up towards the treeline. The man watched him racing away, effortlessly covering the ground and the incline, swiftly receding from him. Gradually he became aware of the increasing whine of the Dodge engine as the Greyhound bus pulled up the gradient towards him. He turned and waved his hat, signalling the driver, then he clamped it back on to his head and picked up the heavy saddle.

The Greyhound drew up alongside him and the hydraulic doors wheezed open, letting out a burst of warm, humid air. The man hoisted the saddle up on to his shoulder and stepped up inside the bus. He turned and looked back through the open door. His horse was standing on a high promontory close to the trees, watching him, still and intent. The man made no move to sit down. He seemed cut off, distant, his eyes clouded.

The driver gestured slightly with annoyance and decided to wait no longer. He pulled the lever, the doors hissed shut, cutting off the man from the horse, and slowly the bus moved away, picking up speed. By the time Harrison reached an empty seat and sat down, the horse had gone.

# PILOT OFFICER BRYCE

The sun was suddenly quite hot on his back. He took off his cap, he could feel the sweat around the leather band inside it, and threw it on to the passenger seat beside him. The narrow country lane dropped away down a hill and he was enveloped in the early morning mist clouding the hollow; it was cold and clammy again in the open-topped MG. He shoved the stubby little lever quickly down through the gears and peered through the narrow windscreen, switching on the wipers. Vaguely he could discern the outline of the high banks bordering the lane, then the red bonnet went up, and as he crested the hill bright sunlight poured over him once more.

Bryce rubbed his eyes. He felt tired, tense. Unappreciative of the rolling Shropshire countryside, too tired to even catch the smell of woodsmoke and dead leaves being burnt overnight. He switched off the wipers and was glad of the slipstream blowing around him, it helped him stay awake, forget the day that faced him. He worked through the gears again, trying to build up some speed, but it was almost impossible in the winding, empty lane. The engine revs changed constantly, the road undulating in front of him,

24

emphasized by the low seat and small windscreen, almost like that of a cockpit. His eyes focused on the tiny, rounded crest on the radiator. He could see through it like a gunsight.

The fighter floated across. Two hairlines, bisecting within the circle, locked on to it. Instinctively he pressed the firing button, keeping it jammed on tight as the eight machine-guns tore raggedly at the forward wing edges, arcing down in front of him. But his prey had gone, there was nothing. The windscreen suddenly shattered, flames engulfed his gloved hands clenching the steering column. He could feel them burning, the leather gloves slowly peeling back, revealing the burnt, blackened flesh beneath. He screamed soundlessly into the roar of the engine, his lips drawn back, teeth bared.

A black shadow flashed across his eyeline and Bryce turned in the driving seat, staring back over his shoulder, terrified. He could see the fighter descending towards him, poised, ready. He slammed his foot on to the brake and the car slithered away from him and stopped in a cloud of dust. He leapt from the seat, running across the road and into a cornfield. The grain was high, almost ready for harvest. It snatched at him, wrapping itself around his legs, slowing him down. He plunged face down to the ground, scrabbling at it with his fingers, trying to bury himself within it. He could still hear the aircraft above him, swooping down, the engine note intensifying as it dived upon him. He covered his ears with his hands, trying to blot it out. But he couldn't . . . it got louder, filling his head, splitting it in two. He turned over on to his back, his arms flung out, eyes clenched shut and screamed for his father . . . his screams unheard.

The Spitfire banked slowly away from the figure lying spreadeagled in the cornfield. Simmonds circled two or three times, but Bryce didn't move. The fighter gained some altitude, then pulled away. Gradually the sound of the engine diminished, then faded altogether. The field was silent, just the sound of the insects and the wind brushing the tops of the corn, like waves on a golden sea ...

# COLONEL BRYCE

The long corridor echoed to the sound of military feet pounding the bare floorboards. Shafts of sunlight speckled with dust slanted down through the high windows. It was hot for late September.

Colonel Bryce, a tall erect man, walked purposefully down the corridor, those in his way falling automatically to one side. Occasionally he would bark out a curt 'good morning' to those with enough courage to greet him.

His assistant, Corporal Watson, recognized his step in the corridor and interrupted the young pilot. 'Hold on will you, I think I can hear him coming now.' She transferred the telephone into her other hand and covered the mouthpiece. Colonel Bryce came in through the door. He glanced at her and noticed her worried expression.

'What is it, Corporal Watson?'

'A Pilot Officer Simmonds. He says he wants to talk to you. It's about your son.'

Colonel Bryce had been in the army a long time. He didn't allow the gnawing anxiety he felt to show, not for an instant.

'All right, Corporal, put it through to my room. I'll take it there.'

He glanced at her jacket hanging over the back of the chair. 'And if you are too warm, open a window. You're improperly dressed, Corporal Watson.'

Diana Watson felt no resentment. She liked working for

the Colonel. He was not a man to take liberties with, but the work at MI9 was interesting, and the Colonel had, once you got to know him, a marvellously dry sense of humour. She hoped his son was all right. 'Putting you through now, sir,' she said into the phone.

Colonel Bryce closed the door quietly behind him and moved quickly across to his desk. He resisted the desire to snatch up the phone and sat down, composing himself for a second before picking up the receiver.

'Hello,' he announced. 'This is Colonel Bryce.'

Simmonds let go of the pencil dangling by a piece of string from the notice board in front of him and faced into the wall, trying to preserve some privacy in the busy corridor next to the officers' mess.

'Hello, sir, it's Pilot Officer Simmonds. I'm a friend of your son.'

'Yes, Simmonds,' Bryce replied, neither friendly nor unfriendly.

'I was up early today, sir, we had a bit of a scare, but it was nothing. Peter wasn't here, he had a forty-eight hour pass.'

Bryce stared out of the window. 'Yes, I know. He was in London I believe.'

'That's right, sir.' Simmonds rushed on, anxious to get to the point.

Colonel Bryce listened carefully whilst Simmonds explained what had happened and his concern for his friend. He waited, not interrupting, until he had completely finished. 'Thank you for calling, Simmonds, but there is nothing I can, or will, do to relieve my son of his duties. If he is ill or unfit in any way he must report this to his MO. However, I thank you for your concern.' He put the receiver down gently before Simmonds could protest, and sat quietly in his chair for a moment, then stood up and walked over to the big bay windows of the country house MI9 occupied at the moment.

This had once been a very elegant drawing-room, and outside he could see one or two cars painted in field grey, standing in the driveway. The lawn was green and still immaculate. It reminded him of home and the games he had played with his son when he had been on leave. It did not seem so long ago. God, it was only ten years, and now Peter was playing a different game, a deadly one, high up there in that blue, innocent sky.

He'd watched a dog-fight once. Tiny silver planes, looking like toys, twisting and turning, chattering to each other like excited school children. One of them had suddenly disintegrated, then he'd heard the faint plop of the explosion as part of a wing spiralled to earth like a sycamore seed.

He crossed the room and picked up the telephone. He pulled rank unashamedly, and eventually got through to his son. He tried not to let his relief show. 'Hello, Peter.'

Young Bryce was in flying gear and feeling the heat in the wooden building close to the dispersal point. The others were outside, lounging in deckchairs or lying on the grass asleep.

'Hello, Father, still catching spies?'

'Doing my best, but I wish you wouldn't talk like that over the phone . . .' He stopped, aware that his normal good humour had deserted him. Once again he'd got off on the wrong foot. He wanted to start again, but did not know how.

The pilot rubbed his forehead with the palm of his hand. He was sweating, tense. 'Of course, Father, I'm sorry. I'm probably surrounded by Nazi infiltrators at this moment, all busily shooting down the Luftwaffe.' He broke off. There was a silence. The older man could hear his son breathing harshly. He was shocked at how brittle and vulnerable he seemed.

'Peter?'

'Yes?'

'I want to come and see you.'

28

'No – it wouldn't be right.'

'Why not? I've got a day off tomorrow. Why don't I just come up, and when you're clear we can have a drink together somewhere . . .'

'I . . . I'd rather you didn't, Father. It might not look right; the other blokes' parents can't get away. Do you understand?'

'Nonsense. I shall be in uniform. No one's going to know who I am. I'll see you tomorrow, Peter; you can count on it.'

The pilot stared distractedly round the small room, wanting to see him, yet fearful of letting him down. 'All right, if you must. Now I have to go – someone needs the phone,' he lied.

His father started to protest, but he slammed down the phone and stared out of the window. The mechanics were swarming all over the fighters parked in the open, baking in the sun. He wondered how they didn't burn themselves on the hot metal surfaces.

His nightmare began to creep back, crawling like a tiny flame along a dry newspaper.

He heard a distant phone ring, glanced down and picked it up – the line was dead, it was somewhere else. A siren suddenly began to wail. He stared out of the window, transfixed as he saw pilots leaping from their chairs, grabbing parachutes and running for the fighters.

Simmonds poked his head through the window. 'Come on, Brycey, last one up pays for Elsie.'

Bryce began to run towards the plane . . .

The RAF Military policeman watched the army colonel emerge from the officers' mess and walk slowly towards the main gate. He could tell by the lack of spring in his step that the officer had been told. He felt sympathy, but he was curious too, from a military point of view, to see how the army colonel took it – how much it showed.

Colonel Bryce stopped by the main gate. He noted the dazzling white gaiters, the gleaming boots, and the salute snapping up like a window blind, rigid, correct. He acknowledged it.

'The cars, sergeant.'

'Sir?'

'The cars. Where do they keep their cars?'

'Go out of the main gate here, sir, bear right up the lane and you'll see them. They're *all* parked there, sir.'

'Thank you, sergeant.'

'Sir.' The salute came up smartly again, and the Colonel turned away after returning it, keeping his shoulders erect, moving slowly but firmly out of the gate and up the lane.

The military policeman watched him go. 'Poor sod,' he muttered under his breath, the hard lines of his face not altering.

The country lane was still and quiet, high banks either side topped with tangled hedgerows. 'Missing.' What did that mean? The Squadron Leader had tried to be kind. He'd arrived to see his son and he was 'missing'. It was such a horrible word, worse in a way than being dead. It meant he didn't know – not for sure – whether his son was dead or alive. But it was clear, at least to him, that there was little hope. He'd headed straight out to sea and his fuel would have run out more than twenty-four hours ago.

He trudged slowly up the lane. If only he had come before, but he'd held back, knowing that Peter resented any idea of special treatment. Didn't want anyone to know that his father was a senior British officer. Now it was too late.

He came to a bend in the lane. The road widened and parked beside it was a long line of MG sports cars, almost a talisman for fighter pilots. He walked slowly past them, looking for Peter's. Some were almost covered by weeds and grass, and he suddenly realized why the military policeman had emphasized the word 'all', when he had said 'They're *all* parked there, sir.'

When the pilots didn't come back, they must leave them here, untouched, open. No one had taken them or looted their contents. As far as he could see, they were exactly as they had been left. A mute epitaph, a token of respect.

Colonel Bryce stared down at the little red car, parked haphazardly, the driving gloves still lying on the passenger seat where Peter had thrown them. He eased himself over the small door and down into the driving seat. He picked up the gloves. They were worn, well used. He pulled them on and stared at them, palm upwards for a moment. Then he placed his hands on the steering wheel and tried to look through the narrow windscreen, but he couldn't, it blurred and he rested his head on his hands and wept.

An RAF aircraftsman, walking to the railway station, passed the red sports car. He looked neither right, nor left, not wishing to intrude or embarrass the army officer – he'd seen it many times before.

# GEHLER

Steam hissed from between the huge iron wheels, enveloping the black-uniformed band standing on the platform. They disappeared for a moment whilst the music of 'Deutschland über Alles' continued to emerge somewhat ridiculously from inside the cloud of grey steam. Then the train was past them and the band reappeared, impassive and still in tune.

Ernst Gehler leaned farther from the window of the carriage, keeping the hand-held camera trained on the reception committee standing rigidly to attention. They were almost entirely military, their black uniforms and highly polished boots contrasting starkly with the plush red carpet. Not for the first time did Gehler regret that he was unable to film in colour with the small camera.

Slowly the huge gleaming engine, bedecked with swastikas, drew to a halt, the entrance to the Führer's carriage stopping precisely in front of the carpet. He emerged immediately, standing briefly at the top of the steps, acknowledging the line of Nazi salutes that snapped up impressively at his entrance. He surveyed them coldly, then casually half raised his right arm, the palm of his hand bent backwards, almost in a cupping motion. Gehler had noticed it before. It was a small but important deviation from the normal salute. No one else dared to emulate it and it served to underline the Führer's total authority.

He kept the camera turning over until Hitler had disappeared between the lines of the reception committee and out of the station, then snapped it off. He ducked back inside the carriage and rewound whilst he ran down the passage to the door Hitler had used. He jumped down the steps on to the red carpet and ran through the exit to the row of open-topped cars waiting outside. No one barred his progress. His uniform and position as Hitler's exclusive personal cameraman ensured that.

The entourage was almost ready to move off and Gehler leapt into the car immediately behind the Führer's. Not by so much as a flicker of an eye did Hitler acknowledge his presence, though Gehler knew he was totally aware of the camera and played to it instinctively. Though physically unprepossessing, there was something the camera liked about him – a magnetism that captured the lens and totally transformed him. He had a power on camera that kept the eye fixed on him alone.

The cars moved off and Gehler checked his exposure and footage, picking up some more shots of the crowds lining the route. As always there were hundreds of children waving flags and women crowding to the front to get a better look. Gehler had noted before the curiously obsessive attraction Hitler had for young women. He had one in his lens now, her lips parted, almost a rapturous expression on her face. She seemed to reach out as though to touch Hitler's car as it passed, then she was gone.

He stopped the camera and refocused it on the Führer, waiting. As the roar of the crowd rose he switched it on again. With perfect timing Hitler waited for it to reach its peak, then slowly he stood up in the white leather upholstered car, one hand holding the rail in front of him, the other raising itself into the familiar half salute. He turned, looking back at the crowd he had passed, directly facing camera. Gehler pulled the focus in closer, trying to keep the camera steady. The face loomed fully in the lens, expressionless . . . then he seemed to smile quietly in triumph as he turned slowly into profile. It was perfect and beautifully judged. Gehler knew he had a great shot, and he'd make it better. He'd cross-cut briefly to the adoring girl he'd filmed a moment before, then back to the Führer just before he turned into profile.

He continued to shoot reaction shots of the crowds thronging the route to the stadium. Faces, hundreds of them. A kaleidoscope of smiles, cheers, tears . . . then something else. Gehler froze. The man seemed to be staring at him, the eyes bulging, blood dribbling down from the side of his mouth. He snatched the camera away from his eye and stared at the place he'd been shooting. Nothing, no one, just a heaving mass of humanity, waving, cheering as his car swept by. He'd seen that face before. He would never forget it.

The little man had stayed on alone in his Chancellery to face them. The *Putsch* had been codenamed Operation Summer Festival, an incongruous name for such a bloody confrontation. Through Party contacts inside the army they had got hold of Austrian uniforms and one hundred and fifty of them had stormed the Chancellery on the Ballhausplatz at noon on 25 July 1934. The omens had been good. The Nazi Party had never been stronger in Austria and Hitler had just reaffirmed his own position by the purge of the Brownshirts in Berlin and the execution of Rohm. But Gehler had not counted on the bravery of Chancellor Dollfuss. The little man had stood up to them, refusing to flee, refusing to co-operate. He had maddened Gehler. The shot had been fired to frighten him. He'd aimed it over his shoulder, but somehow it had pierced his throat. For a small man he had bled a lot. It took him six hours to die and without him as a hostage the *Putsch* had failed. Worse, Dollfuss had become a martyr to Austrian independence, but Hitler's power in Germany had kept them alive – just.

Four years Gehler had waited in that cell for the *Anschluss*. Four years of confinement and beatings. Just remembering it made him sweat with fear . . . he could smell it even in the open car. Automatically he continued to film Hitler, his mind elsewhere.

He remembered the Sunday in March 1938, when he had been released and marched into Gestapo Chief Heydrich's new office on the Morzinplatz. The Nazi machine had begun the neutralisation process within twenty-four hours of marching into Austria. The *Anschluss* was complete. Once Heydrich knew of his part in the attempted *Putsch*, he had been immediately driven out to nearby Leonding. Hitler was there, visiting the place he had been brought up in. The place he had not seen since leaving Austria years before.

The car had driven up through the small community and stopped behind another car standing outside the church. Gehler was ordered out and told to wait beside the car. He could see a figure in a long grey coat standing inside the graveyard, head bowed. He recognized him instantly. The face from a thousand posters was engraved on his memory. Another man stood outside by the wall of the graveyard holding a wreath, later Gehler was to learn that his name was Linge.

The Gestapo man who had accompanied him from Heydrich's headquarters walked over and spoke to Linge briefly, indicating Gehler, then he returned to the car. Gehler continued to wait. He felt cold, numb. No elation. He needed a bath and food. His mind was consumed by the thought of food. How ironic that at a moment like this, all he could think of was his stomach. It seemed unreal, like a dream in slow motion. He'd spent four years locked in a cell. Now, within hours of his release, he was standing by a graveyard watching the man who had inspired him. Was it a trick? Would he wake up in a moment and find himself still wrapped in his single grubby blanket, staring at the white bulb above his head?

He saw Hitler turn and walk slowly towards them. Linge spoke to him while Gehler continued to wait by the car. The Führer said nothing. He looked at Gehler, noting his cropped head, the eyes huge and red-rimmed staring from the drawn pinched face. He motioned him over, but Gehler gazed uncomprehendingly at him. Linge turned and took Gehler's arm, leading him the few paces towards Hitler. Gehler raised his right arm in the Nazi salute. Heil Hitler he tried to say, but nothing came out. His throat was dry, his mouth refused to work. The Führer took one pace towards him and embraced him. 'You are my first Austrian, Gehler. Welcome to Germany.'

Welcome to Germany. He had been welcomed, made almost a hero. He was respected, feared because of the affection Hitler demonstrated towards the man he had appointed as his personal cameraman. But now Gehler was tiring of the circus. How many times could he continue to please the Führer with flattering close-ups and clever editing? He was beginning to realize that politics at this level did not fascinate him as much as the camera. He wanted to get some war footage, perhaps he could make some use of his honorary rank in the Luftwaffe . . . He would try.

The car slowed as the entourage reached the entrance to the stadium. More crowds, more cheering, more bands playing . . . welcome to Germany, *Sieg Heil* little Dollfuss, *Sieg Heil*!

# LIAM QUINN

The dingy church hall was only half full, but still wreathed in a blue haze of cigarette smoke, and he knew his clothes would reek of it afterwards. It surprised him slightly. In Ireland no one would smoke in a church building, whether it was being used for religious purposes or not, and this one certainly was not.

His voice sounded tinny through the microphone. He hadn't wanted to use it, but his American hosts had insisted. Americans, he'd decided, even Irish–Americans, were too fond of gadgets – he'd addressed audiences four or five times the size of this one without amplification.

He pushed the microphone to one side, stood up from behind the table and, ignoring the startled looks of his colleagues on either side of him, stepped to the front of the small stage.

'I don't think I need that,' he said, 'to make myself understood here.' He paused, immediately aware that the move had focused their attention upon him. He could see their faces now, upturned, waiting. 'A chairde gael,' he said in Gaelic. 'I've come a long way to see you. It's a journey that millions of Irish men, women and children have made before me. They came here to America to find a decent life. To hold on to life itself, for that too was being torn from them by the repression and persecution of the English. I've never crossed the Atlantic before. It's a powerful wide ocean to cross and it's near impossible to imagine the suffering of our people that came here before me. Yet I was very conscious of their presence in my warm cabin.'

He glanced around the hall. He had them now; he sensed it instinctively. The coughing had ceased – no one moved. He smashed his fist into the palm of his hand.

'They had to leave to find a place where they would not starve. But the English haven't left . . . not yet. The Brits are still there, occupying a part of our country. We have fought them, forced them out of twenty-six of the counties. We are still fighting them even now as I speak, carrying the struggle across the sea to England. Let them have a taste of the pain!'

There were cheers, yells of agreement. Their blood was up . . . He lowered his voice, assuming the tone of a politician. 'On 12 January of this year we sent an ultimatum to Lord Halifax giving the British Government four days in which to withdraw from the North. I'll read you the last part of this document.' He pulled an envelope from the inside pocket of his jacket and took the letter from it. 'It reads, "We shall be sorry if this basic demand is refused, and we shall feel ourselves obliged to intervene in the economic and military life of your country in the same way your government does in ours."'

Carefully he placed the letter back in its envelope, then lifted his head, gazing directly over the sea of faces. 'They have ignored our ultimatum.' His voice was hardly above a whisper, but every man in the hall heard each word clearly. 'We do not wish to kill or maim any innocent civilians, but our campaign in England will not end until Ireland is reunited. That is our sole aim. We want our people to have all the land that is rightfully theirs. Give generously and we shall succeed . . . thank you.'

He turned and made his way back behind the table to his chair. The applause was thunderous. His colleagues rose, applauding him themselves. He sat quietly in the chair, unmoving, not acknowledging the cheers – waiting for it to die down. He continued to sit while the local Detroit representative of Clann na Gael thanked him profusely.

He was worried. He could not see the FBI agent who had trailed him since his arrival in the USA. Pity. It had been a good speech. Two bombs, as planned, had exploded at King's Cross and Victoria stations in London the previous day. Further, the Royal visit to the United States would soon be under way and it was likely that the American security forces might be jumpy. Surely they were bound to be out there in that crowd, watching. He scanned the audience carefully, but he could distinguish no one who might be police or FBI. They were a strange collection, a few poor, but many were not. Ireland hadn't done badly, he thought.

At last the speechmaking came to an end. He stood up and made his way with the others to the side of the stage. Suddenly two men were either side of him, holding his arms tightly. A third stood in front. He recognized his constant companion.

'Are you Liam Quinn of the Irish Republican Army?'

Quinn smiled to himself. It had worked.

'I think you know who I am,' he said quietly.

A pair of handcuffs were expertly snapped on to his wrists.

'I know you,' the agent said without humour.

# BOOK TWO
## Arrival

Harrison glanced at the altimeter. Ten thousand feet. He must be well out over the Firth of Clyde by now. He'd sighted Stranraer earlier, but the grey mass of cloud below him was unbroken and deepening. Soon he'd have to descend to make landfall on the Mull of Kintyre. He had tried to raise the Fleet Air Arm base there several times, but all he was picking up was static. He felt certain the radio had packed up, but he was not too worried yet, he had another forty minutes' supply of fuel, and the base could only be a few minutes away.

He pushed the stick gently forward and the Hurricane nosed its way down towards the cloud. She began to buck a bit as the first tendrils of the upper layers slipped by the wingtips, but he kept the nose of the tough little fighter down. It was a risk. If he'd been blown off course he could be over high ground and fly into the side of a mountain. He had no alternative. He must get below the cloud base to find out where he was.

Gradually he lost altitude, the turbulence getting worse as he descended. He didn't break clear until he was down to fifteen hundred sweaty feet, and he was relieved to see the white flecked water below him. Visibility was not good, but he'd stay at this altitude until he made landfall. He was better off here where he could see what he was flying into than in the heavy grey cloud just above him.

The engine droned steadily on and he glanced at his watch. He should be crossing the shoreline soon; then it would be a simple matter to find the base. It began to rain, the opaque sheets of water buffeting the plane until he couldn't see the heaving waves below. He kept a steady eye on the altimeter, determined not to drop below fifteen hundred. Still no sign of land. He looked at his watch again. According to his calculations he should have cleared the Firth of Clyde by now, but the headwinds were strong and they would have slowed him down considerably. He knew that if he missed the Mull of Kintyre he would head straight out over the North Channel into the Atlantic, but in spite of the bad visibility he was sure he hadn't missed it.

The single-engined fighter was being thrown about all the time and Harrison had to fight to keep her on an even keel. The weather conditions were really bad, and still there was no sign of land. He tried to raise the Fleet Air Arm base again but it was useless, just a constant jabbering of static. He tore the earphones off. He was nearing the point of no return; it was time to go back before he ran out of fuel, find a place to land somewhere near Stranraer. Harrison knew that if he'd overshot the long promontory of Kintyre there would be high ground somewhere off to the east. He didn't want to waste fuel trying to gain height through the cloud stacked above him, so he began a wide sweep westwards until the compass bearing indicated he was heading south again. Thank God they'd built the little plane tough. Sometimes the downdraughts were so strong he felt the wings would be torn from the fuselage, but the engine note didn't falter and he flew steadily back the way he had come.

Slowly the rain began to ease off and for a moment a shaft of sunlight burst through a gap in the clouds above him, turning the globules of water streaming round his cockpit into a myriad rainbow hues. Then, as quickly as it had dazzled it was gone, but now he could see the water below him and the cloud above. All he needed was the land to put her down. He had about ten minutes of fuel left when he spotted the grey shape of the mountain looming up ahead of him and disappearing into the cloudbase. He felt relief flooding through him, but it wasn't time to relax . . . not yet.

44

He banked slightly to the left, searching for some flat ground where he could put the Hurricane down. At once he saw another smaller mountain rising almost alongside the first. Between them was what appeared to be a valley. He had no time left to search the coastline for an easier landing spot. He crossed the white storm-tossed shore and headed down the narrow valley. He groaned inwardly. Trees, thickly wooded steep hills skimmed by either side of him stretching right down to the valley floor. Desperately he looked for somewhere he could attempt a landing. His options were running out fast. The fuel gauge stood squarely at zero – he was flying on fumes and a prayer.

The valley twisted away to his left and he banked steeply, following the contours. The engine coughed, picked up, then died on him. He straightened her out. The valley widened slightly, a cottage flashed by below him, and then he saw the field. It looked green and flat and very short, with stone walls fringing each side. But he had no choice; it must be better than the trees surrounding it. He kept the nose down to maintain control, then dropped her as fast as he could on to her belly, pulling back the stick just before touching down. Too late he remembered the ignition, then the impact hurled him forward into his harness, the straps biting deeply into his flesh. He covered his face with his arms and waited to die.

The plane skidded along the wet muddy surface, shedding pieces of metal and portions of wings as it slithered towards the low stone wall at the end of the field. A small rise in the ground caught two blades of the propeller, pulling the nose down into the earth. The fighter flipped over on to its back and skidded sideways to a halt three feet short of the wall.

At first Harrison just hung there upside down in his harness, wondering if he was still in one piece. Gingerly he felt the places that hurt, but nothing seemed to be broken. Suddenly he remembered the ignition and hurriedly

45

switched it off. Then he smiled, remembering he'd run out of fuel anyway. The straps were hurting him, but he couldn't release himself until he'd opened the cockpit, otherwise he might just fall and break his neck, which would be a stupid way to go after surviving the crash.

He pulled at the perspex canopy, but it wouldn't budge. It hadn't splintered, but it was wedged firmly into the soft ground and he couldn't shift it any more than he could move himself. The tight confines of the cockpit made it impossible for him to turn around, and already he was beginning to feel dizzy as the blood rushed to his head. He wondered whether anyone had actually died from a rush of blood to the head. He smiled, what a hell of a way for a fighter pilot to go.

He jumped, that is, if it was possible to jump when suspended upside down in a cockpit. A worn weatherbeaten old face was peering at him through the perspex, and it looked strangely frightening seen the wrong way up. The man banged on the side of the fuselage, almost deafening Harrison.

'You all right in there?'

Harrison nodded vaguely. 'Yes; for chrissake, get me out.'

The old man surveyed him quizzically for a moment. 'Ah, there you are, are you.'

Harrison couldn't believe it. 'Right first time . . . I'm here.'

The man continued to gaze at him infuriatingly, before replying, 'Yes – I can see that. Well now, don't you worry, I'll have you out of there in a jiffy.'

Harrison craned his neck round to have a look at this madman. 'Fine, fine . . . I'll just stay here until you do.'

The old man nodded in a friendly fashion. 'Thank you, sir, thank you.'

He disappeared from Harrison's view, then reappeared a moment later. 'Will you look now, I'm just going to get meself a spade to dig you out – I shall be back in a moment.'

46

Harrison nodded sagely, trying to assume the weird normality of his would-be rescuer. 'Good, good. Then I'll see you soon I hope.'

The man disappeared again. Harrison tried to move the straps to ease the pain, but it didn't help. Suddenly the pain disappeared. He sniffed. Jesus he could smell gas . . . Gas! What fuckin' gas? He'd used it all, hadn't he? Maybe he hadn't . . . maybe the engine had just died on him because he'd banked so steeply. He craned his head, peering down the front of the engine nacelle. The canopy had been partially ripped away and he could see something slowly dripping on to the exhaust cylinders. It was fuel and the cylinders were hot.

He hung very still for a moment, then slowly reached into his fur-lined boot and felt around until he found it. He carefully pulled the .38 pistol out; he didn't want to drop it. If he was going to die, he'd sooner go with a bullet in the head than fry. He checked the ammunition and removed the safety catch; there was nothing to do now but wait.

He heard a spade cut into the earth and tapped the perspex to attract the old man's attention. The face floated into view again and smiled, exposing some yellowing teeth.

'Yes, what is it, sir?'

'Could you move as quickly as possible with that shovel, but don't make any sparks. There's a fuel leak and this whole thing could go up like a bomb.'

The face smiled again disarmingly. 'Yes, sir.'

Harrison felt a violent upsurge of impotent rage. 'Have you got that, for chrissake, do you know what the fuckin' hell I'm talking about?'

The old man continued to stare at him calmly. 'Oh yes, sir, I understand your position perfectly. But you see I've been a gardener for a long time and I think I can get you out of there without blowin' us both up.'

He proceeded to dig carefully but with tremendous speed

beneath the cockpit. In minutes he had cleared a space. He placed the spade back on the ground, then gripped the edge of the canopy around the cockpit with his huge horny hands. He began to try and work it loose. Harrison could see the muscles in his arms bulging with the effort, but still it didn't move. The American gripped the edge of the canopy himself and strained to pull it back. It inched open a fraction. Instantly the old man inserted his fingers and it began to open. The smell of petrol was much stronger now. Harrison slid his fingers over the edge of the canopy as well and suddenly the cover jerked back.

The gardener gripped him around the shoulders, while Harrison released the straps; they came free and the old man took his full weight easily without effort and lowered him gently to the muddy ground. Harrison struggled out from under the plane, then they both turned and ran, throwing themselves down behind the wall. Harrison laid there for a moment feeling slightly dizzy, trying to get his breath back, then he glanced at the gardener.

'Thanks . . . seems like I caused you a lot of trouble for nothing.'

A gust of hot air engulfed them as the tank exploded, setting off the ammunition which ricocheted from the wall in front of them. Bits and pieces of metal rained around them and Harrison saw a wheel trundling away until it rolled into a stream. He raised his head from beneath his arms and looked at the old man lying beside him.

'You OK?'

He brushed away a piece of wet grass from the side of his nose.

'Oh I'm fine, sir,' he said, 'just fine. Pity about your flyin' machine there though. It's all in bits and pieces now.'

He stretched out and picked up a piece of metal, then dropped it quickly. 'Mother of God, that's hot!'

Harrison stared at him for a moment, then burst into

uproarious laughter, rolling on to his back. The old man smiled ruefully.

Bryce was falling, tumbling over and over, hardly able to breathe, the wind catching at his clothing, roaring in his ears . . . yet he could see nothing. He reached up, clawing at his face, trying to gulp in the air. His face was wet . . . blood? His fingers scrabbled frantically at his eyes. Was he blind? They were covered by something hard and smooth, glass. He tore the goggles from his face. They were covered in oil.

The sun blazed incandescently in his eyes as he turned over, twisting, falling to earth. Christ, he was alive! He grabbed at the parachute ring and pulled it hard. How long? Was there time? Instinctively he braced himself for the awful bone-crushing impact. He clenched his eyes shut and prayed . . . 'Dear God, please let it open in time.' He heard the silken folds of the chute being plucked from the pack. Then a giant slapping sound as it opened and he was jerked upright, the canvas straps digging into the tops of his legs and arms.

Suddenly it was quiet, still. He felt himself swaying back and forth and tried to open his eyes again. They were hurting as the oil ran down his face into them, but at least he was still able to see and he'd caught sight of a green landscape far below him.

He tried to rub the oil from his eyes but it only made it worse. He kept them half closed and it was bearable. He was descending slowly, gently, towards the earth. The fields seeming to sway from side to side as he dangled beneath the chute. It was beautiful, peaceful, but deceptive. He was suddenly aware that he was falling directly into some woods.

He pulled on the cords, trying to manoeuvre himself away from danger, but he'd left it too late. A branch clawed at his leg tearing his trousers, tipping him head first towards the ground. He grabbed at a branch as he fell, it snapped off in his hand, the parachute shredding on the branches. The cords wrapped themselves around one of the limbs, breaking his fall. He crashed into the ground, his head snapping forward, missing a large stone by inches. He felt pain, disorientation. He tried to raise himself, but he couldn't move. He relapsed into unconsciousness.

The undergrowth was thick, seemingly impenetrable, but the girl was used to the countryside. She found the narrow, almost indiscernible trail of the fox, and pushed her way slowly in towards the heart of the wood. He must be somewhere in here. She'd heard the chatter of machine-gun fire, and seen the fighter pouring black smoke crash into the ground while the German bomber turned away back out to sea, also trailing vapour and losing height. Then miraculously she'd seen the tiny white parachute burst open a few hundred feet from the ground before disappearing into the wood.

A pair of beady black eyes watched her progress, then scuttled away as she drew too close. The girl paused, pushing back the hair from her face. She was about nineteen years old with high cheekbones and a firm jaw. Her dark hair was long, brushing her shoulders and getting in her way as the low branches reached down around her head.

She pressed forward again, bramble bushes catching at her bare legs. She saw a glimmer of white off to her left and turned towards it. There was a small clearing and as she neared it she could see the torn remains of a parachute hanging from the branches of a tree. The crumpled figure of the flyer lay on the ground beneath it, and the girl stopped, frightened of what she might find.

Curiosity gradually overcame her fear and she broke

through the last of the undergrowth into the clearing. The man had not moved. He was lying face down, the cords from his parachute trailing up into the tree above him. She knelt down beside him and put her hand on his shoulder, turning him over. He was heavy, but she was strong and slowly he rolled over on to his back. The girl was appalled, she pulled back from him. His face! It was blackened, his eyebrows gone. She thought he had been badly burnt; then she saw the oil on her hands and realized what it was. She grabbed some handfuls of soft grass and began to wipe the man's face, clearing away as much oil as she could. She pulled a tiny handkerchief from under her sleeve and touched it with her tongue before tenderly removing the black sticky substance from around his eyes.

Bryce could feel something on his face. He tried to move, but nothing seemed to happen. Then something soft and moist on his eyes. He blinked, he could open them. He saw the girl on her knees beside him, her eyes wide, shocked. That was the first thing he noticed, her eyes. He didn't think he'd ever seen anything quite so beautiful. They seemed so young, so full of compassion. God, he must look awful! He tried to move again and the girl leaned over him, pushing him on to the ground.

'No wait, you might have broken something.'

'I'm sorry,' he said lamely. 'I didn't mean to frighten you.'

The girl smiled. 'I'm not frightened. I'm quite used to this sort of thing.'

He gazed up at her, puzzled by the remark. 'You mean you often get people like me dropping in on you?'

She laughed and he realized she was not wearing anything under the simple dress. 'God no . . . it's just that I often have to tend to sick animals on the farm. Now lie still.'

She ran her hands down his arms and legs, then asked him to wiggle his fingers and toes. 'Nothing broken there,' she announced.

51

The harness was still wrapped around his body. 'Can we get this off?' she asked.

He sat up slowly and pressed the quick-release mechanism. The girl pulled the straps gently away from him, then helped him to his feet.

Bryce felt a searing white hot pain down his side and would have fallen if the girl hadn't been supporting him. 'Jesus Christ.' He gritted his teeth, trying not to cry out.

She sat him down carefully on the remains of an uprooted tree and told him to wait. He watched as she swiftly shinned up the tree that he'd fallen into, wrapping her brown legs around the trunk and hanging from a branch while she tore some strips of silk from the parachute, then climbed down effortlessly.

She helped him remove his flying jacket and shirt, then wrapped the strips of silk tightly round his chest, binding his ribs. She did not speak, intent on her task, trying to make him as comfortable as possible. He waited until she had finished, then stood up slowly without her assistance.

'Thank you,' he said simply.

She looked at the ground but didn't answer.

'How did you find me?'

'I saw where you came down; you were very lucky.'

He smiled. 'Depends what you mean by luck.'

'Your parachute didn't open at first,' she said quickly. 'I thought . . .'

He grimaced. 'So did I.'

There was a moment of silence between them, then the girl took his arm. 'Come,' she said.

He allowed her to lead him to the side of the clearing, then he stopped, realizing something.

'What's your name?'

'Nora.'

She led the way along the animal track; he struggled on behind her, his legs like putty. If she hadn't been there he wouldn't have made ten yards. He stopped, gasping for breath, the pain in his side making him sweat.

'Is it far to the road – I must try and get back to my base.'

Nora took his arm and placed it around her shoulders, her arm around his waist. 'That's going to be difficult, seeing as how you're in Ireland.'

At first it didn't sink in, then Bryce stopped, blood from a scratch trickling down the side of his face. 'Ireland!' he said incredulously . . .

Harrison stared at the sergeant. 'Ireland!'

The police sergeant could hardly keep the smug smile off his face. Harrison glanced behind him at the two policemen standing either side of the door.

'Aw shit!'

'That's as maybe, sir, but that is where you are at.'

How the hell had he managed to land in Ireland? The headwinds must have veered round to the east and blown him out over the Atlantic.

The sergeant cleared his throat importantly. 'Now would you mind explainin' a few things to me.' He paused for a moment.

'I see you're wearin' a big American eagle up there on your jacket, and I can tell you're from those parts . . . Canada?'

Harrison shook his head. 'Nope, Wyoming.'

The sergeant scratched his head. 'Yes, yes I see. I'm sorry if I appear ignorant, but I don't know an awful lot about airyplanes. That one that was out there,' he gestured vaguely towards the window, 'that's all in pieces, that's not American, is it? I mean, you're not even in the Emergency, are you?'

It was Harrison's turn to be puzzled. 'The Emergency?'

'The war,' said the sergeant.

Harrison shifted his ground, exasperated by the questioning. 'Of course I'm in the fuckin' war. What do you think that was out there . . . a joyride?'

The sergeant glanced behind him at the policemen by the door. 'So that plane – or what's left of it, was British?'

Harrison began to get worried. 'Sure – a Hurricane. I'm in Eagle Squadron.'

'And that Eagle Squadron, would that be part of the RAF?'

Harrison nodded. 'Right.'

Comprehension slowly flooded across the sergeant's face. 'Well in that case, sir, I have the pleasure to tell you that you're under arrest, prior to detention.'

Harrison looked around him in amazement, the grin of amusement slowly fading from his face. The sergeant was deadly serious.

'But you said this was Ireland. You're in the war. We have bases here.'

The sergeant shook his head. 'No sir, not here. You are referring to Northern Ireland – this is Eire and we are a neutral country. You came down the wrong side of the border, sir.'

'Aw shit,' Harrison said again, and sat down. He felt sick. Six thousand miles to fight in a war and already he was a prisoner.

The copy boy weaved his way between the desks cluttered with clacking typewriters, half emptied cups of tea, rubbers, pencils and the usual untidy mess of newspaper office paraphernalia. The youngster held a piece of paper over his head as though it were a banner. It was, he'd discovered, the usual procedure when relaying something important. One or two of the reporters glanced up at him briefly as he passed but showed no untoward sign of interest. They'd seen it all before.

He paused triumphantly for a moment outside the editor's glass-panelled office, then swept inside and plonked the piece of paper on the desk in front of the middle-aged man who was immersed in a draft front page. 'Just come in, Mr Jordan,' he said.

Bob Jordan continued to study the front page. The boy persisted. 'It's important, sir, just come in on the wire service.'

Jordan lowered the page slightly and peered over the top at the offending distraction. 'Thank you,' he said quietly, then returned to the page.

The boy, undaunted, pressed home the point, reluctant to lose his brief moment of glory. The editor's office was hallowed ground. 'It is important, sir. He asked me to get it to you as quickly as possible.'

Jordan lowered the page wearily and contemplated the eager young face before him. He chewed the end of his pencil for a moment. The boy was new. He hadn't seen him before. He remembered how important it had been for him the first time he was in the editor's office. He pulled the pencil from his mouth. 'Look, young man, I realize you haven't been in here before, but when you have something to deliver to me in my office, all you have to do is put it down on the desk, announce that you've done so and leave. Is that clear?'

The boy swallowed hard. 'Yes, sir.'

Jordan raised his arm and pointed to the door, took in a deep breath and bellowed. 'Then go . . .!'

The boy flew from the room, his feet hardly seeming to

touch the ground. Jordan gazed after the fleeing figure, then resignedly stood up, walked over to the open door and deliberately closed it as quietly as he could. He retraced his steps back to the desk, picked up the piece of paper, then sat down and studied the short message for a moment.

He flicked on the intercom. His secretary answered promptly. 'Get me James Driscoll.' He glanced at his watch. 'He should be at his Newbridge number.'

The phone began to ring, echoing incessantly through the high polished hallway. A tall heavy man about fifty years of age made his way unhurriedly down the wide balustraded staircase: telephones are seldom answered quickly in Ireland. He picked up the receiver.

'Hello . . . Yes, speaking.'

He waited a moment, then Jordan came on the line, the familiar voice as unflappable as ever. 'Hello, Bob, what can I do for you?'

'Couple of things, Mr Driscoll. Just got something in on the wire service. You remember Liam Quinn, the IRA Chief of Staff who went off to the USA earlier this year?'

'Yes, got himself arrested in Detroit while fund-raising, I believe.'

'You know about that then?'

'Yes, heard it from somebody in the Irish Press. I gather the censorship board put the block on that for us.'

'Yes, we couldn't print it, which is the second thing I want to talk about. However, there has been a development on the Quinn thing. You remember his arrest stirred up a hornet's nest amongst the Irish American lobby. Seventy-six members of Congress demanded an explanation from Roosevelt, failing which they threatened not to participate in a Congress reception for King George and Quinn was subsequently released on bail.'

56

Jordan heard Driscoll chuckle. 'It's a powerful lobby we have over there, Robert.'

'There's more,' Jordan replied. 'We've just learnt that Quinn jumped bail in New York.'

Driscoll absorbed that for a while.

'You still there?' Jordan asked.

'Yes. Are we going to be able to print this, Bob?'

'Not if I have to submit my copy to messrs Knightly, Coyne and Connolly, but I believe you know Frank Aiken personally?'

'Yes, I do. Would you like me to have a word with him?'

'Well, he's the Minister who is nominally responsible for the censorship board. I won't get anywhere with this the way it stands. Mike Knightly's OK, he used to be a newspaper man himself. Coyne I can handle. But Joe Connolly will never let this through.'

Driscoll rubbed his jaw. 'OK, leave it with me, Bob. I'll call you as soon as I have something.'

'I appreciate this, Mr Driscoll.'

'It's no problem, Bob, least I can do for my editor at a time like this. Speak to you soon.'

Driscoll replaced the receiver and stood gazing out of the window overlooking The Curragh for a long time, before slowly picking it up again.

Gehler clung to the wing of the Dornier, close to the engine nacelle. The pilot Kinzell and the young gunner Halder were hanging on to the other side; the wing was all that remained afloat. Without it they would have drowned in the heavy seas that surged around them, trying to tear them from their precarious hold on life. The gunner was badly injured and Kinzell knew he could not support him much longer; his hands were cold and numb. He looped his arm around the gunner's chest and clung to the trailing edge of the wing.

The seas swept them high again and Gehler heard something above the sound of the waves crashing round them. He glanced over his shoulder before the wing slid back into the trough. He saw something white and foaming, then he identified the sound. It was shingle, pebbles being rolled up and down beneath the waves pounding a shore. Kinzell was staring at him, he'd seen it too.

Gehler started to kick off his flying boots and Kinzell realized he was going to try and swim for the shore.

'You must help me with the gunner, I can't hold on to him much longer.'

Gehler ignored him, slipping out of his sodden jacket but leaving the camera looped around his neck. He could hear Kinzell pleading with him to try and save the gunner. At last he was free of his boots. He looked across the wing at Kinzell. Halder's eyes were open, staring at him. Kinzell knew then what he intended to do.

'Please, Oberleutnant – he will die without our help.'

The wing seemed to drop lower into the water, one end slowly sinking. A wave crashed down over them and Gehler spat the cold salty water from his mouth.

'We shall die anyway, Leutnant. Leave him.' He raised his legs and pushed away from the wing with all his strength, heading for the shore.

Kinzell felt the cold seeping through his body as he watched Gehler swim powerfully towards the beach. He looked down at Halder's face. It was deathly white – his lips tinged blue with the cold. His right arm was a mess, blood still staining the water around it. Kinzell made up his mind. He waited until the next wave raised them high enough for him to see the shore, then he gripped the fur collar of the gunner's flying jacket, let go of the wing and struck out.

Kinzell could not be sure of where he was going. Occasionally he caught a glimpse of the wing as it rode high in the heavy seas. As long as he stayed in a direct line he should be heading in the general direction of the shore. He used one arm and his legs to propel him and the gunner through the water, but it was painfully slow progress. As one arm tired he would change his hold on the gunner's jacket. All the time the heavy seas and wind tried to pluck him from his grasp. Kinzell knew if he lost him, he would never get him back.

The sound of the pebbles crashing up and down the beach behind him increased. Grimly he hung on to the gunner's jacket, pulling him through the water, not caring if he were alive or dead, intent only on getting him to the shore.

His feet touched something – he straightened up, trying to get a foothold. The sea rolled back towards him and the undertow pulled him face down into the water, almost jerking Halder from his grasp. He stayed on his knees, and inch by painful inch clawed his way up the incline. As each wave receded from the shoreline, seeking to drag him back, he took a deep breath and laid flat, digging his free hand and feet into the beach as the avalanche of pebbles and water tried to sweep him and the gunner back into the deep water.

Gradually the undertow decreased and slowly he dragged the gunner's inert body from the flurry of foam and crashing water until at last they were both clear of the waterline. Only then did he release his hold on the gunner's jacket.

He lay gasping on the beach, his head resting on his arm, coughing up sea water and spitting it out. He pushed himself up on his elbows, scanning the flat inhospitable landscape. Two eyes were staring at him. Gehler was sprawled exhausted farther along the beach. He had watched Kinzell drag himself out of the sea, pulling Halder behind him . . . He'd made no move to help.

Kinzell was on his stomach, unmoving, barely conscious, yet aware of Gehler's unblinking stare, aware too that Gehler had wanted him to fail, wanted him to die. Kinzell crawled over to the still figure of the gunner. He was alive – just. He pulled Halder farther up the beach, then he sat down and dragged off one of his sodden flying boots. It weighed a ton. How he'd managed to remain afloat at all was incredible. He took off a sock and pulled the boot back on again – it felt horrible and slimy, but he had no choice. Somehow he had to stop the blood pumping out of Halder. He wound the sock around the top of his mutilated arm, then twisted it tighter into a tourniquet with a piece of driftwood. That done, he covered him with his jacket and trudged slowly to the top of a small rise about a hundred yards away. Visibility was bad, but not enough to prevent him from seeing they were on a small island, no more than a mile across in any direction. It was uninhabited apart from a few sheep huddled together in a hollow that provided the only protection from the wind howling across the flat landscape. He stared out past the end of the island to the west. Beyond it was the grey mass of the mainland, about a mile and a half and an ocean of grey-white flecked sea away.

It was dark, just a single point of light from the wood fire. A piece of gorse ignited, throwing strange shadows round the hollow that the sheep had occupied. A leg of lamb was suspended above the fire on a make-shift spit and Kinzell didn't wait for it to cook completely before slicing a piece of the meat from it. He took it across to Halder. He was lying close to the fire, sheltered from the wind that still blew strongly by the remains of the wing that had been washed ashore. The parachute packs had been opened, stretched out and added to the protection from the elements. They

60

billowed in the wind, but were strong and wouldn't tear.

Kinzell offered the hot meat to the gunner. He refused it, too weak to even shake his head. Kinzell looked down at the boy. His face was grey, his eyes red rimmed and a film of moisture shone on his face . . . he was beginning to sweat. Kinzell covered him up as well as he could and turned to face Gehler who was sitting on a piece of wreckage from the Dornier, staring into the flames.

'One of us must make an attempt to swim to the mainland tomorrow, otherwise he will die.'

Gehler glanced at him impassively, his eyes expressionless, the flickering light from the fire distorting the contours of his face. Kinzell shivered, and it wasn't from the cold.

The water in the saucepan began to boil and Nora glanced at the big clock hanging beside the dresser in the kitchen, timing the eggs. She'd said nothing about Bryce to her father yet. She'd made a bed up for the pilot in the barn. It was quite warm and comfortable and he hadn't seemed to mind. She took out the two eggs and placed them in the egg cups she had prepared, putting one of them on a tray with toast and butter and a mug of tea, leaving the other egg for Bryce. Carefully she carried the tray upstairs to her father's room. He was lying face down on top of the covers, still wearing his clothes. The dried mud on his boots had marked the counterpane. Nora crossed the room and with her free hand pulled back one of the curtains to let in some light. Her father groaned, turning violently on to his back and shading his eyes from the light of the window. He was confused, his eyes bloodshot.

'Jesus, what the hell . . .'

Nora carried the tray to the bedside. 'I've brought you some breakfast, Da.'

He raised himself on one elbow, squinting at her disbelievingly. 'Breakfast?' He rubbed his eyes angrily. 'I don't want no bloody breakfast.'

Nora was frightened – she stood absolutely still, proffering the tray. He stared at her balefully, her submissive attitude seeming to provoke him further. He reached out and violently knocked the tray from her hands, smashing the crockery and staining the wall with tea. He slumped back down on to the bed covering his face with his arm.

'Get out, you stupid bitch, all I want is some sleep.'

Nora backed away from him apprehensively and started to pick up the broken pieces of crockery. He groaned, rolling over on his side.

'For Christ's sake, leave all that, will you, and let me get some sleep – and pull those bloody curtains before you go.'

Nora stood up, hating him, but too frightened of his violence to protest – she'd felt the weight of his hand before. It had been stupid of her to think she could soften his attitude by bringing him breakfast. He drank himself into oblivion at least three times a week in the village pub. She hadn't heard him return last night – she'd been exhausted and fallen asleep the minute her head touched the pillow. She crossed quietly over to the window and pulled the rough curtain back into place, then left the room, closing the door gently behind her.

Bryce was lying on his back, his eyes closed, his dark hair tousled by sleep down over his forehead. He seemed relaxed, peaceful. Suddenly his eyes opened and he was staring at her. He smiled. 'Morning,' he said, brushing a piece of straw from his hair.

Nora felt confused for a moment, as though she'd been caught doing something she shouldn't.

'I've brought you some breakfast. Did you sleep all right?'

He sat up, reaching for the tray. 'Fine thanks – like the proverbial log. I might decide to sleep on straw all the time after this.'

Nora smiled briefly. Bryce took a sip of the tea, glancing at her over the rim of the mug.

'What's the matter? You look worried. Is it about me? You don't have to, you know. I'll go quietly.'

Nora removed the oil lamp from the box beside him and sat down, not looking at the Englishman directly.

'No, it's not that,' she said. 'I haven't told my father about you yet.' She waited, 'I don't think he's very well – he didn't get back until late last night.'

Bryce dipped his toast into the boiled egg. He was starving. He'd heard someone drive erratically up to the house very late, but it was clear from the raucous singing that the man was drunk, not ill.

'Do you want me to tell him, there's no need for you . . .' He stopped, seeing the look of alarm that crossed her face.

'No,' she said quickly. 'No, I'll tell him.' She smiled nervously, trying to disguise her fear. 'There's no need for you to worry – you can stay here as long as you like. He never comes in here anyway, it's perfectly safe.'

'Yes, I'm sure it is,' he said quietly. He immersed himself in the food. He hadn't realized how hungry he was.

Nora watched him eat, glad to see his appetite was normal. The sleep had done him good. He looked much better apart from the growth of beard around his face, and curiously she quite liked that – she hated it on her father.

The Englishman quickly finished off the egg and toast, then downed the remains of his tea.

A comfortable silence fell between them. She had enjoyed watching him eat, and when he finished, he grinned, stretching luxuriously. The grin turned to a grimace of pain and he clutched his side, leaning back on the straw bed.

Nora kneeled down beside him. 'Is it bad?'

He lay quite still for a moment, then let his breath out slowly before breathing in again.

'No – it's gone again. I suppose it must have been because I stretched.' He shook his head in disgust. 'Bloody stupid of me – I should have remembered.'

'Yes, you'll have to be much more careful,' Nora said, matter of factly, much more sure of herself now she was dealing with something she understood. 'You'd better let me check those bandages.'

Bryce smiled quietly to himself, but undid his shirt without making any comment. He sensed her vulnerability and he didn't want to unsettle her in any way.

She checked the strips of parachute silk she had used to bind him up, and glanced up at him. 'Yes, I thought so. They've worked loose during the night.'

Bryce watched her as she carefully undid the bindings, her long dark hair falling around her shoulders, covering her face when she leaned forward. As the last strip of silk came away Nora leaned back looking at the bruising down his left side. It was quite severe and Bryce pulled a face when he saw it. He glanced at Nora. 'Anything broken?'

'I'm not sure, but I think it looks worse than it is – you'd know if it was broken.'

She hesitated a moment, looking at him, concerned. Once again Bryce was struck by the beauty of her eyes. 'I could find out if there was a fracture, but it would hurt you.'

Bryce gazed directly at her. 'I don't think you could hurt me, Nora,' he said quietly.

The words, though seemingly commonplace, triggered a wave of emotion in Nora. It was the first kind thing that had been said to her for longer than she cared to remember. She felt the tears stinging the back of her eyes and bit her lip, turning her head away, not wanting him to see how much she was affected by the remark.

She was not normally a tearful person, but the strain of trying to run her father's smallholding, and the heartbreaking influence of drink on him since her mother's death nine months before, had finally snapped her resistance. The tears ran down her face and dripped off the end of her nose. She covered her eyes with her hands, trying not to let him see her distress.

He touched her arm. 'Nora, please – please don't cry.'

She began to sob, bending over, trying to hold the pain within her. But now it was unstoppable – a release, all the pent-up grief and humiliation poured from her.

Bryce put his arms around her, not realizing why he had so deeply affected her, but responding instinctively. He held her close, stroking her hair, murmuring quietly to her until the sobbing began to subside. Gradually Nora became aware of his physical proximity. He was bare to the waist, his hard muscled body sweating slightly. She placed her hands on his chest, pushing herself away. Bryce didn't try to hold on to her, though he too could feel himself responding to her sexuality.

Neither of them spoke – there was no need. Bryce wiped the tears from her face tenderly with his hand, then lowered his hands to his sides, no longer touching her. Nora kept her palms on his chest, feeling the short curly hair beneath them. She was incredulous at her physical intimacy with this man of whom she had known nothing twenty-four hours before, but she felt no shame in her desire.

Tenderly she slid her hand down over his bruised ribs. He did not flinch. She touched each one lightly, they were unbroken. She stared up at him, searching his face for an answer, looking for a response. She knew he wanted her.

Nora leaned forward and kissed the bruises on his side,

sliding her arm around his waist, pulling him hard towards her. Bryce kissed her hair, holding her face against his chest – then slowly pulling her down on to the straw bed.

He loved her, she loved him; it was simple.

Harrison sipped the coffee. It was terrible, weak and without flavour. The sergeant was laboriously filing a report after making a phone call. It had taken a long time for him to get through and clearly it was some distance away. Harrison had tried not to make it obvious that he was listening, but the police sergeant didn't seem to care one way or the other. He had informed whoever was at the other end of the line of Harrison's presence and requested instructions – apparently he was to be driven to some place where he would be interned. But Harrison had no intention of allowing himself to be locked away for the duration. He didn't know what kind of a detainment camp he was being sent to, but he hadn't come this far to sit safely locked away somewhere for God knows how long.

He looked slowly round the room. There were two other Garda beside the sergeant, one standing at the door, the other at the single window. The window was old and strong – there was no way he could get through that before they had their hands on him. He waited.

Eventually there was a knock on the door and a young man poked his head around it.

'It's here,' he said. 'Waitin' outside. Do you want me to drive it?'

The sergeant thanked him but declined. 'It's a long trip, Molloy, and we shall not be back before tomorrow – but don't worry about your car, we'll have it back here safely for

66

you and I dare say there'll be a bit of petrol left over in the tank.'

The nod was as good as a wink and that seemed to please the young man. He grinned. 'Thanks, sergeant. Take as long as you like.'

Then he disappeared, shutting the door behind him.

The sergeant glanced at Harrison and smiled disarmingly. 'Difficult to get petrol, but at least the roads are empty.' He looked at Harrison's cup. 'Would you like some more coffee?'

He shook his head hurriedly. 'No thanks.' He couldn't face any more.

The sergeant resumed writing his report. 'We'll be on our way as soon as I have finished this.'

Harrison stood up, stretching his legs. 'Fine.' He rubbed his thighs. 'I'm a bit stiff,' he added by way of explanation.

The sergeant had a thought. 'Look, you might as well go and sit in the car whilst I finish this off. It'll only take a minute and it's more comfortable than that bloody chair.'

He glanced at the two policemen. 'Connor, you'll be driving, and Michael, you sit in the back with the prisoner. I'll be out in a minute.'

The two Garda picked up their caps and one of them opened the door. They each took one of his arms and led him down a short passage, past a desk, then out of the front entrance. Four or five stone steps led down into the road where the car was waiting. A small crowd had gathered, mostly boys and old men. They stood on the far side of the road as though frightened to get any nearer. He heard the buzz of conversation as he appeared and he suspected that they had never seen an airman before.

The road was deserted, just a horse and a small cart with some milk churns on it. The car was at the foot of the steps, and as he rounded the rear he saw that the keys were in the ignition.

One of the policemen let go of his arm, opening the back door. He then bent down to open the front and Harrison jerked his elbow back hard into the chest of the man still holding his arm, kicking the front door into the man who was bending down. It caught him in the face, blood spurted from a gash in his forehead and he fell backwards into the road. The other policeman was bending over clutching his chest, totally winded by the blow. Harrison slammed the back door shut and pushed the half-open front door wide, jumping into the driver's seat. He turned the ignition. He was lucky, the engine was warm and started immediately. He slammed the gears into first, releasing the clutch hastily. The car jerked forward, almost stalling . . . he'd forgotten to release the handbrake. He pushed his foot hard down on the accelerator, snapping down the handbrake as the car shot away along the village street.

The crowd opposite hadn't stirred. They watched petrified as the car disappeared round a bend, the roar of the engine gradually diminishing. The sergeant appeared at the top of the steps still clutching his report. He stared down at the two policemen groaning in the road.

'Shit,' he said, emphatically.

The car bounced unnervingly as it leapt over the small humpbacked bridge before leaving the village behind. Harrison kept glancing in the rearview mirror, but as he expected there was no sign of a chase – it appeared he occupied the only car available, further, he had a full tank. He had no particular plan of escape other than to get back across the border and into Northern Ireland.

He didn't know where he was, but since he had crossed the coastline from north to south, and was in neutral territory, the Ulster part of Northern Ireland must be somewhere to the east. He knew very little of the topography of this part of the world, apart from a vague idea of its shape and history, but certainly the terrain was reminiscent of Scotland. It wasn't surprising that at first he'd believed he was there.

The road twisted and turned, following the contours of the valley, but always heading south. He decided he'd bear eastwards at the first opportunity. He kept his foot firmly down on the accelerator. Even if they could not pursue him immediately, they had phones and would set up road-blocks as soon as they could. He needed to get out of this valley to have a chance.

The road veered sharply round to his left and he put his foot gently on to the brake to ease her down. He saw the enormous pot-hole too late. Hidden by the bend, half full of water, it was in the one place to do him the most damage. He turned the wheel as sharply as he dared, trying to pass it by getting as far to the right as he could. It only made things worse. The front nearside wheel hit the edge of the hole at a slight angle, almost jerking the steering wheel from his hands. He felt the axle snap and the car veered away to the edge of the road, the broken axle tearing into the road's surface.

The low wooden fence splintered as the bonnet ploughed through it. The car dipped forward and downwards as it plunged over the grassy incline that fell sharply away into the shallow river running parallel to the road. Harrison felt the car tip up as the front dug into the soft surface of the bank.

For a moment the vehicle was airborne before it smashed down on to its roof. Harrison's head crashed into the pillar dividing the front side window from the rear, knocking him unconscious. The car rolled over three times before coming to rest on its wheels, right side up, straddling the shallow water of the stream. The engine steamed gently, but did not ignite. For a second time that day Harrison survived the impact of a crash. He was lucky, though it's doubtful that, if he'd been conscious, he would have agreed.

The police sergeant, in a pony and trap, found him ten minutes later, still out cold.

The clock in the upstairs hall ticked loudly, then began to creak as it wound itself up to strike the hour. It sounded like a miniature version of Big Ben as it chimed out its musical introduction, followed by two strikes to indicate two A.M. The house was silent again – just the normal groans of old timber, and the elements' play upon them.

Nora's father turned restlessly in his sleep, his over-full bladder giving him no comfort, and a constant erection. He threw back the covers and sat up suddenly. His feet touched the cold floor and he sat at the edge of the bed for a moment, trying to wake up. He reached down and pulled on his socks, then stood up, swaying for a moment, still only half awake. He felt his way across the room and into the hall, sliding his hand along the wall until he found the switch outside the door of the lavatory. The light blinded him, forcing him to wakefulness. He relieved himself, then groggily pulled the chain. The cistern hissed and flushed and Tracey shut the door behind him to cut off the cacophony of noise. He switched off the light and made his way slowly back along the hall. Nora's bedroom door was open and a patch of moonlight illuminated the faded strip of carpet in her room. He glanced inside – the covers were thrown back across the bed and it was empty, though it had been slept in. He stood uncertainly outside her door. He was puzzled; it was totally

70

unlike her. He went back to his room and pulled on his trousers and shoes, then went downstairs – there was no one; the house was empty apart from himself.

He was now wide awake – the seed of doubt beginning to alarm him. Nora never left the house alone at night without his knowledge, he'd drummed that into her often enough. Secrets were impossible to keep, and most people, including the Garda, knew of his strong Republican sympathies. What he hoped they didn't know about was the cache of arms and ammunition that lay hidden beneath the floorboards of the barn. It was all that remained of the raid by the IRA on the Government's arms depot in Phoenix Park in 'thirty-nine. They'd got away with thirteen lorry loads and a million rounds of ammunition, most of which had been recovered by the Army. What he held was invaluable, and if anyone got an inkling of it he was dead. Several of the men who had taken part in the raid had already been caught and executed by firing squad.

He grabbed his rifle from above the door and walked out into the courtyard separating the main buildings from the barn. A strip of dark cloud cleared the moon and suddenly it was bathed in a white light, shadows of the trees distorted over the cobblestones.

He stood quite still, rifle down by his side, listening. It was quiet, a beautiful night, just the rustling of the trees in the faint breeze coming across the Wicklow Mountains. He tensed, he could hear someone crying. It was a woman's voice coming from the barn.

Nora felt betrayed, she knew that Peter had to leave, but somehow she'd hoped, quite illogically, that it wouldn't happen – that he would stay here with her, that she could hide him, give him civilian clothes, and that he would choose to stay.

Nora, although not much younger than Bryce, had no

concept of a cause – she could not understand what drove him, terrified as he was, to the battle. She buried her face in his makeshift bed, crying bitterly. 'Why did you do it? You don't love me, otherwise you wouldn't want to leave.'

Peter knelt down beside her, not knowing how to console her – disturbed by her tears. 'Nora, I had to let the police know. I'd be termed a deserter if I spent any longer here.'

He didn't tell her the punishment for desertion in wartime. He didn't want to upset her any further. She turned her head to look at him, tears causing some of the straw to stick to her face.

'When will they come?'

'I don't know.' He brushed the straw from her face. 'Tomorrow I expect; I've never been arrested before.'

Nora tried not to smile, but anger lost to her natural good humour and she reached up to kiss him.

Peter saw her eyes widen with shock and she screamed. At the same instant the bullet exploded into the floorboards beside him and Nora pulled him sideways, covering his body with hers.

'No, no, no,' she screamed again and again.

Her father stood holding the rifle to his shoulder some ten feet away.

'Get off him, you worthless bitch – or I'll put the bullet through you.'

Bryce struggled to free himself, but Nora pinned him down, whispering savagely in his ear. 'Lie still, don't move – he will kill you.'

Bryce could see she was right. The man was incensed by her actions, violent and dangerous.

Nora faced him. 'Please, Father, he's a pilot, his plane crashed. He was injured, I only brought him back here to rest.'

Tracey eyed them grimly, absorbing this information,

72

seeing the RAF insignia on Bryce's jacket.

'The bloody Englishman's had you, hasn't he?'

Nora said nothing, instinct telling her not to lie.

'He's been inside you, fucked you in the bloody straw.' Something snapped. All the anger, frustration and humiliation she had suffered from him these past few months she'd been able to bear. The truth caused the explosion. She screamed, flinging herself at her father, clawing at his face, knocking the rifle upwards. Tracey brought the butt round sharply, catching Nora on the side of the head. She fell to the floor stunned. Before Tracey could level the rifle Bryce was on him, pushing the gun barrel back across the older man's throat, pinning him to the ground.

The Irishman's face began to redden, but he'd fought a lot of dirty fights. He managed to jerk his knee up between Bryce's legs. The Englishman screamed with pain as Tracey flung him backwards, but he knew he was dead if he let go of the rifle. Now it was at his throat, pressing down into his larynx. Tracey's face was above him, his eyes bulging, trying to force the life from him. Bryce could not draw breath – he could feel himself weakening, the blood pounding in his head. He could hear bells ringing – was he dead already, on his way to heaven or hell? The rifle was getting heavier, Tracey's face seemed to be pulsating, diffusing into more than one.

Air rushed into his lungs as the two Garda policemen dragged Tracey from the pilot's body. Bryce lay on his back for a moment, staring up at the three men as the Garda struggled to control Nora's father. He raised himself on to his elbow. Nora hadn't moved. He crawled across to her, holding her head in his lap. She was stunned, but coming round slowly. She flung her arms around him, crying with relief. This incensed Tracey further; he tried to break free of the two policemen.

'Do you see what he has done to my daughter – don't you realize what's happened.' He hawked and spat at Bryce. 'Take your bloody hands off her.'

He played it to the hilt – more than anything else he wanted the Garda out of the bloody barn.

One of them held on to him whilst the other went over to the British flyer.

'Come on – the sooner we get you out of here the better.'

Nora clung to him, but she realized he was safer with the police.

Bryce leant over and kissed her once. 'I'll be back – I promise.'

He touched her face tenderly, then allowed the Garda to pull him away from her and lead him towards the open door of the barn. He could see the police car outside and realized why he had heard the sound of bells. The gates of heaven had slammed shut at the sound of a police car and he was more than grateful.

The other policeman warned Tracey not to do anything foolish. He picked up the rifle and Bryce's clothes, gathering them under his arm, making his way to the entrance of the barn. Tracey turned slowly, looking at Nora. He ignored the police and walked towards her, his intention clear.

Bryce realized what he was going to do and tried to break away from the policeman. The Garda yelled a warning to his colleague and they both grabbed Bryce and propelled him towards the car. Bryce heard Nora scream. He twisted around and saw Tracey savagely smash his hand across Nora's face. Blood spurting from her lip as it split. He swore fiercely, struggling like a maniac to escape from the hold they had on him, but they were professionals, more used to dealing with violence. He didn't see the stick the policeman drew from his belt. He just felt the flash of pain slice through his head before he collapsed unconscious between

74

the policemen. Nor did he hear Nora's screams as she begged her father not to beat her. Mercifully he was spared that. The policemen bundled his limp body into the back of the car and drove away.

The only light was from two grilles, high, near the roof of the vehicle. Low fixed wooden benches ran down either side of the van, and it was impossible to get comfortable. Bryce realized that was probably quite deliberate. He had never been arrested before, but he had seen the way the RAF Military Police handled prisoners, and he had no reason to believe the Irish equivalent would be any different. The military van had bounced its way across the country for what seemed like an eternity and Bryce was feeling cold and miserable, finding the half light oppressive.

He heard the engine level change as the vehicle slowed down, then stopped. At first he thought it was just another crossroad, but then he heard one of the doors slam and somebody get out of the cab. The heavy boots stopped at the back of the van and Bryce prepared himself to leave. He heard the rattle of keys, then the two doors were flung wide and Bryce shielded his eyes from the bright light that flooded in, making them water slightly. He saw the outline of two men standing outside the van, then they were bundled in and the doors slammed shut. He heard the MP laugh derisively as he got back into the cab. The van moved slowly forward again and began to pick up speed.

The two men were seated opposite and as his eyes quickly readjusted to the gloom Bryce could see they were in uniform. The Luftwaffe insignia glinted in the dim light and he felt the shock of surprise run through him. Gehler too was surprised at the presence of the RAF pilot, but four years of close confinement in Austria had taught him how to survive and he didn't expect to be a prisoner for long.

He appraised Bryce carefully. He was very young, not more than twenty, he guessed, and he looked more than a little apprehensive. He smiled to himself – one thing to incinerate an anonymous person in a dog-fight. Quite another to sit a few feet away and look into his eyes. He decided to take the initiative.

'It seems we are faced with a long journey – together for a change,' he smiled. 'My name is Gehler, Oberleutnant Gehler. My colleague is Leutnant Gunther Kinzell.'

He stretched out his hand – Bryce stared at it. He could see the glove melting, peeling slowly back as the flesh beneath it slowly blackened with heat. He drew back from Gehler, pulling his knees up to his chest, sliding along the bench seat into the corner, as far away from the German as he could get.

Gehler couldn't see his face, but he heard the whisper from the corner.

'Bryce – Pilot Officer Bryce.'

Gehler and Kinzell exchanged a look, but said nothing. Their internment had begun.

Quinn wiped the sweat from his eyes on the damp rag that was tied loosely around his neck. It was filthy and only served to move the coal dust and perspiration around his

76

face. He was stripped to the waist, the work hard and grinding, constantly shovelling the coal into the heart of the furnace below the boilers. In the fierce heat of the engine room he'd lost more than twelve pounds in weight. This crossing had been very different from the last, the old coal burner had taken nearly five weeks to drag itself across the Atlantic and half the Mediterranean. He glanced up at the streaming steel walls that surrounded him, aware that he was far below the water line and that if they'd been hit by torpedo he would have had little or no chance. The merchantman would not have been the first neutral vessel to be hit thus. He shovelled coal and tried to forget about it. The brass-plated clock on the bulkhead moved slowly. Another fifteen minutes and his shift would end. It would be his last. Soon they would be docking.

The rusty hull nosed its way slowly through the crowded harbour of Genoa. On her flaking prow and stern could just be discerned her name – *Abraham Lincoln* – almost hidden by years of grime and rust as though the old vessel were slightly ashamed to carry such an august name. Quinn had changed and washed himself down, his duties completed, his voyage nearly over. He stood leaning against the rail in the forecastle watching her slow progress into dock, wondering whether there would be anyone to meet him, whether his message had reached its destination. If not his pay for this trip would not last him long, nor could he attempt to reach Ireland without assistance. Germany occupied Europe right to the Channel coast, and even though Eire was neutral, there were, as far as he knew, no regular sailings from Europe. He scanned the quayside anxiously, his contacts in New York had relayed all the details relating to his voyage and arrival. In spite of her age and condition the *Abraham Lincoln* was into Genoa on time.

It was hot, the midday sun baking the metal surfaces,

glittering on the water. Quinn squinted, shading his eyes from the harsh light. He spotted him almost at once. His white suit standing out incongruously amongst the dock workers busily tying the merchantman to the quay. Even an old tub like the *Abraham Lincoln* gathered a few spectators. The man that Quinn had focused on stood a little to one side, unmoving, his spectacles glinting in the sunlight.

Quinn left the deck and went down to his quarters, picked up the battered suitcase which was all he had allowed himself and, without a backward glance, walked to the gangplank that had just been swung into position. No one took the slightest notice of him as he made his way down it. The ground felt hard, and slightly disorientated him for a moment. He paused. The quay was alive with activity and slowly Quinn moved off, slipping anonymously into it.

The man hadn't moved and, as Quinn made his way towards him, he smiled expectantly. The Irishman stopped, facing him, saying nothing. He did not intend to identify himself yet.

The man smiled again, slightly embarrassed. 'I'm expecting someone to arrive on that vessel. My name is Hoffner. I am an interpreter here on behalf of the Foreign Office of the Third Reich.' He poked his glasses nervously back on to his nose.

Quinn studied him for a moment. 'Hoffner?' he enquired.

'Yes, yes of course, I'm sorry.' He fished around in his pockets, sweating slightly. 'I do have something.' He smiled with relief. 'Ah, here it is. I should have shown you this first. They told me you might be suspicious.'

He held a small leather wallet out in front of him. Quinn glanced at it briefly; it seemed in order. He stuck out his hand.

'Glad to see you.'

Hoffner grasped it enthusiastically. 'Good, good. I did not know quite how to make contact. I thought it best just to make myself conspicuous, hence the white suit.' He grimaced, still ill at ease.

Quinn looked at the motley collection still surging around them. 'You certainly did that. What happens now?'

Hoffner began to walk towards the dock gates. 'I have a car. We go to the Legation first, where you can clean up and have a meal. You must be exhausted.'

Quinn swung in alongside him. 'And after that?'

Hoffner stared straight ahead. 'We go to Berlin,' he said.

The roads had been almost deserted of cars, though there had been plenty of horse-drawn traffic. Bray had reminded him of the old yellowing photographs of Dublin one sometimes saw in the estate agents' offices. Hansom cabs and horse-drawn trams, frozen in time. Driscoll was lucky. As an influential member of the establishment in Dublin he received as much petrol as he required. Though the newspaper he ran, *The Sunday Irish Times*, was small by London standards, it was well respected and carried some weight politically, particularly within the newly-formed structure of Irish politics. Ireland was perhaps one of the few places left in a modern world where important decisions were still made in dim, smoky back rooms. Real power surfaced in strange places, and very little went on in Ireland that could be considered truly confidential. It was hardly surprising in a country where the population was so small and power so concentrated, and it was one of the reasons why Driscoll was making this trip out to the golf course at Delgany.

He turned up the long drive that led to the clubhouse.

The incline was steep and trees crowded in on either side. Shafts of sunlight occasionally penetrated the gloom, then the road swept round to the right and the trees disappeared. He drove up to the clubhouse, built a few years before in the mid-thirties. It was an attractive building, white pebble-dashed walls with black windows and doors. A small balcony crossed the front of the building, facing the high tree-studded hills backing on to the course. They dominated the landscape dramatically. It was a spectacular setting and appropriate for what Driscoll had in mind. Most of the diplomatic corps played golf here, and no one would think twice about a round of golf between himself and the German Ambassador.

He parked the car in front of the clubhouse. The Ambassador's limousine with the swastikas on the bonnet had already arrived. The chauffeur was sitting in the driving seat, where he would wait until the Ambassador left. Driscoll's pulse quickened a little; the meeting could be decisive.

They trudged up the long hill to the last tee before the treeline at the end of the course, pulling a mobile caddie behind them. Delgany Golf Course had been known to finish off a few weak tickers because of its steep hills, and already Driscoll was breathing heavily, though Herr Hemmrich seemed less affected. The Ambassador glanced at Driscoll. He was overweight and red in the face.

'Would you like to rest for a moment, we have plenty of time.'

Driscoll nodded gratefully, and they both sat down on the grassy bank at the edge of the tee. The view was magnificent. Looking eastwards down the valley and over Greystones they could see the calm water of the Irish Sea glinting below them. A white sail drifted slowly from north to south. It looked infinitely peaceful, and it was hard to believe that farther out in the straits between Liverpool Bay and the North Atlantic U-boats were waiting for any stragglers that hadn't managed to stay in convoy.

The course was empty, few people could play golf on a working day. Fewer still could get this far out of Dublin with petrol in such short supply. The Ambassador had chosen well.

Driscoll's colour had returned to normal, and Hemmrich decided to make it easy for him.

'It's beautiful, this valley.' He waved an arm and shook his head in appreciation. 'I am constantly surprised at how the light keeps changing, altering the perspective, adding to its beauty. You are right to be proud of your country.'

Driscoll realized it was his cue. 'I wanted to talk to you privately, Ambassador. There are things I feel your Government should be aware of.'

Hemmrich said nothing, but he nodded in a friendly fashion, encouraging the Irishman. Driscoll gazed down between his feet. A caterpillar was humping itself slowly across the grass.

'You know that Churchill's representative, Mackay, was here?'

Hemmrich looked at him and smiled. 'Yes, I had heard.'

'He wanted Ireland to participate in the war against Germany – and he offered Dev a very powerful inducement.'

Driscoll could see that the Ambassador was interested now, though he tried to disguise it.

'Indeed . . .'

'He proposed a joint committee to work out the Constitution for a United Ireland, provided we joined the war against Germany.'

Hemmrich contemplated the white sail as it slowly disappeared behind the point. He fully realized the implications. He had considered it highly likely that Ireland would join Britain against Germany, and had been surprised when the Irish Premier had steadfastly maintained his neutrality. But Driscoll was right. A United Ireland was a powerful inducement.

'Since Mackay has already returned to England, I imagine the decision has been taken.'

Driscoll glanced down. The caterpillar had made another couple of feet. 'It has, and Dev has turned it down flat. He has no intention of fighting on Britain's side. Besides, he knows the North would never agree. It was a sprat to catch a mackerel.'

Hemmrich followed Driscoll's eyeline and saw the caterpillar's methodical progress. 'Then the situation has not altered.'

Driscoll ground his heel angrily into the caterpillar, crushing it into the soil. 'Wrong. Churchill will invade Ireland from the North!'

He turned, gazing directly into Hemmrich's eyes. 'He needs these ports in the South, Ambassador. Your U-boats are throttling the life from England and he will not sit by when it is a matter of life or death for his country. He will take us over.'

'But surely, Driscoll, England only has the remnants of her army left. Most of her equipment was left in and around Dunkirk.'

Driscoll gripped his arm. 'They still have a navy, Ambassador, and an air force. The Luftwaffe will testify to that. We have neither. All that stands between them and the ports are seven thousand badly equipped soldiers and reservists. And that will not stop Churchill if he needs those ports. Admiral Doenitz will know better than anyone whether the U-boats are succeeding. I beg you, Ambassador, to inform your Führer of this development. This is the moment we have been waiting for, Herr Hemmrich. I believe that now is the right time for Hitler to approach De Valera and offer him some of the arms and equipment abandoned at Dunkirk, which are of the type and calibre already in use by the Irish Army, and also guarantees of protection against invasion from the North. I should be most willing to act as an intermediary – there are many people I can approach in confidence. I think a majority would welcome Germany as an ally. Without you I fear we shall become a satellite of England again.'

Hemmrich removed Driscoll's hand, which was still gripping his arm tightly. He knew of this man's connections. They had proved useful in the past. And this information was vital. Strategically Ireland was extremely important.

'I understand your fears, Driscoll, and believe me your message will be with the Führer before the week is out. I shall also make sure they know of your generous offer.'

Driscoll felt an enormous sense of relief. He pushed himself upright and offered his hand to the Ambassador. Hemmrich gripped it and hauled himself to his feet.

'Thank you, Driscoll.'

He picked a club from the caddie. 'Your shot, I believe.'

Quinn sat huddled in the corner of the black limousine, his hands thrust deep into the pockets of the long grey overcoat. They felt cold, though the night was humid and still, the air heavy. All day he had felt the tension growing. He rubbed the back of his neck; his head throbbed painfully. He recognized the symptoms: soon there would be a storm. His head always ached when there was thunder about. He hoped they would have taken off before it broke; the flight had already been postponed once because of bad weather. Not that the Schloss Hotel at Wilhelmshoe had been uncomfortable, but the questioning and briefings had gone on too long. Before his arrival at Kassel there had been a month of interrogation in the bank director's house at Grunewald in Berlin. The *Abwehr* were thorough; clearly they recognized that his organization could pave the way to German involvement in the struggle to free Northern Ireland, but he wasn't sure how deep their commitment went. However, he had got a promise of arms and supplies, and he felt sure that if he could get back and demonstrate his ability to sabotage the British war effort, he could bring the Germans in much more directly. Now all Quinn wanted was to be home. He admired much of what he had seen in Berlin and Kassel, but Germany was too clean for him . . . too neat.

He glanced out of the window. They were passing through a small village, but it was completely blacked out, not a crack of light to be seen. He wondered how his driver managed to stay on the road with headlights so heavily shrouded. How ironic if he were to be killed running into a tree in the dark after coming this far. He shivered and pulled the collar of his coat up around his neck.

God, it had been so cold in New York last winter. He'd hated every minute of it, being shifted from one 'safe' house to another, only allowed out at night, but he knew the restrictions were necessary. His face had been plastered over the newspapers when the Congressmen had protested about his arrest and there had been even more publicity when he had jumped bail. He'd had to lie low for a long time. All the normal shipping routes back to Ireland had been suspended and those that remained were too risky for him to chance. For a while he had despaired of ever getting back – then the contact had been established with the German Legation in

Genoa and his hopes had risen. But it had taken months of negotiation before the perilous journey had finally been arranged. It was more than a year since he had left Ireland and what had he achieved?

The *Abwehr*'s interest was positive. They would not have gone to this trouble to effect his return to Ireland if it wasn't to their advantage. A special minister had been appointed from the German Foreign Office to deal with Irish affairs and liaise with the *Abwehr*, Dr Edmund Veesenmayer. He was young and committed, and also very shrewd. Quinn had done his best to convince him how important Ireland could be to Germany. He sensed that Veesenmayer was his best bet.

They were back in the open countryside again and a half moon was struggling to break through the cloud cover. He peered at the luminous face of his watch – it was just before eleven P.M. – they should be arriving at Fritzlar Airfield soon. He'd got as far as the base last time. Now he felt the car slowing down and leaned forward in his seat. He could see the low line of hedgerows that bordered the airfield, then the wheels crunched as they swung into the entrance and stopped before the gate post while the guards checked identification. They'd arrived.

Thankfully, the briefing was short. He'd already had instruction on how to use his parachute. His pilot, as before, was Leutnant Drexler, but he hardly noticed him, just a blurred impression of a pleasant face surrounded by a leather flying helmet, the straps flapping loosely beneath his chin.

The door banged shut behind them and they walked side by side across the tarmac, Quinn's parachute bumping uncomfortably against the back of his legs. A breath of wind suddenly whipped up over the flat landing strip, blowing grit into his face. He spat it out and grinned in the darkness at his companion. 'The storm is coming.'

The pilot glanced at him, sensing his effort to repress his fear. 'Nothing to worry about. We'll be up and above it long before it breaks.'

Quinn said nothing, but he was grateful for the other man's confidence. He knew he wasn't a coward, but he'd never flown before. The *Abwehr* didn't know that, though he suspected they knew everything else, including the mole in his armpit.

He almost bumped into the plane. It was painted jet black and he hadn't seen it in the dark. He mumbled an embarrassed apology to the pilot, who grabbed his arm and led him to the hatch in the belly of the twin-engined bomber.

'No need to apologize, Quinn. We don't want anyone to see it.'

He climbed up inside, banging his knee painfully on the metal supports. Then the cloud cleared momentarily and he saw the latticed perspex nose of the Heinkel 111.

The Leutnant sat him down in the co-pilot's seat beside him, flicked on the dull red cockpit light and commenced his pre-flight check-out.

Two mechanics materialized out of the darkness and removed the chocks from the wheels. Drexler checked with the radio tower and was given clearance for take-off. He glanced at Quinn, who had strapped himself in.

'All right?'

Quinn nodded and Drexler fed some juice into the engines and switched on, first the port, then the starboard engines. The noise shattered the silence of the night, and settled into a steady drone. The Leutnant taxied the bomber to the take-off position, then signalled he was ready. The runway stretched ahead of him, straddled on either side by twin rows of lights merging imperceptibly into the darkness. He pushed the throttles forward and the Heinkel trundled down the runway, gathering momentum.

Quinn sat immobile, gripping the edge of his seat, the lights flicking past him like a train at night roaring through a station. Then suddenly the bumping ceased, the lights dropped away below him and disappeared as the Heinkel bore into the low cloud. He was on his way.

As he sat in the bus and the old bones of the seats of him shaking beneath him. He could feel his through him. They had only the band and cases and then directly to the ... she said and asked if he could ... and asked if it would be safe ...

BOOK THREE

# INTERNMENT

Provost-Marshal Tynan was curious. He wondered what the American would be like. What had prompted him to come this far, to engage himself in a war in which, so far at any rate, his own country played no part? Tynan had seen the newsreels. They'd got a lot of mileage out of Eagle Squadron: idealistic young Americans flocking to the cause of democracy and a free world. He didn't believe it – at least, he didn't believe all of it. But like all good propaganda there was an element of truth in there somewhere. It remained to be seen how much.

He heard heavy military boots clumping along the passage to his outer office, followed a moment later by a respectful knock. His Executive Officer poked his head around the door. 'The American is here, sir.'

Tynan nodded and the officer beckoned the escort in. The boots thudded into the floorboards as the two Military Policemen marched Harrison in between them. Tynan was shocked, but remained impassive. Harrison looked terrible. His face was marked and a thin trickle of blood emerged from the hairline close to his forehead where he had only partially managed to parry the blow from the guardstick of one of the MPs. His body ached from the prods and sharp digs he'd had to endure since his recapture. He felt weak from hunger and exhausted by the endless journey. An MP pushed him roughly towards the desk. He staggered and was promptly dug sharply by the guardstick again.

'Stand to attention,' the MP barked.

Harrison flinched. The MP's mouth was only inches from his ear and the words reverberated in his head.

91

Tynan had seen enough. 'All right. Leave him. Dismissed.'

Two pairs of heavy boots crashed to attention, then thudded from the room. The door closed quietly, deferentially, behind them. Harrison looked at the man behind the desk for the first time.

He was clean-shaven, his hair greying, cut short, no attempt to disguise the fact that it was thinning. He was about forty-eight years old with a wide, generous mouth and deep-set eyes, the heavy brows casting shadows over his sharply-etched cheekbones. As the light was directly above his head, Harrison could not see his eyes clearly. But there was something else, something Harrison was only vaguely aware of, a presence? Or was it only his weakened state and fevered imagination? He swayed slightly.

Tynan indicated the chair in front of his desk. 'Sit down.'

The American did so gratefully. Tynan studied him.

'You seem a little the worse for wear.'

Harrison felt the cut in his hairline gingerly. 'Your MPs aren't exactly gentle.'

'No, but I hear you roughed up some of our constabulary.'

Harrison grinned. 'I needed the transport.'

'You didn't get far.'

'I might have, if you built roads instead of holes.'

Tynan almost smiled. 'I doubt it.' He paused momentarily. 'A car in Ireland these days is as noticeable as an aeroplane in 1918.' Opening a drawer, he lifted out a bottle of whiskey. 'Would you like a drink?'

Harrison nodded his acceptance and Tynan poured out two small glasses.

'Thanks,' Harrison said. He tossed it back in one gulp, Tynan sipped his.

'Where are you from?'

Harrison rubbed his unshaven chin. 'Name, rank and serial number, and that you've already got.'

92

'Of course – I was just referring to your insignia, Eagle Squadron. I'm curious. Why would an American come this far to fight in a war?'

Harrison sat back in the hard wooden chair. Tynan took another sip of his drink, but Harrison was aware that there was a good deal more than simple curiosity behind the question. He smiled. 'Who knows, maybe I just needed the job.'

Tynan surveyed him coldly, unamused. Harrison sensed an immediate change in the man, like a steel shutter coming down, primitive and menacing. He shifted in his seat instinctively straightening up as though to ward off a blow. Yet Tynan hadn't moved, his face was as impassive as ever. But it was there, Harrison knew it, recognizing the same elemental fear he had once felt in the mountains when he had turned from his camp fire and seen a huge grizzly standing only a few feet away. Luckily bears did not much care for fire and it had lumbered quickly away when he grabbed a flaming stick and wielded it.

Harrison heard him speaking as though from a distance. 'There are a few things you need to know. Attitudes here are a bit mixed. Some pro-British, some anti-. It depends. We have a long history with England, though that will be complicated in your case by the fact that you are American. However, let me make it clear what the position is. Ireland is a neutral country and all combative belligerents that fall into our hands are interned for the duration of hostilities. There is a parole system that has to be authorized by me and countersigned by your own CO in the camp. His name is Burroughs and he will explain to you how it works.' Tynan took another sip of the whiskey, then paused momentarily. 'I know it is your duty to try and escape; that I understand. It is also mine to try and keep you in Ireland one way or another. I hope I make myself clear?'

Harrison stared at him curiously. Was it a question? His

mind refused to function clearly. He rubbed his eyes wearily.

Tynan raised his glass. 'Good health.'

It seemed incongruous. Harrison looked at him without expression, but did not raise his glass. Tynan waited. Then Harrison reached forward and placed his glass upside down on Tynan's desk.

'Empty,' he said.

Bryce listened. The van had halted and he could hear voices, shouted instructions. Then it jerked forward again, this time over what seemed to be a dirt track. He opened his eyes and swung his legs down on to the floor. The vehicle stopped again, and this time he heard the military policemen climb out of the cab and walk around to the doors at the back. The two Luftwaffe officers in the seat opposite began straightening their jackets. A key fumbled in the lock and the doors were flung open. A burly figure was silhouetted against the light and an Irish voice commanded them to get out.

Bryce waited until the German officers had slid along the bench and been marched off, then he emerged stiffly, blinking in the light. Immediately two Military Policemen grabbed his arms and marched him swiftly towards a high solid wooden gate.

As his eyes adjusted to the light Bryce could see it was the outer entrance to a depressingly well-organized POW camp, and it was immediately clear that there was nothing temporary about it. Two high coiled wire fences about fifteen feet high and eight feet apart formed the outer barrier and another barbed-wire inner barrier surrounded a number of corrugated-iron huts raised on concrete blocks. As he was marched through the gates he noticed a second similar structure forming the entrance to another camp of slightly larger dimensions farther to his right. The two gates were separated by a small wooden hut. In fact it was one single camp divided in two by a high corrugated-iron fence sunk into a ditch, and Bryce saw several Luftwaffe officers clustering around the two new arrivals before he was marched through the inner gate and surrounded by a number of RAF officers and men.

One of them, a short, stocky man, back-pedalled in front of him as he was propelled forward by the two MPs. He grinned up at Bryce, exposing a row of gold-lined upper front teeth that gleamed brightly in the sunshine.

'How is war, sir – we win yet?'

The accent was heavy and from the insignia on his jacket Bryce could see he was Polish. He tried to return the grin, but the MP to his left reached forward and pushed the Pole roughly aside. The little man, who was already having difficulty walking backwards quickly enough, tripped and fell sprawling into the dirt. The two MPs stepped quickly over him without pausing or releasing their hold on Bryce.

A number of the RAF began to boo and slow handclap the MPs. They drew threateningly closer, jeering. One of the two drew his riot stick, looking nervously from side to side.

A line of officers formed in front of them and they stopped short, gripping both of Bryce's arms tightly. He could feel the tension in their grip. The man on his left with the drawn stick was trembling slightly, and sweating.

Nobody moved, the chanting died away, the atmosphere was electric. All it needed was the spark and Bryce felt the MP on his left tense himself as though to charge forward, but it didn't come.

'All right, what's the problem? Let's see the wood for the trees.' The voice was cool, authoritative, and the men facing them glanced behind and shuffled apart. A Flight Lieutenant walked slowly through the gap. He was older than the majority of the other officers, of medium height with a quiff of hair that continually flopped around his forehead. He brushed it back with his hand, put on his cap and smiled. He did not look particularly impressive but there was no doubt that he was in command, and the response was automatic.

The two MPs saluted, and Bryce sensed their relief at the appearance of the senior officer.

'This is Pilot Officer Bryce, sir, and we have been instructed to formally hand him over to you.'

They saluted again in unison. The CO responded casually. They stepped one pace smartly back, about turned and marched from the compound. Bryce faced the senior officer and saluted.

He stretched out his hand. 'I'm Flight Lieutenant Burroughs. Welcome to K Lines, Bryce.'

Burroughs' room was shabby, but clean. A battered desk in one corner, a couple of chairs and a bookcase the only furnishings. Bryce slumped into the chair in front of the desk and gratefully accepted the offer of a cup of tea. A sergeant brought it almost immediately.

Burroughs sat in the only other chair behind the desk, and glanced at the young officer while he shuffled a few papers about. He looked exhausted, on edge. Dark rings around his eyes. He decided on a few general questions – the debriefing could come later. There was no urgency.

'Did you see Tynan?'

Bryce looked puzzled. 'Tynan?'

'The Provost-Marshal. He sometimes has a talk first with new detainees.'

Bryce sipped the tea and looked out of the window at one of the gun posts. 'Looks more like a prisoner-of-war camp.'

Burroughs smiled automatically. 'Yes, it's a moot point. But there are differences.'

'In what way?'

Burroughs stood up and walked to the window, his back to Bryce. 'Well, there is a parole system that enables you to visit certain local areas during the day, but you can forget any ideas you might have about using it to break out.' He paused, then added quietly, 'All three governments, British, German and Irish, have agreed that if anyone uses it as a method of escape – under international law, they will be sent back.'

Bryce stared incredulously at Burroughs. 'Are you saying that there is no way to escape?'

Burroughs turned and faced him, his face set, eyes boring into Bryce. 'Virtually, that is true. The only way you, or anybody else, will be accepted back into the war, is if you escape legitimately from inside the compound, and that is almost impossible.'

Bryce rubbed his eyes tiredly. He was finding it difficult to take in the implications. 'Why?'

Burroughs remained by the window, silhouetted by the light behind him, which made it impossible for Bryce to see his face. 'Because the Irish Military Police have had nearly twenty years' experience of keeping hot political prisoners firmly locked away.'

Bryce shook his head. 'But why should they care what happens to us?'

Burroughs showed the first sign of agitation. He began to

pace up and down behind his desk. 'They do care. There is a very strong German delegation in Dublin. Their Ambassador visits the detainees nearly every Sunday, and if both sides were not seen to be treated exactly the same – well, who knows? Anything could happen. We don't want to give the Nazis any excuse for occupying this country. We're stretched enough as it is. So, you will not break your parole, and I will be informed of any escape attempts from inside the camp.' He halted immediately in front of Bryce. 'Is that clear?'

Bryce rose from his seat and faced Burroughs. 'Perfectly clear, sir.'

The CO stared at him icily for a moment, then smiled suddenly.'Good,' he said, then walked around behind his desk and sat down. 'Now I expect you'll want to clean up and get some rest – though I don't suppose you'll get much of that until you've been pumped dry. We're a bit short on news around here.' He waved an arm dismissively. 'Off you go.'

Bryce turned, then halted by the door, remembering something. 'Sir?'

Burroughs looked up. 'Yes.'

'Will you let the authorities back in England know that I am safe?'

Burroughs brushed the quiff back from his eyes. 'I expect the Irish have already done so, but I shall confirm it.'

'Thank you, sir.'

Bryce saluted and left.

Gehler was surprised but delighted. That there should be a bar at all in an internment camp gave him cause for hope – that it should be so well stocked was a bonus.

The bar had been constructed with characteristic thoroughness, using whatever materials were available. And since barbed wire was in most plentiful supply, it had been used as the motif for the bar, which was promptly christened the Barbed Wire Bar.

The room was crowded. Most of the Luftwaffe officers were present, anxious to hear the latest news from home. Gehler estimated that there must be between forty and fifty airmen in the room. Kinzell was trying to answer some questions, but as yet the senior officer had not appeared. Gehler decided to wait no longer. He thumped the bar several times to gain their attention. Slowly the hubbub died down as they turned to face him. He waited until they were completely silent.

'The news is good. A week ago I accompanied the Führer to a rally.' He paused, allowing that to sink in. 'The response was magnificent, as always. But perhaps more important, the German people are in great heart, sensing that victory is almost within our grasp. We now occupy all of Europe from Germany to the Channel, the eventual occupation of England is merely a matter of time, as is our release.'

Instantly the men began to cheer and clap, responding as he had intended they should.

He saw a senior officer enter the room and slowly make his way through the crowd towards him. The men fell back and the cheering subsided. The Commanding Officer, Hauptmann Carl Von Bernstorff, halted in front of Gehler, who brought his arm up smartly into the Nazi salute.

'Heil Hitler.'

Von Bernstorff responded automatically and regarded Gehler without enthusiasm. 'I see you have already been regaling the men with news of our successes to date, and I too am interested in your confident predictions for the future.'

The irony was not lost on Gehler.

'Perhaps,' added Von Bernstorff, 'you could tell me how we . . . the Luftwaffe that is, are doing. Have we gained air supremacy over the RAF?' He smiled deprecatingly. 'We only receive the news via the English newspapers, and they, though somewhat biased, do seem to indicate that the skies over England are not ours yet.'

Gehler stared icily at Von Bernstorff but made no reply. The crowded room was silent, waiting to see whether Gehler would respond. He did not.

Von Bernstorff smiled again. 'I thought not. Perhaps you would be kind enough to brief your commanding officer, Oberleutnant, now that you have spoken to everyone else.'

He turned and strode quickly from the room. No one moved or made a sound, aware of Gehler's humiliation. Gehler glanced at Kinzell, then they both followed Von Bernstorff from the room. Immediately an excited buzz of speculation broke the silence.

Dietrich Bech pulled out the small red diary from his tunic pocket and began to make some notes.

Bech could hear the mumble of voices from Von Bernstorff's office; but not what was being said. Kinzell emerged, glanced briefly at him, then turned away down the passage and out of the entrance to the hut. Bech continued to lounge against the wall as though he were waiting to see the CO. The voices were getting heated now, and it was clear that Gehler was defying Von Bernstorff, ignoring his seniority, which surprised Bech. The repercussions, even under these circumstances, could be severe. Bech wondered why Gehler took such a risk. The argument continued for a few more minutes, then Bech heard the commanding officer dismiss the Oberleutnant. The door opened; Gehler saluted, then jerked it shut behind him.

He stood for a moment staring at the door, his eyes glittering with rage. Then he became aware of Bech's presence in the corridor. He turned slowly and stared at him.

'Well.'

The single icy word brought Bech smartly to attention. 'I have been instructed to show you to your quarters, Oberleutnant.'

Gehler nodded curtly and Bech led him down to the end of the corridor, opening the last door. Gehler stalked past him and glanced briefly round the room.

'At least it is clean.' The remark was dismissive, but Bech ignored the unspoken command and stepped into the room, closing the door quietly behind him. Gehler studied this behaviour without curiosity and waited for an explanation. Bech fumbled with the flap of his pocket, then pulled out the red diary. He offered it to Gehler.

'I'd like you to look at this, Oberleutnant.'

Gehler accepted it. 'What is it?'

Bech smiled obsequiously. 'A record that I have kept. It contains references, dates and witnesses of conversations I have heard, or that have been reported to me, that were in any way derogatory to the Führer, the Party or the war effort.'

Gehler began to flick through some of the pages, interested.

Bech smiled again. 'As you can see, the last entry is of Von Bernstorff's remarks to you.'

Gehler read it carefully, then looked up at Bech. 'Good, this is excellent, Leutnant . . . ?'

He allowed himself the flicker of a smile.

The Leutnant clicked his heels together. 'Bech, sir, Dietrich Bech'.

It was raining, a fine misty haze, cold on his face. He shivered and realized he was sweating, yet cold. He must be running a fever. The man's face loomed strangely above him, upside down as he struggled up the stairs with the stretcher. Halder couldn't see the bearer in front. The stretcher tilted and he rolled slightly. The pain in his arm was terrible, but seemed more bearable than before, almost numb.

He saw a white ceiling and white walls, and heard the footsteps of the two stretcher bearers echoing in the bare corridor curiously distorted – the sound coming in waves.

He felt the stretcher lift, then the softness of a bed as he was gently lowered on to it. Strange how everything seemed indefinable, like a dream. He wondered if he were dying and examined that thought carefully. Why didn't it frighten him?

Another face appeared above him, wearing a thin moustache. He closed his eyes and pretended to be asleep. The doctor carefully removed the bloodstained bandages from the injured gunner's upper arm. A thick putrescent smell assailed his nostrils at once. The flesh had been torn open to the bone, which was visible but unbroken. It was a dreadful mess, but he could have saved it if the boy had got here twenty-four hours earlier. Now it was too late. His nose wrinkled distastefully and he called out sharply, 'Nurse!'

He turned, seeking assistance. The young nurse was standing a couple of paces behind him, gazing fixedly at the mangled arm. Her eyes were wide, horrified, then the vile stench reached her and she covered her mouth and nose with her hand.

The doctor faced her, 'I need your help,' he said gently. 'This man's arm is gangrenous, I want you to prepare him for an operation – it will require amputation.'

The nurse seemed to steady for a moment. Then her eyes flicked past him and stared at the patient. The doctor felt a steely grip on his arm, pulling him round.

Halder dragged himself upwards until his face was almost level with the doctor's. His eyes glittered with fever, sweat standing out on his forehead and upper lip. But the voice was hard, no sign of delirium.

'No, there will be no amputation.'

The doctor, though surprised, still noted the quality of the man's English, hardly a trace of accent. He tried to help the gunner to lie down, but he gripped the front of his white coat, pulling his face towards the doctor's.

'Fetch Kinzell for me, promise you will do nothing till he is here?'

The doctor gently disengaged his hand. 'It's all right, I promise I will speak to him. Lie down please.'

The young man allowed him to lower him back to the bed, but did not take his eyes off him for an instant. 'I will not let you take my arm, doctor.'

He stared up into the doctor's eyes, willing himself to remain conscious, fear pumping adrenalin through him, the pain in his arm almost unbearable now. Yet if it hurt, it could not be dead. He hung on to that. It gave him hope.

He heard the doctor order the nurse to clean him up. He saw her face appear above him. Her eyes looked frightened – the boy smiled.

Captain Slye was sitting behind a huge littered desk, playing cards with himself and losing. He usually did. It was a source of constant frustration to him. He was a short, rotund man, almost Dickensian in appearance, with long sideburns sprouting down to his jawline.

He slammed down one hand of the cards irritably, then picked up the other and tugged at his whiskers, more than a little perplexed. The phone rang. It was a welcome relief – it got him off the hook.

'Captain Slye,' he announced, a little portentously, then added, 'liaison officer.'

He listened as Dr Martin explained the position. 'He is badly injured, and I must operate on his arm. However, he speaks English and insists that he wants to see a German officer by the name of Kinzell. I presume that is one of the Luftwaffe officers who were with him.'

Slye nodded unconsciously in agreement. 'That's right, Leutnant Kinzell. He's just arrived in K Lines. Shall I get him?'

'Please, and could you bring him up here, Captain. I can't delay this too long.'

Captain Slye replaced the receiver. He took his cap from the top of the table lamp on his desk and placed it at a jaunty angle on his head, then eased himself with some difficulty from his swivel chair, making his way to the door. He opened it, then paused, glancing at the cards on the table. He scuttled back, picked up one hand surreptitiously and replaced one of the cards with another from the other hand, then put both face down on the table.

A look of satisfaction spread across his face. He beamed, delighted with himself, glowed his way across the room, out of the door, and closed it with a thud of approval.

The blanket of fine, hazy rain still enveloped the grey Victorian buildings of the barracks and military hospital. Kinzell, Slye and an MP ran up the steps to the outer entrance of the medical wing and Slye ordered the MP to wait for them. The Captain removed his cap, flicking it up and down a number of times to remove the rain while he led Kinzell down the corridor to the Casualty Department.

Dr Martin and the nurse were stripping away the last of the gunner's clothing as they arrived. Halder was still clinging to consciousness. He saw Kinzell and weakly raised his good arm.

Kinzell strode across to him. The doctor waved the nurse away and joined Captain Slye, who was trying hard not to show his distaste for the smell.

Kinzell leaned down over the young gunner, speaking to him quietly in German.

'Paul, how are you?'

Halder felt an immense sense of relief. He gripped Kinzell's hand tightly.

'Leutnant, listen to me . . .' He swallowed. His throat was dry. Kinzell took a glass of water resting on top of a set of bedside drawers and lifted Halder's head, allowing him to sip some of it. His face was grey, like putty, a film of moisture glistening in the light from the electric bulb hanging above them. Halder licked his lips.

'Kinzell.' His eyes pleaded with the Leutnant. 'They are going to cut off my arm.' The boy bit on his lip, trying to hold back his tears. 'You must stop them. Please, make them understand, explain about my work.'

The gunner clutched at the officer's tunic, pulling him closer. 'Don't let them do it, Kinzell,' he whispered. 'I would sooner die.'

Kinzell held the boy's hand, knowing that he was telling the truth. He could see it in his tortured eyes. He brushed the damp hair back from Halder's forehead and tried to reassure him.

'I will speak to the doctor, Paul. I will make sure he understands, and I promise, nothing will happen without your knowledge.'

He squeezed his hand and had to swallow hard when he saw the gratitude in the gunner's eyes. He turned away and walked over to the doctor, who was waiting with Slye and the nurse. He spoke to Slye in German. 'Would you ask the doctor if I may have a word with him privately for a moment?'

Slye translated this and Dr Martin nodded his agreement, then asked the nurse to stay with the patient. The girl had completely overcome her initial fear. She sat down beside Halder, wiping the moisture from his face with a damp cloth.

Martin led them down the empty ward. Kinzell didn't speak at first. He was trying to decide how best he could explain and convince the doctor. It wasn't going to be easy through an interpreter. He glanced at Captain Slye.

'Would you ask the doctor if he has a nice home?'

Slye's eyebrows shot up, visibly surprised by the question. He glanced enquiringly at the German.

'Ask him,' Kinzell said.

Slye shrugged his shoulders and put the question to the doctor, who studied the German thoughtfully for a moment.

106

'Yes,' he said. 'I think so.'

'Are you a cultured man?' Kinzell asked.

The doctor nodded. 'I read, I like poetry, paintings.'

'So does Paul, my gunner.' Kinzell stopped and faced the doctor. 'He is a painter – he is very good. I have seen some of his work. It is his whole life, doctor. You must save his arm. Without it he will not live anyway.'

The doctor listened to the translation, wanting to protest, to explain the necessity, the risk, how close the gunner was to death. But Kinzell just stood there mute, waiting for his reply. He looked back up the ward to where Halder was lying, then nodded his head wearily.

'I will do what I can.'

In his heart he thought it was useless, but he had seen the implacable will in the gunner's eyes and he did not doubt that Kinzell was telling the truth.

The German smiled. 'Thank you, Herr Doktor,' he managed to say in English.

Bryce emerged from his meeting with Burroughs confused and depressed. He felt drained and for the moment there was no resentment at the CO's insistence that escape was almost impossible. All he wanted was sleep. He stood on the top of the steps and glanced around the compound, a fine rain was descending and it was beginning to look like a mud patch with a couple of shingle paths criss-crossing it. In the distance he could hear the strains of a Sousa march being played by a brass band. Most of the men in the Allied compound had gathered by the wire fence nearest to the road outside the camp. Bryce crossed the compound and stood beside them. The music grew louder. Then the band emerged round the corner from the general area of the main Curragh Military Barracks. They were all in Irish Army uniform, solidly in step and tempo. In front, striding somewhat unsteadily, was an Irish officer leading the band. A small man, not much more than five feet in height, his heightened colour betrayed the reason for his haphazard progress. The band ignored him and his tempo to a man. An RAF sergeant strolled casually over and stood next to Bryce watching the band's approach. Bryce glanced at him, instinctively he guessed he was a Londoner. There was something about his cheerful, uncomplicated face. He was a big man, broad shouldered, looming over him, grinning at the leader of the band.

'Looks as though he's had a skinful,' Bryce said.

The sergeant turned to him, still smiling. 'Brendan's always a bit like that, sir. I don't think he likes the army much, but the band are always in tune.'

'And in step,' Bryce added. He was right, the south London accent was unmistakable.

The sentries on the main gate were preparing themselves for the familiar ritual changing of the guard. The sergeant continued to watch the band's progress. 'It's Pilot Officer Bryce, isn't it?'

'Yes, that's right,' Bryce replied automatically.

'Sergeant Reed, sir, the CO's asked me to help you settle in.'

But Bryce wasn't listening. His whole attention was focused on the bloodstained figure being marched along behind the band towards them.

Harrison could feel the blood trickling down over his forehead, but made no attempt to staunch it. He was having too much trouble just staying on his feet and keeping in step.

The music helped. His legs were like rubber, and his eyes refused to stay open. He'd never felt so tired. He staggered and felt the MPs grab his arms. He shook himself loose and continued to march stiff-legged between the redcaps. The blood was blurring his vision, but he could see RAF officers behind the barbed wire watching him intently. It only increased his determination to make it under his own steam.

One man began to clap rhythmically in time with Harrison's step, encouraging him, it was quickly picked up by the other officers. Harrison could see they were clapping in unison, though he couldn't hear it very well. It was distorted, like a radio set not properly tuned to the station. Although he did not know it, he was suffering from mild concussion.

The band came smartly to a halt, Harrison stopped too, swaying unsteadily. The officers continued to clap their hands together, recognizing that he was close to collapse, willing him to remain upright.

The two redcaps marched Harrison over to the Parole Hut and left him standing to attention while the formalities of signing him in were completed. Harrison blacked out for a moment and almost fell. The handclapping grew in intensity. He jerked himself upright, blinking, trying to focus his eyes on the line of flyers behind the barbed wire. The main gate was finally swung open. The MPs lined themselves either side of the American again and began to march him into the compound. As he passed through the second gate the handclapping gradually turned into loud applause. Harrison and the two MPs were surrounded by jubilant officers, jostling, pushing, cheering.

He felt his legs turn to water. They collapsed beneath him. There was nothing he could do to prevent it. Bryce and Reed grabbed his arms before he fell headlong into the mud. They half carried, half dragged him towards one of the huts, while the two MPs were manhandled away by the internees and were relieved to make it back to the safety of the main gate.

Bryce and Reed found an empty room and laid Harrison on a bed. Reed took off the American's boots, the small calibre pistol had gone, taken by the Military Policemen. Bryce had a look at the wound in the American's head.

Harrison opened his eyes. 'How is it?'

'You'll live.' He handed him a handkerchief. 'Use this.'

The American took it and dabbed some of the blood away, glancing up at Bryce. 'You don't look so good yourself.'

Bryce sat down in a chair beside the bed. 'I've only just got here as well.'

Harrison grinned. 'Yeah, I know, these roads are hell.'

Bryce smiled at the irony. 'You suffered too then?'

'Yep, and I thought it was only the English they didn't like.'

Sergeant Reed dropped the American's boots on the floor and sat on the end of the bed. 'That depends on which house you visit.'

Harrison punched up the pillow. 'Choosy.'

Bryce remembered what Burroughs had said. 'I gather we're allowed out on parole.'

'That's right, sir,' Reed said. 'But not in uniform, and we have to sign in and out of the Parole Hut.'

Bryce pursed his lips. 'Sounds all right.'

Reed nodded unenthusiastically. 'Yes, but it's bloody frustrating.'

Harrison looked at him curiously. 'You mean no fraternization?'

Reed's gloom lifted momentarily. 'No, that's no problem, sir, plenty of that.'

He didn't enlarge on his previous remark, but Bryce was curious. 'What, then?'

110

'Difficult to explain, sir.' He paused, searching for a way to start. 'You see, you can walk around, apparently a free man, money in your pocket, surrounded by people who speak English. Half of them have relatives working in England in munition factories and so on. But you can't make a break for it.'

Bryce stood up and stared out of the window at the gun turrets. 'Is there no way?'

'Only one,' Reed replied. 'From here, inside the camp. That way you don't break parole.'

Harrison, whose eyes were closed, grunted sardonically and rolled over on to his side. Bryce turned, staring at the American, then exchanged a look with Reed.

'What about at night?'

The sergeant stood up, walking over to Bryce by the window. He pointed at the arc lamps positioned round the camp. 'All the huts are floodlit, underneath as well as from outside. There's no way.'

Bryce felt weariness cloak itself around him.

'Has anybody done it?'

'A few, sir, but not as many as you might think.'

Bryce rubbed his face tiredly. Reed could see he was exhausted. 'Shall I show you to your quarters?'

Bryce glanced down at the American, who was fast asleep. 'Please.'

The sergeant led him from the room and down the passage. He stopped outside one of the doors. 'This is your room, sir. You'll have an Irish orderly who will look after you. The washroom for the officers is outside at the end of the hut, and you get hot water from nine-thirty in the morning until eight o'clock at night.'

Bryce opened the door and looked inside. 'I might be tempted to stay.'

The sergeant's face hardened. 'There are a few who think like that, sir.'

Bryce turned, looking at him sharply. 'But you don't.'

'Me, sir?' Reed stared at Bryce, then smiled suddenly. 'Not bloody likely. I might be only a navigator, but I'm not going to sit here on my arse for the duration.' He saluted. 'Good day, sir.'

He turned and strode off down the corridor. Bryce watched him go, beginning to sense the tension lying just below the surface. He shut the door carefully and lay down on the bed, fully clothed. He was asleep almost instantly.

Captain Slye paused despairingly by the white double doors that led into the ward and looked back at the tall elegant figure of Dr Martin standing implacably farther up the corridor watching his progress. He waved him impatiently forward. Slye sighed and pushed through the twin doors.

A young nurse was standing beside one of the beds, which was partially surrounded by a white screen. She beckoned to him and he advanced nervously towards her, ashamed of his fear of death, yet fearful nevertheless. The nurse smiled reassuringly and Slye sat down on a chair beside the bed. The gunner's eyes were closed, dark rings surrounded them, emphasized by the grey pallor of his skin and the dark stubble of beard round his chin.

Slye leaned over the young man and whispered his name, using the German pronunciation. 'Paul.'

His eyes flicked open, staring at the Irish officer.

Slye spoke in German. 'Paul, my name is Captain Slye. How do you feel?'

Halder licked his lips. 'You speak German very well.'

112

Slye smiled gently. 'I try. I have been to Germany many times to study the language, listen to the music.'

The gunner studied him for a moment, then said weakly, 'You like music?'

Slye nodded. 'Yes, Beethoven, Chopin. I have many records. You must come and listen to them when you are better.' He paused. 'You like Chopin?'

Halder nodded. There was a silence. Slye sat twiddling his fingers nervously, unable to broach the subject. Halder watched him, sensing his difficulty.

'You have come to tell me they are going to take off my arm.'

Slye rubbed his jaw quickly, shocked by the directness of the German, desperate to find some way of diluting the dreadful truth. It was impossible, and somewhere within himself he found strength, a calmness. He stood up beside the bed.

'Yes, it's true, Paul. They must do it; otherwise you will die. I know how much your work means to you. We all understand that. But surely it is better to live and lose an arm than it is to die?'

The gunner stared at him, his eyes feverish. Slye wondered whether the boy had understood him. Then slowly, agonisingly, the gunner began to push himself upwards on his injured arm. Slye was frightened. He turned towards the nurse, who saw the look on his face and walked quickly across the ward. She paused momentarily when she saw what Halder was trying to do. Then, fearful he would injure himself further, she leaned forward to help him. The gunner's teeth were bared with pain.

'Nein,' he said. The voice, choked with an implacable determination, halted the Irish girl in her tracks. He rested his full weight on his elbow, his eyes bulging, looking first at the captain, then at the nurse.

'See,' he said triumphantly. 'I can already use it to

113

support me. It is getting better. They – must – not – cut – it – off.'

He gripped Slye's lapels with his free hand. 'Tell them if they leave it I will recover, but if they cut me I will die – I promise. My death will be their guilt. I will have no reason to live.'

'Do you understand?'

Slye nodded. 'I will tell them, Paul. I promise.'

The gunner's head drooped and Slye glanced at the nurse and nodded imperceptibly. She took the boy's shoulders and gently lowered him back on to the bed. His eyes were pleading with her and she stared down at him for a moment before turning to look at Slye. She was close to tears.

'Do what you can,' she said quietly.

Slye nodded, sniffed and turned away.

Bryce was surprised at how decrepit and shabby the huts and general areas surrounding the Allied compound were. Where there was grass it was overgrown, weeds growing in some profusion.

'It looks a mess,' he said disgustedly.

Reed glanced at him. They were sitting on boxes outside one of the huts.

'What is?'

Bryce waved an arm at their surroundings. 'All of this.'

Reed contemplated the Allied compound silently for a moment. 'There is a reason, sir.'

Bryce raised an eyebrow. 'Really?'

'If we cleared all this up, made it all shiny and spotless like Gerry has, people at home might get the wrong idea.'

Reed gestured to the other side of the galvanized-iron fence that separated the two camps.

'That lot over there *know* they're never going to get back unless Hitler wins the war. They've got a whole propaganda exercise going on. Christmas carols for the kids in the hospital, a local labour force prepared to work anywhere to make a few bob – they've almost become a permanent fixture. We don't want anyone at home to think we're content with our lot, making the place look bright and cheerful – so, we just leave it like this.'

Bryce absorbed this, then glanced towards the CO's hut. 'How do you think the Yank is making out?'

'Dunno – depends on the Yank.'

Bryce looked at him sharply. 'What do you mean?'

Reed stared moodily at one of the gun positions. 'Everybody sees Burroughs differently.'

'How do you see him?'

'He's all right,' Reed said cautiously. 'Very straight.'

'Come on, man, speak up. Give me an honest answer. I promise it will go no further.'

Reed considered this, then made up his mind. 'Right. Well, for one thing he's been in the RAF longer than any of us, sir – joined up way back at the beginning of the thirties. He gets on very well with the Ambassador in Dublin, the Irish Liaison Officer and the Provost-Marshal.'

'Tynan?'

'Yes sir.' He paused, weighing his words carefully. 'I get the feeling, sir, that our commanding officer doesn't want anything to upset the boat. He likes it the way it is.'

He looked hard at Bryce. 'What about you, sir? Where do you fit in?'

Bryce sat quite still, aware of the implications. He'd been

115

asked for honesty and he couldn't duck the question. The temptation to sit tight and stay safe was almost irresistible. He looked down at his hands and began to sweat.

He tore his eyes away and looked up at the sergeant.

'What's the best way out?'

Reed grinned, delighted. A door slammed and Harrison emerged from the CO's hut. He looked angry and frustrated. He glanced across at the two Englishmen, but ignored them and walked to the other end of the hut. There he squatted, cowboy fashion, on his haunches, staring at the ground in front of him. He took off his flying helmet and threw it into the dirt.

'Shit,' he said.

Bryce glanced at Reed, then stood up and walked across to the American. They stood either side of Harrison, waiting for him to look up. When he did so Bryce stuck out his hand.

'Hello again. Welcome to Ireland.'

Harrison debated whether to ignore the gesture. He decided against it and rose languidly, without effort, gripping the outstretched hand.

'Harrison,' he said. 'Roy Harrison.'

Bryce glanced at the sergeant. 'This is Sergeant Reed. My name's Bryce. We were just trying to think of ways to get out of here.'

Harrison looked at the sergeant, then grinned. 'Sounds good to me.'

Outside Von Bernstorff's office a group of German officers were in singlets and shirts playing handball. Inside Gehler was angry. He paced the room fiercely.

'I must see the Ambassador immediately.'

Von Bernstorff surveyed him coldly from behind his desk. 'That is not possible. You are only allowed into Dublin once a week and I cannot arrange it immediately. Tynan has to countersign each application and he might become suspicious if you went so soon. He has the instincts of a bloodhound.'

Gehler stopped pacing. 'Does the Ambassador come here?'

'Frequently.' Von Bernstorff smiled thinly. 'Sometimes with company.'

Gehler ignored the implication. 'Then ask him to do so at once.'

Even Von Bernstorff was taken aback at the arrogance of the Oberleutnant. 'I will pass on your request, Gehler, but I hardly think he is likely to respond.'

Gehler recognized the mocking sarcasm implicit in the remark. He stared coldly at the Hauptmann. 'I make no request – show him this, Herr Hauptmann.'

He took from his wallet his authorization to accompany Hitler at all times as his personal cameraman. Von Bernstorff stared at the grey card in the perspex case. He felt sick. He knew now he was finished, his authority merely token.

The bald patch on the crown of the driver's head fascinated Driscoll. It gleamed beneath its spurious covering of long hair licked over from the low parting close to the ear. He wondered whether in a high wind it billowed like a flag. Driscoll doubted the poor man had any conception of what he looked like from the rear.

'Coast Road', the signpost had said after they had put Limerick behind them, but as yet he hadn't glimpsed the sea. The train journey from Dublin had been uneventful. He'd covered his tracks pretty well and had spotted no one who might have been following him: not that anyone should, but in Ireland you could never be sure, least of all with a secret. The man with the bald patch had hardly uttered a word, just asked for confirmation of his name at the railway station. Since then, nothing. Not that he minded the silence.

They'd just passed through the narrow bottleneck at Askeaton when he noticed that the driver was glancing continually in the mirror. Driscoll turned and looked behind. An old Ford was sticking close to the rear. There appeared to be four men inside, but he could not distinguish their features because of the grime on the windscreen. He leaned forward in his seat. 'Is everything all right?'

The driver did not answer. He looked in the rearview mirror again. Driscoll repeated his question, phrasing it differently.

'We seem to have company.'

He heard the engine of the Ford rev, and as it shot past them Driscoll's driver began to brake. The other car slewed into the side of the road ahead and bald patch pulled Driscoll's car in behind it. A man jumped quickly from the rear of the Ford almost before it had stopped, slamming the door behind him. As soon as he did so the Ford accelerated away. The man ran to Driscoll's car and jerked open the back door. He stopped when he saw the pistol levelled at his stomach.

'No need to be alarmed, Mr Driscoll, it's just that I prefer talking in a moving vehicle. Besides, the man in the front seat can shoot as well as drive.'

Driscoll turned. The barrel of the Webley was not six inches from his ear. He smiled wryly at the man in the doorway. 'I hope the rest of your organization is as efficient.'

Quinn sat down beside him and waved the driver on. The road was still deserted and the exchange had taken only moments. He waited until the car had picked up speed again, then glanced at Driscoll. 'You know you could have got your head blown off, aiming a gun at me.'

'Perhaps, but your driver is singularly uncommunicative

and the arrangement was that we meet in Tralee.'

'He was under instructions to say nothing, I needed to be sure you were not followed.'

'I resent the implication, Quinn.'

'No need. I wouldn't last two minutes without precautions, and I'll take just as good care of you.'

Driscoll tried to relax, but his stomach still churned and his mouth felt hot and acidy. He was too old for this cloak and dagger stuff.

'What are the arrangements?'

'Better you don't know,' Quinn said shortly.

Driscoll sighed with exasperation. 'I see. So I must leave it all in your hands.'

'Better for yourself if you do. That way you know nothing and it's easier than lying. However, you will leave tonight. That has been confirmed by Berlin. Do you know who you are to see when you arrive?'

'No, but Herr Hemmrich told me that the request came from the highest level.'

Quinn gazed unseeingly out of the window. He wasn't sure how much he could tell Driscoll. Instinct warned him to be careful, but he'd been curious about Driscoll for a long time. Certainly he'd proved himself a good ally in the past and the political information that he fed down had been confirmed as accurate for a number of years.

'There's a man named Veesenmayer. He's from the German Foreign Office, though he works in close collaboration with *Abwehr* II in Berlin. I met him before they got me back here and I know he believes that Germany and Ireland should be more closely involved.' He turned and faced Driscoll. 'Now he must be able, through the Foreign Office, to make contact with the German Ambassador in Lisbon. Tell him that I *know* the Allies are using the civilian flying boats to ferry back escaped British POWs.'

Driscoll stared at him.

119

'You mean they are bringing them into Foynes?'

'That's right. They bring them in on the Sandringhams. We are neutral. So is Portugal. What could be safer? Then they go by train to Dun Laoghaire and across the Irish Sea back to England.'

Driscoll was astonished. 'What about the authorities? Surely they must know!'

Quinn laughed. 'They know all right, but they are all in civilian clothes and so customs turn a blind eye.' Quinn gazed out past the driver.

'Tell Veesenmayer that I intend to stop their little game,' he said quietly. 'Tell him that they cannot trust Dev, that he is practising a very benevolent neutrality so far as the Allies are concerned.'

Driscoll thought about that for a while. He sensed the bitterness behind Quinn's remarks, but his attitude totally conflicted with his own plans.

'Do you think that is wise, Quinn? Supposing I can convince whoever it is that wants to see me that I can bring Ireland in on Germany's side if they will guarantee a United Ireland?'

Quinn studied him for a moment. 'Can you?'

Driscoll smiled. 'Let us say that I have the ear of certain prominent politicians who believe, as I do, that this is Ireland's best chance. More than that, Hemmrich tells me that an Irish Army officer has been in contact with him. They want Ireland in on the side of Germany, and are also putting pressure on the Government.'

Quinn watched the road ahead. They were coming into Foynes. Driscoll was telling the truth. He knew about the General . . .

'All right, you do it any way you like. But remember this. They might decide on a pre-emptive strike if they thought Dev was collaborating with the British. Make sure you get them to check out the Lisbon connection. It may not just be POWs that they are bringing in through Ireland.'

Mentally Driscoll heaved a sigh of relief. Thank God for that. He needed the co-operation of Quinn and the IRA if his plans were to succeed. He glanced out of the window. It was time to change the subject.

'Is this Foynes?' he asked.

'Yes, you'll see the pier soon where they tie up.' Quinn tapped the driver on the shoulder. 'Drive easy past the pier, Brendan.' Bald patch nodded. They passed some grey stone buildings on the right, then Driscoll caught his first glimpse of the sea behind them. A strong wind was blowing up the estuary that separated the mainland from Foynes Island and one of the Sandringham flying boats was heaving at its anchor in the middle.

Rain began spotting on to the windscreen of the car and quite suddenly the visibility cut down. The Sandringham was reduced to a grey distorted shape, almost obliterated by the squall.

Driscoll peered up to his left at the high ground that faced out into the estuary. 'I wouldn't like to take off in this.'

Quinn turned, following his eyeline. 'No, if the wind is from the south-west they have to clear that after unsticking from the water. Must be nearly two hundred feet from the estuary to the top of that hill.'

The car crossed slowly past the pier, then up over the shoulder of the hill before passing into Foynes Woods. Driscoll watched Quinn, who was still gazing out behind him at the hill. He made a mental note not to fly on any plane coming in or out of Foynes.

It was pitch black. The light from the storm lamps flickered wildly as they swung in the wind that gusted and sighed through the trees fringing the graveyard. It was bizarre, like the set of a Hollywood horror film, yet it still sent chills up Driscoll's spine. As curious a collection of individuals as one could imagine stood round the open grave. He tried to fix their faces in his mind, but the lamps cast such strange shadows over them, intensifying the darkness outside the weak circle of light, that it was impossible to do so. They remained dark and indistinct and vaguely menacing.

He could discern six German seamen in black roll-neck sweaters, a naval officer wearing a peaked cap, the gold braid on his sleeve occasionally gleaming as it caught the light. The priest was murmuring the burial service, incongruously in English, and beside him a lean spare little man whom Quinn had rooted from his bed. He was the local undertaker.

There were more shadowy figures in the background, and Driscoll presumed they were local IRA volunteers protecting this odd little ceremony in the dead of night.

Eventually the priest stopped and the officers uttered a short command in German, then saluted. The other sailors followed suit and Driscoll lowered his head in respect as the two coffins slowly disappeared into the ground draped in swastikas.

Another more violent gust of wind shook the trees as though it would tear them from the earth. Curiously the wind did not touch the small group clustered round the grave. It was as if they were suddenly sheltered by an invisible wall of glass. It was weird. Driscoll wondered whether anyone else had noticed it. He heard the coffins scrape as they reached the bottom. The men who had lowered them slowly pulled the ropes free and silently looped them round their elbows and forearms before slipping away into the darkness. The naval officer called his men to attention then marched them away towards the cars that waited outside the low wall that circled the cemetery. Driscoll listened to their boots gradually fading down the gravel path, then turned to Quinn.

'How did they die?'

'I don't know. The undertaker said that it was machine-gun fire, so it was probably an exchange with a Sunderland flying boat. They must have been caught out in the open on the surface. They had to come here to pick you up and the Captain requested a land burial rather than risking a burial at sea.'

Driscoll was surprised. 'Has it happened before?'

Quinn started to crunch his way down the path to the entrance. 'Once, I believe.'

Driscoll fell into step beside him. He was pleased. He would be able to pass this on to Berlin.

'How widespread are the connections?'

'Just a few arms shipments. Occasional requests for supplies. That sort of thing. But it is increasing.'

Driscoll pulled his collar tight around his chin. He was cold. 'It's got to,' he said.

The tall wrought-iron gates materialized through the gloom and Quinn waited for Driscoll to pass through before shutting them. He faced Driscoll in the dark.

'That's your job.'

Driscoll got into the car and Quinn slid in beside him. He watched the driver turn the key and slip the car into gear, but he didn't hear anything. The engine noise was drowned in the wild threshing of the trees outside. Quinn was right, of course, and the fact that the German High Command had responded so quickly to his request through Hemmrich proved that they too recognized the strategic value of Ireland. Now the politicking could begin, and he did not intend to fail. That strange little ceremony had somehow drawn him closer to these German sailors. He had to succeed, but he could not help wondering what awaited him at the end of this long and hazardous journey. He hated ships, and the thought of plunging beneath the surface of the sea in a submarine terrified him.

'Is it far?' His voice sounded strained even in his own ears. He felt hollow, empty.

Quinn recognized the symptoms. 'No, just a mile or so down to the beach. Once the submarine descends it's perfectly calm.'

Quinn, he knew, was trying to reassure him, but Driscoll's stomach had turned to water. He could hear the sound of the surf now breaking heavily against the rocks below. He took a deep breath and tried to compose himself.

By the autumn of 1940 it was clear to Hitler that the Luftwaffe were not going to overpower the RAF. The Stukas that had terrorized Europe had proved totally ineffective against the faster and more manoeuvrable Spitfires and Hurricanes. The losses had been so great that Goering had withdrawn these planes from the air battle. The rest of the Luftwaffe's hardware did little better, and if the invasion plans for southern England, Operation Sea Lion, were to take place at all, air supremacy was crucial.

With the failure of the Luftwaffe in the Battle of Britain, Hitler's fertile imagination lit upon another, perhaps weaker link in Britain's defences – Gibraltar. If Gibraltar were in Germany's hands, the Axis forces could command the Mediterranean and close the Suez Canal to Britain's vital oil routes. With the Mediterranean closed, then the Middle East and Africa would be within his grasp. Further, if he could persuade the Arabs, because of their hatred of the Jews, to join his cause against England, then Britain would be isolated from all but America.

Gibraltar was strategically one of the most vital of Britain's possessions. The idea appealed to Hitler, but without the participation of Spain and Vichy France it was unworkable. Immediately, he arranged through Franco's Minister of the Interior, Serrano Sumer, a meeting for 23 October at a small town called Hendaye near Biarritz, on the borders of Spain and France. A further meeting with Marshal Pétain, Leader of Vichy France, was arranged for 25 October, two days later, at Montoire.

Hitler boarded his special train, 'The Amerika', on 22 October 1940. It was to be a fateful journey.

*29 October 1940*

He'd found it impossible to sleep, waking in the early hours, the steady clicking of the wheels only tormenting him further as he tossed and turned in his bed, going over the events of the last few days again and again.

Franco's train had arrived an hour late at Hendaye. At first he had paid it no heed. The weather had been perfect, and Hitler had been elated with the possibilities of his plan for the taking of Gibraltar. Later, as the clever, podgy little Spaniard had spun his web of flattery and deceit, always claiming spiritual kinship with Germany, yet constantly finding reasons why Spain could not immediately enter the war against England, Hitler had come to realize that the lateness of Franco's arrival at Hendaye was probably deliberate: another ploy to keep him off balance.

He rolled over on to his back and groaned at the memory of the humiliation. Never before had he been so out-manoeuvred by a statesman. Chamberlain at Munich had been a child compared to the cunning 'Caudillo'. He'd taken nothing from Hendaye but promises. He stared at the tiny light above his bed as it swayed to the motion of the carriage. His tactics with the elderly Marshal Pétain had been different. He had told the vanquished Frenchman that someone would have to pay for the cost of the war, was that to be England or France? He'd reminded Pétain of the Royal Navy's destruction of the French Fleet at Mers el Kebir. The Marshal had seemed to agree with Hitler's opinions about the need to bring Britain to her knees quickly and end the war, but like Franco he had sparred for time, asking when the two million French prisoners would be returned to their homes. Hitler sweated with anger. The final straw had been the hastily arranged meeting with Mussolini in Florence. Il Duce had marched into Greece. No warning, no collaboration on this operation. It could only have been deliberate. Seeking glory for the Italian Army to counterbalance the increasing influence of Hitler in the Balkans. He should have crushed the puffed-up Italian. Instead he had been cautious, fearful of losing a certain ally when neither Spain nor the beaten French could be persuaded to fight against England.

He had also been deflected in his attitude by the incredible reaction of the Italian people. Time and again the two dictators had been forced to appear on the balcony of the Palazzo Pitti where the talks had taken place. Hitler had glowed in the rapturous reception, standing like a modern Caesar on a balcony above the cheering crowds. It had been impossible later to take the tack he had intended with Mussolini. They had parted swearing eternal brotherhood.

He squirmed with embarrassment and flung back the covers of the bed. The train was too warm, cosseting him from the rigours of the cold outside. He pulled aside the curtains of his window. The Alps were breathtaking, the early morning sun was just catching the top of the mountains. They gleamed frostily high above him, dwarfing the toy train that wound its way slowly up the valley between the high peaks.

For a moment his depression lifted. He was reminded of his Eagle's Lair in Berchtesgaden and the increasing pleasure he got from Eva's company. She was amusing to be with and some of the films they had of their meetings had reflected that pleasure, the affection they shared.

He stared moodily at the soaring peaks as the train slowly crawled up the steep incline. Gehler had been foolish to risk an assignment on a Luftwaffe mission. He had done it without his direct knowledge, though Gehler had often talked longingly of shooting some exciting war footage. The new cameraman was efficient, but servile, and his work lacked the imagination that Gehler's had always contained. He missed the quick smile of encouragement when Gehler had seen him tiring in the public's eye, and his intuitive understanding of how to get the best shots of the Führer. Hitler was saddened by his loss. His plane had not returned and, diligently as he had probed for information, nothing had been found; and no amount of power could bring back the dead.

There was a knock on his door. He turned.

'Come in,' he said.

It was Linge, his valet, with some breakfast. He glanced past Hitler out of the window and smiled.

'It's a lovely day, Mein Führer.'

It was as well, perhaps, at that moment, that Hitler remained unaware that Franco was, at least in part, a Jew.

# BERLIN, 30 OCTOBER 1940

The high marbled hall echoed to his footsteps, and to those of the black uniformed SS Officer in front of him. The Chancellery was impressive, and used as Driscoll was to marbled elegance and power, his stomach churned.

He could see two German SS guards on either side of a pair of doors that seemed a mile away. He guessed that was the entrance to Hitler's chambers and tried to pull himself together and marshal his thoughts for the crucial meeting as the doors grew steadily closer.

The officer halted in front of him and asked him to wait for a moment. He went inside while Driscoll tried to concentrate his mind and absorb his surroundings. He felt a tap on his shoulder and started nervously. He hadn't heard the officer re-emerge.

'You can go in now,' he said.

He opened the doors for him. Driscoll entered the huge room and heard the doors click shut behind him. He was alone. A huge map of Europe dominated the room, almost filling one wall completely. A large desk stood in front of the windows, a tall leather chair behind it. Driscoll saw a flicker of movement and the grey-uniformed figure of Hitler detached itself from the tapestries near the window where the shadows were deepest. He was slightly disconcerted, realizing that Hitler had been watching him from the moment he had entered the room. The Führer was looking at him curiously.

'I believe you speak German?' he said.

'That is correct, Herr Hitler.'

Driscoll was impressed – they'd clearly done their homework. Hitler waved his arm at a chair in front of the desk.

'Sit down, Herr Driscoll. You must be tired after your journey.'

Driscoll smiled. 'Recovered now after a good night's sleep, but very gratified that you were able to see me.'

Hitler sat down in the leather chair, placing his elbows on the desk, fingering his small moustache. This man from Dublin intrigued him. Ireland intrigued him, particularly her neutrality. He had fully expected the former colony of the British Empire to take sides against him, and De Valera's impartiality was surprising. In truth, he knew little of Ireland's history, nor had he taken any serious interest in it politically beyond sending a few agents from the *Abwehr* to collaborate with Republican forces in the South.

'The information that you gave to my Ambassador, Herr Hemmrich. Is that to be taken seriously? Do you consider that there is any real possibility of British forces invading Southern Ireland?' The question seemed straightforward enough, though Driscoll knew that his credibility depended a great deal upon his reply.

'You must know, Führer, that I am the publisher of one of Ireland's most influential newspapers. That in itself, however, would not make me privy to the innermost secrets of a country such as Germany or England. But Ireland, although the size of Southern England, has a small population, something like three million in the South; and power is concentrated among a relatively small number of people. Those like myself, therefore, are constantly rubbing shoulders with the power structure, as indeed are the populace in general.'

Hitler cut across him, 'Therefore making secrets harder to keep?'

Driscoll saw the trap opening before him. 'In normal

circumstances, yes. But the war has made a difference. Security is tighter.'

Hitler sat back in his chair. 'Then how do you know so much?'

'Because of my connections with Fleet Street.' It was Driscoll's turn to smile. 'It's almost impossible to keep secrets there.'

That seemed to please him. Hitler had no love for the British press, particularly Lord Beaverbrook.

Driscoll pressed home his advantage. 'Churchill is concerned about his supply lines. There are two main areas. First, the Middle East, where he obtains most of his oil. And since the Italian Navy cannot, as yet, cut that supply, your only hope there would be to command the Straits of Gibraltar by taking the Rock. But neutral Spain prevents your mounting a land offensive.'

Unwittingly, Driscoll had played his best card. Of Hitler's fruitless journey he knew nothing.

'However,' he continued, 'your U-boats are wreaking havoc on Churchill's Merchant Fleet in the North Atlantic. So much so that an American reporter, Ed Murrow, had his report on a typical convoy from America censored. Britain needs those supplies from America. Without them she cannot survive. That is why the ports of Ireland are so valuable. At the moment Churchill only has one, Belfast in the North. If he could take control of Southern Ireland without extending himself, I believe he would. Now that he has been unable to persuade De Valera to participate in the war against you with promises of a United Ireland, I think it is more than just a possibility. I think it is imminent.'

Hitler was listening now, and Driscoll felt a surge of elation. He stood up and walked across to the huge map on the wall. 'If Churchill possessed the whole of Ireland, he could secure the Western Approaches for his shipping – protecting them much farther out into the Atlantic – making it much more difficult for your U-boats to press home their attacks.'

He paused, picking up the long marker stick. 'But if the positions were reversed, if you held the whole of Ireland, all of this . . .' He swept the stick up the western side of Britain. '. . . all of this coastline would be at your mercy. It is one thing for the Royal Navy to protect the coastline of Southern England down here from invasion across the short distance of the Channel. It is impossible for them to continue to do that, and to cover the whole of Britain's west coast as far north as Scotland.'

He stopped, breathing heavily. He was not used to long speeches, or to the stress under which he had put himself on this journey. He waited.

Hitler remained huddled in his chair. He was shaken by the reference to Gibraltar. What did this Irishman know of his politicking of recent weeks? Or was it merely what it seemed, an accurate assessment of Britain's vulnerability. He was impressed by the Irishman's logic. What then of Ireland?

Was it possible to effect an alignment with the Irish that would enable the Wehrmacht to use their country as a starting point for an invasion of Britain? Churchill had rejected his peace proposal outright, though he still found it difficult to believe that the British people wanted another war to the death with Germany. Only the bombing of Berlin by the RAF had finally convinced him that he must conquer Britain. Then he could move on to deal with the Slav. Russia was his real aim, yet he did not want a simultaneous war on two fronts. Next month Molotov, the Soviet Foreign Minister, would be arriving in Berlin to begin talks on a German-Russian Peace Treaty. Then he could turn his attention fully towards England. He leaned forward in his chair, peering at the Irishman standing near the wall map.

'If a constructive dialogue could be mounted between

ourselves and the politicians in Dublin, how would you see it materializing as a base for a German foothold in that country?'

This was the crucial question, the one Driscoll had been preparing himself for ever since he had set out from Dublin. He pointed to the map again.

'Here,' he said, 'on the south-west corner of Ireland, is Bantry Bay. It is twenty-six miles long, seven miles across, with a draught of forty fathoms. It will take the biggest ships as well as the smallest. If a force were landed there – one Panzer division would be enough – they, with the willing co-operation of the Irish Army, could assemble on the Northern Border, sweep through and take Belfast in one night. British reserves there are limited, not enough to resist for long, even if they knew of the impending attack. With surprise, the attack would devastate them overnight.'

The idea was persuasive, but Hitler was too experienced to make any comment at this stage. He stood up and walked over to the wall map, looking at the spot Driscoll had indicated.

'Bantry Bay,' he repeated.

Driscoll pointed to it again. 'It is more than just a bay for most Irishmen, Führer; and if you were to land there it would have enormous psychological as well as historical significance for my countrymen.'

Hitler looked at him expressionlessly. Driscoll explained. 'In 1796 a French Republican force of some thirty-five ships dropped anchor in Bantry. On board were some of the finest soldiers Napoleon had commanded. They had been brought there by a man named Wolfe Tone, a leading Republican figure in Ireland at the time. There were no British troops within miles of the area, and the road to Cork was open. But headwinds in the Bay were strong and increasing, and a storm developed. It lasted five days. Twenty of the ships had to slip their cables and make for the open sea. Fifteen held on for a while, but finally had to give up.' He paused. 'The weather beat Napoleon, Führer – not Britain. I think Germany can do better.'

The flattery was blatant, but the idea was good. Hitler could see that. Still he hesitated, a lot needed to be looked into before he could trust this man as an intermediary between himself and Dublin. He had no official authorization, that much he knew, but it was worth exploring.

'I will think about what you have said, Herr Driscoll. When are you due to leave?'

'The day after tomorrow, Führer.'

'Then perhaps you will hear from me by then. Goodbye.'

Hitler held out his hand – Driscoll gripped it. It was damp, seemingly without strength. He thanked Hitler, turned and walked to the door. As he opened it he glanced back into the room. Hitler was still standing by the wall map, his hands clasped behind his back. Never had Driscoll felt so disappointed.


*1 November 1940*

He gazed out over the slopes of the Obersalzburg. A fine frost glinted in the early morning sunshine. Already he felt better, relaxed and fresh. Amazing how simple basic things like a good night's sleep and a perfect breakfast improved one's well being. Eva too, had made him feel good. Her welcome had been so warm and affectionate, blanking out his feelings of anger at the wasted journey to Hendaye and Montoire.

One of his alsatian dogs came padding into the room and sat by his chair, eyes pleading for a scrap. He fondled the dog's ears. He would take them all for a walk later. He glanced up. Linge, his valet, was standing beside the breakfast table holding a communiqué. He was beaming.

'What is it, Linge?'

The valet continued to smile. 'Good news, Mein Führer. Forgive me, but the operator told me what it was when he gave it to me.'

Hitler shook his head exasperatedly. 'Well, don't just stand there grinning foolishly. What is it – tell me?'

'It's Gehler. He's been found. He's alive, Führer.'

He gave the sheet of paper to Hitler, who read it quickly. He rubbed his forehead with his hand, not looking at his valet. 'This is good, Linge, the best news for a long time. Tell Eva. She'll be delighted.' He looked at the communiqúe again. In Ireland, it said, in an internment camp. He remembered Driscoll's visit in Berlin. He was due to go back today. Linge was just leaving the room. Hitler called after him. 'Ask the Communications Officer to see me at once.'

Linge nodded deferentially and closed the door behind him.

The three engines of the JU 52 steadily consumed the distance between Berlin and Bordeaux. He gazed out of the square window. The night was cloudless; he could see the stars glittering in the inky sky above. Normally he enjoyed flying, but he felt cold and utterly depressed. He'd waited in his Berlin hotel until the last possible moment before leaving for the airport, but he'd heard nothing. Now he was on his way back, empty handed. Thank God no one but Hemmrich knew of his mission to Germany. The failure of a fellow countryman was something the Irish seemed to take a perverse delight in, and he wondered how long his meeting with Hitler could remain a secret. He fell into an uneasy sleep.

He woke abruptly. The engine pitch had altered and he glanced out of the window. The stars and sky were almost level with the wingtip as the plane banked steeply to port. He wondered if they were about to land. Then he felt a hand on his shoulder. It was one of the crew. He leaned forward

towards him so that his voice could be heard above the roar
of the engines.

'We are going back to Berlin,' he said. 'You are wanted
there. We should be landing in about another hour.'

Driscoll nodded dazedly. Going back! His heart began to
thump against his chest and he felt a sense of huge elation
pass through him. It had worked. Now Ireland had a
chance.

# BOOK FOUR

## Plans

Bryce gazed up at the red-brick Victorian barrack lines. Lights blazed from every window and it was hard to adjust. Every instinct prompted him to yell at them, make them go out, scream at whoever was responsible. But Ireland was neutral – at least this part of it – and blackouts did not apply. He was so intent on taking in everything, getting his bearings, that he stepped in a puddle and swore as the cold water splashed up inside his trouser leg.

Reed grinned in the half light. 'Better watch your step, sir. Irish roads are full of holes.'

Harrison glanced sharply at him. 'Thanks, Sergeant. It's a sore point.'

Reed gazed glumly at the wet macadam of the road. 'Sorry, sir.'

They strode along in silence for a while, just the squelching of Bryce's wet shoe making its own comment. Bryce tried to ignore it. 'Where is the station cinema, Reed?'

'Not far, sir. It's on the other side of the barracks, just past the church.'

Some Irish soldiers emerged from one of the buildings, laughing uproariously. They swung into the road and walked towards them. Harrison tensed; the beating up he had received after his attempted escape still hurt. He trusted nobody. Reed sensed the American's uneasiness.

'It's all right, sir. They never bother us when we are out on parole.'

Harrison did not reply, but continued to watch them carefully until they'd passed, still laughing amongst themselves. Then slowly he let out his breath.

'Well, they seemed happy enough,' he said, relieved.

'They're all right most of the time, just a few hard nuts who sometimes have a go when the Guinness has been flowing. It's the redcaps you've got to watch, Tynan's lot – they can be real bastards.'

Bryce was curious. 'Any idea why they split their duties between them, Sergeant?'

'No sir, unless the Military Police are just there to stiffen up the Army, keep them on their toes. Tynan takes it very seriously.'

Bryce glanced towards Harrison. 'You saw him, didn't you, Roy? Before you came marching down behind that band.'

'That's right,' Harrison said non-committally.

Bryce looked at him curiously, but made no comment. Harrison thrust his hands into his trouser pockets, gazing unseeingly at the road.

There was something about Tynan. He couldn't pin it down. It was odd, but when he had been in the room with the man all his senses had sharpened. Nothing had been said, yet everything seemed to have a subtext, a different meaning.

They were coming to a junction in the road and Reed gestured to his right.

'That building on the corner is the church, and behind it is the water tower.'

Bryce peered through the darkness. He could just discern an oblong building with latticed windows and behind it, looming high against the night sky, the square sharp sides of the water tower. In the gloom it looked more like the battlements of a castle than a means of pumping water.

'How big are the barracks, Sergeant?'

Reed thought about that for a moment. 'The main military area covers several square miles. K Lines is away from the built-up area near the golf course to the east. The barracks are surrounded on all sides by The Curragh, which is as flat as a pancake, no trees, nothing. That's something else that doesn't help us. We have to clear that lot before we reach any cover. Newbridge is the nearest town. That's about three miles to the north, but there are plenty of big houses round The Curragh where we are welcome. The Barracks used to belong to us until 1922 so there are plenty of Anglo-Irish about, mostly ex-service and so on.'

Reed turned left at the junction and they began to descend a sharp hill. He pointed to some low wooden buildings to his left.

'That's the Dobuyn sisters' shop. They have an ice-cream parlour in there and they're open most days. Gerry uses it too, of course, when they've got the money, but I never share mine.'

Harrison grinned. 'Starving them out, Sergeant?'

'Something like that, sir.'

Reed crossed the road to his right. 'Here we are, should be in time for the main feature.'

Harrison called after him. 'Hey, Sergeant, you never told us what was on.'

Reed turned and faced them, walking backwards. 'Thought you might not come, sir,' he grinned. 'It's about the Navy.'

Bryce and Harrison exchanged a look, then crossed the road to look at the stills outside the front entrance. It was *The Sea Hawk* starring the Warner Bros current hero Errol Flynn. Bryce looked at the sergeant, who was buying the tickets.

'The Navy!' he said sarcastically. 'The closest he'll ever get is a beach house on Malibu.'

Harrison tapped Bryce on the shoulder. 'Don't mock. I hear he operates very well on a boat.'

Bryce smiled. 'Depends what you mean by operate.'

Reed handed them their tickets. He was the only one who

had any money until the new arrivals were put on the pay-roll, and the pretty girl inside the foyer tore them in half. She smiled shyly at Harrison.

Bryce raised his eyebrows. 'It's the accent, Sergeant. Gets them every time.'

'Yes, I suppose so,' Reed said, gloom returning. 'See you after the show. Your seats are upstairs.' He began to walk towards the door at the end of the corridor.

'Wait a minute,' Bryce said. 'Where are you off to?'

'Sorry, sir, should have told you. Officers are upstairs, NCOs down.'

Bryce was torn. He liked the sergeant. His bright London chatter had cheered him, lifted the depression he'd felt since he had had to leave Nora. But there were also certain rank barriers that had to be preserved and he couldn't see a way round this one.

'That's a pity. All right, well, in the foyer then after the show.'

The American was stunned. 'Hey, just a cotton picking minute. We don't have to put up with all that bullshit over here do we?'

His voice had risen angrily and two Luftwaffe officers gazed icily at him as they climbed the stairs together. Harrison caught the look and whirled around, raising his right arm mockingly in the Nazi salute.

'Heil Hitler and up yours too!'

Bryce was embarrassed. 'Come on, Roy, can't be helped.'

Harrison stared at him, his eyes cold, without depth. 'Stuff you as well, Bryce – I'll go with Reed.'

The sergeant stepped forward a couple of paces then stopped when he saw the look on the American's face.

'You can't do that, sir, only NCOs allowed downstairs.' For a moment Bryce thought that Harrison was going to hit Reed. The moment hung there, silent, dangerous, then

142

imperceptibly passed. Harrison looked at Bryce then at Reed.

'You know, sometimes I wonder why I'm fighting in this fuckin' war at all.' He turned and walked back towards the entrance, stopping in front of the girl who had torn their tickets.

'Next time,' he said, dropping the torn half of his ticket into her palm, 'I'll come with you.'

She gazed at him wide-eyed for a moment, then lowered her eyes. Harrison turned and without looking back strode from the cinema.

Captain Slye was conscious that every eye in the crowded balcony was on him. He was sweating and he knew that too. Oh sweet Jesus, why did this always have to happen to him? He tried to be fair, to treat each side as decently as he could, yet they despised him totally and it was a familiar syndrome. He didn't blame the Germans or the English; it just happened. He was always nice to people and yet they always seemed to turn against him. He couldn't understand that it was simply because he tried too hard.

Despite his bulk he was a sensitive man and he felt that everyone in the balcony was enjoying his predicament. He tried again.

'You must leave these seats, Oberleutnant. The Provost-Marshal always has two seats reserved when the internees visit the cinema each week. Please. He will be here any moment.'

Gehler surveyed him without warmth. He found it hard not to be openly contemptuous of this oily little man.

'I do not see why Leutnant Bech and myself should do so. We have been here for at least ten minutes and I see no reservations on these seats. I will talk to the Provost-Marshal if and when he arrives. I presume,' he added, 'you would prefer not to.'

Slye was aware of the disdain. He glanced nervously around the audience. Their amusement was plain to see. He could have wept. Bryce, who had just found a seat near the back, felt sorry for him. He was plainly out of depth with the Oberleutnant. Gehler was a cold fish; that afternoon, when they had been together in the van, the German had been curious. Several times he had tried to start a conversation. Bryce wondered why. It would be interesting to see what would happen if Tynan did arrive.

The rain had returned and was spattering down on to the windscreen of the car. He glanced at his watch; he was late. He tapped the driver on the shoulder.

'As quick as you can, Corporal.'

The car sped between the lines of red-brick barracks, the road gleaming wetly in the reflected light. It was miserable weather, but Tynan was used to rain and he was looking forward to the film. The car drew up outside the cinema in a shower of spray and he leapt from it, his greatcoat flapping like great wings around him. He ran up the stairs to the balcony. Tynan didn't have to pay. It was one of the perks that came with the job.

Before he reached the balcony he knew something was wrong. He could hear catcalls and jeering, and as he entered a slow handclap was starting. Slye, perspiring freely, was standing in the centre aisle at the front arguing volubly with two Luftwaffe officers. An English voice yelled out.

'Come on, Paddy, show Gerry who's boss!' This was followed by a mixture of derisive laughter and cheers.

Tynan stood motionless at the back of the balcony, water dripping from the brim of his cap. Slye looked around despairingly, then saw him. His face visibly paled. He broke off the pointless dialogue and hurried up the aisle towards him. Tynan brushed aside his explanations and made his way to the foot of the balcony. The catcalls died away and a

144

quiet expectant hush replaced it. Slye could feel the tension and tried desperately not to wring his hands.

Tynan stopped beside the two Germans. Gehler knew he was there, but did not betray the fact by as much as a flicker. He continued to gaze directly towards the curtained screen.

Tynan looked down at the two officers, who avoided his eyes, staring steadfastly to the front.

'Get out!' he said. His voice was low, yet edged with menace. He pushed back his long overcoat and rested his hand on the holster attached to his belt.

Gehler turned slowly and looked up at him. The eyes were cold, implacable, and he did not doubt the Irishman's determination. He weighed the possibilities. Tynan was the Provost-Marshal. He outranked him and there was no dishonour in obeying an order from him. He'd made his point. He stood up, stepped one pace up the stairs so that he was above the tall Irishman and raised his hand in the Nazi salute. He turned and, followed by Bech, walked up the aisle. Immediately the RAF officers began to hoot and jeer. Gehler ignored them, looking neither right nor left, he made his way to the exit and left.

Tynan watched them go. Slowly the noise died away. He waited until they were completely silent. A curious anticipatory silence settled over the cinema.

'All of you,' he said in a quiet toneless voice, 'are privileged to be interned here. You are given a civilized parole system that enables you to exist with some dignity in this country. In any other camp, either in Germany or England, none of this would be yours. Yet you continue to behave either in some arrogant Teutonic manner or as stupid English schoolboys. In future I shall expect your conduct to be more suited to officers, otherwise these privileges will be removed. I hope that is clearly understood.'

He stared at them, scanning the audience in the balcony, daring them to catch his eye. None did.

Then he glanced up at the projectionist, who was watching fascinated through the aperture. Tynan nodded, and the man remained frozen for a moment before springing into action.

Tynan sat down in the seat vacated by Gehler and waited for Slye to sit beside him.

'I hope,' he said quietly, not looking at the Captain, 'that this isn't a war film.'

Slye smiled nervously. 'Indeed sir, so do I.' Then hastily, 'No sir. No, it certainly isn't.'

The lights began to dim and, after the usual certificate had been flashed on the screen, the Warner Bros credit music thundered, followed by the opening bars of Eric Wolfgang Korngold's score for *The Sea Hawk*.

Tynan was relieved. The situation had been entirely unexpected, but it had clearly put his position under public scrutiny. He had no way of knowing how deliberate that had been. Mr Gehler would have to be watched.

He enjoyed the film immensely. It was good swashbuckling stuff. But the evening still had one more surprise in store. The film had almost reached its end, and after numerous adventures Flynn had unsurprisingly, but entertainingly, triumphed. Elizabeth, the Queen, stood up to address her admiring subjects, but the speech was not merely for them:

'And now, my loyal subjects, a grave duty confronts us all. To prepare our nation for a war that none of us wants. Least of all your Queen.

We have tried by all means in our power to avert this war. We have no quarrel with the people of Spain or of any other country. But when the ruthless ambition of a man threatens to engulf the world it becomes the solemn obligation of all free men to affirm that the earth belongs not to any one man but to all men. And that freedom is the deed and title to the soil on which we exist. Firm in this faith we shall now make ready to meet the great Armada that Philip sends against us. To this end I pledge you ships, ships

146

worthy of our seamen. A mighty fleet hewn out of the forests of England, a navy foremost in the world not only in our time but for generations to come.'

The meaning was clear, and Tynan could see the effect it was having on the audience in the cinema. He glanced to his right across the aisle, looking at a group of RAF officers. Some faces were shining; many were proud.

As the speech ended and the credits appeared someone began to clap. It was picked up and as it gathered momentum the Englishmen began to cheer, the volume swelling to a thunderous roar of approval at the message from Hollywood.

This time Tynan did not feel called upon to show his disapproval. He heard a sniff beside him and dug Slye sharply in the ribs.

'Captain, remember who you are. Flynn may be an Irish name, but the message was for them, not us.'

Slye surreptitiously blew his nose, then tucked his handkerchief into his pocket. He'd enjoyed it too.

For once the sky was blue and cloudless, just enough nip in the air to remind one that winter was not far away. Off to their right, behind the golf club, someone was burning dead leaves and the smoke drifted lazily across the dirt track that ran past the edge of the course. The smell was pungent but not unpleasant.

Here, close to the track that led away from K Lines, were a few clumps of gorse, bright yellow against the green of the plain surrounding them. Bryce, Reed and Harrison strolled past the clubhouse, then down and round a short incline.

Harrison could hear some boys playing with a dog in the bushes nearby and he stopped, looking over the golf course away to his right.

'Any chance of us getting a game there, Reed?'

The sergeant followed his gaze. 'Sure, no problem other

than clubs, and they'll let you hire those if you can afford it.'

He didn't mention the fact that NCOs were not allowed to play. Last night's scene was still fresh in his memory. He appreciated the American's point of view, but it didn't help much. Bryce was surprised.

'Do you play, Roy?'

Harrison laughed. 'Nope, but it might pass the time.'

They resumed their walk, Harrison kicking a small stone in front of him.

'What about a tunnel, Sergeant?'

The question didn't surprise Reed. Sooner or later everyone asked it.

'Easier said than done, sir. Trouble is the bloody floodlighting. All the huts are raised off the ground, and because there's no blackout they have arc lamps under every hut as well as searchlights on the towers.'

The American took a kick at the pebble and sent it spinning off into the bushes.

'Shit! The whole bloody situation is ridiculous. We can walk around like free men during the day, yet we can only make a break for it while we're locked up at night. It makes no sense.'

Bryce too felt the same sense of frustration.

'Might be better if there was no parole system. At least that way we'd know where we stood.'

Reed shook his head. 'Wouldn't go down too well with some, sir. They've formed relationships, seem to have settled in. Besides, it does help us set up an escape route once we can get out of the camp.'

Harrison noticed that he couldn't hear the children any more, but he knew they were still out there. A branch brushed back into place away to his left behind some bushes. He realized the children were tracking them. A shoe struck a stone behind him and he whirled around, dropping to one knee and sticking out his hand as though there were a gun in it, firing three imaginary shots.

A red-headed boy about seven years old who had been stalking them down the path froze for a second, then ran off into the bushes deliciously frightened.

Bryce grinned and the sergeant stared open-mouthed at the American.

'Bloody hell!' he said, totally forgetting rank. 'You must have ears like a fox. I didn't even know the little bugger was there.'

Harrison and the two Englishmen continued their walk. The American was silent, listening.

'There's three of them,' he said quietly, 'away off to the right, and they've got a dog with them.'

Declan was ten, he ran as fast as he could through the gorse bushes, the dog panting alongside him. He'd left his two younger brothers behind; he wanted to get ahead of the three airmen. He came to the thick trunk of the tree that stood close to the track and gripped the dog's collar, forcing him to sit.

'Be quiet, Billy,' he whispered. 'Be quiet.'

The dog sat dutifully by his side and Declan waited. He could hear his heart pounding in his ears and he was beginning to feel quite scared, but he was determined to see if he could outwit the American after what he'd done to Red.

He heard the men talking as they came round the bend in the track towards him. He knelt down beside Billy, whose ears had pricked up. The dog began to growl far back in his throat, sensing the boy's fear. Declan waited a moment, then harshly in the dog's ear he shouted:

'Go fetch them, Billy!'

The dog bounded from behind the tree and stopped in front of the three men. They stood motionless watching the animal. It was a mongrel, small, with a lot of terrier in him,

149

and Bryce knew if he got his teeth into something he wouldn't let go.

The animal snarled, its lips rolled back over its teeth, ears flat against its head. Harrison didn't move a muscle. The dog was poised, waiting for someone to make a sudden move.

'OK,' he said to the others. 'Stay there. Let me handle this.' Reed was happy to oblige. Coward he was not, but animals were his weak spot and he felt sure the little beast knew it. He saw Harrison slowly reach his hand into his trouser pocket. He pulled something out – it looked like a sweet. Harrison very carefully got down on one knee and offered the lump of sugar to the dog.

'Here y'are boy, here y'are.'

The tone was quiet, gentle, but firm. The mongrel's tail twitched then started to wag. The hair on its spine flattened and slowly it shuffled forward and sniffed Harrison's hand before taking the sugar.

Reed relaxed, but Bryce was staring fixedly at the dog.

'That's it,' he whispered half to himself. The sergeant looked at him, wondering if he was still frozen by fear.

'What?'

'The dog,' Bryce said, 'the bloody dog.' He slapped Reed enthusiastically on the shoulder. 'That's the answer, don't you see?'

The sergeant looked at Harrison, perplexed. 'Do you know what he's talking about?'

Harrison shrugged his shoulders. Bryce gripped the American's arm.

'Look, it's simple. First we persuade Captain Slye to let us have a dog. Right?'

Harrison nodded.

'Then, if we've got a dog, we must have . . .' he paused, 'a kennel. And where do we keep a kennel?'

He waited. He saw the penny drop. Then they both

grinned and slapped him on the back. They began to laugh uproariously, and Declan, who was watching from behind the tree, thought they'd all gone quite mad. He was more than ever convinced when they began to do a wild Irish jig of pure delight. Billy, recognizing the familiar ritual, began to bark, joining happily in the celebration, his tail wagging furiously. That really disgusted Declan. He thrust his hands deep into his pockets and began to walk back to where he'd left his brothers. My god, would he have a tale to tell them . . .

Reed very carefully eased back the inside edge of the curtain and peered through the gap at the floodlit compound outside the hut. It was bright, but bare and still as the grave. He looked up at the guntower in the corner, but could see no sign of the sentry. Probably fast asleep below the waist-high level of the balcony. He crawled back across the floor of the hut.

'Nothing,' he said. 'You'd think they were dead.'

Harrison grinned in the darkness. 'Don't say dead, Sergeant.'

Bryce smiled, 'OK, let's see what we've got.'

Close to the outside wall he pulled back the lino, then poked a finger into a small hole in the floorboards in the centre of a knot. Slowly he lifted and the trapdoor rose noiselessly on its well-oiled hinges. Harrison helped him lay it back on the mat.

The sergeant stretched himself out on his stomach and reached down into the space below the floorboards. Immediately below the floor was the roof of the kennel he'd constructed. He inserted his fingers either side under the lip of the roof and slowly lifted. It came away easily, and he raised it until Bryce and Harrison could lift it from him. They carried it into the corner, then rejoined him.

They peered down into the kennel and two wide, soft

151

spaniel eyes gazed back, the tail gently slapping the side of the kennel.

Reed grinned at Harrison. 'Good choice of Captain Slye's, a spaniel.'

'Yeah, he was right too about not having a bitch. Puppies are all we need.'

Bryce smiled at the memory of the good captain's interest and concern. In a way he regretted having to deceive him.

Harrison leant down and tenderly gathered the puppy into his arms. The tail continued to wag, but the dog made no sound.

Bryce slid the box he had prepared across the floor and Harrison laid the puppy on the cushion inside. The dog curled up, closed his eyes and went back to sleep instantly.

They sat staring at it for a moment, then Reed took the box and placed it out of the way in the corner.

'We'll need a bigger one when he starts to grow.'

He crawled back to the trapdoor. 'All right, now comes the tricky bit. If you'll just grip my legs, sir, I'll reach down and remove the bottom of the kennel.'

Bryce and Harrison held on to him as he slid face down through the hole in the floor. First he handed up the dog's blanket, then gripped the two small rings he had placed either side of the floor of the kennel. He pulled and it came away easily. He tipped it sideways and Harrison grabbed it while Bryce still held on to the sergeant's legs. Bryce helped Reed back up into the room and grinned at him in the darkness.

'Marvellous. Well done, Sergeant. It went like clockwork.'

Harrison carefully placed the bottom of the kennel next to the roof and picked up two shovels and a garden fork. He handed the shovels to Bryce and Reed, then slid down into the gap. First he checked each side of the kennel. No light was getting through, the sergeant had done a good job. He stood up; his head and shoulders cleared the floor of the hut.

'OK, it works. Sergeant, you get the sacks – now we start to dig.'

Nora sat in the truck. She'd parked it opposite the Town Hall in Newbridge, as arranged. The road was wide and there were one or two cars on either side, which made her feel less conspicuous. The town was crowded with shoppers. It was Saturday morning and the market stalls were surrounded by women and children. The women, she knew, would be trying to lay their hands on whatever tea and sugar were available. There was plenty of dairy produce, and meat was selling cheaply. Livestock farmers had been badly hit, when the main export market to England was cut off and they could hardly give their animals away. Her father was lucky. His produce was unaffected so far.

She watched a couple on the other side of the street. The girl was clinging to the arm of the man, talking animatedly. The town bustled around her, but Nora felt cut off – stranded high above them in the cab of the lorry. She knew the internment camp was close by and she wanted desperately to go there to try and see him, but she daren't. Too many people would know within twenty-four hours if she visited Bryce.

She was startled by a tap on her window. She turned and looked down at the man standing by the door to the truck. His hair was fair, eyebrows so blond they almost merged with the colour of his skin. He was smiling and he had good teeth. He would have been handsome if it hadn't been for his eyes. They were almost colourless.

153

'Are you Nora?' he said.

She rolled down the window. 'Yes, I'm sorry. I was miles away. You must be Mr Gehler?'

'That's right,' he said. He smiled again. 'Aren't you going to let me in?'

Nora felt the colour rising round her throat. 'I'm sorry,' she said again. 'You surprised me.'

She leant over and fumbled with the near-side door-latch. He walked around the front of the lorry, opened the door then climbed in, sitting beside her.

She stared at him, unaware of her gaze. She'd never been this close to a German before. He glanced down at the keys hanging from the ignition.

'Is there any reason for delay?'

Nora fumbled with them and switched the engine on, pumping some petrol into the engine. 'No, of course not.'

The Bedford engine sprang to life at once and she carefully eased the small truck into the stream of traffic.

Gehler said nothing while she manoeuvred the lorry through the crowded streets. She drove well, he thought – surprisingly so for a girl. They cleared the town, turning right off the main road and heading eastwards towards the Wicklow Mountains.

'Why are you alone?' he said quietly. 'I thought Mr Tracey was supposed to be with you?'

Nora didn't look at him, concentrating on driving the truck through the narrow twisting lane.

'He didn't want to come. Lots of people know him round here, so he sent me.'

Gehler made no comment. He didn't like unexplained changes of plan, any more than he liked being driven by a slip of a girl, but it made sense.

The country lane was beautiful, deep browns and golds of the last leaves clinging to the trees. The still wintry sunshine

154

dappling the road ahead turned the mountains beyond purple and blue through the faint mist.

Nora wanted to ask him about conditions in the camp, in particular the RAF section of it, but thought that he might be suspicious of her interest. Her father had told no one of that night in the barn, and the Garda were not likely to broadcast it. They cared little for family quarrels, especially between those whom they knew had Republican sympathies.

They crossed another main road and Gehler smiled when he saw the name of the village on a signpost.

'Hollywood?' he laughed. 'Do any filmstars live here?'

Nora glanced quickly at him. He seemed friendly enough.

'No – it's just a name.'

She remembered something. 'One of those film stars did come from Dublin though.'

Gehler wasn't really interested, but he wanted to get her talking.

'Who?'

'Maureen O'Hara. I saw her once in a film with Charles Laughton.'

'*The Hunchback of Notre Dame*,' he said, smiling. 'I saw it too.'

'In Germany?' Nora exclaimed.

'Oh yes. We do have films there you know.'

'No, I didn't mean that,' said Nora, missing the irony. 'I was just surprised that you got American ones.' She looked at him with renewed interest.

'Oh yes,' he said reflectively. 'Lots of American ones.' He sat quietly for a while, remembering how he'd studied their film techniques, trying to improve his own.

'Many of the best German film people have gone to work in America,' he said, trying to keep the conversation flowing. 'Actors, writers, directors – all of them.'

He watched her from the corner of his eye as she

155

concentrated on her driving. She looked so young, not more than nineteen, yet somehow she was already caught up in this conflict with England. Then he remembered that he too had been active politically in Austria at the same age. Perhaps it wasn't so surprising after all.

'Do you want to be an actress?' he asked suddenly.

She glanced at him surprised. 'Who, me?'

'Yes, why not?'

He saw her colour rise again. She was young.

'No, not me. I don't think I'm the right sort of person for that.'

He knew she meant that she was not pretty enough.

'I think you could do it. You have good bone structure. I should know – I am a cameraman myself.'

She turned and looked at him incredulously. 'What, you?'

The truck hit a pot-hole and swerved unnervingly.

'Mind the road,' he yelled, his voice harsh, the banter dropping away like a cloak.

She quickly regained control of the vehicle, frightened by the sudden coldness of his eyes. They were climbing now, up between the mountains through the Wicklow Gap. The terrain was spectacular. High rounded hills, screes and rugged clefts dropping vertically into the valley away to their right. The road grew narrower, twisting its way up towards the shoulder of the mountain. Gehler was tempted to take over the wheel, but Nora drove well, and clearly she knew the road. He decided against any more surprising remarks – at least until they were clear of this hazardous route over the mountains.

Nora felt confused, ill at ease with this German officer whose mood changed so abruptly. She didn't know where he fitted in, or why her father had instructed her to pick him up in Newbridge and take him back to the farmhouse. Her father had always hated the English. She understood that. He had preached that message to her for as long as she could remember. Yet now she felt he had rejected her. She'd tried so hard to fill the gap left by her mother, to ease the despair that made him drink . . . Yet the harder she tried the more he seemed to despise her. Oh god, if only she could find Peter again. There must be some way that she could reach him. The road crested the highest point between the mountains, narrowed still further and began to descend towards Glendalough and Laragh.

Gehler broke the long silence. 'Is it much farther?'

Nora didn't look at him. 'About twenty miles,' she said tonelessly. She didn't care about Gehler any more. She knew what she was going to do.


Tracey heard the whine of the engine as the truck came up the hill. He eased himself out of the battered armchair and walked over to the window.

'They're here,' he said.

Driscoll was relieved. He found conversation with this man heavy going. They had exhausted what few topics they had in common. No doubt he was a stalwart Republican and would die for the cause if he had to, but apart from exchanging their credentials and a few general pleasantries they had nothing to talk about.

The truck pulled into the small yard in front of the farm buildings and Driscoll followed Tracey to the front door. The Oberleutnant jumped down from the cab and walked over to the two men. He looked enquiringly from one to the other.

'I'm Oberleutnant Gehler,' he said.

Driscoll stuck out his hand. 'Pleased to see you at last, Oberleutnant. This is Tracey. He owns the farm.'

Gehler shook hands with both of them. Driscoll was about to step back inside when he saw Nora approaching. He paused. Tracey shifted uncomfortably, not sure whether he should introduce her or not.

157

'This is my daughter Nora,' he said eventually.

Driscoll nodded affably and thrust out his hand again. 'Hello, Nora. Thank you for bringing our German friend to us.'

Nora smiled automatically. 'It was no bother at all.'

Driscoll turned back briskly to Gehler. 'Well, shall we go inside?'

The Oberleutnant nodded and they all made their way through the door into the large kitchen. Driscoll pulled a chair from beneath the table and sat down, indicating that Gehler should do the same. He glanced up at Nora.

'I wonder if it would be possible for us to have some tea.' He looked enquiringly at Gehler. 'Is tea all right?'

Gehler sat down opposite. 'That would be fine, thank you.'

Tracey stood awkwardly for a moment, realizing that he was not wanted.

'. . . er. I have to feed the animals now. I'll see you before you go.'

Driscoll smiled expansively. 'Splendid,' he said, dismissing him.

Tracey grabbed his jacket from the back of one of the chairs and left while Nora moved around the kitchen preparing the tea. Driscoll ignored her and looked across at the German.

'I've heard a lot about you, Oberleutnant.'

Gehler made no comment.

Driscoll cleared his throat. He felt it was necessary to establish the level of this meeting at once. Gehler did not seem the sort of man who would be easily impressed, so he wasted no time on chit chat, plunging straight to the point.

'I have only recently returned from Berlin,' he said. 'I had long and detailed discussions with Herr Hitler. He asked me to express his relief at knowing that you were alive and well. He . . . er, also seemed a little put out that you decided to

158

attempt this flight without consulting him. It seems he values your work highly.'

Gehler inclined his head politely. 'I'm pleased to hear it, but I am sure you did not bring me all the way out here to discuss my work for the Führer.'

Driscoll pulled a silver cigarette case from his pocket and proffered it to Gehler, who declined.

'No, I did not.' He lit the cigarette and took a lungful of smoke. He glanced behind him. Nora was at the end of the long, low kitchen by the range, pouring boiling water into a teapot. Driscoll leant across the table, lowering his voice.

'I asked you to meet me here because this is a safe house, and I cannot afford to be seen anywhere with you. Not even your Commanding Officer, Von Bernstorff, knows of my mission to Germany. Herr Hitler asked me to show you this as proof of what I am saying.' He pulled from his wallet a small photograph taken when Gehler had been shooting some footage of the Führer at Berchtesgaden. The German's face betrayed no emotion. He looked up from the picture.

'So, the photographer is photographed. I hadn't seen that picture.'

Driscoll pulled his chair closer to the table. 'Mr Gehler, I cannot stress too much how important to Ireland, and indeed to Germany, my meeting with the Führer was. From it I hope will stem the final victory that we all want. I am sure you are aware of how strategically valuable Ireland is to the German war effort.'

He paused while Nora put a tray down on the table. She looked down at Driscoll.

'Would you like me to pour?' she asked.

The Irishman leant back in his chair. 'No, my dear, I'm sure I can manage that – you run along now.'

Nora went back to the kitchen range and picked up the mug of tea she had poured for herself, then went through the beaded curtains into the hall and sat down on the stairs, out of sight of the men in the kitchen. She sipped the tea reflectively.

Driscoll poured milk from a small jug into one cup.

'Do you take milk and sugar?'

The German nodded, impatient to continue. Driscoll poured the tea into the cup and handed the sugar bowl to the Oberleutnant, who helped himself to a single teaspoonful. Driscoll didn't put any sugar in his. He was trying to lose some weight. He filled his cup, then had a sip before putting it back on to the saucer.

'That's good,' he said.

Gehler ignored the pointless comment. 'You were saying, Mr Driscoll?'

The big Irishman chuckled deep in his throat. 'Good, good I can see you are impatient to get to the point.' The twinkle left his eyes. 'The point is, Oberleutnant, that the Führer has ordered certain tasks you are to carry out. Naturally nothing could be put down on paper in case I fell into Allied hands on my return journey. However, they are crucial to the overall operation.'

Gehler interrupted. 'What operation, Mr Driscoll? Precisely what are you attempting to do?'

Driscoll looked at him coldly, puffing gently on the long cigarette.

'Nothing less, Oberleutnant, than the occupation of Northern Ireland by forces of the Third Reich and the Irish Army, together with considerable Republican forces. It's my task to prepare the ground politically for this united effort. It's yours, Oberleutnant, to carry out certain duties in order to prepare the way.' He waited for the German's response with some anxiety.

Gehler picked up the spoon and stirred his tea, then took a sip, looking over the rim of the cup at Driscoll.

'What tasks, Mr Driscoll? Exactly what do you want me to do?'

160

The Irishman sighed with relief. 'Good. One. Clearly the German Officers in K Lines will have key roles to play. Without telling anyone the extent of the operation, or its purpose, you must form them into a cell structure. Their task is mainly, at this stage, reconnaisance: to look for key positions where they can assist, or, in the event of certain areas of non-cooperation, and there will be some, be ready to take over. However, the most important object is preparing a plan for the release of the political prisoners in "Tintown". These men are vital to the Republican cause and the Provost-Marshal will be reluctant to let them go. That's where your men come in.'

Gehler weighed this carefully. 'I take it you expect that there will be some elements of the Irish Army who will not choose to co-operate with the German Forces?'

Driscoll nodded. 'Yes, I'm afraid so. There will be some, but I am sure you are aware that the majority of the soldiers are pro-German. It's just a few of the officers that I am concerned about, and you and your men are perfectly placed to deal with that. We must be prepared to act quickly and effectively when the time comes.'

'Of course,' Gehler said, 'there is one other thing.'

Driscoll looked for an ashtray, then, not finding one, stubbed the cigarette out on the sole of his shoe.

'Yes?'

'When will this operation take place and has it been coded yet?'

Driscoll shook his head. 'Can't answer your first question, but as soon as I can initiate the expected response in Dublin. Then I would expect it to be some time early in the new year. The code name is Osprey, Operation Osprey.'

Reed slowly hauled the heavy bucket of earth up from the bottom of the tunnel. His legs were braced either side of the open trap door in the floor of the hut. Gradually he eased the rope between his hands, letting the slack drop loosely beside him. It was backbreaking work, but now his hands had hardened and the real progress they were making took some of the pain from his back.

The bucket emerged into the flickering light of the oil lamp. The sergeant grabbed its handle and placed it on the floor beside him. He undid the rope and tied an empty bucket to it, lowering it back to the bottom again. When all the spare buckets were full the dirt would be put into sacks and distributed on the new vegetable patch that was being dug outside the hut, with the enthusiastic support of their Irish cook.

Whistler groaned and rolled over in his box, overflowing from it in every direction. Reed had placed an old blanket down beside it, but Whistler doggedly stayed in his old box, from which he refused to be parted. The sergeant grumbled quietly to himself and the animal.

'It's a dog's life, isn't it, Whistler, lying there all night watching everyone else do the work. Pity you can't be trained to lift buckets, rather than fill them.'

He felt the bucket strike the bottom of the shaft and waited for Harrison to release it. They'd rigged electric lights on an extension cable in the tunnel. It ran diagonally away from below the hut, taking the shortest possible route towards the outside wire barriers. Harrison knew they could not expect to be below the fence before Christmas, and for the American every hour in the tunnel seemed like wasted time. He found it almost impossible to reconcile himself to the parole system. The so-called code of honour was a curiously European concept. For the American it was an anachronism; he wanted to fight a war – not play games.

He tied the full bucket of earth to the rope and gave it a couple of tugs, signalling Reed to pull it up. Then he crawled on hands and knees through the narrow tunnel supports that they had gleaned from old wardrobes, the linings of drawers, any timber they could lay their hands on.

He reached the end of the tunnel. Bryce was on his knees, stripped to the waist, digging at the face. He paused momentarily as Harrison crawled up behind him.

'We'll have to put some more supports in soon.'

Harrison contemplated the roof above their heads. It looked firm.

'Should be OK for a couple more feet. Do you wanna swop round for a bit?'

'No,' Bryce replied. 'I'll stay on this till we put the new supports in. Then you can have a go.'

Harrison grabbed the bucket that was full and replaced it with an empty one.

'Suit yourself.'

Bryce watched him crawl backwards down the tunnel and took a swig of water from the flask tied round his neck. He replaced the cap on the bottle and wiped the sweat from his forehead with the back of his hand. The moisture partially cleared some of the dirt, exposing his white skin beneath. Bryce stared at his hand. He suddenly felt he was choking, short of air. He knew it was stupid and he tried to breathe deeply, but the air was heavy and fetid. It only seemed to make it worse. The close confines of the tunnel were bulging inwards, trapping him. He could not take his eyes off his hand. The white patch seemed to be on fire. It darkened, then started to peel back, exposing the red flesh beneath. He screamed and jumped backwards, trying to escape down the tunnel, cannoning into one of the supports. He felt it crack behind him. He twisted round, trying to hold the support, but it collapsed before he could grip it and he looked up terrified at the roof of the tunnel. He saw the earth furrow and crack and he flung himself face down, his hands around his head as the roof collapsed on to him, his scream cut off as the earth buried him.

The cloud of dust billowed around Harrison then up the tunnel, causing Reed to leap away from the trap door. He heard the American shouting for help, took a deep breath and began to climb down as quickly as he could.

Harrison had heard the scream and the crack as the support had given way. He crawled through the choking cloud of dust calling Bryce's name. Luckily the light circuit hadn't broken, but it was like trying to see through a thick glutinous fog. The dirt kept getting into his eyes, making them water. He scrabbled his way blindly forward until he reached the earth fall. At first he could see nothing. He clawed at the loose earth and then saw Bryce's boot sticking up towards him. He grabbed it, then found the other, working his hands up his legs until he could get a purchase. He pulled, but Bryce's body didn't move. He screamed back down the tunnel for Reed, then felt him crawl up beside him. Desperately they each grabbed Bryce's legs and braced themselves against the side of the tunnel. They heaved and Harrison felt some movement.

'Again,' he yelled.

This time Bryce moved perceptibly. Quickly they pulled again and this time his body came clear.

Harrison rolled him over on to his back and carefully wiped the dirt away from his eyes and mouth. He leant down, putting his ear close to Bryce's face. He was breathing – just. Harrison slapped his face lightly and Bryce groaned, then started to cough. Harrison lifted up his shoulders and pounded his back. The coughing subsided and Bryce wiped his eyes, blinking away the dirt. He tried to smile, but couldn't quite make it.

'Sorry,' he mumbled. 'My own fault.'

Reed peered at him anxiously. 'You all right, sir?'

Bryce sat up and gingerly felt his arms and chest.

'Yes, I think so. No bones broken anyway.'

The sergeant heaved a sigh of relief. 'Thank god for that.'

Harrison eyed them both. 'Why?' he said disgustedly. 'So that he can go back into that again and maybe bring it down on all of us.' He glanced at them through the dim half light. 'Jesus Christ, we must all be crazy. Any time we like we can walk out of this camp, free as a bird except for some stupid code of honour. Well, I didn't come this far to get myself buried beneath some soggy Irish field. That's it for me.' He paused, his eyes red-rimmed, staring at them. 'Now,' he said. 'I make my own way.' He crawled back down the tunnel.

Bryce and Reed sat slumped, saying nothing, listening until they could hear him no more. It was Reed who broke the long silence.

'What do you want to do, sir?'

Bryce shifted himself wearily, picking up the shovel. 'I think we had better clear this away, don't you?'

Reed nodded tiredly and pulled the empty bucket up for Bryce to fill.

Harrison leaned the bicycle against the Parole Hut and tucked his trousers into his socks. The Irish MP pushed the parole book across the sill and the American straightened up and signed it.

'Nice day,' the military policeman commented.

Harrison smiled. 'Yep. Cold but bright.'

He pushed the bike through the Main Gate, nodding affably to the guard who had opened it, then mounted, cycling carefully along the rutted track until he turned the corner out of sight of the internment camp. There he dismounted and fiddled with the inner tube cap, pretending he was losing some air. After a couple of minutes he began to make his way back to the Parole Hut, after speaking to the guard on the Main Gate. He leaned the bike on the wire, this time just inside the gate, and went back to the hut.

The guard smiled sardonically. 'That was a quick trip.'

Harrison tried to look as embarrassed as he could. 'Sorry, I'd better sign back in. I forgot my gloves . . . is it all right?'

The guard sighed exasperatedly and pushed the book towards him. 'You'll forget your head one of these days.'

Harrison scribbled his name in the book as quickly as he could and thanked him, striding back across the compound to his hut. He waited just inside the door for a moment, then took the gloves from his pocket and returned the way he had come, through the inner gate to the Parole Hut. He waved the gloves at the guard and smiled, trying to look as relaxed as possible. The next few moments would be crucial. He reached his bike and then, as casually as he could, slowly pulled on the woollen gloves. The guard in the hut wasn't watching him. As quietly as he could he reached for the bike and began to push it back to the Main Gate. The guard opened it wearily again and Harrison waited, sweating, until there was a gap big enough for him to pass through, all the time listening for the yell of realization. It didn't come. He mounted again and cycled down the lane and out of sight, elation lending wings to the bike's progress. My God, he'd done it! He'd got out of the camp without signing the parole book a third time. Legally he was in the clear, having already signed back in. The question was, would he be able to get across the border to the North before the oversight was noted? He glanced at his watch. It was 9.25 A.M. and he had all day before he had to be back in camp. His chances were good.

Tynan transferred the telephone abruptly from one hand to the other. He was finding it extremely difficult not to interrupt the British Ambassador, Sir John Maffey, who was attempting, as diplomatically as he could, to justify the American's escape as legitimate.

Group Captain Burroughs, who was sitting opposite Tynan, tried not to look apprehensive. He could see that the Provost-Marshal was seething with anger, quite rightly in his opinion; but Tynan was a formidable man and quite terrifying when he was angry. The Irishman could restrain himself no longer.

'I don't give a damn about the gloves, Sir John. The ruse is a mere technicality and I have to deal in realities. As far as I am concerned, the parole system has been broken by Harrison, and I am suspending it as of now for both the Luftwaffe and the RAF internees. You can inform your Government of that. I want that American back here quick.'

He slammed the receiver on to its rest and directed his gaze at Burroughs, who tried hard to return it, but couldn't. Tynan leaned across the table to emphasize his words.

'Listen, Burroughs, I meant what I said. Parole is suspended for both groups. Now if Sir John has any sense he'll get that bloody Harrison back here PDQ. When he is back, he's your responsibility. I cannot vouch for the behaviour of my men or even consider resuming the parole system unless he is *seen* to be punished. Do I make myself clear?'

Burroughs understood perfectly. There were other

reasons, too, why this escape could not have happened at a worse time. Reasons that even Tynan was unaware of.

'Yes, sir, you do; and I am certain that Sir John will see to it that the American is returned. Also, when the men understand just what the repercussions are, not only for themselves, but also the Luftwaffe officers, just what the behaviour of this one man has cost them in terms of honour as well as privilege, then I think they will deal with the matter effectively.'

Tynan stood up. 'Then I hope that we understand each other – good day.'

Burroughs stood up too and saluted, turned and left the room. After he'd gone Tynan picked up the telephone and dialled an extension.

Slye was, as usual, playing cards with himself, and his luck had not improved. He was still losing. Miserably he picked up the phone.

'Yes?'

The voice came through clear and harsh, and Slye began to sweat. He listened to the order with increasing apprehension.

'But sir, why are you suspending parole for the Germans if it was one of the RAF officers – I don't understand.'

Tynan took a deep breath. 'No, I don't suppose you do, Captain, but tell Von Bernstorff nevertheless.'

He slammed the telephone back down again before the Captain could bleat any more.

Slye protested, but the phone was dead. He gazed at it unhappily, acutely aware of the confrontation he would have with Von Bernstorff. He tried to think of some way round it. But there was none. Tiredly he picked up his hat from its usual spot on top of the table lamp. He peeped furtively at the other hand of cards, then played his own. He stood up, cheered momentarily by his success, then left the room.

\* \* \*

The mess hall was full. All the RAF personnel were gathered in the long L-shaped room, and an excited buzz of conversation animated most of those present as they speculated on the possibilities following Harrison's breaking of the parole system. Bryce and Reed stood in the corner, not indulging in the general air of expectation. Bryce anticipated repercussions and his fears were confirmed when he saw the grave face of the Commanding Officer.

Burroughs shouldered his way through the crowd to the end of the room, then stepped up on to the slightly raised dais. The conversation died away and he waited until the room was silent. He glanced at his notebook, then looked out over the sea of faces.

'Right, no doubt you all know about Pilot Officer Harrison's escape.' Stanley of the gold-lined front teeth grinned, exposing his expensive eating equipment, and cheered loudly, clapping his hands. Stanley the stocky little Pole was known simply by his first name, his surname being totally unpronounceable. His escapades on thin ice were legion. He would go where others feared to venture, but on this occasion the others boisterously joined in.

Burroughs held up his hand for silence. 'There will be no more of that, and by the time I am finished I hope none of you will echo those sentiments.' He paused, waiting for that to sink in. 'Harrison,' he continued, 'is now in Belfast. He left your bicycle, Pilot Officer Bryce, outside the railway station in Dublin. His "escape", for want of a better word, was perfectly easy and without any risk at all. It would,' he added, 'be equally easy for any of you if you too decided to break the parole system. I have just come from Commandant Tynan's office and he has informed me what the repercussions are to be. One. All parole and privileges are to be suspended forthwith for all RAF personnel. Two . All parole and privileges will also be suspended for all Luftwaffe personnel.' Reed glanced at Bryce in dismay.

'Further,' Burroughs continued, 'the parole system will not be reinstated until such time as the British Authorities return Harrison to this camp.' He stopped. There was absolute silence from the room. 'Yes,' he said, 'I thought that might surprise you.' He looked directly at Stanley and raised his eyebrows. 'Any comments?'

The Pole lowered his head and looked at the floor.

'I thought not,' said Burroughs. 'Some of you may take the view that the Provost-Marshal's reaction is too harsh. I have to tell you that, if I were in his place, I would do precisely the same. Harrison has broken the "code of honour" with a ruse – a technicality. The Commandant takes the view, and it's one that I share, that he operates a very civilized system for all of us here. He understands the pressure that you are under to escape – unlike the Germans, who settle happily into this system because there is no way back for them to occupied Europe. He knows that there is an extreme shortage of pilots and crews back home, and that it is your duty to try and rejoin them. All he asks, and I insist on, is that you do *not* break the parole system which is supported by International Law. But it is more than that. We are all members of the Royal Air Force and there is a code here – a code of honour. It may not exist in other areas of this war, but it will be observed here to the man while I am your Commanding Officer. Harrison has broken that code. He has dishonoured the Royal Air Force in the eyes of the enemy, and also amongst those whom we would wish to be our Allies. If we are lucky enough to see Harrison in this camp again, this will be made clear to him, by all of us . . . Dismissed.'

He closed the gate of the low stone cottage and stood perfectly still, trying to gauge the night. He looked out across the bay. The last glow of light was disappearing below the horizon and a fine grey mist, creeping in off the water, crawling up the inlets, softened the harsh rocky shoreline. Already the intermittent flashing light of the Fenit Lighthouse was diffusing into a pale watery glow. The night would suit him fine. He turned and looked up at the mountain. Mount Brandon loomed huge and black against the night sky, but soon that too would fade into nothing as the mist crept insidiously up its slopes.

Quinn pulled the shoulder straps of his backpack down into his chest and started up the rough stony track leading to the lower slopes; he wanted to reach his vantage point before the mist enveloped him. The conditions did not concern him; he had played on these slopes often enough as a child and he knew the terrain like the back of his hand.

The track disappeared as he struck out across the soft springy turf and high tufts of coarse grass. The slope steepened quickly and he settled into a short climbing stride that gradually took him clear of the grass on to the rocky lower reaches of the mountain.

He passed the first of the metal posts that led, at thirty-yard intervals, directly to the ruins of the ancient oratory at the summit of Mount Brandon. They were there to help the pilgrims that still climbed to the summit to kneel and pray. It was said that Saint Brendan had prayed there before his legendary voyage to America. Mount Brandon was a corruption of the saint's name. Quinn was grateful for the

171

metal posts. They would serve his purpose tonight, though not for guidance, or for prayer.

The light was fading in Lisbon too, and Jimmy Proctor had deliberately positioned himself next to one of the large, square windows of the Sandringham Flying Boat so that he could watch the huge floats lift clear of the water. It was his first trip as an assistant steward, and although they'd landed and taken off a number of times on this round trip to South Africa and back, he still hadn't got over the excitement.

All the passengers were seated and strapped in ready for take-off; all the formalities completed. He felt the hull beside him vibrate as the pilot fed power into the four engines. The water below them began to fleck and spray as the huge plane slowly gathered way, forcing itself through the slightly choppy water. The Sandringham increased its momentum. Gradually the hull was rising in the water; but Jimmy could still feel the waves slapping sharply against the hull, the deep padding of the seat taking most of the faint jarring.

It seemed as if the plane did not want to part company with the sea. The sharp crest of the hull continued to smash through the water, but suddenly all the bumpiness ceased and the floats were clear, streaming, flinging spray back into the sea as the huge seaplane clawed its way into the darkening sky on the last lap of its journey to Foynes.

Quinn dragged the boulder to one side and shone a torch into the short narrow cave behind it. He'd often played here, pretending to hide from the 'indians', waiting to see if his friends could find him. No one would find him tonight.

The mountain was blanketed in a soft cold mist. It seemed only he inhabited it. He pulled out the battered suitcase he had placed in the cave two nights before, setting it down flat on the soggy ground. He undid the latches and threw back

172

the lid. There were two luminous dials, one measuring the milliamps and the other the RF output. Three knobs painted bright yellow, one for the PA coupling, the other the Driver and the lower knob indicated the beacon frequency in megacycles.

He moved his backpack and lifted out the Lellanche heavy-duty battery and plugged it into the high-tension sockets on the beacon. Then from inside the case he lifted a twelve-volt liquid accumulator. He checked the acid level then plugged that into the low tension socket.

He slid a long copper rod from the top of the suitcase and uncoiled the wire wrapped around it, plugging it into the earth socket. That done, he trailed the wire a few feet from the set and plunged the copper rod into the soggy ground near the cave's entrance. Now all that remained was the aerial.

From his pack he took two aluminium rods and slotted them together, forming a small Y. He picked up the torch and carried the rods about three yards to one of the hollow metal posts that climbed the side of the mountain. He flicked on the torch then slotted the lower part of the aluminium rod into the top of the post until it reached the fork in the Y. It was loose, but it would do. He took the connecting wire back to the set and plugged it in. Now it was nearly ready. He switched on the beacon and adjusted the controls until the DC milliamps was at 750 and the RF output read 10 watts.

He was now transmitting a VHF signal with a range of between twenty and thirty miles. The signal was identical with the one at Foynes. He flashed the torch on to the dial of his watch. It was just after two-thirty A.M., and by now, if his instructions had been carried out correctly, the transmitter at Foynes would be dead.

The four men were still talking, sitting opposite one another in deep conversation. They intrigued Jimmy. They'd all boarded the Sandringham in Lisbon, their clothes ill-fitting and poor, unlike everyone else on the aircraft. Yet they spoke like gentlemen, and Jimmy wondered whether they were spies. He'd heard a lot from the Chief Steward about Lisbon being the centre of espionage in Europe. He would like to have eavesdropped on their conversation, but it was impossible. A Swiss diplomat was sitting immediately behind them and an American officer in front. Most of the passengers were asleep or dozing and the conversation between the four men was beginning to flag. Jimmy closed his eyes. He was tired. It had been a long trip and the sound of the four engines gradually lulled him to sleep.

The pilot glanced at his watch. The luminous dial glowed in the half-light of the flight deck. It was coming up to four-thirty A.M. and they had made good time from Lisbon. Strong tail winds had pushed them ahead of schedule, but they would not be able to land at Foynes until dawn. They had picked up the local radio beacon and now they were circling in a wide holding pattern at two thousand feet. It was raining heavily and getting a little bumpy. He glanced at his co-pilot.

'I'll take her up a bit, Reggie. No point in waking everyone just yet.'

Reggie smiled. 'Always rains in Ireland,' he said.

The pilot began to pull back on the stick and feed a little more power into the engines. The stick dropped suddenly and he felt a jarring crash. Quickly he straightened her out, glancing hurriedly behind and to his left. The port float had gone! Jesus Christ, they'd hit something! He reacted instinctively, pushing the throttle up to maximum and pulling right back on the stick, trying to gain some height. He peered through the wipers flicking back and forth across the windscreen. Something loomed out of the rain and mist ahead of him. He swore and banked sharply to the left. In so doing he saved himself and fourteen other lives of the twenty-five people on the Sandringham.

The huge flying boat's engines roared as the plane clawed its way up, turning away from the sheer rock face directly in front of it towards the rocky scree and great boulders that covered the sides of the ravine up which the aircraft had been lured.

Another twenty feet and the quick reactions of the pilot might have saved them all, but he didn't have those few life-saving feet. The port wing struck first, shearing clear away. The main body of the flying boat powered into the rocks, breaking up, scattering its wreckage and human cargo over an area of nearly half a mile.

Jimmy Proctor woke up still in his seat, the harsh wind tearing at his clothes, rain soaking him. He was cold, dazed and totally disorientated, but otherwise quite unhurt.

He stood up, leaning into the wind in order to stay upright. It was pitch dark and thankfully he was totally unaware of the carnage that lay around him. Some lights were blinking farther down in the valley. They seemed deceptively close. He wrapped the thin steward's jacket tightly round him and began to make his way slowly down the lower slopes of Mount Brandon.

Quinn's beacon had worked perfectly, and the Sandringham was only the first. Less than four weeks later an RAF Sunderland would share its fate, crashing into the mountain less than a mile away.

'Is it far?' he asked.

The small, wiry Irishman driving the car shook his head emphatically.

'No indeed it isn't, sir.' Dolan wasn't quite sure how to address Lord Parker. He'd never been in the presence of a lord before. He glanced in the driving mirror and smiled nervously. 'We'll be there shortly.'

Colonel Bryce leant forward, looking out through Parker's window.

'That must be Mount Brandon. It's the highest peak. The aircraft came down on one of the lower slopes near the sea.'

Lord Parker looked up at the mountains rising to his left.

'Daresay we'd bag a few grouse, Bryce. What say you, Mr Dolan?'

'I wouldn't be knowin' much about that, my Lord. Me work keeps me fairly busy.' The undertaker concentrated on his driving, unaware of the grim irony implicit in his remark.

Lord Parker chose to ignore it and continued affably.

'Yes, I believe you buried four of the passengers from the civilian plane locally?'

Colonel Bryce turned away from Parker and concentrated on the terrain. The Minister for War sounded as if he were discussing the weather. He knew what Parker was doing but he still found the manner offensive. Dolan slowed the car to a crawl while he negotiated a hairpin bend over a narrow bridge.

'That's right, sir. Four of the bodies were unidentifiable and your embassy man asked me to do that. All of the others I took personally up to the border and handed over.'

'Anything else?'

176

'What do you mean, sir?' Dolan asked anxiously.

Parker waved an arm expansively.

'Oh, I just mean personal effects, things of that nature.'

Dolan sighed with relief. 'Yes, I handed all that over to your people in Dublin. I had a terrible job getting all the papers and briefcases together – God, there were a terrible lot of them. I think they must have been all going to a meeting or something.'

Bryce and Parker exchanged a look.

'Yes, that's right,' Parker said blandly. 'There were a number of South African businessmen on board – heading for a conference in Dublin, I believe.'

Dolan nodded and smiled. 'I see. Then of course there was the money that I handed to you before.'

Bryce took up the gentle probing. 'I expect that too must have been difficult.'

Dolan laughed. 'God, you wouldn't believe it, Mr Bryce. It was everywhere like it had been raining pound notes. The Army had to block the road until it was all collected, but I'm afraid some of it must have got lost in the process, if you get my meaning.' He peered into the rearview mirror at Bryce.

Bryce smiled reassuringly. 'Bound to happen, Mr Dolan. It would anywhere. How did the money eventually reach your hands?'

Dolan pushed the car through the gears and they began to climb the shoulder of the hill. 'A young lieutenant signed for it first. Then he handed it to a police sergeant who eventually gave it to me when he knew I was dealing with your embassy man in Dublin.'

Bryce looked out of his window over Tralee Bay. He could just see the rocky promontory near the centre on which the Fenit Lighthouse stood. It looked for all the world like a dark grey warship anchored in the bay.

'Those men you buried, Mr Dolan?'

'Yes.'

'Would it be possible for us to see the graves?'

Dolan nodded. 'Yes, of course, though it's only one grave, Mr Bryce. It was impossible to separate them.'

Bryce closed his eyes momentarily, sickened, though he was sure the undertaker had meant nothing by his remark. The insensitivity must be necessary to shield himself from the horror of what he had to do in such circumstances.

Lord Parker continued imperturbably. 'You'll have some lunch with us later, Mr Dolan? The food in the hotel is excellent. We don't see such spreads in England these days.' He laughed. 'One of the fruits of neutrality, eh Dolan.'

The Irishman turned the car up an even narrower lane that climbed steeply. 'No, not many things are short here, sir, just tea and coffee – things like that. The youngster that was on the Sandringham, Proctor I think his name was. First thing he did when he got to Tralee was buy a huge box of chocolates for his mother – though I think he finished up eating most of them himself.'

'He had a remarkable escape,' Parker said quickly.

'Miraculous,' Dolan agreed. 'Unbelievable when you see how badly wrecked the plane was.'

'No need for that, Mr Dolan. Bit gruesome gawping at wreckage. No, Mr Bryce and I are just over for the weekend from the Ministry getting a bit of a break. Nothing official, you understand. Just wanted to pay our respects, if you get my drift.'

Dolan was surprised, but relieved. He hadn't been looking forward to the stiff climb. 'That's perfectly all right, sir. I understand your meaning.' He turned into a little bit of flat ground at the top of the lane and parked the car. 'This is as far as we can go.'

He jerked up the handbrake and climbed out, opening the door for Lord Parker. Bryce got out the other side. He was annoyed that Lord Parker had decided against examining the crash sites, though he realized how important it was not to give any undue weight to their presence in Ireland. The whole visit had been arranged to look like a social weekend at the Knights of Glin's residence so that he could sniff around and get the feel of the place. He had examined the reports and photographs meticulously, but nothing was so effective as being there. The reports had revealed nothing untoward. Both crashes had been at night in bad weather conditions. The only odd circumstance was that although the radio beacon at Foynes had been temporarily out of action, due to a power failure when the first crash occurred, the pilot, who had survived, insisted that he had used it as a guide for his circling pattern. If the second crash of the Sunderland had not occurred so quickly and so close to the same spot he would have been inclined to think that the pilot was making excuses for hitting the side of the mountain in bad weather. Now he wasn't so sure. Two flying boats in the same place within four weeks of each other was too much of a coincidence for his liking. He followed the other two men up the lane past a stone cottage to their left until the lane petered out into a track on the lower slopes of Mount Brandon.

They stopped, gazing silently up at the great bulk of the mountain above them. It was a clear, bright sunny day, the mountain etched sharp against the blue sky above. Behind them the bay glinting, white horses occasionally tossed high by the wind. A peaceful, beautiful scene, but Bryce was not satisfied.

'Where did the Sandringham crash?'

Dolan pointed up and to his left. 'You see that headland rising from the bay up towards the mountain above us.'

Bryce followed the line he had indicated. 'Yes, I see that.'

'Well, there's another ridge the other side of it which you

179

can't see from here. The plane flew up between them, then tried to turn away to its left when the pilot saw the mountain in front of him. It crashed about three-quarters of the way up the ridge. You can just see the tailplane sticking up.'

Bryce gazed up at the spot. He could see some wreckage. It looked tiny, and forlorn, like a piece of silver paper reflecting the sunlight. He turned and looked out over the bay.

'How far away is Foynes?' he asked, though he knew the answer.

'About fifty miles as the crow flies,' Dolan said. 'Nearly home,' he added.

Bryce said nothing. Fifty miles. How the hell could an experienced pilot make such an elementary error? There was more, there had to be. He glanced at Lord Parker.

'Shall we have a look at the grave now, sir?'

The Minister for War nodded. 'Yes, let's do that.' He shivered. 'I feel cold.'


They retraced their steps down the track to the car parked close to the cottage. Bryce saw the curtains twitch as they passed. He knew they were being watched, but he could see no one, nor did he have any authority in this country. Strictly speaking, as a member of the armed forces, he should not be here at all.

Dolan opened the front door, then the back one for Lord Parker. The Minister clambered inside. Bryce paused for a moment, leaning on the roof of the car, watching the cottage. He sensed the presence of someone behind those curtains but could distinguish nothing, just the vaguest of shadows. He climbed into the car and Dolan backed it out into the lane – turned round and drove off.

Quinn carefully placed the camera down on the side-

180

board and walked to the door. He lifted the latch and stood gazing thoughtfully down the lane, listening to the sound of the car's engine fading into the distance.

Dolan led them through the graveyard. The grass was untended. Some of it grew up to their knees. Lord Parker, and Bryce who was following, tried to stay on the narrow little paths between the graves, but the undertaker did not seem to care whether he walked over them or not.

The small stone church stood back from the wrought-iron gates, isolated, surrounded by the forlorn and over-grown cemetery. The trees seemed to sweep angrily towards them as they passed on as though annoyed at their presence.

Dolan stopped eventually by the low stone wall border-ing the graveyard and pointed to a new headstone in front of a single freshly-dug grave.

'I had this put up at the request of the embassy in Dublin.'

Bryce stopped beside the Minister and looked at the stone. It was simple and uncluttered. The four names, followed by the inscription:

WHO LOST THEIR LIVES IN THE SUNDERLAND AIR CRASH
AT MOUNT BRANDON

Bryce glanced at the Minister. 'That's a mistake surely?'

Parker leant forward, staring at the stone. 'What?'

'The Sunderland air crash. That came later. These men were from the Sandringham.'

Parker looked at Dolan. 'That's right.'

The undertaker grew nervous. 'Well, that's what I was told to do by the embassy. You can check with them.'

Bryce shook his head. 'Easy enough to make the mistake,

I suppose. The Sunderland is in fact the RAF version of the civilian Sandringham. It's not vital, just confusing.'

Parker took the point. 'Yes, I suppose so. But I'll have a word with the embassy.' He turned to the Irishman. 'They might want you to alter that slightly.'

Bryce turned away, there was little more to be learnt here. At least the embassy had got one thing right. The headstone carried no ranks. It did not reveal that at least two of the men were escaped POWs. He walked past the church and up the other side, glancing at the names of the dead. Churchyards had always fascinated him. There was some more freshly turned earth, sheltered by an alcove of trees. He stopped in front of it, his attention riveted to the names on the headstone. They were German. Their ranks indicated they were seamen, the date barely two months before. He turned quickly, Dolan froze.

'I was looking for you,' he stammered.

Bryce could see the fear in his eyes, but it would not do to upset this man – he already knew too much about the Sandringham. He smiled.

'Sorry,' he said, 'just looking around. Are you ready to go?'

Dolan looked relieved. 'Yes, Lord Parker is waiting in the car.'

Bryce began to walk briskly down the path. 'Then we must go. Can't afford to keep the Minister waiting. You will join us for lunch, Mr Dolan?'

The Irishman grinned. 'Be delighted, sir, delighted.'

The six Spitfires flying in V formation flew in from the west, the setting sun behind them. As they crossed Tralee Bay the formation broke up and each in turn made a separate approach to the lower slopes of Mount Brandon. They spiralled and swooped around the mountain, several of them following the precise route of the Sandringham up the ravine, breaking away to port and starboard before reaching the vertical face of the precipice at the end.

Local people stood in their doorways, excited and curious, watching the display. Children ran around waving their arms, yelling at the sky as though to attract the attention of the pilots. A nervous fireman at the fire station in Tralee sounded the alarm and a solitary car slowed and bumped quietly into a horse-drawn cart; neither driver seemed to notice. The small elegant little planes eventually reformed and flew off towards the north and their base in Ulster, the sweet sound of the six Merlin engines gradually fading into silence.

The women in the doorways continued to buzz excitedly; the children, arms extended flew in flights of imagination, buzzing lamp posts and each other. The two drivers who had collided almost imperceptibly parted good friends, and slowly life went back to normal. But the buzzing of Mount Brandon would be remembered many years hence.

The heavy black Mercedes crunched slowly up the drive, followed by its faithful police car. The headlights flicked across the front of the half-timbered house. Both cars stopped in the driveway as Toller came to the door.

Herr Hemmrich leaned forward and tapped Carter on the shoulder.

'Tell the Garda in the police car I am having dinner with my Counsellor.' He glanced at his watch. 'I shall be at least four hours, possibly more. Toller's cook has got something for you in the kitchen.'

Carter climbed out and opened the door for the Ambassador. 'Thank you, sir, I'll pass that on.'

The Ambassador strode to the door, where Toller greeted him, then led him inside, shutting the door behind him.

'This way, Herr Oberst,' he said quietly. He led him out through the french windows at the back of the house and down to the bottom of the garden. The small wooden gate in the fence was covered in cobwebs and slightly rusted. The Ambassador was about to warn him of the possibility of noise when Toller reassured him.

'I oiled the hinges this morning. It will make no sound.'

The gate opened noiselessly and Toller gripped the Ambassador's arm. 'It's not far. This back road leads to the entrance to the golf club. Come.'

They walked quickly to the end of the dirt track, where Toller gestured him back. 'Wait. I'll just check.'

He emerged into the road and looked right, then left. A car was waiting on the side of the road. He saw a cigarette glow briefly, then the engine engaged and the car drew up beside him.

'Mr Hemmrich?' an Irish voice enquired.

Toller shook his head 'No, but he is here.'

He waved the Ambassador forward. Hemmrich emerged from the shadows and gripped the Counsellor's hand.

'Thank you, Toller. I shall be back here in three hours. If I am a little late, don't worry. The Garda do not expect me to leave before midnight.'

Toller indicated his understanding. 'Good luck, Ambassador.'

Hemmrich nodded and climbed into the car. The Counsellor watched it until it was out of sight, then made his way back to the house.

Hemmrich was the last to arrive and Driscoll took him through to the main lounge where the others had already gathered. Driscoll made the introductions. The Ambassador had already met General Lynch and they greeted each other warmly. Gehler too had had one meeting with Hemmrich, but Quinn's greeting was more formal and guarded. Driscoll was concerned about him. The General had, understandably, been somewhat cool in his response to the IRA leader, but Quinn had remained aloof from the others too, seldom exchanging more than a few words, and Driscoll had had to work hard to cover the gaps. He filled the Ambassador's glass with white wine and recharged some of the others.

'Gentlemen, I hope you will forgive me, but as the host may I suggest we sit down at the table and get the discussion under way.'

Driscoll stood by one of the chairs and offered Quinn the place next to him as the five men arranged themselves around the large oval table.

'For obvious reasons,' Driscoll resumed, 'there will be no

record of this meeting, or the subject under discussion, but I think it's clear that none of us would be here tonight unless we fully realized that we have reached a decisive point in Ireland's history – one which could, if we handle it correctly, see all Ireland's national aspirations achieved.'

Lynch raised his hand. Driscoll paused. 'Yes, General?'

'I'm sure we can all identify with that, James, but I should like to get straight down to brass tacks and ask Herr Hemmrich whether we can count on any definite help from Germany in the military sense, should we decide to take action ourselves. I know, for example, that the Wehrmacht picked up huge supplies from the British Army after its retreat from France and Dunkirk. Our men are usually equipped with British weapons, and they are used to them – but we have nothing like enough to tackle even the limited forces opposing us in Northern Ireland.'

The Ambassador glanced at Driscoll. 'May I answer that?'

Driscoll nodded. 'I think we'd all like to hear your views, Ambassador.'

Herr Hemmrich smiled, appreciating the hint. 'Curiously, only today I have had direct communication from von Ribbentrop in Berlin. He has asked me to make it clear to De Valera that, if the Allies were to threaten the borders of Southern Ireland in any way, we could indeed supply the arms you require, General. Further, I know that Frank Aiken, the Minister here for External Affairs, is greatly concerned about the possibility of an invasion from the North. So in brief, the answer to your question is yes. We can supply equipment.'

Quinn picked up a leather briefcase from the side of his chair, opened it and selected two photographs. He threw them on to the table.

'I've not been waiting for arms. I think I realized a long

186

time ago that if I waited for other people to act nothing would be done.'

No one spoke. Driscoll watched the smoke from Hemmrich's cigarette curl silently up to the ceiling. He'd dreaded this.

Quinn resumed. 'You may not have heard anything about this, because a security blanket has been thrown over the whole affair. But I would ask you all to take a look at these pictures. They were taken by a local photographer in Tralee.'

Lynch picked one up. It was the wreck of an aircraft. Only the tail was recognizable and a few of the markings. He glanced up at Quinn. 'Is this the Sandringham that came down on Mount Brandon?' He knew of the civilian crash and the terrain was not unfamiliar.

Quinn nodded. 'That's right, General, and the other one is the Sunderland that followed it four weeks later.'

The General glanced briefly at the second photograph and handed it on to the German Ambassador. 'Why do you show us these, Mr Quinn?'

Quinn glanced around the table, the others were watching him now, waiting for his reply.

'I think you already know the answer, General. Perhaps you are the only one here that would know.' He pointed to the photographs. 'Those crashes were no accident. That was my doing.'

Hemmrich was shocked. He stared at the Irishman. 'But why, what for? The Sandringham was on a civilian route from Lisbon. I knew the Swiss Ambassador who was killed, he was a decent man . . .'

His voice trailed off. He was clearly upset.

Quinn leaned forward over the table to emphasize his words.

'Because, Mr Ambassador, that civilian route, as you call

187

it, is being used to smuggle escaped British prisoners of war from Lisbon back into England, where they can rejoin their units and kill more of your people.' He paused, waiting for that to sink in. 'The Sunderland was an RAF plane and, as all of you are aware, *I* am at war with England. So are my volunteers. We shall remain so until Ireland is united.'

They digested that. The clock in the corner ticked, its sound suddenly noticeable in the silence that followed Quinn's speech.

Gehler took the pencil he had been chewing from his mouth.

'How did you do it, Mr Quinn? They are both big well-equipped flying boats. It's unlikely they would fly into high ground, even at night. Mount Brandon is the highest mountain in Ireland and is well documented.'

The implication was clear, and Driscoll began to sweat. The last thing he wanted was disagreement between these men. It was vital that some coherent policy should emerge from this meeting. He looked at Quinn. The eyes seemed dead. He rushed in. 'I'm sure Oberleutnant Gehler did not mean to imply anything, Liam, his curiosity as a member of the Luftwaffe . . .'

Quinn cut him off. 'I'll answer it.' He paused, staring straight at Gehler. 'The pilot did not know he was approaching Mount Brandon. He thought they were circling over Foynes. It is fifty miles farther north and there are no mountains. As you know, they use dead reckoning plus the radio beacon at Foynes to identify their position. I'd had the electricity at Foynes cut off, apparently accidentally. It happens all the time. And the back-up generator failed to work.' He smiled. The eyes remained cold. 'I'd arranged that too.'

Gehler nodded, 'I see, and you had another beacon on the mountain.'

Quinn acknowledged the deduction. 'That's right,

supplied to me by parachute drop from the Luftwaffe.'

Gehler and Quinn exchanged an appreciative look. Driscoll felt the atmosphere relax. He sighed with relief as quietly as he could.

The General seized the opening. 'So you have had some supplies from Germany, Quinn?'

Quinn nodded. 'Some,' he replied tersely.

Lynch turned to Driscoll. 'But it seems the attitude of Germany is to help us only if there is an invasion from the North.'

'Surely,' Gehler interrupted, 'that is more likely if the Republican forces under the control of Mr Quinn are actively sabotaging British planes?'

The General shrugged his shoulders. 'That depends on whether or not they are aware that it is sabotage.'

Quinn picked up another photograph from his briefcase and handed it to Lynch. 'His name is Bryce. He and the Minister for War, Lord Parker, have been to Kerry and the mountain. They stayed at Glin Castle, supposedly on a weekend visit, but they took the opportunity to wine and dine the undertaker Dolan. I think they wanted to see how much was known or suspected generally. But you can't hide anything in a place like Tralee. Everyone knew that there was something strange about who was on that plane. The survivors in the local hospital were all Smiths and Joneses. There was a large sum of money on the plane, and the opinion is that some sort of conference was going to take place. One of the survivors even let it out of the bag that he was an escaped POW. He said to one of his colleagues after he had been rescued that he'd really hurt his back this time. It was twice as bad as the first time he'd crashed in France.'

Gehler took the photograph from the General and looked at it. 'You say this man's name is Bryce?'

'That's right,' Quinn answered. 'I had him checked out.

He's from Military Intelligence, MI9. He's a Colonel.'
Quinn looked across the table at General Lynch. 'They
know that these planes were sabotaged. A week after the
Sunderland crashed a flight of Spitfires came in from the
sea and buzzed the mountain trying to see what the
attraction was. They may have thought it was magnetic or
something, but they'd have found nothing.'

Hemmrich hadn't recovered from his revulsion. 'In that
case, surely Aiken is right. Isn't it more likely that Britain
will invade if they think their aircraft are being sabotaged?'

Quinn allowed himself a smile. 'That's why I did it.' He
stared at the German Ambassador, who tried to hold his
gaze but could not.

'I want Germany in on our side, Mr Hemmrich. I want
them here on Irish soil fighting alongside us.' He glanced
at Lynch, 'And anybody else who wants to be rid of the
English – how we get them in I don't give a damn!' He
stopped, and Driscoll felt the moment was opportune to
pull this together and spring his news.

'Gentlemen,' he said, 'I think we are all agreed on the
need for Ireland and Germany to work together to defeat
England. It's a matter of how and when. I returned from
Berlin with the direct order of the Führer to try and
persuade political opinion at the highest level to form an
alliance with the Third Reich in order to carry out precisely
what we have been discussing. Oberleutnant Gehler and I
have already had a meeting, and I brought him specific
instructions from Herr Hitler which I am sure are already
being advanced.' He glanced at Gehler for confirmation.
The Oberleutnant inclined his head.

Driscoll turned to Quinn.

'When these plans are put into operation you will be
reunited with many of your colleagues who are at present
locked away in the Internment Camp called Tintown on
the other side of the main military barracks on The

Curragh. Now you asked, and I think quite rightly, how soon will German Forces be involved. I can tell you this. I put to Herr Hitler a proposal for a liberating army to be landed in Ireland. I have every reason to believe that this is already being acted upon. Through the German Legation a communiqué was handed to me yesterday. I will not read it to you as you can do that yourselves.' He pulled a sheet of yellow paper from his jacket pocket and placed it on the table. 'Suffice to say it indicates that a volunteer group of top SS troops, to be designated No 1 Special Service Troop, is already being trained at the Totenkopf Barracks in Berlin. They are being taught to use captured English weapons, and though they do not know it yet, their destination is Ireland.'

Quinn said nothing, but felt a surge of elation at these words. His face, however, betrayed none of his exultation. Gehler glanced quickly round the table. He sensed the effect on Lynch. He turned to Driscoll. 'You said you were working to get political acceptance of Germany's role in Ireland. Has De Valera given you any response yet?'

Driscoll lit the cigar he had been preparing and inhaled deeply. Gehler was a dangerous ally. He could undermine the success of this meeting, which was almost within his grasp.

'Things have a funny way of happening in Ireland, Oberleutnant, as I am sure you will discover. It isn't always possible to go straight to the top. Nor is it always the best ploy. It may not be suitable for the Prime Minister to give me the answer I seek, even if he should want to. However, that does not mean that he cannot indicate his willingness to co-operate by turning a blind eye. There are certain Ministers I am in touch with who have the ear of De Valera. The mere fact that at this table we have General Lynch, who holds the second highest position in the structure of Army Command, while sitting opposite him is the officer who commands the forces of the IRA, which, as you can see,' he waved an arm at the photographs on the table, 'are considerable and effective. That in itself should indicate the breadth and scope of the movement in Ireland for an alliance with Germany.'

He took a puff on his cigar. He felt good and the speech had been impressive – certainly he'd re-established himself after allowing his composure to crack when Quinn had so very nearly proved disruptive.

Gehler picked up the photograph of the man standing by the car. The face was vaguely familiar. 'What did you say this man's name was?'

'Bryce,' Quinn said, 'Colonel Bryce, Military Intelligence.'

Gehler looked again at the photograph. Yes, of course, the pilot in the van with him when he had arrived. He looked across the table at Quinn and smiled. 'Thank you,' he said, handing back the picture. 'Thank you very much.'

Halder pushed the bicycle across the compound and out through the inner gate. The military policeman in the small hut saw him approaching and placed the parole book on the sill of the counter.

'Read the declaration, Leutnant, and sign at the bottom if you please, sir.'

Halder had done this several times and knew the routine. He smiled at the guard. 'Lovely day for this time of year.'

192

The guard grinned, exposing some discoloured teeth. ''Tis that, sir, beautiful.'

Halder signed his name and pushed the old-fashioned bike forward past the guard, who had opened the Main Gate for him. Then he mounted it.

The arm gave him no trouble now. Despite the general detention of the internees since Harrison's escape he had been granted special parole in order to exercise in the fresh air. He'd been lucky in all his treatment to have a nurse as dedicated as the young Irish girl who had tended him. He smiled to himself. He'd probably fallen in love with her, as all patients were supposed to, but Maureen had an Irishman and was far too sensible to make the mistake of becoming entangled with him. It was a pity – she was very attractive.

He cycled eastwards, clearing the grassy plain of The Curragh and entering a lane bordered with high trees. He'd always been interested in wild life and there was a patch of woods down by the river that he wanted to explore. He passed some big houses set well back from the road, then turned off on to a narrower track that led into the woods. The trees were bare now, the last of the leaves almost gone, but each season had its different beauty and he loved the starkness of the branches reaching up to the metal blue wintry sky as though appealing for help.

He parked the bicycle next to a tree and walked slowly through the wood. The soft matting of grass and fallen leaves made his passage almost silent, and sometimes he'd stop and listen to the furtive scurryings in the undergrowth. Once, briefly, he saw the startled face of a fox; then it was gone and he wondered if it were just his imagination.

He found some blackberry bushes and made a mental

note of their position. Blackberry pie would be a welcome addition to the menu next September. Paul had slowly come to realize that he didn't mind his partial imprisonment. He had never wanted to be involved in the war, but the thought of conscientious objection and its subsequent publicity and shame had frightened him more than the idea of flying. Flying was for him still terrifyingly real. He hated the insubstantial feeling of nothing beneath him. Here on the earth, in the woods, he was at home, he felt easy. Ireland was beautiful and different. Every day he cycled somewhere new, finding something fresh to explore, to contemplate.

He could hear the sound of the river bubbling away to his left somewhere. He turned towards it, then stopped. Directly in front of him was a blackbird, its wing hanging uselessly by its side. It didn't move, the black beady eyes studying him intently, waiting to see what he would do. Paul stood absolutely still, then very slowly he reached into the pocket of his jacket and found the piece of bread he had brought to throw upon the stream.

Slowly and carefully he withdrew his hand, talking softly to the bird, using all his skill not to frighten it. He crumbled the bread and tossed a small piece of it towards the bird. It hopped away for a moment, then stopped and slowly retraced its steps. The broken wing looked ugly. The natural aerodynamic shape of the bird distorted. How it had been injured was impossible to tell. It could have been hit by something, a car or a lorry. In any case it would not survive long in the coming winter in the wild.

Paul tossed it another piece of bread, this time a little closer, and the bird hopped obediently towards it. He knelt down on his haunches, talking continuously, throwing each small piece of bread less and less distance away. Finally the bird was within reach, but Paul did not make a grab for it. The blackbird was starving, close to death. The feathers matted and unresistant to rain. Some of the feathers on the broken wing were missing, but it might be possible to save him. Halder intended to try. He held out his hand, a piece of bread in his palm. The bird looked at him enquiringly and cocked his head to one side as though to gauge his intentions. Paul smiled.

'Come, little bird, I only want to help you. Let me help you, the bread is here.' He held out his hand. The bird did not move at first, then slowly it hopped towards him, its wing trailing in the dirt. He pecked at the bread in his hand and did not try to escape when Paul slowly brought his other hand towards it. Tenderly he picked up the injured creature and held it up examining its wing.

'Don't worry. I think I can fix it. We'll try, shall we?' Carefully he tucked the blackbird into the front of his jacket, cuddling the bird in the crook of his arm. He walked slowly between the trees, back to where he'd left his bicycle.

The gentle, sweet curve of the opening bars from Beethoven's Pathétique rippled quietly from the grey stone church, the deep chords of the organ giving new strength to Beethoven's work, yet sounding strangely unfamiliar within the context of a rural Irish setting. Those that lived within earshot had grown used to these winter afternoon interludes. Some would open their windows and listen; others would continue to do their daily tasks. Yet most welcomed the return of the German flyer who played so beautifully.

Father Hogan delighted in the presence of Gehler. He played the church organ so sensitively and yet, although not in uniform, his manner was always vaguely military and polite. Hogan liked him. He knew he had some organ music somewhere; and this time he was determined to find it before the officer departed. The chest of drawers was all open, papers and rubbish that he had collected over the years strewn about the place. The music was not there. He slammed the drawers shut irritably.

'Where the divil is it?' he muttered to himself. He looked around the room. A huge oak bureau stood staring at him malevolently in the corner, as though waiting to pounce. Hogan's eyes lit on it with glee. 'That's where you'll be hiding, I'll bet.'

He crossed the room and grabbed the key to the lid, pulling it open and down. A cloud of dust enveloped him momentarily and he spluttered and coughed, wiping his eyes with a handkerchief plucked from his soutane. He descended on the pile of letters and yellowing unpaid bills looking for the music and the mound of rubbish in his room grew steadily. The tattered carpet had almost disappeared beneath it when suddenly his piercing cry of triumph stopped his housekeeper dead in her tracks. His voice floated up the stairs.

'I've found it, Mary, I've found it. It was in the bureau.'

Mary continued to tidy the bedroom, not bothering to answer. She was tight-lipped, anticipating the chaos that would greet her when she went downstairs. Father Hogan waited, smiling broadly, listening for her response. When it didn't come he pursed his lips and called up the stairs again.

'I'm just takin' it over to the Church for the German. I won't be long.' Still no reply. He shook his head, annoyed. 'Oh, to hell with the woman.'

He stopped, realizing what he had said and crossed himself reverently. He gazed up at the cracked ceiling and mouthed silently, 'I'm sorry.' Then, clutching the dusty music sheets, he fled from the study, along the short corridor, out of the house, across the graveyard to the entrance of the church. The doors were open and he knelt

196

and crossed himself briefly before walking more composedly between the empty pews towards the altar.

The organ was to the right, opposite the pulpit, the terraced organ pipes ascending close to the stone wall. Father Hogan stopped, waiting for the music to end. The rich tones of the organ seemed mellowed and sweetened by the sad strains of the Pathétique. The natural acoustics of the high timbered ceiling gave the sound great presence, and once again the priest marvelled at the beautiful subtlety of the music.

He glanced back towards the entrance as a tiny speck of dust glinted in the watery sunshine that streamed through the narrow stained-glass windows. The speck slid slowly down the beam of light as if fearful of losing its warmth. It flashed then disappeared into the shadow. Hogan turned back to look at the organist as the music ended.

Gehler seemed unaware of his presence. He had his back to him, sitting perfectly still. Hogan coughed gently and the officer turned and looked at him, saying nothing. The priest felt vaguely uncomfortable, almost an intruder. He waved the sheets of music, distributing more dust into the atmosphere.

'I found this, Oberleutnant. It's the organ music I told you about before.' He smiled, indicating the state of the sheets. 'As you can see, it's been gathering a certain amount of dust over the years. Perhaps you'd like to have a look?'

Gehler stood up and descended the stone steps towards him. 'That's kind of you. Thank you Father.' He took the music from the priest, who rubbed his grubby hands on his soutane. 'Sorry about that,' he said, apologetically.

Gehler lifted one of the sheets up to the light and examined it briefly, then took each sheet in turn, noting the

197

composer's name. He handed them all back to the priest, who stared at him surprised.

'Is something wrong, Oberleutnant?'

Gehler paused reflectively, then said, 'I don't play Mendelssohn, Father.'

Hogan was puzzled. 'But it is his organ sonata. I would have thought it was perfect . . .' He stopped, suddenly aware of the implication. He was shocked, finding it difficult to comprehend. Gehler continued to stand in front of him, unmoving, silent.

'You mean,' Hogan paused, clearing his throat, finding it almost impossible to articulate the thought within the confines of the church. 'You mean because he was a Jew?'

Gehler said nothing for a moment then repeated without emphasis, 'I don't play Mendelssohn, Father.'

The priest spread his hands mutely. One of the sheets of music slipped from beneath his arm and fell to the floor. 'But all music is welcome here, Oberleutnant, just as you are.'

Gehler inclined his head sharply. 'Good day, Father.' He walked past the priest and down the aisle, his footsteps echoing hollowly until he had gone.

Father Hogan waited, staring at the organ until the church was totally silent again. Then he knelt down and picked up the sheet of music. Carefully he wiped the dust from the composer's name with the worn sleeve of his soutane. He turned and slowly left the church.

Bryce sat up in bed, wide awake instantly. 'Come in,' he said.

The door to his room opened and an Irish orderly poked his head around it somewhat hesitantly. 'Sorry to be wakin' you, sir, but can I do the room now?'

Bryce stared at him fascinated, not quite sure whether he was still dreaming.

The orderly looked puzzled. 'Is anything wrong, sir?'

Bryce swung his legs off the bed. 'What? No, nothing wrong.' He slipped on his trousers and flying jacket. 'Come in, man, come in.' He tried not to stare. 'Have you got much to do here?'

'Yes,' the Irishman said, slightly relieved. 'I've only just started today and I'm findin' me way about as it were.'

Bryce pulled on his boots. 'Right, carry on; the room is yours.' He shut the door behind him and almost ran along the corridor. He crossed the compound as quickly as he could without attracting attention to the NCOs' quarters. Sergeant Reed was sitting on his bunk examining his feet. He stood up as Bryce came in. The officer grabbed his arm. 'Have you seen Stanley anywhere?'

The sergeant sat down again and began pulling on his socks and shoes. 'He'll probably be in his room, sir, sleeping off last night.'

Bryce swore, 'Shit! You mean he was drunk?'

'As a lord, sir, and picking fights with the Luftwaffe in the hotel bar.'

Bryce clapped a hand to his forehead. 'Any injuries?'

Reed smiled, 'Only to them.'

Bryce grinned. 'Great, let's get him.'

The sergeant grabbed his jacket and led Bryce past the NCOs' bunks towards a passageway at the end of the hut.

'What's all this about, sir?'

'I'll tell you when we find Stanley.'

Reed came to a door on the right off the passageway. He opened it without knocking and walked straight in. Bryce followed. Stanley was stretched out on the bed fast asleep, his mouth open wide, snoring like a buzz saw. Reed shut his mouth and the snoring ceased.

'We have to stick him in here when he's over the eight, otherwise we'd get no sleep.'

Right on cue Stanley's jaw snapped open again and the buzz saw resumed, his gold-lined front teeth gleaming.

'Well, we'll have to keep his mouth shut or he'll give it away.'

Reed looked at him incredulously. 'What?' he said, mystified.

'The teeth, man, the teeth.'

Reed stared blankly.

Bryce turned and closed the door behind him, then faced Reed again. 'Look, there's a new Irish orderly presently cleaning up my room who is the living spit of Stanley, only he hasn't got gold-lined teeth.'

Reed's eyes widened as the penny dropped. 'Right.' He turned, dropped on one knee and began to slap the face of the sleeping Pole. At first nothing happened, then the buzz saw began to hiccup, finally stopped and two red-rimmed eyes peered cautiously up at the sergeant.

'What you want? Has the war been ended?'

Reed hauled Stanley into a sitting position. 'How's your Irish accent, Stanley?'

'I speak it very no damn good.'

Bryce moved towards the door. 'OK Stanley, get dressed, come over to my quarters and we'll have a new uniform for you. You're going out today, but you'll have to keep your mouth shut.'

'Me no say word,' Stanley said determinedly.

Bryce smiled and turned to the sergeant. 'You come with me, Reed. We have a little tying up to do.'

'Sounds good to me, sir,' Reed said enthusiastically.

Stanley pulled on the jacket. It fitted quite well though the shoulders strained a bit at the seams. He stared down at the hapless orderly, who was bound and gagged and wearing

200

nothing but long johns. 'He is quite good fit,' Stanley said affably.

Bryce pulled him round, facing him. 'Now listen, all you have to do is walk naturally and say nothing. Have you got that?'

Stanley nodded vigorously. 'Walk nothing, speak naturally – I will.'

Bryce looked at Reed hopelessly. The sergeant took up the impossible task.

'No, you must not speak at all, Stanley. Do you understand?'

The Pole looked at each of them apprehensively, opened his mouth, changed his mind, shut it tightly and nodded. Reed turned away exasperated and Bryce resumed.

'OK. Let's not waste any more time.' He picked up the orderly's pail and mop and handed them to the Pole. 'Take these, walk as casually as you can across the compound. No one should stop you at the inner gate during the day. When you get to the Parole Hut try not to look at the guard. Remember what you learnt when you were square bashing – never look the sergeant in the eye. Do that and you should be all right. Now once you get through you can make your way to Dublin by bus and get the train to Belfast.' He looked at Reed for confirmation. 'Is there anything else?'

The sergeant shook his head. 'No sir, on a quick patch-up job like this it's just a question of keeping your head down and hoping for the best.'

Bryce propelled Stanley towards the hut door. 'Good luck, Stanley.' He grasped his hand and shook it. 'Remember, not a word.'

Stanley, his lips still firmly closed, rolled his eyes. Reed opened the door and Stanley squared his shoulders, almost splitting the seams of the jacket. Reed closed his eyes as some of the stitching popped. When he opened them the

Pole was halfway across the compound, gripping the pail tightly and holding the mop like a spear.

'Oh, God,' Bryce muttered. 'He'll never make it.'

Reed crossed his fingers and said nothing.

Stanley reached the first gate and passed through it without any trouble. The MP was standing outside the Parole Hut lighting a cigarette as Stanley approached. He nodded affably and took it from his mouth. 'Lovely day,' he said.

Stanley, the thought that he must not talk totally obsessing his mind, nodded vigorously, then smiled in what he hoped was a friendly fashion. The sun bounced off the gold-lined teeth, dazzling in their brilliance. The MP's cigarette dropped from his nerveless fingers and he stared fascinated at the molar display.

'Would you believe that,' he muttered to himself, recognizing the teeth instantly. He blocked Stanley's path. 'And just where do you think you're going?'

Stanley decided the time had come to break his silence. His smile broadened fiercely. 'I out go,' he said with some authority. The Military Policeman gripped him gently but firmly by the arm and led him back towards the compound. 'Stanley, you really are a pain in the arse.' Stanley smiled, glowed, proud and incandescent. 'I know – I also cause much trouble, yes?'

The guard nodded resignedly, 'That would not be a lie, Stanley. Now where would you be puttin' the man whose clothes you're wearin'?'

Stanley pointed to the hut where Bryce and Reed were watching. They looked at each other in consternation, then turned and fled.

The black van drew up outside the small country police station. Two Military Policemen sitting in the cab alighted and walked slowly towards the entrance. A local Garda officer emerged before they reached it, followed by a dishevelled RAF pilot, his leather flying jacket torn, carrying his helmet loosely in his hand. He was slight, lightly built and round-shouldered. There was some bruising above his left cheek which only accentuated his clear blue eyes. He was about twenty-three years old. The two MPs advanced towards them. One of them glanced at the bruise, then at the Garda.

'Would he be after causing you any trouble?' The Garda policeman smiled benignly at the RAF officer.

'No, no trouble at all. His name is Crawford, a Pilot Officer. The villagers brought him in early this morning. His plane ran out of fuel and crashed into the sea off Wicklow point. He landed by parachute, luckily not in the water.'

The MP who had spoken first gestured to the prisoner. 'We'll be after takin' him off your hands now. You'll be havin' a piece of paper for me to sign?'

The Garda nodded and found the appropriate form after rummaging through various pockets with a certain amount of embarrassment. At last he came upon it and smiled with relief. 'Ah, here it is. Have you got a pencil?'

The two MPs exchanged a look and Crawford found it hard not to smile. They searched through their pockets and between them eventually found a scrubby piece of pencil. They handed it to the Garda, who duly signed, giving the paper to them for countersignature. Some barefooted children had gathered to watch and when these formalities had been completed they cheered enthusiastically, annoying the two MPs still further. They grasped Crawford roughly by the arms and propelled him towards the back of the van. The Garda called out, reluctant to allow this brief moment of glory to pass altogether.

'You taking him to The Curragh?'

One MP unlocked the door of the van while the other gripped Crawford's arm tightly. 'That's right,' he called over his shoulder. Then, to Crawford, 'There's another one of your "fly by nights" in there. Thought he could escape, but we got him back.'

The doors were flung back and Crawford was bundled in. He sat down on the bench seat as the doors banged shut behind him. He heard the two MPs march round to the front of the van and, as his eyes adjusted to the gloom, saw the other officer sitting opposite him. The engine started and they jerked into motion. There were cheers from the children outside, a few of them running beside the van banking on it for as long as they could keep up. Gradually the sounds of pursuit faded and Crawford stuck out his hand, smiling.

'My name's Crawford, pilot until this morning.'

Roy Harrison eyed him speculatively, neither friendly nor unfriendly. Finally he gripped the other man's hand.

'Hello,' he said without warmth.

Crawford was surprised by his manner, but put it down to fatigue. He was only half right. Harrison felt mean and had no desire to communicate with this fresh young British officer. He'd had a bellyful of the British.

Crawford persisted. 'I see you are with Eagle Squadron.'

No reply. He tried again. 'They said you tried to escape – is it difficult?'

Harrison absorbed that for a while, then said, 'You bet, especially when I get sent back by your guys.'

Crawford was puzzled, not sensing the sarcasm. 'I'm sorry. I don't follow.'

Harrison eyed him coldly. 'Oh, you will and you'll be just the same as everyone else.'

Crawford continued to stare at him uncomprehendingly. Harrison felt a wave of irritation. 'Look,' he said shortly, 'it seems I had some crazy idea about coming over here to fight Germans. I made it back to the North, right? But apparently your people would sooner preserve some stupid code of honour than get up there where it hurts.' He pointed upwards.

Crawford was beginning to understand. Wisely he decided to say nothing. The American gestured angrily.

'Maybe I should have stayed back in Wyoming with my horses. I understand horses,' he added. He relapsed into silence, stretching out on the bench seat, trying to relax. Only his eyes betrayed his bitterness.

Flight Lieutenant Burroughs stood gazing sightlessly out of the window of his office in the compound. He had reports to type, work that he should be doing, but his mind was on other things. He was deeply worried about some of the actions he was being forced to take as a result of top-level negotiations presently in progress. But he was in a cleft stick and could see no alternatives – none, at any rate, that were acceptable.

He jumped as there was a sharp knock on his door. He knew what it was. He made a conscious effort to pull himself together.

'Come in,' he said, still facing the compound.

A pilot officer opened the door and took a pace into the room, pausing when he saw Burroughs with his back to

205

him. The Commanding Officer turned.

'Yes, what is it?'

The pilot officer saluted. 'The American sir, Harrison; he's about to arrive.'

Burroughs glanced at his watch. 'Has the German Commanding Officer been informed?'

'Yes, sir.'

'Good.' Burroughs nodded curtly, dismissing the young officer, who turned and shut the door as he left. Burroughs stood staring at the closed door for some time. Then he picked up his cap from the desk and placed it on his head, straightened his uniform carefully and left the room.

Harrison could tell they were approaching The Curragh Military Barracks. Shouted commands, booted feet, the occasional burst of raucous laughter indicated a military establishment and he began to recognize the route the van was taking, the tyres of the van swishing on the wet macadam. Crawford glanced across at him anxiously. 'We there yet?'

Harrison swung his legs down off the bench seat and stuck his cap on his head. 'Any minute now you'll be seeing your future home for the duration.'

Crawford shook his head. 'Not me. I intend to get back as soon as possible.'

Harrison unwrapped a stick of chewing-gum and stuck it in his mouth. 'Yeah, well, you're welcome, young Crawford. You get on with it.'

The van jerked to a halt and Harrison heard the key go into the padlock. A moment later the doors were opened. A burly MP stood outside. Methodically he slapped his guardstick into the palm of his hand, grinning at Harrison.

'Now why don't you step out here so that we can all have a good look at you.'

The stick continued to pound his palm menacingly. Harrison glanced briefly at Crawford, then smiled.

'Why not. I've missed the sight of your ugly face, Brady.'

He stood up, then jumped out of the rear of the van, avoiding a large puddle behind it. Immediately the grey misty rain began to seep into his clothing. Brady grabbed his arm, squeezing it brutally. He grinned obscenely at the American.

'Don't want you to fall over now, do we, Harrison, 'specially when so many people have turned up just to see you come back.' He waved the stick towards the compound. It was crowded. It seemed every RAF Officer was there watching him, oblivious to the rain. He could see Burroughs standing at the top of the steps that led to his office. His gaze shifted. On the roofs of the huts in the German Compound stood the Luftwaffe internees. They were crowded together on the three nearest huts, silent, waiting. It was then that Harrison got an inkling of what was in store.

'You see,' Brady said, pointing with the stick. 'They're all here, Germans and British alike, all waiting to see you, Harrison. Now don't you think that's altogether very good of them.'

The question was rhetorical, mocking, and Harrison didn't bother to answer it. Brady dug him sharply in the back with the guardstick.

'Over there to the Parole Hut. Believe it or not, Yank, you have to sign back in.'

He pushed the American towards the hut and Harrison looked behind him. Crawford was following. The MP in the Parole Hut turned the book towards him and proffered a pencil.

'Sign there,' he indicated a spot.

Harrison signed his name, then deliberately broke the

pencil by pressing it too hard into the book. It snapped in half. He glanced up at Brady. 'Sorry, Sergeant,' he smiled. 'Not much lead in it, I guess.'

Brady stared at him, his eyes cold, unamused. Harrison knew he would have beaten him with the stick if the others hadn't been watching. Brady indicated the compound.

'On your way, Harrison. I hope they make you feel welcome.'

Crawford stepped up beside him. 'I'll join you.' He looked nervous, but determined.

Harrison shook his head. 'No, you stay here.'

Crawford stuck his flying helmet in his pocket. 'Look, I don't know what this is all about, but I stay with you.'

Harrison shrugged his shoulders. He began to walk steadily towards the group of RAF flyers standing just inside the second gate. He ignored the puddles, his feet squelching through the mud and water, Crawford just behind him. He walked directly towards the centre of the group, who didn't move. At the last moment they broke ranks to allow him passage between them. He did not hesitate for an instant. His objective was Burroughs, who was still standing, waiting at the top of his steps. The nearer he could get to him the better.

He heard a scuffle behind him and a muffled blow as Crawford was pinned down. He knew what to expect. He spotted the thickset stocky man standing just to one side on his right. As he passed him he saw a flicker of movement as the man aimed a punch at his kidneys. He turned swiftly, blocking the blow, and swung up his foot with all his strength. It crashed into the man's groin. He screamed in agony and fell to the muddy ground. Another man tried to tackle him and Harrison managed to get only a handful of blows in before they all descended upon him with a collective roar of anger, smashing punches and kicks into

208

him, crushing him into the ground, which churned into a soggy morass. He broke free of them briefly, covered in mud and blood, swaying, punching, trying to fend them off. Faintly, as though from a great distance, he could hear the Germans cheering, yelling obscenities at him and America. Then they were on him again, pulling him into the mud, clawing at him.

He felt nothing; his blood was up and his only instinct was survival. He kicked, elbowed, bit, used every trick he could, but he had no chance. He could feel himself weakening, slowly giving up, seeking to protect himself rather than inflict pain. He heard a yell, his name was screaming in his ear, he looked up from beneath an arm. Bryce, Reed and Stanley were hauling bodies from him, lashing out, screaming encouragement. Suddenly Crawford reappeared, dragging him upright, fighting off those who could still stand. Now the odds had changed, there were five of them, but they were still massively outnumbered. The fight became quieter, more savage. Men contained their energy, picking themselves off the ground, kicking and punching when they got a glimpse of the target.

Burroughs watched the pitiful display. Now the Germans had fallen silent, sickened by the brutality. Burroughs held up his hand. 'Stop – stop it. Leave them alone.'

The fighting gradually came to a weary, messy halt. The five men backed away from the group and stood swaying, heads down, trying to draw breath through battered teeth and nostrils.

Bryce tried to smile, but gave it up. 'Welcome back,' he said with a grimace. Harrison, covered in mud and blood, tried ineffectually to clear some from his face. He winced.

'Beats Saturday night in Wyoming.'

Bryce took his arm and led him towards the hut. Crawford, Reed and Stanley followed.

'Think you've got enough energy to help out with the tunnel? We're almost there now.'

Harrison stopped, turned and faced him, his eyes glittering. He swallowed. 'Nope.' He paused, drawing in a shaky breath. 'From now on I stay here and enjoy myself.' He looked back at the welcoming committee, who were slowly and painfully disbanding. 'I reckon that lot over there and the Nazis just about deserve each other. You're welcome to try whatever you like, Bryce – I stay put, OK?'

He stood, sagging slightly at the knees, hardly able to hold himself upright and Bryce could not blame him, nor could he help. Harrison stared at him balefully, blood dripping down his face. Then he made his way doggedly towards the hut and disappeared inside.

Bryce finally prised the piece of granite loose from the heavy damp soil at the face of the tunnel and rolled it round behind him to be carted away by Stanley. Sergeant Reed appeared at his elbow.

'Just as well we didn't lose the Pole, sir – I could never have shifted that stone.'

Bryce paused for a moment, wiping the sweat from his face.

'How's Crawford making out?'

'Oh he's fine, sir. I've got him up in the room hauling the stuff up. He's very keen.'

The sergeant glanced up at the roof of the tunnel. 'We'll have to reinforce this bit that we have cleared tonight before we pack it in.' He paused, looking at the face. 'We must be getting close now, sir.'

Bryce could sense the elation just beneath the surface. He grinned at the sergeant. 'Get the rope,' he said.

Reed was delighted. 'Right.' He crawled back down the tunnel and called out, 'The rope, pass the rope.'

Stanley, who was at the foot of the well that led vertically up into the room, heard him and unhooked a thin coiled rope staked to the side of the tunnel. He passed the end of it to Reed. The sergeant took it and crawled back the way he had come, handing it to Bryce. Bryce pulled it taut and held the end up to the face where he had been digging – right into the hole that the piece of granite had occupied. There was about four feet to spare. Bryce rolled over on to his back and stared up at the sergeant, his eyes gleaming with excitement. He held up the spare piece of rope.

'That's how far we are from the wire. We could be out of here in a week.'

Reed stared at him incredulously. 'Jesus, only another week,' he whispered. He looked weary but triumphant. Bryce and Reed began to laugh. At first it was just a chuckle of amusement and delight, but it grew into something else with the realization that this self-imposed ordeal would soon end. Reed ventured to slap the officer on the shoulder and Bryce put an arm around the sergeant and waved the rope.

'Only four feet.'

For some reason this caused them to collapse into more paroxysms.

The earth above them quivered. Their laughter cut short – they stared riveted at the roof. Another great thud struck the ground above their heads and the earth cracked. Rivulets of dirt cascaded round them and into their hair. They stared at each other frozen with horror. Bryce was the first to recover.

'Quick,' he said. 'Out.'

Another bone-shaking thud crashed into the roof and Reed needed no second bidding. He crawled as fast as he could towards the foot of the well. Stanley was shouting a warning, and Reed yelled at him to get out. Bryce followed the sergeant as quickly as he could, desperately trying not to panic as he felt the tunnel vibrating and cracking around him.

The sergeant reached the foot of the well and began ascending the ladder. He paused half way up to make sure Bryce was behind him. Stanley had already cleared the well.

Reed climbed the ladder, hanging on to the rungs as the heavy vibrations continued to shake and shatter the tunnel below. Suddenly a wave of damp humid air rushed past him causing his ears to pop and he was engulfed in a blinding, choking cloud of dust. He realized the tunnel had collapsed. Keeping his eyes tightly closed, he stuck one hand up in front of the other, gripping each rung in turn. He felt somebody grabbing his arms and hauling him up. It was Stanley, pulling him into the hut. He could see nothing. He rolled over beside the Pole on the floor and screamed into his ear, 'Bryce was right behind me.'

They peered down the well, trying to shield their eyes from the dirt still billowing upwards. It was impossible to see anything. Reed was about to climb down again when a hand appeared, reaching towards them, clawing for another rung. Stanley grasped it and hauled Bryce bodily out of the well and into the room.

They rolled away from the trapdoor, crashing it down into place. Gradually the air began to clear and their coughing subsided. Bryce sat up. He could see Crawford sitting on the bed holding the dog by the collar. The dog was growling deep in his throat staring into the corner of the room. Bryce raised himself. It was Captain Slye, his back to the wall, gazing fearfully at the animal. He turned thankfully to Bryce.

'I am glad to see you got out safely.' He gestured towards the animal. 'Is that thing safe?'

Bryce didn't answer him. He rose, facing the Irish

officer. He heard a grunt of anger behind him and restrained the Pole as he tried to get at Slye. Reed came and stood beside him; outside they could hear the cheers of the Irish soldiers as they pummelled in the rest of the tunnel.

'How did you know?' Bryce asked simply.

Slye beamed, pleased with himself. 'Oh, we've known for some time as a matter of fact.'

'How long?' Bryce repeated tonelessly.

Slye straightened up, feeling more confident now. 'Well now,' he said. 'To be honest with you, almost since the beginning.'

Bryce stared at him expressionlessly. 'You mean you just let us sweat our guts out down there uselessly?'

Captain Slye felt good. For once he'd got it all right and he knew that Tynan would be pleased. He smiled at the thought. 'We . . . er . . . we thought it might keep you all occupied for a while, out of trouble so to speak.'

It was Sergeant Reed who lost control. He leapt forward, seizing the Irishman by the throat. 'You fat slimy bastard.' He tried to throttle the officer and it took the combined strength of Bryce and Stanley to haul him off. Slye's face went red, then puce, his feet scrabbling the ground as he fought to release himself. Finally they wrestled Sergeant Reed away and Slye gasped in air, choking in the dust still circling the room. He was very frightened. He realized he had completely misjudged the situation. Reed still looked murderous and the Pole was clenching his fists. The Captain turned his attention to Bryce.

'Look, I'm sorry,' he gabbled. 'I didn't understand. But really it wasn't my doing, it was Tynan's.' He looked quickly from one to the other, clearly they didn't believe him. 'It was Tynan,' he repeated. 'It was almost as if he wanted you to escape. He just ignored what the Ambas-

213

sador had said . . .' Slye stopped. He'd revealed too much.

Bryce took a step towards him and the Captain flinched, expecting another blow. 'The Ambassador,' Bryce said. 'You mean the British Ambassador?'

Slye nodded dumbly, almost crying with mortification.

Bryce looked at the others. 'Then the Ambassador must have got it from somebody here, somebody in the camp.'

There was a silence as the implications began to sink in. Slye looked frantically from one to the other, desperately aware of how vulnerable he was. If only he hadn't insisted on coming in here alone, believing he could command the situation in the way Tynan had in the cinema. He could scream for help, but it was impossible to bear the thought of the jibes that would follow, the mocking sarcasm of his fellow officers if he had to be rescued. He appealed to Bryce.

'Please, look, you mustn't say how you found out about this, otherwise I'll be sent away.' He could almost feel their contempt. 'I, I don't want to leave, you see. I'm very happy here with you in spite of Tynan.'

Reed wiped his mouth with the back of his hand. Slye jumped, staring at him fearfully.

'Who told the Ambassador, Slye, who told him?'

The Captain licked his lips nervously. His eyes slithered from one to the other. 'Look, if I tell you, will you promise to say nothing of my involvement?'

The sergeant reached forward and grabbed him by the lapels, almost lifting him from the ground. 'Who was it, you little shit.'

It spilled from Slye, like peas from a pod. 'The Commanding Officer, it was Burroughs who told him – I don't know why.'

Reed put him down slowly. Slye collapsed against the wall of the hut. They gazed at one another uncomprehend-

214

ingly. It didn't make any sense. Crawford stood up, still holding on to the dog.

'But why would the Ambassador inform Tynan?'

The door slammed open, banging against the inner wall and rebounding shut behind Bryce. He strode over to the bed and grabbed the commanding officer from it. Burroughs, only half awake, staggered and would have fallen if Bryce hadn't hauled him upright by the front of his pyjama jacket.

'Did you know that we were digging that tunnel?'

Burroughs could see the fury in the young officer's eyes. He knew what this was about, and he also knew that unless he re-established his authority quickly, Bryce would finish up in a court martial.

'Let go of me, Bryce,' he said coldly. He gripped the fist holding his jacket. Bryce resisted at first then let go. The older man disengaged himself, putting some space between them.

'Did you know?' Bryce repeated.

Burroughs turned and picked up his dressing-gown, slipping it on. 'Yes, I knew.'

'And did you inform Tynan?'

Burroughs faced him. 'There are things here you do not understand, Bryce.'

'Then why don't you tell me, sir.' Bryce made no attempt to keep the sarcasm out of his voice.

Burroughs contemplated the young officer for a moment, trying to decide how much he should reveal. 'If I do so,' he said finally, 'it is because of the circumstances. No one else must know yet.'

Bryce stared at him contemptuously. 'I'm not making any promises – not to you.'

Burroughs weighed the possibilities. 'When I learnt of

your escape tunnel I decided to speak to our Ambassador in Dublin. It was he who decided to inform Tynan. I don't expect you to appreciate this, but he is involved in delicate negotiations with the Irish Government to have us transferred from here, and eventually back to the UK.' He paused to emphasize his next point. 'Any escape attempt now could ruin these negotiations. Since I could not ask you not to tunnel without disclosing this to you, I left it in his hands. Coming as it did from him, the Irish Government would know he was acting in good faith.'

'Good faith!' Bryce spat out. 'You have Harrison beaten up because he wants to fight Germans. You cynically allow us to dig in that filthy hole for weeks, knowing that the Irish would stop us before we could get under the wire. Good faith! My God, there's no such thing any more, not here.'

He turned disgustedly to leave, then stopped by the door, staring coldly at Burroughs. 'I don't know if you realize what you have done, but neither you nor the Ambassador have the right to stop me from trying to get back to my unit – and I am going to get back, Burroughs, I promise.'

After he'd left the commanding officer gazed blankly in front of him for a long time. Then wearily he sat down on the bed and buried his head in his hands. Bryce, he knew, was right. He realized now that he'd made a calamitous mistake.

Nora paused outside the square grey church hall. She could hear the sound of the dance band drifting through the open double doors at the side of the building, then a thin high male voice began to sing:

'Heaven, I'm in heaven . . .'

She smiled in spite of herself: the unconscious irony did not escape her; then glanced down the main street of Newbridge. Although still early for a dance, a number of girls were already making their way towards the hall. Platform soles and squarish shoulders seemed to be the smart thing to wear and Nora felt another pang of apprehension. She was wearing her best party dress, which was simple and clinging. Nora looked up again at the sign pinned to the church notice board:

GRAND PRE-CHRISTMAS DANCE
BY SPECIAL ARRANGEMENT FOR
ONE EVENING ONLY,
A VISIT BY THE WORLD-FAMOUS

VICTOR SYLVESTER AND HIS BALLROOM ORCHESTRA

She wondered whether Bryce would be there. Everyone knew that the orchestra had been brought over specially from England by the local Anglo/Irish committee for the RAF internees. Nora thrust her fears behind her. She'd come this far and she intended to go through with it. She walked up the path and round to the door at the side, paying for her ticket with a display of confidence she certainly didn't feel.

Light poured through the vestibule and the inside of the church hall was bedecked with streamers, red and yellow balloons and Christmas decorations. A huge Christmas tree stood just to one side of the stage. It shimmered and twinkled, gold and silver bells flashing reflected light from the cut-glass ball that hung from the ceiling. The band, dressed formally in dinner suits and silly hats, were on the stage and an elegant figure in tails was conducting the orchestra through Irving Berlin's 'Cheek to Cheek'.

Nora had never seen anything like it, not even on her sole visit to the Metropole in Dublin on her sixteenth birthday. She stood and quite unashamedly stared.

Crawford accepted the pint of Guinness from Bryce and took a sip, the froth leaving him with a white moustache on his upper lip.

Reed laughed, 'Better watch out, sir. Otherwise you might get mistaken for Santa Claus.'

Crawford wiped his lip with the back of his hand. 'I wonder who pulled the strings to get us a band like this for the local hop?'

'It's the Ambassador's idea,' Bryce said shortly. 'Maybe he's feeling a pang of guilt because we're still here.'

'Yeah, just to let us know the boys in blue are not forgotten at Christmas,' Reed said disgustedly. He took a swig at the beer. 'Bloody hell! Imagine Christmas on The Curragh.'

Crawford groaned, 'Sounds like an Irish jig.'

Reed shot him a dirty look. 'I'd sooner have Bing Crosby.'

'He's Irish,' Bryce said maliciously.

Reed looked startled. 'In that case, make it Bob Hope.' He thought for a moment.

'You know what they say about The Curragh, don't you?'

218

Crawford glanced at Bryce and raised an eyebrow. 'No, what?'

Reed smiled, 'Sheep, shit and soldiers . . . try saying that quickly.'

Bryce laughed and began to relax. He sipped his drink and looked around the room. Some of the German internees had turned up and Tynan was standing with a priest in a small group of people. He was not just there for the dance and Bryce was glad of his presence. Too many drinks and there could be trouble, especially if Stanley decided that Poland needed to be defended. He noticed Harrison standing by the bar. He had remained a distant and withdrawn figure since the beating up and had shown no inclination to respond to his gestures of friendship. Bryce could hardly blame him.

He felt someone tap him on the shoulder and he swung round.

'Hullo, Peter,' she said.

He just stared, unable to speak.

Nora smiled. 'You seemed miles away.'

Bryce continued to gape. He swallowed, trying to get the lump from his throat. She looked so beautiful. The soft simple dress emphasizing her young body. Her hair long and straight, flecked with auburn. But it was her eyes that struck him dumb. They smiled at him, warm and friendly yet with a trace of sadness that made him want to crush her to him. He glanced quickly at Reed and Crawford, wondering whether they knew what he was thinking.

Reed broke the silence. 'Aren't you going to introduce us, sir?' He leaned towards Nora. 'I think it must be something he ate, miss. The grub isn't too good at the camp.'

Nora smiled shyly. 'Maybe I ought to make you some pies.'

Bryce took her hand. 'I'm sorry,' he said, not looking at the others. 'This is Nora Tracey, the girl I told you about. She helped me when I came down.' The band were just beginning a slow waltz. 'Would you like to dance?' he asked.

'Yes,' she said quietly, 'very much.'

Crawford watched them go. 'Do you ever get the feeling that you are invisible, Sergeant?'

Reed took another swallow at his beer, 'Now that would be helpful, sir.'

Crawford laughed.

Bryce held her lightly, gazing intently at her. 'How are you?'

'Fine, I'm fine.'

'I'm so glad you came, Nora. I wanted to come and see you. I tried to find out where you were, but it was impossible. They took me away at night and . . .'

She put her finger over his lips, stemming the rush of explanation. 'I know that, Peter. I realized you'd never be able to find the farm again, not knowing the district. I wanted to come to you, but there are reasons why I cannot visit the camp.'

He would have held her tightly, caressed her, but there were only two or three couples dancing and he was becoming aware that every eye was on them.

'Your father,' he said quietly. 'Are you all right?' He swallowed, finding it difficult to put into words.

'He's no trouble, Peter. It was just that night – seeing us together for the first time, and he had been drinking.' She looked at him. She could see how concerned he was. 'Don't worry, Peter. I can handle my father. He never used to be like that. It's only since mother died – but I can manage.'

'Your farm,' he said. 'Tell me where it is. We'll meet somewhere close. I can come when I'm on parole.'

She nodded her head in agreement, delighted. 'Yes, we

220

can do that. The farm is near Glencree, which is the other side of the Wicklow Mountains. You'd know it once you got there, but,' she added hastily, 'you must never come to the farm.' She thought for a moment. 'Look, Powerscourt Gardens are not far away. They allow visitors there during the day. We could meet in the tea rooms. What's a good day for you?'

'Any day,' he said quickly. 'What about tomorrow?' She smiled at his eagerness. 'Yes, tomorrow then, in the afternoon.'

'What time?'

'I'll be there at 1.30. He leaves the farm then.'

He smiled broadly. For the first time he seemed happy. 'And we still have the rest of this evening.' He began to whirl her round and round exuberantly, not caring who was watching, or what they thought.

A flinty grey-haired woman about sixty years old, standing in the group with Tynan, gripped Father Hogan's arm, brusquely interrupting the Provost-Marshal.

'That young man, Father, dancing with the dark-haired girl. I want to talk to him.' It was hardly a request.

The priest followed her eyeline and nodded his agreement. 'Yes, of course.' No one disagreed with Mrs Hawley.

The dance ended. Stanley, who had also been on the floor, joined Bryce and Nora as they breathlessly made their way back towards Crawford and Reed. Stanley's teeth glinted almost as brightly as the cut-glass ball whirling above their heads.

'You dance good, sir. Pretty girl,' he added, flashing his teeth at Nora.

Mrs Hawley glared at the priest. 'Well,' she said, 'what are we waiting for? Let's go.' She set off.

Father Hogan agreed nervously and followed in some confusion towards the RAF flyers.

Reed saw them approaching. 'I think we've got company.' He indicated Mrs Hawley, who was cleaving her way through the crowd like a battleship through the Atlantic, dragging the helpless Hogan in her wake. She came to a halt beside them and waited impatiently for the priest, her grey eyes surveying each of them beadily.

Hogan cleared his throat. 'Gentlemen, I'd like you to meet someone for whom I have always had a very high regard. This is Mrs Hawley.'

The old lady acknowledged gracefully. 'Thank you very much, Father.' She turned and glared at him again, waiting for him to take his cue. He accepted the unspoken hint, coughed and excused himself. 'Yes, well, I'll be off now and er . . . leave you to it.'

Mrs Hawley waited until he was out of earshot. 'Charming man the Father, but like all of his calling, inexcusably nosey.' She pulled herself upright. Stanley was fascinated. 'Well, how do you do.' She ignored their silence and continued imperturbably, 'I'm sorry my husband can't be here tonight, but he took a tumble on one of the horses – never could dance anyway. Now,' she said without pausing, 'which one of you is Bryce?' She stared straight at Peter.

Bryce, somewhat awed, almost snapped to attention. 'I am, Mrs Hawley, Peter Bryce.'

'Yes,' she said, looking him over carefully. 'You do look a bit like your father. Knew him briefly before he got mixed up in all that intelligence business. My husband was in the British Army for nearly thirty years. We retired here some time ago, my home of course. Now then, who else is here?' Bryce introduced them one by one. Stanley seemed apprehensive. Mrs Hawley grabbed his hand and crushed it. 'Come along, no need to be afraid of me. What's your name?'

He looked at Bryce then back at Mrs Hawley. 'Me Stanley, how do you do.'

Mrs Hawley beamed at him. 'I'm very well, Stanley. Perhaps I ought to change my name to Livingstone?'

The others laughed, Stanley looked bemused.

'Sorry,' he said. 'I thought your name Hawley.'

The old lady dismissed him with a wave of her hand. Clearly he was foreign and inferior. 'Never mind,' she said. 'We'll soon sort you out.' She turned to Bryce. 'Now then, I'd like you to dance with me young man.'

'What!' Bryce exclaimed, startled. Then, hastily, 'Yes, yes of course.'

Before he could waver Mrs Hawley took him firmly by the arm and led him to the floor. 'Years since I've danced,' she chattered, whirling him around. 'I wish James would try, I do like it so.'

'How did you know I was at the camp?' Bryce asked.

She tapped the side of her nose. 'Difficult to keep secrets here, young man. Truth is, I'm a member of the committee and I saw your name on the list of new arrivals some time ago. I wondered if you might be related.'

'You say that you know my father?'

'Yes, years ago of course. James did too, but only briefly. It was James who insisted that I should find out. "Can't let old Bryce's boy wander around unattended," he said. He liked your father. How is he?'

Bryce smiled. 'Oh, he's fine. I spoke to him on the phone just before I . . .' He stopped. 'He was going to come and see me at the station.'

'Good.' She nodded her head vigorously. 'How are we doing?' She stared at a group of German internees and raised her voice. 'Are we beating that lot?'

Bryce saw several people glance towards them. 'I think we will, if we can get America into the war.'

She stared at him haughtily, then conceded. 'Yes, I suppose you are right, but it's a pity we can't manage it ourselves . . . which reminds me, which one is the American?' She looked around the hall.

Bryce indicated Harrison. 'The man standing at the end of the bar: fair hair, wearing a blue jacket.'

Mrs Hawley's eyes fastened on Harrison. 'Right, I can see him. Now listen carefully. James and I live in a big house on The Curragh, about a mile and a half from the camp. It's called The Old Mill. Ask anyone. They'll tell you where it is. Now I want you and your friends to know that you are welcome there any time, by day or by night. Is that clear?' She looked directly into his eyes, 'Do you understand me?'

Bryce nodded, 'I think so.'

'Good.' The old lady almost smiled. 'We are ready to help you in any way we can. There is a small window near the kitchen that will always be open at night, and we can shelter you in the loft should you manage to escape, providing it is a legitimate break from inside the camp. During the day, of course, when you are on parole, you can come down for lunch or whatever quite openly. I want to help.'

Bryce began to appreciate the old lady's spirit. 'You're marvellous, Mrs Hawley.'

She waved that aside impatiently. 'Never mind all that rubbish. Take me back now, please. I want to talk to someone else.'

Obediently Bryce stepped back and allowed her to precede him off the floor. Stanley watched her return with some trepidation.

'Thank you, Peter.' Mrs Hawley turned to Nora. 'You can have him back now, young lady.' The tone was formal but her eyes sparkled with amusement. 'Gentlemen,' she said, turning to the others, 'I hope to see you all again soon. That goes for you too, Stanley.'

'Thank you, Mrs Livingstone,' he said nervously.

224

Mrs Hawley gave him an old-fashioned look. 'Are you from Poland?'

'Oh yes, Poland.'

'I thought so,' she said, her suspicions confirmed. 'Goodnight all.' She waved a hand dismissively and strode across the hall towards Harrison.

Reed watched her go, then let out a sigh of relief. 'Phew, I'm glad she's on our side. I don't see how we can lose.'

Harrison had seen her approach but ignored it until she spoke to him.

'I believe you are the American?' The voice was imperious. Harrison turned slowly. 'That's right, ma'am, from Wyoming.'

She looked him up and down, appraising him. 'I believe you ride horses?' Harrison towered above her. 'Yes, my father used to own a string of them back home.'

She raised her eyebrow. 'Used?'

'He died, ma'am.'

'Oh,' she paused. 'I'm sorry.'

'Thank you.'

She inclined her head. 'Not at all.' She gazed up at him curiously, but she was not to be diverted. 'I think you ought to know that I do not approve of what you did, or perhaps I should say, the *way* that you did it.'

Harrison remained impassive.

'However,' she continued, 'at least you showed the right spirit. You wanted to get away.' She turned and raised her voice deliberately, 'which is more than I can say for them.' She stared contemptuously at the group of German internees. The hall had gone very quiet. Harrison could feel the tension. Mrs Hawley could feel it too. She tossed her head arrogantly and virtually addressed herself to everyone in the hall. 'All they seem to want to do is sit out the war in safety and comfort.'

Harrison shifted uncomfortably from one foot to the

other. 'They do have a lot farther to go, ma'am.'

The old lady glared at him. 'Nonsense. Our boys are coming back all the way from inside Europe. They know we need pilots. That lot,' she addressed herself to the Germans again, 'that lot, don't even try.'

Harrison said nothing. He did not want to precipitate another onslaught.

'However,' Mrs Hawley resumed, 'what they do is of no interest to me. Since you know about horses I could use your help. One of mine is unaccountably lame. Perhaps you'd come and look at him for me?'

'I'll do what I can, ma'am.'

'Good.' She eyed him cheerfully, in no way put out by the situation she had created. 'I shall expect you for breakfast at nine. Goodnight, Mr Harrison.' She thrust out her hand and he held it lightly in his. Her grip was surprisingly strong. She stared triumphantly round the hall, daring anyone to challenge her. No one did. She strode to the vestibule, grabbed her coat from the startled attendant and disappeared into the night.

Victor Sylvester whispered urgently to the orchestra. They struck up the opening chords and the singer began to croon:

'You're the tops, you're the Eiffel Tower . . .'

Mrs Hawley descended the wide staircase, her feet making no noise on the carpet but clipping loudly as she crossed the polished wood floor of the entrance hall. She opened the front door. Harrison, wearing his leather flying jacket, jeans and a wool scarf round his neck, turned to face her.

'Good morning, ma'am.'

'Good morning,' she exclaimed. She glanced at the tiny fob watch she carried on her dress. 'My word, you are prompt.'

Harrison's breath steamed on the frosty air. 'I've looked

at the horses. There are three jumpers, but none is lame.'

She pulled the door wide. 'I see. You'd better come in.'

Harrison stepped inside and Mrs Hawley closed the door behind him. 'This way, Mr Harrison.' She led him across the hall and opened a pair of double doors. The most delicious smell of bacon, eggs and mushrooms wafted out. A large table was set for breakfast and on a serving hatch from the kitchen were some silver salvers. Mrs Hawley crossed the room and lifted one. 'What would you like?' she asked, looking at him enquiringly.

He stood awkwardly in the middle of the room. 'Why did you invite me here?'

The old lady smiled. 'Let's have some breakfast first, then we can talk. There's bacon, eggs, mushrooms, kidneys?'

'Just ham and eggs would be fine.'

Mrs Hawley proceeded to fill two large plates. 'Sit down, Harrison,' she called out over her shoulder. 'Take your jacket off if you want to.'

He undid the scarf and took off the heavy jacket, looking for somewhere to place it. Without turning round Mrs Hawley said, 'Just leave it over the back of the chair.'

He slipped it over, then stood behind the chair waiting for her. Mrs Hawley bustled across the room carrying the two plates. She placed them on opposite sides of the table. 'I've given you two eggs. There's plenty of toast and marmalade afterwards.' She indicated his chair. 'Do sit down before it goes cold.' He did so and after Mrs Hawley had begun to butter a piece of toast he started to eat. The smell of the cooked bacon had made him ravenous. Mrs Hawley smiled approvingly. 'James will be down in a moment. He is dying to meet you.'

He wiped his mouth with the napkin. 'I don't understand.'

'Don't you.'

'Why are you doing all this?'

'We do it for everyone, Mr Harrison. May I call you Roy?'

'Why not?'

'It's just that I get so confused by ranks, though my husband enjoys it. What is your rank?'

Harrison swallowed some food. 'Pilot officer.'

The double doors opened and a tall, elegant, slightly stooped figure came in. James Hawley was elderly but still retained much of his stylish appearance. He had a prominent nose and blue eyes which were scanning Harrison keenly.

'Ah, I see you beat me to it.' He stuck out his hand.

The American rose and gripped it. 'Sir.'

'Sit down, sit down, man, finish your breakfast.' He walked over to the salvers, lifted one of the lids and began to help himself.

'This is Pilot Officer Roy Harrison from America, James.' The old soldier looked over his shoulder. 'Yes, I know. Heard about your escapade of course. Pity, bloody business. Damned stupid rule, but there it is and there's no way round it, I'm afraid.'

He came back carrying his plate and sat down beside Harrison. The American looked at him quizzically. 'I hear you took a fall?'

Hawley began to eat. 'A fall! Good God no. I told Jilly to say that – didn't want to mix with all those bloody Germans.'

Harrison looked from one to the other. Mrs Hawley was studying him intently, her husband determinedly sawing a piece of bacon in half. Harrison resumed his breakfast, not sure whether he was exasperated or filled with admiration.

*  *  *

Frost crackled beneath the wheels of the bicycle and Leutnant Halder rode carefully. The bends in the lane were sharp and the wheels could easily slip from beneath him. A dog was barking somewhere; the air was still and cold. It was difficult to judge how far away; sounds travelled easily in such conditions. Paul loved mornings like this; apart from the dog's faint barking and the sound of the tyres on the road it was uncannily quiet and peaceful. He seemed to be suspended above the hedgerows, gliding along in a world of his own. Green fields sparkling in the cold hard sunshine as the frost gradually melted. Long shadows of trees outlined on the grass where the frost still lay untouched. The lane began to wind up the side of a hill and he dismounted, pushing the bike. His hands were cold inside the woollen gloves and he blew on them, guiding the bike with his elbows on the handlebars.

Trees lined the road to his right and through them at the bottom of the hill he could see the big old house. He stopped by a gate leading into a field. He pushed it open with his back then pulled the bike through, closing it after him. The grass was wet and he was glad of his wellington boots. He saw a flash of movement close to the bottom of the field where it began to slope down the hill and the small white tail of a rabbit bounded out of sight into the trees.

He pushed his bike to the edge of the field and leaned it against one of the trees. This was as good a spot as any. He glanced around; nothing stirred. He unstrapped the wicker basket from the handlebars and carried it to the centre of the field, then set it down on the grass. Slowly he lifted the lid an inch or two and slid his hand inside. The bird had long since grown used to him and allowed him to pick him up. Once he had the blackbird softly in his grasp he opened the lid fully and lifted it out, holding the bird in both hands. He stroked the shiny black feathers and carefully pulled out the wing that had been injured. He examined it, then folded it back again.

'There,' he said softly. 'I think it's better now.' He held the bird in front of his face. The beady black eyes stared unblinkingly at him. The bird cocked his head to one side. Halder smiled.

'It's time for you to go now. I've done all I can. Your wings are strong. Now you must try to fly.'

He held the blackbird out at arm's length and gently threw it into the air. The bird fluttered as though it would fall to the ground. Then instinctively it balanced itself, glided for a moment, then flew powerfully upwards. Halder shielded his eyes from the rising sun and watched it circle until it disappeared into the trees.

He felt pleased, yet sad. The bird had adapted well to its enforced captivity, allowing him to tend its injury twice a day. That in itself had been a breakthrough and only achieved after long and patient attention, breeding familiarity and trust. And now it was gone, as he knew it always would be. But he was glad the bird could fly. He picked up the empty basket and walked to the line of trees. No sign of the blackbird. He hadn't really expected to see it.

He gazed down the slope of the hill to the big house tucked into the valley beyond, its grounds laid out neat and green, the drive winding its way up to the front door. Behind it he could see the red-roofed stables and a pile of straw and horse dung steaming gently in the frosty air. He tucked the basket under his arm and strode down the hill towards the house.

Harrison finished his second cup. 'The coffee is good.' He smiled appreciatively.

'I told cook to do her best. It's hard to get these days, but I explained that you were an American and that did the trick.' Mrs Hawley's old grey eyes twinkled mischievously and Harrison nodded his assent.

'It's fine.'

James Hawley looked up from his breakfast at his wife. She gave him a look which brooked no countenance. He cleared his throat nervously.

'Yes, well, I expect you are wondering why we got you out here this morning on a wild goose chase.'

Harrison pushed back his chair a little. 'It had crossed my mind, sir.'

'Truth is, I wanted to talk to you before the others arrived.'

Harrison was curious. 'The others?'

'Some of the boys from the camp. They come here all the time.' Mrs Hawley gave him another piercing look and he decided he'd better enlarge on that. 'Listen, I want you to understand, Harrison, that I feel badly about what happened to you up at the camp. So do some of the other officers now.'

'Some,' Harrison said laconically.

The old man stared at him fiercely, considering the implication.

'I understand how you feel, but it is a dilemma. However, I don't want to dig all that up. What's done is done. Let me tell you what is afoot. They have an escape plan. It's a good one. No tunnels this time. They intend to go over the wire. They are making ladders here out of angle iron which can be taken back to the camp in sections, hidden in golf bags. Then it is reassembled when the time comes.'

He paused and Mrs Hawley interrupted impatiently. 'Come to the point, dear.'

James Hawley looked at his wife then back at Harrison. 'The point is, young man, I want you to join them. I think this time you would have an excellent chance. Once you

231

have got over the wire you come straight here and we'll have a car ready to get you to the North.'

Very deliberately Harrison replaced his coffee cup in its saucer. He realized that both James and Mrs Hawley were in a sense trying to help him, bring him back into the fold. But he didn't like the fold any more, nor did he much care for those who ran it.

'I'm sorry, sir, but I don't want to get back to England. Now if you'll excuse me.' He rose from his chair. 'Thank you for my breakfast and the coffee.' He picked up his jacket from the back of his chair.

Mrs Hawley stood up. 'Look, Roy, I want you to be sure of one thing. Whatever happens, you are welcome here at any time.' She turned to her husband for confirmation. 'Isn't that so, dear?'

The old boy nodded dispiritedly. 'Yes of course . . . goes without saying.'

Mrs Hawley's eyes glinted. 'Not in these circumstances, it doesn't, especially as you understand horses. James does worry about my riding, and I don't hunt anymore, but I'd love you to join us one day.'

Harrison acknowledged the invitation. 'That's a date ma'am. They're fine horses.' He slipped his jacket on and started towards the door. Mrs Hawley suddenly remembered something. 'Just a minute, Roy.' She went to the mantelshelf and took down an oblong sweet tin, then fished around inside. She smiled at Harrison. 'It's here somewhere . . .' She broke off, staring out through the verandah windows. Harrison followed her eyeline. A man was walking up the drive to the front door.

'Who is that, James?'

Harrison recognized him. 'It's one of the Luftwaffe internees. His name is Halder, I think.'

'Is it indeed,' the old lady said indignantly. Harrison saw

232

the gleam of battle in her eye as she rushed from the room. He was glad he was not the unfortunate German.

James called after her . . . 'Wait!' But she was gone. He looked at Harrison, exasperated. 'God damn the woman!' He left, trailing after her, and Harrison smiled to himself.

Mrs Hawley threw open the front door before Halder could reach it. She watched him coldly as he climbed the few steps to the door. He stopped and took off his hat, holding the wicker basket under his arm.

'Yes,' she said abruptly.

The young man twisted his hat nervously in his hand. 'I saw you yesterday at the dance.'

'Did you indeed.'

The hat stopped its circular movement. Then he spoke quietly. 'I heard what you said about us, how you think we have no courage to go back to Germany and fight.'

The old woman stared at him, flinty eyed. 'Precisely.'

Halder was stung for the first time by her arrogance. 'No, you do not understand. I think there are too many people like you who love to fight this war. There are many in Germany also who love it.'

'Only when they think they are winning,' she replied.

'And that is what you would think if you were winning?'

She raised her head imperiously. She was shorter than Halder but she seemed to dominate him. 'We are winning,' she said quietly.

He looked at her. She was magnificent, he thought. He shrugged his shoulders. 'So, you love it too. I have always believed it was madness. It kills and it maims and I am so happy to be here where the madness has not reached.'

He seemed a nice young man, but she did not allow her face to soften. 'It will one day.'

'Perhaps,' he said.

They gazed at each other silently, trying to understand.

233

'Why did you come here?' the old lady asked him.

'Because you insult me.' He bowed his head deferentially, then put his hat back on. 'Good day.' He turned away and walked slowly back down the drive.

Mrs Hawley closed the door. Her husband was behind her in the hall. 'What did he say?'

She whirled around angrily, suddenly aware of his presence. 'Bloody man! I'll bet he was spying.' She strode back into the breakfast room. It was empty, the verandah doors open. She crossed the room and looked outside but she could not see Harrison. 'Oh dear,' she said, looking at the small package in her hand that she had taken from the sweet box. 'I wanted to give him some chewing gum...'

Bryce was early. He'd managed to get a lift in a tradesman's van from Newbridge, through the Wicklow Gap to Newtown-Mount-Kennedy. The driver had gone out of his way to bring him to Powerscourt and now he had time to kill.

The grounds and gardens were open to the public and he had paid his entrance fee to a lady in a small lodge at the beginning of a long row of lime trees called, not unnaturally, Lime Avenue. It led past some paddocks and a small building on the left where tea and cakes were sold, and eventually to Powerscourt Mansion itself which sat on the crest of a hill overlooking a magnificent terraced garden. The view from the top of the steps leading down to the lake below stretched out like a tabloid. Patchwork fields and tiny white-walled houses in the distance dotted the landscape and over it all dominated the Sugarloaf Mountain, violet blue in colour and, from its shape, rounded and conical, clearly of volcanic origin.

He walked down the steps towards the lake. In front of it, cast in iron, were two winged horses of Pegasus. He stared up at one of them. It was beautiful, the ironwork seemed almost to be flesh and blood so skilfully had the statue been cast, the lines, tendons, muscles clearly and naturally delineated. A horse like that, he thought, and I could fly home.

Spray from the fountain that rose in the centre of the lake showered him as it was caught by a gust of wind. He glanced at his watch. By the time he had walked back to the entrance Nora would be due. He climbed the wide stone steps, returning the way he had come.

He waited just inside the entrance and heard the sound of the old battered truck before he saw it. It steamed gently round the bend in the road and he recognized the driver instantly. He was surprised to see how well Nora handled the truck, but a lot of young girls in the services back in England were showing just how little their potential had been used before. Nora was no exception.

He stepped forward from behind the gates and Nora pulled the lorry into a wider part of the road near the entrance and parked it. Her heart was pounding in her throat and she could feel her hands shaking. She switched off the ignition and opened the door. He was looking up at her, smiling, he didn't say anything. He merely proffered his hand to help her down and she felt tears stinging the back of her eyes. Somehow, at the dance, with people watching, they had maintained some semblance of normality; but now, out here, alone together for the first time since he had been dragged away by the Garda, she felt her composure slipping.

Bryce held up his hand and she gripped it, squeezing it tightly. Then he held up his arms and gently lifted her to the ground. Nora held him close, burying her head in his chest, clinging to him. He stroked her hair tenderly, kissing the top of her head.

Gently he pushed her away from him so that he could see her face. Tears were running down her cheeks and he wiped them away with the palm of his hand.

'Don't cry, no need to cry,' he said. 'I've got you now.' He held her face between his hands and kissed her. She put her hand on his and pulled it down, sliding it round her waist, pushing her body hard against his, holding him tightly.

Neither of them was aware of the lady in the lodge who collected the entrance fees. She watched them for a moment, then turned away from the window, a lump in her throat, remembering . . .

They walked down the long road between the lime trees until they came to a small tin-roofed building that was the tea room. They munched thick currant bread and butter and drank watery tea. They hardly noticed either; they were oblivious of the world around them. Later, as they strolled around the gardens, they came to a small animal cemetery on the side of a hill. They read the brief inscriptions together. Busky, Chow Chow, Sting – faithful beyond human fidelity; Jack the Cocker Spaniel, Modger; but the one they both liked best was for Doodles, a Chow who had died in 1938:

> Loved and faithful friend for 14 years
> You've gone old friend
> A grief too deep for tears
> Fills all the emptiness you've left behind
> Gone is the deep companionship of years
> The love that passed all love of human kind.

Bryce turned away and gazed up at the Sugarloaf Mountain in the distance.

'Is your farm far away?'

'No, three or four miles, that's all.'

He took her hand and walked with her down to the

bottom of the hill. There was something he needed to know.

'Nora,' he began, 'I know how difficult this is for you, but I don't want to be the cause of any more trouble between you and your father. You must tell me if you think he could be violent again . . .'

She stopped him. 'No, he won't. I think that it was just because he was drunk that night and frightened.'

'Frightened?'

Nora wondered how much she could tell him. She loved her father. She knew why he had behaved so badly, but things had eased off at the farm after Peter had been taken away. She realized now that she could not replace her mother, nor did she try any longer. Her father's Republican connections were no secret, but she didn't want to frighten the Englishman away and she had no intention of betraying what she had overheard between Gehler and Driscoll. She knew what could happen both to herself and Peter, yet there was something he had to know.

'Peter, do you know any of the Luftwaffe internees?'

'A few.' He looked at her curiously. 'Why?'

'Do you know a German named Gehler?'

Bryce remembered the man in the prison vehicle when he had arrived at K Lines.

'Yes, he's tall, deep-set eyes . . .'

She nodded, 'Yes, that's the man.'

They reached a path and turned left, their shoes crunching on the hard frosty ground. He looked at Nora.

'What about him?'

Nora thought carefully. 'I think you ought to be keeping an eye on him.'

'Why?'

'I'm not sure, but he has been to the farm to meet someone and I think they are planning something.'

Bryce was curious. 'Do you know what?'

237

'No!' she said quickly. 'They were just talking and I think I heard them mention The Curragh.'

Bryce knew that she was lying, but he didn't want to press her. He understood the risks she was taking. He pulled her round to face him.

'Listen to me, Nora. I know your father is mixed up in something. That's probably why he reacted so quickly when he saw me in the barn. I don't care about that – I don't care what he and Gehler may be up to, but I do care about you.'

She started to protest, but he stopped her.

'No, you must be careful, Nora, not to get involved. Is that why you couldn't come to the camp?'

Nora bit her lip, saying nothing. She feared he might decide not to see her any more.

'We must be careful no one sees us together.' He glanced around the gardens. They were deserted – hardly anyone in the middle of a working day just before Christmas.

'This place seems to be OK for the present, but we cannot take any chances.' He looked at her, concerned. 'Do you understand?'

She nodded dumbly, then flung herself into his arms. 'Oh Peter, I love you so much.'

He nestled his face in her hair, kissing her ear. 'I love you too,' he whispered.

The noise was shattering: the hounds milling round the yard between the stables, anticipating the hunt to come; their yapping and the clatter of the horses as they pranced nervously making it difficult for some of the less regular riders to keep their seats. They were a motley collection, some wearing the traditional pink, but not all.

Tynan, in uniform, sat astride a magnificent black stallion that gleamed from the attentions of one of his horse troopers. The horse, like Tynan, seemed calm, sure of itself, waiting.

Harrison was in cords and a sweater. Mrs Hawley had said it didn't matter, and such was the variety of dress in the hunt, no one had given him a second look, apart from Tynan. Not that Harrison had noticed any particular attention from him, but he sensed that there was something: an old feeling, the anticipation of danger, was back.

The Huntsman blared a blast on his hunting horn and the hounds began to move out of the stable area behind Hawley's house and down the drive. Harrison rode loosely, cowboy style, reins held in one hand. He saw Mrs Hawley on the doorstep and she waved to him as he rode by. He touched his forehead, acknowledging the greeting, then looked round quickly at Tynan, whose eyes were on him. Harrison grinned at him insultingly, then dug his heels into his mount, moving his horse into a trot, following the hounds. Tynan's expression did not alter; he followed quietly.

Mrs Hawley watched him depart. She felt a vague sense of unease. She waited until the back markers had cleared the front of the house, then shut the door and went inside into the lounge. There were four men sitting quietly.

'All right,' she said. 'You can begin now.'

They started unpacking and silently set to work.

The baying of the hounds drifted back across the fields. The tone had changed and Harrison knew they'd picked up the scent. It was more intense and oddly chilling; the hunt was on. A deep hedgerow loomed up before him. Harrison tightened his knees and thighs around the horse, lifting himself forward as the stallion took the jump. The horse

239

landed easily on the other side and quickly resumed his rhythmic loping run.

Harrison looked back over his shoulder and watched Tynan's mount rise effortlessly over the hedge. He was right behind him. They'd opened a big gap between themselves and the rest of the hunt, which had scattered and widened, stretching back into the early morning mist that eddied and drifted, trailing through the hollows, gradually disappearing as a pale watery sun crept unobtrusively into the sky as though ashamed to show its face.

Harrison heard the soft pounding of Tynan's horse as he slowly drew level with him. They took the next jump together, landing simultaneously the other side. Tynan looked across at him and yelled hoarsely, baring his teeth. It was unintelligible and had no meaning, except to Harrison. He recognized its primitive challenge and accepted it instantly, wheeling his horse savagely away from the hunt and setting off diagonally eastwards towards a line of violet blue mountains rising eerily from the mist in the distance as though they were floating.

It all fell into place. The curious sub-text, the anticipation, the instinctive recognition of Tynan as one with himself. A man he understood without words.

Tynan reined in his horse and trotted it towards a round clump of trees circling a hollow. Once inside the cover of the trees he sat quietly and waited. Gradually the sounds of the chasing horsemen drifted closer. They began to thunder by in twos and threes, spattered with mud, pursuing the hounds. Some had obviously fallen already.

The last of the rag-tag hunt trailed by, dishevelled but determined. He waited until he could hear them no more. Then he dug his spurs lightly into the stallion and set off after the American.

Harrison hauled tightly on the reins, thrusting all of his weight backwards in the saddle to offset the steep gradient.

His horse slithered and leapt in short jumping motions down the deeply wooded side of the valley, the trees clinging close to each other. He needed all his skill as a horseman to avoid being swept from the saddle.

Tynan must have been confident to have given him such a lead. Why? There was little time to consider it. His horse half jumped, half slid down an almost vertical six feet of muddy bank, jarring to a halt on a narrow pathway, which traversed the side of the valley, climbing back towards the top. He ignored that and turned right, descending to the bottom of the narrow tree-lined gorge. The track twisted back and forth, with heavy undergrowth on either side, dropping steeply all the time. It began to level out and he emerged into a grassy clearing. Through the centre ran a wide deep stream. The track disappeared. He reined his horse to a stop and tried to work it out.

He had a number of choices. He could go back the way he had come. He rejected that as too risky – Tynan could be descending now. He could try and force his way up through the undergrowth and trees to the other side of the rim, or he could follow the stream either up or down.

Tynan would know this valley. He would also know from his tracks that Harrison had descended into it. But why had he allowed him such a lead? It nagged away at the back of his mind, worrying him. Since Tynan knew this terrain like the back of his hand, it could only mean that he knew the choices that now faced him and would try to anticipate his next move.

If that were the case, how could Tynan expect to know which way he would go, since there were three alternatives? But did he have three choices? Maybe he didn't. Maybe the river was impassable in one direction or the other. He listened intently, trying to hear above the sound of the running water. There was something, a very faint muffled roar from upstream. That must be it, fast water. If he'd chosen upstream he would have had to come back. He made up his mind, he would not choose either.

Harrison spurred his horse towards the other side of the clearing; almost at once his mount began to have difficulty climbing its steeply wooded sides. He dismounted and led the horse carefully upwards, choosing what seemed the safest route, sometimes having to make wide detours around vertical stone bluffs. But gradually he ascended foot by painful foot, scrabbling his way up through short close-packed trees and undergrowth. Half way up he stopped and looked back the way he had come. No sign of Tynan, but he'd been right about the rapids. White water thundered down through the neck of the ravine and he would never have got through it.

Eventually the trees began to thin out and he was able to mount and ride the last fifty yards or so to the rim. Before he came to the edge of the tree line he dismounted again, tying the reins around a convenient branch.

He moved forward slowly on foot until he could see the green fields glistening with early morning dew between the trees. He dropped down on to his knees and crawled forward. There was no more cover, and he scanned the terrain carefully. It seemed empty, deserted. Then a flicker of movement caught his eye away to his left. He noticed that the trees seemed to close in and descend at that point. It must be the lower end of the ravine. Then he saw another movement and realized it was the sun flickering on a highly-polished bridle. Tynan was there, concealed by the tree cover, waiting. Suddenly Harrison realized what had happened. The Irishman had not followed him down the ravine at all. He knew there were only two alternatives, downstream through the gorge below him, or up this side and out from the tree cover. By circling the end of the gorge, he'd been able to station himself in the right position and wait.

Harrison was beginning to realize now just what this was all about. He'd sensed from the start, from the first time their paths had crossed, Tynan had been gauging him, testing him, setting him up for this. But this was just a game, a rehearsal for something else. But what? There had to be more: he'd known that the moment he'd accepted Tynan's almost animal challenge. Suddenly it was clear to him. For the first time since his enforced return to the internment camp Harrison felt alive. Now he had a purpose, and he knew what he must do.

Quietly he crept back to where he had left his horse. He mounted and deliberately dug his spurs deep, forcing his animal to leap forward and charge through the last of the trees. He leaned low over its neck as the branches whipped across his back, seeking to pluck him from the saddle. Then suddenly he was in the open, thundering across the wet fields. He did not look back, but he knew Tynan was behind him, staying close, tracking him all the way.

Harrison began to circle back towards The Old Mill, Mrs Hawley's house. He pushed the game stallion as hard as he could. He wanted to give Tynan a run for his money. Mud spattered up from the hooves of his horse and he wiped some of it away from his face and grinned to himself. He'd not played all his cards. There was plenty of time for that. Time was the least of his enemies. He looked towards the mountains. That would be his battleground, where he would fight his war.

He waited in the courtyard by the stable. Tynan was only moments behind him. He trotted his horse along the drive.

The animal, like Harrison's, was exhausted, foam around its mouth and working up under the edge of the saddle. Tynan rode erect, shoulders square, moving easily with the animal's rhythm. He reined his mount to a halt facing the American. They surveyed each other curiously for a

243

moment, neither of them dismounting. Tynan took off his cap and wiped his brow.

'You're a fine horseman, I enjoyed that.'

'Me too. You stick close.'

Tynan put the cap back on his head. 'I have to – otherwise you might get away.'

Harrison watched him carefully, not deceived by the casualness. 'I gotta get out first,' he said.

Tynan almost smiled. 'That's right. You're learning.'

There it was finally, the open invitation, the challenge.

'Maybe we both are,' Harrison replied laconically. He waited for the steel trap to come down the way it had once before in Tynan's office. The eyes filmed over for an instant, cold, deadly. Then they cleared and this time he did smile.

'I think we understand each other very well. Now, if you will excuse me, I have some work to do here.' He indicated the house and then dismounted, handing the reins to Harrison.

'Perhaps you would be kind enough to give him to the stable lad.'

Harrison gazed down at him for a moment, then accepted the reins without comment. He watched Tynan stride across to the front door of the house and saw the startled face of Mrs Hawley appear for a moment at a window before ducking back behind the heavy curtains. He dismounted and led the two exhausted horses back towards the stables.

Tynan lifted the heavy, ornate knocker on the door and rapped twice. He could hear Mrs Hawley scurrying about, then finally the door was opened and she stood before him smiling broadly.

'Ah hello, Commandant, I thought you were still out with the hunt.'

244

He'd tried several times before to explain to her that he was not a commandant, but she persisted in calling him that. He protested no longer, it was like water off a duck's back.

'Indeed I was,' he answered, not bothering to explain. 'It's a lovely day to sniff the air, wouldn't you say?'

She looked at him uncertainly, 'Yes, yes I suppose so.'

He waited, but she did not invite him in. He indicated the hallway behind her. She seemed flustered.

'Yes of course,' she said. She opened the door wide and led the way. 'Would you come into the dining-room. I'll ring for some coffee.'

He shut the front door and called after her, 'No, don't put yourself to any trouble. I'd just like a word with Mr Hawley if I may.'

She hesitated just beside the dining-room, waiting for him to sit down. She hovered until he'd done so.

'I'll go and fetch him,' she said, not wanting to leave at all. 'You sit there. I shall only be a moment.' She left finally and Tynan sat utterly still in the chair, his head raised, listening. He looked slowly around the room, observing everything. His attention gradually focused on the double doors to the lounge across the hall.

He rose silently from his chair and began to move towards them. As he reached the door to the hallway James and Mrs Hawley came bursting down the staircase. He stopped, waiting for them to reach him.

'I found him,' Mrs Hawley said unnecessarily.

James stuck his pipe in his mouth and offered his hand to Tynan, who grasped it.

'What can I do for you? Jilly tells me you want a word.'

Hawley wanted to lead him back into the dining-room, but Tynan held his ground.

'Yes, that's right. Sorry to drop in unannounced, but I

know how experienced you are with horses and I wanted a little advice.'

'What sort of advice?'

Tynan had positioned himself close to the double doors of the lounge. 'I'm thinking of starting a string of my own.'

He turned suddenly and threw open the doors. The room was empty, but there were cups and saucers for a number of people on the table and lying on the floor a solitary piece of angle iron. Tynan took it all in, then gently closed the doors again. He turned and faced both of them. Mr Hawley betrayed his apprehension, chewing instinctively on the end of his pipe. Mrs Hawley returned his cold hard stare, raising her chin haughtily, saying nothing. The flinty old lady had spirit.

'I was wondering,' Tynan said softly, 'if you could suggest the right person.'

The old soldier jumped. 'What!' he said nervously, expecting something else, then relieved. 'Oh yes, yes of course. Tell you what, let me have a think about it and I'll be in contact.'

'Yes, I think we shall,' Tynan said slowly. Then, to Mrs Hawley, 'Sorry to have troubled you, I'll let myself out.'

They watched him walk to the front door and close it silently behind them. His footsteps faded on the gravel drive, then a door slammed and they heard his car drive away. Mrs Hawley glanced at her husband, then leaned forward to open the double doors. They saw the piece of angle iron together and looked at each other anxiously.

It was cold; the sky, slate grey, threatened snow, but so far none had fallen. It was a disappointment to some who still clung to the idea of a white Christmas, but it did not disappoint Sergeant Reed; he knew how cold it could get in these iron-roofed huts during winter. The last thing he wanted was snow or a white Christmas. Some of the German internees had invited them to the Barbed Wire Bar for a drink that Christmas Eve but Burroughs had refused permission which Reed felt was bloody stupid. Tynan had allowed the parole system to be re-introduced after Harrison's return, and as far as Sergeant Reed was concerned any change of scene was preferable. What was wrong with mixing with Gerry anyway? This was perhaps a little unfair on Burroughs who realized only too well that to fraternize with the enemy could lead to a weakening of the resolve to fight them when the time came. All the same, Christmas Eve lunch had been better than usual, chicken and roast potatoes. And tomorrow there was the promise of turkey and plum pudding. Now it was church parade, for a special carol service, and on this occasion everyone had been allowed to wear full uniform for the first time.

All thirty-seven Allied internees were lined up in the compound ready to be marched up to the church, and Reed could just hear the German commands in the other compound as the Luftwaffe were prepared for the short march. The Irish Military Policeman at the gate gave permission and Burroughs brought them smartly to attention. They were left-turned and led out through the first gate, then brought to a halt in front of the heavy main gate.

Harrison stood in the line of men, waiting a little impatiently for the usual formalities to be completed before they were allowed to leave the compound as a company. The Germans too had reached the same point in their departure, and Captain Slye was overseeing the movement of the two sets of internees from their compounds to the church on the other side of the main barracks.

He signed the necessary forms accepting responsibility for both groups and then two MPs began to unlock the main gates leading to both compounds.

Harrison watched idly as the heavy gate was slowly swung open. This time it grated harshly on its hinges, the cold had thickened what little oil was left and they were badly in need of more lubrication. He flinched as they swung rustily open and looked up at the offending hinges at the top. He stiffened slightly, noticing something, then casually switched his attention to the lower hinges. The gate was made of heavy oak beams, built like the entrance to a castle, and was virtually immovable. Certainly nothing could break it down and it must weigh a ton. But Harrison was excited. He'd noticed something for the first time, maybe there was just a chance. How strange he had never seen it before.

The RAF internees were first to arrive outside the church. They were stood at ease until the Luftwaffe group joined them. Then Tynan, Captain Slye and the other Irish Army Officers entered the church. They knelt and crossed themselves after passing through the vestibule.

The Luftwaffe Officers came in, not sitting until they had lowered their heads in prayer. The RAF contingent were ushered in and placed on the other side of the aisle. They sat down; some prayed, others did not.

The church was quiet, yet Tynan was aware of an underlying tension. Men coughed and fidgeted waiting for the carol service to begin. Sidelong glances were quickly averted. It was not much, but enough for Tynan to be watchful. This was the first time both sides had been brought together, it was also the first time they had been allowed to wear uniform, and he suspected that it was the uniform that heightened their awareness of each other.

At last the priest mounted the pulpit and, after a short prayer, he announced the first carol, 'Silent Night'. The organ played the opening bars and as the internees began to sing Tynan felt a cold hard shock of surprise. It was so unexpected, yet so natural. The Germans were singing it in its original form in German, the English, the Anglicized adaptation. Immediately there was a sense of competition, and Tynan knew he should have foreseen it. He saw Captain Slye watching him anxiously from the corner of his eye and ignored him for the moment. There was no way of knowing what was going to happen and any moves on his part might precipitate trouble. He waited.

The singing grew in intensity, each side vying with the other to demonstrate its identity. Tynan stopped, one by one the other Irish Officers stopped singing also, realizing they were not involved in this. The Provost-Marshal watched carefully, conscious of the feelings these men were expressing in their own languages. He had always understood the mental state of those who were imprisoned. It was necessary if he was to keep them thus. Over the years this sharpened awareness had become instinctive. Yet he hated it, despised himself for being part of it. For nearly twenty years, since the Civil War in 1922, he had been responsible for keeping the hard core members of the IRA locked up in 'Tintown'. Of necessity it was a harsh regime. On all sides were those who would help them escape back into the great family of 'safe' houses in Ireland. Yet these same men had once been his comrades when he fought against the British in the Flying Columns around Cork and the south-west. Then had come the Civil War, the worst of all bloody and brutal dilemmas. And so they had become his charge, his duty – his prisoners.

Now these other prisoners were expressing their anguish, their loneliness at Christmas. Their singing was fierce, patriotic; and now the organist, confused, had faded from this battleground of music.

The men of both sides continued to sing, they looked not at each other, but in front, towards the pulpit, singing as though their hearts would burst. Tynan could almost feel the electricity. The hair on the back of his neck seemed to shiver, grow cold. But now something else began to emerge. As the intensity of the singing grew, so did the beauty of Franz Gruber's music. A strange metamorphosis took place. The more feelingly the carol was sung, the less competitive it became. Both languages seemed to diffuse, grow as one, the music, the church, capturing their expression, taking both sides, bringing them together.

What emerged from each set of prisoners, through each language, was a curious mixture of hope and despair and a universal longing for home. Captain Slye swallowed hard, but the lump in his throat would not go away. He blinked furiously, determined not to disgrace himself further. He would not cry, but he felt such sadness for these men.

The carol ended magnificently, the last strains of the last note fading into the rafters of the church above them. The priest climbed slowly into the pulpit, his shoes echoing flatly in the silence that followed. He cleared his throat.

'Let us all, on this Eve of Christmas, say together the Lord's prayer.' He began:

'Our father, which art in heaven . . .'

This time all in the church were in unison, whatever the language.

He raised his arm and peered at the luminous dial of his watch. It was nearly two in the morning. He pulled back the covers and swung his feet down on to the floor. Christ, it was bloody cold. The thin layer of linoleum did little to keep out the chill from these corrugated-iron-roofed huts. Quickly he pulled on his socks and trousers and pulled a thick polo-necked jersey over his head. From under the bed he dragged a pair of light rubber-soled plimsolls and tied the laces securely.

He stood up and padded silently over to the window, moving the curtain slightly so that he could peer out over the compound. It was brightly lit as usual, but totally deserted. He grabbed his fur-lined jacket, slipped it on then opened the door to the corridor. He glanced quickly up and down it, shut the door behind him and moved quickly down the passage to the outer door of the hut, pausing for a moment to glance behind. The corridor was empty, not even a creak. He opened the outer door and the floodlighting poured into the passage momentarily. He shut it behind him and he stood with his back to the door, blinking in the harsh light of the arc lamps positioned round the outside rim of the first wire barrier.

He waited for his eyes to adjust, then stepped openly on to the compound, making his way as quickly and quietly as he could to the first gate. An Irish MP opened it for him and he slipped through and strode across to the Parole Hut. Another MP opened the Main Gate just wide enough for him to pass through. He crossed the short open space from the Parole Hut and out of the Main Gate. Tynan was waiting outside.

He said nothing, but led him down the rough track to a black saloon car that waited by the intersection leading to the main barracks. He leaned down to open the back door, but Tynan put his hand on it, preventing him.

'I don't know what you are involved in, Leutnant Bech, nor do I wish to know. I'm sure you are aware of the dangers. But there are two things I ought to tell you. I do not approve of this,' he paused, 'arrangement.' He spat out the word as if it offended him. 'I can promise you one thing, Leutnant. It will not happen again while I am Provost-Marshal.'

'And the other?' Bech asked.

Tynan took his hand off the door of the car and straightened up, facing him. 'Whatever happens to you in the future, whether inside or outside the camp, I can no longer be responsible for your safety. Your superiors have exposed you to me, and to my men. Some of them are not entirely on your side. Goodnight, Leutnant.'

Tynan turned his back on him and walked away. Bech watched him go, his face expressionless. He climbed into the back of the car, which moved off at once.

The car drew up outside the main hotel opposite the Town Hall in Newbridge. Bech climbed out and was met by two MPs, who escorted him up the steps and through the main door as far as the lounge. They positioned themselves on either side, staring straight in front, avoiding his eyes. He looked from one to the other, then turned the knob of the wide double doors and stepped inside. The room was dimly lit and smelt of stale tobacco smoke and drink. He shut the door and walked across to the sofa set against the wall. He sat down and waited. He did not have to wait long.

A narrow door at the end of the bar opened and a medium-sized man, about fifty years old with greying hair, emerged and strode quickly towards him. His bearing was faintly military, and it came as no surprise when he introduced himself as a Colonel Bryce. They shook hands and the Colonel waved him back down on to the sofa, seating himself opposite in a rather battered leather chair.

Bryce wasted no time. 'How long have you been infiltrated into the camp, Walker? Six months, isn't it?'

He nodded, waiting for Bryce to come to the point.

'So you would have been there when Oberleutnant Gehler arrived?'

'That's right.'

'What do you make of him?'

Walker surveyed him coolly. 'Before I answer that, sir, you are going to have to explain why you dragged me out here in the early hours of the morning. I could have come out and met you any day on parole. Now Tynan and his military police know I am not a German and they have no love for us, Colonel. They'd gladly reveal my true identity if it suited their purpose.'

Bryce pulled out his pipe and began stuffing it with tobacco which he selected from a small pouch. 'Sorry I can't offer you a cigarette, I only use this.'

Walker waved an arm impatiently. 'That's all right. I don't smoke.'

Colonel Bryce lit the pipe and puffed at it a few times until it was glowing nicely. 'You're quite right to put that to me, Walker, and I'm sorry I had to bring you here for this meeting. But my hands are tied. I'll tell you as much as I can.'

He blew out a cloud of smoke, watching the young Englishman for a moment before making up his mind. 'For some time we have known that there has been a build-up in various contacts between Berlin and Dublin. We know too that the IRA have been active against British targets recently, not just in England, but particularly in the south-west of Ireland around Kerry.'

253

Walker was puzzled. He knew nothing of the Sandringham and Sunderland crashes and the Colonel didn't enlighten him. Instead he continued:

'We do not think that this is coincidence. But as yet we have not been able to penetrate their cells or discover precisely what is going on.'

'You say we, Colonel?'

Bryce smiled wryly. 'That's right. We have been co-operating fully with the Irish Secret Service, G2. That in itself is something of a coup. Liddell at M25 hasn't been able to get anything out of them. However, that's by the by.' He puffed again on his pipe, surrounding himself with a halo of smoke, wondering if perhaps he'd gone too far. Perhaps not. The man had been put at risk and he was entitled to some explanation. 'Usually,' he said. 'Irish Intelligence are very good at infiltrating the IRA structure, and to get something out of them I had to reveal that I had a contact within the German Internment Camp. I might say, Walker, that it's almost certain that they already knew; so it was better that your presence was on the table, so to speak. Unfortunately their political head, Joseph Walshe, insisted that any meeting between you and me would have to be under their jurisdiction, hence all this cloak and dagger stuff.' Bryce waited, puffing gently on his pipe.

Walker was disturbed that his infiltration had been revealed to the Irish, but there was nothing he could do. 'You wanted to know about Gehler, sir?'

Bryce nodded affably.

'Well, he certainly carries some clout. I don't know why, but I think even the German CO Von Bernstorff is taking orders from him, and clearly it is not because of Gehler's rank, which is junior. It must be some other connection, and I am getting pretty close to him, sir.'

'In what way?' Bryce said quickly.

'Well, I've been keeping a diary as it were on anything

254

said within the German Camp that is in any way derogatory about the war effort of the Nazi Party, and there is always some amongst the Luftwaffe.'

'Thank God for that,' Bryce muttered.

Walker grinned. 'I ought to tell you that it does not make me very popular. But it does serve to endear me somewhat to Gehler.'

Bryce leaned forward. 'Have you got anything definite?'

'No sir, not yet. But something is up. He asked me to prepare a short list of people whom he can trust to do exactly as he says, obey his orders implicitly. My feeling is it must be some sort of break from the camp.'

Bryce sucked on the stem of his pipe. 'I wonder.'

Walker was curious. 'What do you mean, sir?'

'Oh nothing, just a feeling, that's all.' He paused for a moment, thinking. 'Look, Walker, something clearly is on. What it is I don't have the foggiest at the moment. What with the increase in communications between the German Delegation in Dublin and Berlin, the incidents down in Tralee, which are I believe connected in some way, plus what you have just told me, I begin to feel very uneasy. Keep a sharp eye on Gehler. The minute you have anything contact the Ambassador in Dublin through your usual channel. Which reminds me, the RAF side of the camp may not be there much longer.'

Walker was surprised. 'But why?'

Bryce shrugged his shoulders. 'Political, mainly. London are hoping to conclude an agreement with the Irish Government to take the RAF internees out of the K Lines, ostensibly to go to a separate camp at Gormanstown. In fact, all pilots will go back to the UK and a few NCOs will be kept in Ireland for a while to offset any comment from the German side. Dublin is anxious not to be seen favouring one side or the other, but they do see that putting us together like this is not good policy. It's good

255

news for us, of course. It means we shall have some badly needed pilots back in the fray.'

'So I shall be on my own?'

Bryce peered at Walker through his pipe smoke. 'In a sense yes, more isolated certainly. However, it may be that Gehler will feel less constrained by our presence and open up a bit more.'

Walker raised his eyebrows. 'Let's hope so.'

Bryce stood up and picked a couple of glasses from the bar, then took down a bottle of Scotch from the shelf. 'Care for one?' he said, smiling. 'We might as well avail ourselves of the hospitality.'

Walker accepted the drink gratefully. He was cold and not a little worried about Bryce's visit and the implications for his security. He felt vulnerable. He gulped his down and waited while Bryce sipped his.

'I daresay,' Bryce began, 'you know my son is in the RAF camp?'

Walker nodded. He wondered why the Army officer hadn't broached the subject before. His contact in Dublin had informed him of the link with MI9 as a matter of form.

'How is he?' Bryce asked.

'As far as I can tell, he's well and active. I don't know how much of this got back to you, sir, but when the American, Harrison, was sent back after breaking his parole your son and a couple of others tried to defend the Yank when the other officers were giving him a going over.'

Bryce smiled ruefully. 'Sounds like Peter.'

Walker remembered something. 'When Gehler first arrived he came in the same transportation as your son. I was outside Von Bernstoff's office that day and although I couldn't hear what was being said, I think the name Bryce was mentioned. In fact the CO and Gehler had a row about something.'

256

Colonel Bryce didn't like it, but he couldn't see where it fitted in. There were so many pieces lying around, but no overall pattern was emerging, just the growing conviction that something was brewing. However, he allowed none of his apprehension or frustration to show but smiled broadly at Walker.

'Well, thank you for your information. Keep an eye on Gehler. He represents the crux of whatever is developing in that camp. Now I think you ought to be getting back. Care for another drink before you go?'

Walker declined. He would have liked another drink, but it was necessary to have a clear head. He didn't like the open compound that he knew he had to cross . . .

Halder sketched in some of the background. The low stone bridge over the stream was very attractive, the setting idyllic and Gehler, seated on the parapet in full uniform, stood out prominently from the washed-out colours of winter, his buttons, newly polished, gleaming in the angled shafts of pale sunshine filtering down between the stark bare branches of the trees.

Gehler called out behind him, though in deference to the artist he did not move his head:

'Caught anything, Bech?'

Bech's voice echoed hollowly from beneath the bridge. 'Nothing yet. I think like the leprechauns the fish do not exist.'

'Nonsense,' Gehler shouted back. 'There are many fine fish to be caught in Ireland if you have the right bait.'

Bech recast his crude rod and line in the flowing water and looked up at Gehler, who was still maintaining his pose on the wall of the bridge. The remark seemed innocuous, yet his stomach tightened involuntarily – he didn't trust Gehler. He concentrated on his fishing and rebaited the hook. He kept losing his bait in the stream. Perhaps Gehler was right; maybe he needed something more tacky and substantial. He heard Halder calling his name.

'Yes,' he answered.

'Keep an eye open in case anyone comes along. I don't want the Oberleutnant to be seen in his uniform.'

Gehler smiled. 'You worry too much, Halder. I have my coat, and it will only take a moment to slip it back on again. Besides, no one is likely to come this way.'

Halder was right of course. He was not supposed to be in uniform at all, but if Halder insisted on painting him he intended to be at his best.

'When can I stand up, Leutnant?'

Halder examined his sketch. 'I think I have enough to complete the preliminary drawing. No need for you to stay there.'

'Good.' Gehler stood up and stretched, then walked over and stood behind the artist.

Halder glanced up, 'It's not finished yet, of course, just a drawing.'

Gehler was impressed, 'Nevertheless, the likeness is very good.' He put his hand on Halder's shoulder. 'You are a fine artist, Leutnant.'

Halder did not like the proprietary hand, but he tried to ignore it.

'Thank you, Herr Oberst.'

Gehler squeezed his shoulder. 'No need for such politeness, Halder,' he said quietly. He felt the artist tense beneath his grip as though he were frightened by his touch and experienced a sudden surge of anger. He took his hand away and stepped back a pace. Halder could almost feel his eyes drilling into the back of his head. When Gehler spoke, however, his voice was cold, unemotional.

'Do you mind if I take a stroll now?'

Halder leaned forward on his stool and examined the drawing. 'Of course not. I do not need you any more for this. I just want to fill in some background.' He was relieved when Gehler walked in front of him to the bridge and leaned over the parapet.

'I'm taking a walk,' Gehler said. 'Would you like to join me, Bech?'

Halder watched from the corner of his eye as the Leutnant scrambled up the bank reeling in his line. They strolled off down the path and disappeared between the trees. He was glad to see them go.

'A talented man Halder,' Gehler commented. 'But curious, don't you think?'

Bech glanced at him, 'Curious?'

'Yes, you remember the blackbird he nursed back to health. He seems to spend all his time with waifs and strays.'

Bech thought about that. 'I suppose so, Herr Oberst. Perhaps he sees himself as some sort of evangelist. Ireland affects people in different ways.'

'Well, that may be harmless in a non-combative zone like this, but we shall not be here for ever, shall we, Bech?'

The Leutnant glanced at him uncertainly. The question seemed to be rhetorical. But again the remark hung there, vibrating. 'I hope not, Herr Oberleutnant,' he replied.

Gehler turned swiftly, grabbing Bech by the throat, thrusting him up against a tree. The suddenness of the attack took Bech completely by surprise. A wickedly curved hunting knife had appeared in Gehler's hand and he held the razor-sharp point up under the fleshy part of his chin, just pricking the skin. Bech could feel the blood trickling down on to his collar.

Gehler leant up hard against him, giving him no room to manoeuvre, his face inches away from Bech's.

'Tell me who you really are, Leutnant?'

Bech strained away from the knife, but Gehler kept the point cruelly into his flesh. Then he lowered it slightly to allow him to speak. Bech tried to play for time. 'I don't know what you mean, Herr Oberst. I have been in the camp longer . . .' he choked, not speaking as the knife was thrust back into his flesh again.

'Don't waste time lying to me, Bech. Where did you go last night when Tynan so kindly loaned you his car?'

Bech said nothing for a moment. He was trying desperately to think of a convincing story – there was none. Gehler removed the knife from under his chin and inserted the blade into his nostril. Bech could feel the urine trickling down the inside of his leg.

'Don't even think of lying to me, Bech, or I will slit this nostril wide open. I heard what he said to you. Who are your superiors?'

The words tumbled from Bech's mouth, spilling over one another like corn from a split sack.

'My name is Walker, Military Intelligence. I was infiltrated into your camp to try and keep an eye on things.'

Gehler leaned closer. 'And why did they smuggle you out the other night?'

Bech paused momentarily. Gehler turned the knife in his nose. He screamed in agony, blood spilling down into his mouth. 'They wanted to see me,' he gasped with pain. 'The Air Attaché in Dublin.' It was only half a lie. 'They are trying to get the RAF flyers moved to another camp.'

But it was only half the truth and Gehler knew it. He ripped the knife upwards, tearing open the nostril, blood pumped on to Gehler's face. Walker screamed again, his voice echoing horribly through the empty stark wood. Gehler thrust the knife back towards the wound, his face distorted with hatred and spattered with blood.

'No,' Walker screamed. 'Please, I'll tell you. The airmen are not just going to another camp. There are talks between Dublin and London to have the pilots taken back to Northern Ireland. They need the pilots – the move to another camp is just a cover up.' He had told him one truth, but nothing of Colonel Bryce or his suspicions.

Gehler studied Bech's mutilated face. The terror was real. He was satisfied.

'Thank you, Walker. If only you had told me that earlier you could have saved yourself so much pain.'

He took the knife back from his face, pushing himself away from Walker, his hand flat on the other man's chest.

Walker put his hands to cover his wound and he saw Gehler smile. He realized in that instant, in that frozen moment of horror, that Gehler intended to kill him. The long knife smashed into his diaphragm just below his rib cage, tearing through his contracting muscles and plunging upward into his heart. Walker's eyes widened in shock. For a fleeting instant before he died he saw someone standing beneath the trees, then they glazed in death and Gehler savagely jerked the knife free and whirled around as Walker's body slid to the foot of the tree.

Halder was standing in the shadows rooted with fear. Gehler crouched, staring at him, waiting for him to run. Halder didn't move.

Gehler called to him softly. 'Come here, Halder. Come here.'

For a moment he didn't stir. Then slowly he walked towards Gehler, stopping in front of him, his eyes avoiding the body lying on the ground.

'He was a traitor, Paul.' Gehler used his Christian name for the first time. 'He was a spy. He confessed it. All spies are executed in a war. There are no exceptions.' He took the Leutnant's arm. 'Now you must help me. It is your duty as a German officer.'

Halder said nothing. He seemed to acquiesce. Gehler slipped the knife back into his boot and stooped, grabbing the arm of the dead man to drag him away from the path.

Halder made no move to help him – he was in shock. Gehler studied him for a moment, then rose abruptly and slapped his face.

'Take his arm, Halder.'

The young man stared at him blankly for a second, then looked down at the blood-stained body. His face betrayed no emotion. Slowly he reached down and took hold of one of Walker's arms. Gehler was relieved. He took the other one and between them they dragged the body into the undergrowth about twenty yards, until the ground began to slope gently upwards. Gehler stopped and looked around for an implement. He found a broken branch. It would do. Quickly he tore off his jacket, then found another piece of wood and handed it to Halder.

'Help me,' he ordered.

Halder stared at the broken branch, then dropped to his knees and began to tear at the earth with it. Gehler knelt beside him, dragging the loose earth away, digging himself. Halder saw some of Walker's blood on the back of his hand. He rubbed it off frantically, then dug savagely at the soil, tears streaming down his face.

The rain fell pitilessly, bouncing high off the pavement, gleaming wetly in the light from the street lamps. The gutters were awash, huge puddles filling the road like miniature lakes where the drains couldn't cope. Gehler was soaked to the skin; but he didn't mind the rain. It kept the roads around The Curragh empty, and he stayed in the darkness, close to the hedgerows of the big houses set well back from the road.

He paused at the end of Driscoll's driveway, making quite sure no one had seen him. He looked up and down the streaming road. It was empty of everything except the rain. Satisfied, he moved up the side of the gravelled road, walking soundlessly on the sodden grass verge. He reached the front of the house. The light in the vestibule was out as arranged. He quickly crossed the open space in front of the building and rapped on the door twice. Almost at once he heard someone cross the entrance hall inside. The door opened soundlessly and Driscoll peered out.

Gehler slid quickly inside and Driscoll shut the door. He led Gehler towards the kitchen. 'You'd better come in here. It's warmer and you can take off some of that clothing.'

Gehler followed him into the wide red-tiled room. He took off his hat and shook some of the water out of it into the enamelled sink. Driscoll helped him with his raincoat and hung it on the door.

'God man, you're absolutely soaked. What forced you out on a dreadful night like this?'

Gehler sat down and began to unlace his boots. 'I had to see you. That's why I telephoned.'

He stood the boots in front of the solid-fuel Aga glowing in the corner and warmed his hands on the covers to the cooking rings.

'How good are your connections with the British Ambassador?'

Driscoll opened a cupboard and took out a bottle of whisky and two glasses. 'Sir John Maffey? Not too bad. We meet from time to time. He likes the paper and sometimes passes on snippets of information that he would like published.'

Gehler turned, warming his back on the stove. 'What he didn't tell you is that the RAF pilots are being moved out of K Lines.'

Driscoll paused, holding the bottle above one of the glasses. 'Moved! Where to?'

'The pilots go back to England via a staging camp at Gormanstown which will be used as a cover.'

Driscoll poured some of the whisky into a glass and

handed it to him. 'Are you sure about this information?'

Gehler swallowed the whisky in one gulp. 'I'm sure.' He wiped his mouth with the back of his hand. 'The agreement is all but completed. The Government in Dublin must have been discussing this with London for some time.'

He leaned forward, staring coldly at Driscoll. 'Where does that fit in with your so-called top-level political contacts? Someone is playing both ends against the middle, a ploy the Irish are fond of . . .' He let it hang there, waiting for Driscoll to respond, watching him carefully. The Irishman was dismayed, and there was no faking in his reaction. He poured himself a drink, offering Gehler another. He declined.

Driscoll swallowed quickly, thinking fast. It must be a result of Mackay's recent visit. A sop to the British Government after turning down Britain's proposals to bring Ireland into the war against Germany. It was not something that would involve his contact in the Government, and it was typical of Dev to say nothing until the deal was a *fait accompli*. He tried to explain this to Gehler, but the German brushed it aside.

'It matters not why they did it, Driscoll. The fact is this deal has been made and we must not regard it as a setback; we can use it.'

Driscoll stared at him. 'How?'

Gehler began to pace the kitchen. 'Don't you see? They are going to return pilots to fight against us. They have engaged in secret negotiations with the British. They have allied themselves with London.' He turned triumphantly to Driscoll. 'Get this information back to Berlin. Inform the Führer of their duplicity and then he has the perfect reason to land military forces in Ireland.'

He could see the dislike on Driscoll's face. 'Look, Driscoll. It's perfect. Sit down, let me explain.'

The Irishman slumped into a chair and Gehler poured

him another drink, placing it in front of him. He sat opposite. 'I understand how you feel, Driscoll, that it means the end of your role as an intermediary. But don't you see, this is even better? If you inform Berlin of what has happened then your status will be improved in their eyes. When we take control here a Government will have to be appointed that will be sympathetic to our aims, our military strategy. They would look naturally to someone outside the present administration. How could they trust any of them in view of what has happened? They will look to you, Driscoll. You would have to form the new Government.'

Driscoll took a sip of the whisky, not looking at Gehler. It was persuasive and, the way he had put it, not unattractive. But he was too long in the tooth to fall for the unsubtle flattery. There were other factors too. His own credibility was severely undermined by Dublin's actions. How would Hitler respond to that? After all, had he not journeyed all the way to Berlin to try to persuade the German Government that Dublin could be brought in on their side? He still felt that could be achieved. It was impossible for a man like Gehler to understand how these two apparently contradictory attitudes from Dublin could still be resolved. He would have to be careful. Gehler was dangerous. He looked up.

'I shall see Herr Hemmrich tomorrow, arrange to have this information transmitted to the German Foreign Office in Berlin. I shall also suggest that, perhaps, in view of this, I should go back to Germany to discuss how best we can make use of it.'

Gehler studied him for a moment, then turned away, picking up his glass and refilling it. Driscoll was lying. He would deal with him later. It was vital that Berlin should know what had happened. There was another way . . .

\* \* \*

Quinn listened carefully. When Gehler had finished, he took from his pocket a large-scale map of Ireland and spread it on the kitchen table. Nora removed the teapot and mugs to give him room. Quinn pointed to Bantry Bay in the south-west.

'Driscoll's original plan is still good. If we make use of von Ribbentrop's suggestion for delivering arms, but instead have Irish cargo vessels arriving from the direction of the Western Approaches with a Panzer Group, then they could certainly land here. It's far enough away from Dublin for my volunteers to be able to cut communications and prevent any news of the landing reaching the Government for at least twenty-four hours. Then, if they move them up the west coast here and link with General Lynch's second Spearhead Group facing the border to the North . . .' he traced a route across the map . . . 'then I think that with our knowledge of the terrain we could set up an invasion across the border before any effective resistance could be mounted.'

Gehler liked it. It was a bold plan yet relatively simple, as all good military procedures needed to be, particularly when large forces had to be deployed.

'Have you arranged the rendezvous?'

Quinn nodded. 'Yes, your man will be met here.' He pointed to a spot on the map. 'They'll be back in Germany within hours of their arrival.'

Gehler smiled and drank his tea. 'Good. I want the High Command to see these plans in their entirety. How soon can you liaise with General Lynch?'

Quinn shrugged his shoulders. 'Within the next forty-eight hours. We have met since our first conference in Driscoll's house. Like me, the General does not entirely trust Driscoll. He is useful and has given me good information in the past, but I am surprised that he was unaware of the negotiations to have those RAF men taken out. That's unlike Driscoll.'

Gehler was emphatic. 'We must forget him. Both he and Herr Hemmrich must know nothing of this operation. It's possible, in view of what you said about this Colonel Bryce, that the German Legation is already under surveillance. Warn Lynch not to go there again.'

Gehler glanced across the room at Nora, who was preparing a meal for them. He lowered his voice. 'What about the girl and her father?'

Quinn shook his head. 'Tracey's a good man. He's been in this movement since before 1917. He safely kept the arms from the Phoenix Armoury here until we needed them.'

Gehler repeated the warning. 'It is vital that this does not reach anyone outside these four walls. You must see that.'

Quinn knew he was right, and he realized the implications of Gehler's remark. But he was not having any part of a ritualistic killing, not when it was totally unnecessary – he needed good men like Tracey. 'All right, I'll deal with it in my own way. They are my people.'

Gehler had to be content with that. He was beginning to understand the Irish, but sentiment was weakness. He looked at the girl again and indicated his assent, after all, she did drive well, and he might need that transportation.

Quinn waited until Gehler had left in the truck with Nora. Tracey stood next to him in the doorway watching the lorry disappear up the lane towards the mountains.

'Did the meeting go well, sir?' he asked.

Quinn glanced at his watch. 'Yes it did.' He looked at the older man. 'Now I want you to do something for me, Tracey, and I can't give you a reason.'

He nodded gravely. 'That's all right sir, I'll obey whatever orders you give me.'

Quinn knew he could trust him. 'Good. I don't want either you, or the girl, to leave this farm until I say so. Is that clear?'

Tracey looked at him incredulously. 'Not leave at all!'

Quinn repressed a smile. 'Not even for a drink.'

Tracey was stunned. 'Not even for a drink!' he repeated. He looked sorrowfully at Quinn. 'I'll surely die of thirst,' he said gloomily.

The mess was almost full and there was an anticipatory buzz in the conversation. Something was up. Nothing travels faster than news on the grapevine in a closed society, and they were aware that Burroughs was being quite deliberately excluded from this meeting. Harrison had insisted upon it. He'd been backed up by Bryce, Crawford, Reed and Stanley.

Bryce waited until the last of the internees had arrived, thirty-six excluding Burroughs, then he posted 'eyes' on each window to warn him if any guards got interested in what was going on. He nodded to Harrison, then made his way to the end of the mess where a blackboard had been set up on a slightly raised dais. He lifted his arms for silence and eventually the talking died away. 'Are all the "eyes" in position?' he asked. The men on the windows indicated their presence and Bryce was satisfied.

'Good. Now I want you all to listen to Pilot Officer Harrison. He's come up with something that I think could work.' He looked to the back of the mess where the American was standing and called his name. Harrison straightened up from the wall against which he had been lounging and walked slowly through the assembled officers.

They eyed him curiously as he passed between them. There was a strange parallel which Bryce sensed immediately from the platform. The officers parted to allow him through just as they had when he'd faced them in the compound on his enforced return to the camp. Bryce was very aware of the tension; the electricity could almost be felt. He was relieved when Harrison stepped up on to the dais and grinned at him.

'I thought maybe I wasn't going to make it,' he whispered from the side of his mouth. He faced the assembled flyers and eyed them silently for a moment. 'I guess you don't need me to tell you that most of the other escape attempts have failed. One of the main reasons, I think, is because they've been in the areas where the barriers are toughest, either over or under the wire . . .'

He was interrupted by the burly sergeant who had been the first to go for him in the compound. 'What about your escape, Yank?'

There was a burst of laughter from the crowd, which died away as Harrison showed no sign of amusement. Then quite suddenly he grinned.

'Yeah, but look how far that got me.'

Relief sounded in the real laughter that followed. Many of the men had felt disgusted by what had happened and were glad of an opportunity to show some warmth towards this withdrawn and ambivalent American.

'The point is,' Harrison continued, 'they've had nearly twenty years' experience in keeping men locked up. That IRA camp the other side of the barracks has been there since the Civil War in 'twenty-two. They also speak the same language, which makes it very easy for them to read us, especially a guy like Tynan. No one is going to get over those three barriers of wire, or under the trenches. There's only one place, one spot where this camp is new and different so far as the guards are concerned.' He paused to let them consider that. 'The main gate and the parole hut. The inside gate is opened on request for parole purposes. Once the sentry there is surprised, we can all rush the second inner gate without too much trouble. It's the main gate that is the barrier, but let me show you something.'

He picked up a piece of chalk from the blackboard and drew the main gate and the posts to which it was attached. 'OK,' he said. 'That's the gate as best I can do it. But I want you to look up here.' He pointed to the hinges on the posts. 'As you can see, they are neither sealed nor bolted on top.' There was an excited reaction amongst the flyers. 'I guess,' Harrison resumed, 'whoever designed it figured that the gate was so goddamn heavy that no one could lift it anyway. And he was right, up to a point. But if we could rush the inner gate, overpower the guards and insert leverage under the main gate, four heavy guys could topple it.' He held up his hand to quell the speculation. 'Wait a minute!' he yelled. Gradually the hubbub died away. 'I reckon everybody could be outside in seconds and cause plenty of confusion, but if anybody is going to make it back to the North there have to be some diversionary tactics to split the Irish Army up, otherwise we all get caught as usual in the roadblocks over the river.' He stopped for a moment. They were all listening. 'Some will have to head south to draw them away.'

There was a shocked silence, then someone yelled out, 'Suicide!'

Harrison stared at him unblinkingly. 'I know, you're right. They're bound to get caught eventually, and it's not for me to say who should do it. But what they need back in England right now is pilots. One more thing. Once outside the gate it's up to each individual to decide if he wants to rendezvous with someone else or try to make it on his own.' He shrugged his shoulders. 'That's it.'

Harrison rubbed the board clean, making quite sure nothing remained. Bryce and the others joined him.

Harrison glanced around the mess, where everyone seemed to be talking at once.

'Not here. Let's talk in my room, OK?'

Once there they all crowded in, and Stanley moved to shut the door, but Harrison stopped him. 'Leave it ajar and keep your eye on the passage. I don't trust anyone, right?'

Stanley nodded emphatically. 'OK. Me watch.'

Harrison looked out of the window at the compound. The skies were grey, leaden. He faced them. 'There's something I didn't talk about up there in the mess, but I guess it's no secret that the majority of the guys that break out are going to finish up right back here inside twenty-four hours.'

Bryce sat down on the bed. 'That's a chance we all take surely?'

Harrison stared at him for a moment. 'Not all of us.'

'What do you mean, sir?' Reed asked.

'I mean,' he said, 'that I can get three horses.'

They stared at him incredulously.

'Horses?' Reed repeated.

'Right, with horses we can stay off the roads. There are hardly any cars about because there's no gas, so anything moving after the break will immediately be under suspicion. We'd stick out like a sore thumb. On horseback we can make good time and head for the high ground . . .'

Crawford interrupted. 'But that's east, not north.'

'Right,' Harrison turned to him. 'But if we travel north, even if we avoid the roadblocks, we would still be heading the way Tynan would expect us to go. There are no mountains between here and the North and the border is heavily guarded on both sides. I say head south. The Wicklow Mountains to the east extend more than fifty miles down, almost as far as Wexford. After that we make a break for the coast, pick up a fishing boat and head for the coast of Wales.'

There was a moment or two of silence while they all

271

weighed this up. Bryce was the first to speak. 'He's right. Once we get into those mountains no vehicle is going to catch us. We don't need roads.'

'You said three horses,' Crawford reminded him.

'That's right. Three good jumpers, and I don't want to risk trying to get more. If Tynan gets to know . . .' He left the rest unsaid.

Reed glanced at Stanley, who was standing by the door. The Pole shrugged his shoulders eloquently. 'Me never ride horses ever.'

The sergeant knew then that the die was cast. Besides, he didn't much care for open ground and mountains. He was a city boy and would sooner take his chances on foot. He looked at Bryce, who had been watching him. 'That's it then, sir. Stanley and I aren't pilots. Besides, I hate horses. A donkey once threw me on a beach when I was a kid. I don't like beaches either.' He grinned at Stanley. 'And there's always Rosie.'

The Pole returned the smile, bathing them all in his golden glow. Bryce looked puzzled.

'Rosie's a girl we know, sir,' Reed explained. 'She's not ungenerous, if you know what I mean, sir, and I think she might help us.'

Bryce tried to keep a straight face. 'You should have introduced me.'

The sergeant shook his head. 'She doesn't like officers, sir.'

This time Bryce smiled appreciatively, enjoying the joke. He put his hand on the sergeant's shoulder. 'Thanks, Reed, for making it easy. But when we all get back, I buy the first drinks, right?'

The sergeant raised a finger. 'But only the first round, sir.'

Bryce turned to Harrison. 'That's settled then.'

The American felt a surge of exultation – it was on. Now it could begin . . .

Halder concentrated on the eyes. He couldn't get the eyes. Gehler was sitting on the parapet of the bridge a few feet in front of the easel looking down at the stream below. The rest of the portrait was beginning to jell, but he needed to have Gehler's attention if he was to get it right.

'Herr Oberst.'

Gehler glanced at him. He tried to engage his attention. Without thinking, Halder brought to the surface what had been eating into him since Bech's death. 'You said that Bech was a spy?'

Gehler stared at him expressionlessly. That was it! That was why he could not get the eyes. They were almost opaque, telling him nothing.

'How did you know he was spying?' he asked.

Still the eyes said nothing.

'He confessed it, Leutnant. I was suspicious and eventually he confessed it.'

There! He'd got something on the canvas. It wasn't complete, but it was coming. Halder kept probing. 'Why were you suspicious, Herr Oberst? He seemed to be loyal to the Party. He even kept a diary, they say, of those who said anything against policy.'

If he could keep him talking, maybe jar something out of him, he knew he would have it. Gehler surveyed him coldly.

'My suspicions must remain private for security reasons, Leutnant. I am sure you appreciate that.'

Halder nodded understandingly, shading in some colour around the eyes. 'Yes, of course, Herr Oberst, but if he was a spy why is Hauptmann von Bernstorff passing on to

Germany details of him simply as a missing airman? Everyone at the Camp thinks he has escaped.'

Halder's attitude had worried Gehler for some time. He made no secret of his dislike for war, but he was tolerated because he was an artist, and here, as a prisoner, his loyalty could not be tested. Yet Gehler didn't trust him, and it was a pity he had witnessed the British agent's death.

'I haven't told von Bernstorff, Leutnant. Nor do I intend to. There is no reason for him to know. The danger has been eliminated and the fewer that know the better under the circumstances.'

Halder had seen something that time, the merest flicker of what? 'But isn't it our duty to inform Hauptmann von Bernstorff so that he can pass on this information to Berlin? Surely Berlin have a right to know?'

There was no gainsaying that, but Gehler had no intention of revealing how or when he would pass that information on.

'I think you can safely leave that in my hands, Leutnant,' Gehler said softly.

Halder continued to work swiftly on the portrait. He almost had it now. He was so obsessed with his work that he wasn't picking up the warning signals from Gehler. He didn't believe what Gehler had said. Nor did he believe that Bech had been a spy. He remembered very clearly his ordeal in the sea when their plane had crashed, how Gehler had left him to die. If it hadn't been for Kinzell he would not be here now. He needed to know what was behind those dead eyes. There was no depth, no feeling. The colour was wrong, he rubbed it out irritably.

'Whether Bech was a spy or not, Herr Oberst, is not for me to say.' He brushed in some more strokes, watching Gehler intently. 'But I am certain that Von Bernstorff should know, and if you will not tell him, Oberleutnant, I will.'

274

My God, there it was finally. An intensity of feeling that he had never seen before. It almost made him flinch. Then it was gone again in an instant as the Oberleutnant stood up, moving away from the bridge. It didn't matter; he didn't need him anymore; he had it in the eyes on the canvas. He applied the final stroke and stopped horrified. It was there, that which he had not recognized in reality, staring at him from the painting. It was murderous; the intention was transparent. He turned, sensing a presence behind him. The hunting knife was raised, Gehler's face immobile, sweating slightly. Halder saw the blade glint in the light as Gehler plunged it downwards towards his neck and shoulder. He leapt sideways from his stool, the knife ripped through his heavy jacket, slitting the arm of it open. He stumbled, but didn't fall, running towards the trees, running for his life.

The undergrowth and trees closed around him. He crashed through it, sobbing, running blindly. He could hear Gehler's feet pounding into the soft rotting leaves close behind him. Flying had frightened him, compounded by his revulsion of war, of killing, but he'd felt nothing like this. The terror was in his throat, turning his legs to water, like a nightmare, the more he strained to escape the slower he seemed to move. His arm was beginning to pound like a dull hot knife. He clutched at it and his hand came away red, covered with blood. He stared at it, horrified. His arm, his right arm. It had taken so long to heal. Now the blood was pouring from it, dripping from his fingers. He was going to die. Gehler would spill his life away in this Irish wood. He should never have baited him. It had been stupid. Gehler was a ruthless killer and he had seen him kill once before. He should have recognized the possibility that he might do it again. But he had been obsessed by the portrait, by what lay hidden behind the eyes Gehler presented to the world. Now he had seen it, the face of a predator, and he was its prey. That was something Halder understood very well.

275

Suddenly his feet were flying over the surface, without effort. He moved freely, swiftly – released from his fear. Instinct took over and adrenalin pumped into his veins, widening his perception, pouring new strength into his limbs. He didn't want to die. He would not submit weakly to the knife. In that instant he knew himself finally – and what he must do to survive. He held tightly on to his arm, saving his life's blood. Gehler had made a mistake. He should never have tried to murder him here. He knew these woods, this ground. He was a naturalist and familiar with the contest in nature to survive, the fine balance between life and death, between the predator and the prey. His survival was in his own hands and he had certain advantages, but first he needed some time, some space.

He crouched, running swiftly, circling gradually towards the stream, putting more distance between himself and his pursuer. He easily avoided the branches now, using the terrain, widening the gap between them. He came to the stream. It was heavy, swollen with rain, but perfectly passable. He took his hand away from the wound in his arm and let some of his blood drip on to the ground, then he leapt across the stream and ran as far as the nearest undergrowth, repeating the procedure.

He wrapped his arm in the sodden sleeve of his jacket and carefully retraced his steps, placing his feet in the footmarks he had made before. Using stones protruding from the water or immediately below its surface, he moved downstream about twenty yards until he came to a hollow tree. Carefully he stepped from the stream, keeping as much as possible to firm ground. He slid into the hollow trunk and waited, listening intently.

A branch brushed back into place after it was released and Halder stood very still, breathing shallowly, making no sound. He peered through the crack in the gnarled old bark.

He could see Gehler crouching down by the stream examining the bloodstains. His head turned slowly. For one heart-freezing moment his eyes seemed to be gazing directly into his. Then they slid by and came to rest on the bank opposite. Halder saw him stiffen slightly. Then he rose and ran swiftly, leaping the stream and disappearing into the undergrowth on the other side. Halder let his breath out slowly, then eased himself out of the jacket. The wound was not as bad as he had feared. It was superficial. The knife had ripped down through the sleeve, not cutting him until it had sliced across his forearm. The bleeding made it look worse than it was. He took his handkerchief from his pocket and bound the wound, using his free hand and teeth, staunching the flow of blood. He pulled the heavy jacket back on again.

He went through his pockets one by one. All he had that resembled a weapon was his penknife. He opened it and examined its short stubby blade. It was sharp, but no match for Gehler's knife. He folded it back again. Perhaps there was another way.

Halder slid from the cover of the hollow tree and began to run along the bank upstream. When he was certain of his position he set off diagonally away from the brook into the denser undergrowth until he finally broke through into a circular clearing about thirty feet across. A patch of washed-out blue sky brightened the gloom beneath the trees and Halder circled the clearing until he found what he wanted.

He began to work swiftly, listening all the time for Gehler, stopping once when something moved then bustled away, disturbed by his presence. He continued working steadily, using his skills as a naturalist until he was satisfied.

Carefully he removed all traces of his presence, leaving the ground as undisturbed as he could. He backed into the clearing until he was on to the grass, then turned and made his way back the way he had come.

Gehler knew he had lost him. He'd seen no traces of blood since the stream. Nor had he heard a sound other than that of a startled rabbit. His sense of direction had always been good.

'Put me down anywhere and I'll find my way home,' he'd boasted as a child to his schoolfriends, and he always had. It was something that he took pride in. Methodically he made his way back towards the stream. The silence beneath the trees was oppressive, as though all its creatures had stopped and were listening, watching. He thrust the stupid thought aside, pushing through the undergrowth until he emerged back beside the stream.

He was just below the point where he had crossed and he started to make his way upstream. He saw the stunted, hollow old tree almost at once. From downstream of the crossing the open side was visible. Gehler knew instinctively what had happened. He jumped across the narrow bubbling water and climbed the short bank on the other side. The dark interior of the tree was perfect cover, and caught on a splinter of wood was a fibre of wool from Halder's jersey.

Gehler almost smiled with satisfaction. So, he had an opponent instead of a victim. That made it more interesting. He moved back down towards the stream. As he had expected, he found tracks moving up past the point where he had crossed the water to follow the false trail. He moved slowly, carefully following the occasional disturbances that indicated Halder's path. Gehler was no expert, but it wasn't too difficult in that heavy undergrowth where nothing had been disturbed before. He stopped. He'd heard something, not too far away. He stood stock still, listening. There it was again, a movement somewhere up ahead of him. He watched the spot intently, unblinking. He saw a momentary flash of colour between the trees and a shadowy figure for just a second; then it was gone again. He started forward stealthily, making sure he trod on no dead twigs, pushing the branches aside carefully and holding them until they were back to their original position.

He could hear Halder now. He had veered away from the stream and it became more difficult to make progress as the trees huddled closer together, blanking out what little there was of the light. He was getting closer. Halder seemed to be trying to find his way out of the densely-packed wood towards a patch of green. Gehler could just see light flickering between the trees. He slowed. If Halder stopped in the clearing to rest he could outflank him.

He crept silently towards the clearing. He could see the long wild grass green beneath the circle of blue sky. Halder would be there. If he could get close enough to him he would slit the artist's throat before he knew of his presence. The wood was quiet. No sounds, not even a bird's song, disturbed the silence. Gehler hoped that Halder would not notice the unnatural calm. A breath of wind sighed through the close-packed trees, swaying them; a last few dead leaves spun slowly to earth. The grey sapling in front of him did not move. It seemed rigid, strangely immobile. He stopped staring, a sliver of fear ran icily down his back. A small white cloud rolled away and the winter sunshine poured down through the trees. Gehler saw a flicker of light as Halder's penknife cut the string holding the sapling branch to the ground. Gehler saw the leaves on the ground in front of him cloud outwards as the branch sprang up released from its tension. Too late he saw the white sharpened point of the spear slice towards him. He heard its awful whine as it rent the air like an arrow. It thudded into his chest, emerging from his shoulder blades, lifting him off his feet, suspending him, twisting like a butterfly stuck to a page.

Halder emerged from behind the bush holding the penknife. He gazed horrified at the still live figure of Gehler impaled upon the bough of the sapling. His eyes bulged grotesquely, staring at him. Gehler's arm lifted weakly, still holding the knife. Halder knew his intention, but found it impossible to move, his body refusing to function. The arm went back to throw the knife, but Halder could not take his eyes from those of Gehler. They seemed locked, imprisoned. He waited for Gehler's knife. But then Gehler's eyes ceased to bulge. The cold emptiness returned. He gazed unseeingly at Halder and the knife slipped from his dead fingers and plunged into the damp soil, the hilt quivering, the blade glinting in the sunlight.

It seemed to Halder that he remained rooted to that spot for minutes, gazing up at Gehler's dead eyes. It may only have been a moment; he had no way of knowing; but then suddenly he was running, crashing through the wood, unmindful of the cruel branches clawing at him, seeking only to put as much distance as he could between himself and the impaled body of Gehler floating inches from the ground. He cleared the last dense patch of trees and ran beside the brook, back past the hollow tree, through the last of the undergrowth towards the bridge. Gehler's face danced before his eyes, staring at him coldly, mocking his efforts to escape.

He reached the easel and gazed at the painting. The eyes were real. The killer stared at him ready to pounce. Halder screamed and flung himself at the canvas, crashing it to the ground, ripping at it with his penknife until it was shredded, just splashes of red and brown amongst the dead leaves, trampling the pieces into the earth until he could see them no more. Only then did he stop. But the picture in his mind remained. It would never go away.

Tracey blinked and opened his eyes. He must have dozed off in the warm room. He watched Nora moving round the kitchen, clearing away the dishes after their meal. She seemed different, composed, more sure of herself somehow. Or was it him? Since Quinn had ordered them both not to leave the farmhouse his enforced abstinence had certainly improved his temper. He'd found no reason to vent his anger on her. It was peculiar, but he felt no anger, no sense of resentment in her presence any more. She turned to pick up one of the mugs from the table and saw he was awake.

'Would you like a cup of tea, Da?' she said.

He smiled. 'I would indeed, that'd be grand.'

She filled the large flat-bottomed kettle and put it on the range to boil. Then she took down the precious tea caddy and measured two small helpings into the pot. His eyes were half closed and he could feel her movement around him. It was comforting and suddenly he felt tears stinging the back of his eyes. He leaned forward in the chair, clasping his head in his hands, trying to hold back the emotion. Nora crossed the room quickly and knelt down beside him, concerned, trying to move his hands away from his face.

'Oh Da. What's wrong? Tell me, please,' she implored, distressed by his tears.

'I can't,' he said. 'I can't.'

He shook his head, his body racked by his sobs. Nora put her arms around him, trying to comfort him, stroking his wiry hair. Slowly the emotion died away. He tried to

281

wipe his eyes, embarrassed by his display. Nora took off her pinny and tenderly dabbed away the tears.

'What is it, Da? Can't you tell me?'

He looked down at her kneeling in front of him. 'I don't know, Nora. It was so sudden. I, I was watchin' you, you see. Thinkin' how nice you were, how you looked after me so. And I started to cry.' He stopped and swallowed, his voice breaking for a moment. He continued. 'It was your mother I could see, Nora. You're so much like her and . . .' He stopped again, distressed, and rubbed his face with his hands. When he spoke he covered his eyes as though he could not bear to look at her. 'I've never cried for your Ma, Nora. I don't know why. I was so angry that she had to die so young. I bottled it up and tried to forget her. It, it hurt so much,' he whispered, his voice muffled, almost to himself.

Nora said nothing. She had never seen her father like this, his defences down, vulnerable. She took his hand and squeezed it. He wiped his eyes on the pinny again.

'I'm sorry,' he muttered. 'I didn't mean to upset you. I know you're doin' your best to help me forget.'

'That's all right, Da,' she said softly. 'Don't think about it. I know how much you've missed her. I miss her too.'

He looked at her, putting his hand to her cheek. It felt so soft. He remembered suddenly how swollen her face had been after he had beaten her in the barn. He bit his lip, holding back the pain he now felt so keenly. He crushed her to his chest.

'Nora, I'm sorry, I'm sorry.' He rocked her gently in his arms as though she were a child again, as though he were comforting her. She patted his back and held him close.

The dining-room of the Shelbourne Hotel was half empty. Not many visitors to Dublin, thought Driscoll, certainly few in the middle of this winter of 1940. He glanced at his watch. The Minister was late, though he only had to come from his office in Kildare Street around the corner. He erected a copy of the London *Times* in front of him. Some of it had been blanked out by the censor, but it was still readable. He felt someone tap him on the shoulder, glanced up and rose from his seat.

'My dear fellow, how nice to see you.'

They shook hands and the Minister sat down opposite. 'Sorry I'm late,' he said. 'But we got into a long discussion about the lack of importation from Britain and it dragged on.' He picked up the menu, 'Have you ordered yet?'

'No,' said Driscoll. 'Thought I'd wait for you.'

'How about the lamb?' the Minister asked. 'That's usually pretty good here.'

They indulged in some smalltalk until the waitress had taken their order. Then Driscoll decided to get straight down to brass tacks.

'Minister, I know it's not your brief, but I have heard some rather disturbing news about the internment camp on K Lines.'

The Minister raised his eyebrows and stared at Driscoll. 'Really, what?'

'The RAF side of the camp are being transferred to Gormanstown.'

The Minister buttered some bread. 'Well, there's nothing wrong with that, surely. Better for them to be separated from the Luftwaffe I would have thought.'

Driscoll waited for the waitress to put down his soup. 'As you say, sir. However, my information is that only the NCOs will remain at Gormanstown; the RAF pilots are being smuggled back to the North.'

The Minister's spoon stopped between plate and lip. The surprise was real. 'When?' he said.

'Fairly soon, I gather.'

The spoon splashed back down into the soup plate. 'Good God!'

Driscoll seized the initiative, lowering his voice and leaning forward over the table. 'You can see the position that places me in, Minister, in view of our previous discussions. It effectively removes any credibility I might have had and will destroy any confidence that I have built up in Berlin.'

The Minister was clearly shaken. 'Does anyone other than yourself know of this yet?'

Driscoll nodded. 'Yes, I'm afraid so. I learnt of it from a Luftwaffe officer at the camp. He is utterly reliable.'

The Minister pushed the soup bowl away from him. He had no appetite any more. He looked at Driscoll. 'I assure you I had no knowledge whatsoever of this.' He was rattled, but he recovered quickly. 'I'm sure you realize, however, that this would not be the first time that the left hand didn't know what the right one was up to.'

Driscoll waved the comment aside. 'Of course, I understand that. I know how the Dail works. But will Berlin? No one keeps secrets from Hitler. He dictates all policy. How am I going to convince him that we mean what we say? Is Dev interested in an alliance or not?'

The waitress returned and took away their plates. The Minister fumbled for his cigarette case and extracted one. 'Do you mind?' he asked.

Driscoll shook his head. The Minister was so disturbed he forgot to offer the case. He lit up and drew deeply on the cigarette, not looking at Driscoll. 'It's a very difficult situation.' He was sweating, knowing that he was about to stick his neck out. 'Very difficult,' he repeated.

Driscoll waited. 'However,' the Minister continued, 'all is not lost. I have it on good authority that our Ambassador in Lisbon has been in touch with a German representative from their Foreign Office, a man named Veesenmayer, I believe?' He glanced at Driscoll enquiringly.

'Yes, I've heard of him. He's a good man,' Driscoll volunteered.

'Yes, well, apparently our Ambassador made it clear that under certain circumstances something to our mutual advantage could be worked out. Of course,' he added hastily, 'there would have to be guarantees.'

Driscoll nodded. That was not unreasonable. His hopes began to rise again.

'This meeting. How much reliance can I put on it?'

The Minister coughed. 'Well, of course it was informal. We don't want anyone to know that we are making these contacts with Germany. But it is reliable. Kerney, the Ambassador, knows De Valera well and I doubt that he would arrange such an important meeting without Dev's knowledge.' He leaned towards Driscoll. 'The important thing is to make damn sure no knowledge of what is happening up on K Lines gets back to Germany. That's your job, Driscoll.'

It was Driscoll's turn to sweat. How did he stop a man like Gehler? Was it even possible? He tried not to let his own anxiety communicate itself to the Minister. 'I'll deal with that,' he said confidently. 'You get to work on ironing out the details. I want to give Berlin something positive very soon.'

The waitress brought the two helpings of lamb and a bowl of vegetables. This time they both tucked in. Somehow they felt better.

# BOOK FIVE
## Escape

Harrison, Crawford and Bryce pulled the collars of their coats up round their ears and put their heads down against the wind that buffeted across the compound. Harrison glanced up at the black night sky beyond the glare of the arc lamps. Dark clouds scuttled low across the sky from the west, propelled by the strong prevailing winds.

They walked through the first inner gate, discussing, loudly, the possibility of a lift into Newbridge. Bryce watched the sentry at the second gate. He emerged from his sentry box and started to unlock the gate so that they could reach the Parole Hut and sign out. Bryce timed his walk so that he reached the sentry just as he was swinging the gate open. He whipped the wood truncheon from under his overcoat and brought it down swiftly on to the sentry's head. He grabbed him as he slumped to the ground and bundled him back into the box.

Crawford ran to the Parole Hut and, before the guard could unlock the door and get out, stuck a specially prepared cork into the keyhole, effectively imprisoning him. Harrison turned and signalled towards the mess hut. The doors opened and all the RAF internees began to pour out. Some were carrying metal rods torn from the shower area, and four others carried small barrels they they had taken from the bar.

A sentry who had been dozing in one of the gun towers suddenly realized that something was wrong and gave the alarm. Almost at once the warning siren began to wail, dipping and rising as it was caught by the wind and snatched away.

Tynan sat up in his bed, awake instantly. He threw back the covers and moved quickly across the room, flinging back the curtains. Beyond the treeline that bordered the barracks about two miles away he could see the suffused glow of the arc lighting around K Lines. A searchlight pierced the sky momentarily, then swung back down to sweep the grassy plain surrounding the camp. Tynan strode back to the bed and proceeded to dress himself as quickly as he could. The telephone rang. He picked it up, pulling on a shoe with the other hand. It was Slye.

'There's a break-out, sir.'

'I know. I'm on my way. How many?'

'Not sure. The situation is confused. But just the RAF flyers as far as I know.'

'Right. Don't flap, Slye. Throw a cordon round the outer perimeter of The Curragh. Organize pursuit and search parties. I'll be there shortly – got that?'

Before Slye could reply Tynan slammed down the phone and picked up his gunbelt, notching it around his waist. He headed for the door.

The sentry in the gun tower began to fire sporadically over the heads of the milling prisoners. They had orders not to shoot at any prisoners interned on K Lines.

The metal rods were all inserted under the main gate, and Harrison yelled for the barrels to be run below them. There was no shortage of willing hands, and the barrels were quickly slid beneath the metal rods. Stanley threw himself on to one of the rods and Harrison swore at him to wait for a concerted effort. Six men were placed on each rod and, on the American's command, they all pressed their weight down on to them. Still there was no sign of the Military Police or Reserves from the barracks half a mile away, but Harrison knew they would not be long. The gate creaked;

the rods quivered; but it didn't budge. Bryce waved more men on to the rods. Once more they all heaved, throwing their weight down upon them. This time Harrison heard the familiar rusty screech of the hinges. The gate was lifting. It was slow, the enormous weight of the thick heavy wooden structure defying their combined efforts. As a small gap appeared below the gate more men crouched, sliding their hands underneath it, risking crushed fingers, heaving upwards with all their strength. It was coming. Harrison called for one more effort and slowly the gate inched up to the top of the rusty hinges. It shuddered momentarily on the top then began to fall outwards.

Harrison shouted a warning to the men lifting the gate. It fell backwards and the men on the rods leapt away as the massive wooden structure toppled slowly over, crashing thunderously to the ground, dirt spouting from beneath it. The men yelled triumphantly and began to pour through the gap over the fallen gate. By now German internees were lining the roofs of their huts to see into the RAF camp. They waved and yelled encouragement as the searchlights began to probe the plain of The Curragh, trying to pinpoint as many of the escaping prisoners as they could. It was impossible. The RAF flyers split and dispersed as they had planned, swallowed up by the darkness and the rain that began to pour from the sky as though on cue. The elements tonight were on England's side, and by the time the Military Police and Army had reached the fallen gate the RAF camp was empty, the plain deserted.

Bryce, Harrison, Crawford, Reed and Stanley managed to stay together. The rain was coming down in earnest now and they sheltered beneath some trees for a moment at the edge of the plain. The searchlights had a strange eerie glow as their light was diffused by the distance and the rain. Like white misty fingers they probed and flickered over the sodden grassy surface, reaching out blindly, trying to find them.

They were all gasping for breath, soaked by the downpour yet elated by their success. Harrison put his hand on the trunk of the tree, leaning on it, and shook some of the water from his cap.

'I guess this is as good a place as any to split up.'

'How far to the horses?' Crawford asked, still watching the searchlights.

'About a mile,' Harrison replied. 'The Old Mill.'

Bryce was surprised. 'That's Hawley's place, I didn't think you were fraternizing with that crowd.'

'I wasn't until I rode her horses. She's expecting us.'

Bryce turned to Sergeant Reed. 'What about you and Stanley?'

'We're sticking together, sir.'

Bryce saw Stanley's teeth gleam in the darkness. He knew he was smiling. He turned back to Reed. 'Will you be all right, Sergeant?'

'Don't worry about me, sir. I know a lady who might be able to lend us a hand.'

Harrison clapped Reed on the shoulder. 'Come on. We've got to break this up.'

Bryce gripped the sergeant's hand. 'Good luck, Reed.'

'We'll be all right, sir, probably get back before you do.'

He looked at Harrison. 'So long, gang.'

Harrison tapped the peak of his cap. 'Take it easy.'

Crawford shook hands with Stanley. 'Look after the sergeant and don't smile until you're over the border.'

'My smile pretty no damn good. I frown all the way home.'

Harrison, Crawford and Bryce left Reed and Stanley and began to run diagonally through the trees, keeping well away from any roads heading in the north-easterly direction. But

The Old Mill lay on the other side of the main road and there was no way they could avoid crossing it. They flung themselves down on the wet grass behind some bushes and watched it carefully for a few moments. Nothing disturbed the streaming macadam. It was empty of traffic this late at night.

Bryce gripped Harrison's arm. 'If we don't make a move they may use this to ring The Curragh. It's about the only road available.'

'OK. We all go at once. No splitting up.' Harrison looked at Crawford. 'All right?'

Crawford nodded his assent. Harrison crouched, looking first right, then left. Still no sign of anything. He dropped his arm and ran, the others pounded softly behind him. He heard the whine of the military lorries as his feet hit the hard surface. But there could be no turning back. For once the rain was working for them, cutting down visibility. He increased his pace, sprinting across the road. There was a low hedge the other side. He had no way of knowing what lay beyond it, but there was no time for half measures. He dived headfirst over it, tucking himself into a ball and somersaulting as he landed. He was lucky. The ground was soft and yielding. Bryce and Crawford landed safely beside him and he leapt to his feet still running for the cover of the trees. The ground began to slope down to the river that ran past The Old Mill. The rain hissed and spattered on to its surface. They turned left, running along its bank. The heavy overcoats were sodden by now, increasing their weight. Bryce was panting, mouth wide open, drawing in the night air. His heart felt as though it would burst and his legs were like two lead weights. Still the American did not slow down, running it seemed without effort over the soaking spongy surface. They came at last to a stone bridge that carried the Hawleys' drive up to the house. Harrison stopped beneath it, waiting for Bryce and Crawford to catch up. He put his finger to his lips for silence, indicating that they should stay put. He moved cautiously up the bank beside the bridge, peering round the end of the parapet. There was no one yet, but he knew that this place would be one of the first that Tynan would search. He called softly to the others and they ran along the drive towards the house. The drive began to widen; it opened out to a wide courtyard in front of the building. Some lights were on downstairs, but Harrison ignored the house, circling the courtyard and staying close to the shrubbery. He stopped by the high brick arch that marked the entrance to the stables and stood silent, trying to distinguish any sound above the splatter of the rain on to the cobbled stone surface. He heard a stable door creak and saw a figure move in the shadows. He pushed the others back against the wall then stepped forward. 'Mrs Hawley,' he called softly.

A torch switched on and the beam flashed across his face. He stopped, then he heard her familiar haughty voice. He relaxed.

'You made good time, Roy. I heard the alarm. Are the others with you?'

Mrs Hawley lowered the torch and stepped out into the rain. Bryce and Crawford emerged from behind the archway. They were drenched.

Mrs Hawley waved them towards the stables. 'Come inside quickly. You're like drowned rats.'

They followed her into the stables. Three horses, already saddled, were standing in their stalls. She tucked the torch into her pocket and switched on a low-powered light, then picked up a flask, pouring out three cups of steaming tea. 'Drink this,' she ordered them. No one felt like disobeying.

While they drank the tea she took three oilskins from the back of the stable door and handed one to each of them.

'Wear these. Try and find some cover as soon as possible and light a fire. You need to dry out.'

Harrison was almost reduced to silence. 'Yes, ma'am,' he muttered.

She put her hands on her hips, surveying them one by one. 'I wish you could hide here for a while. I do have a bolt hole, but if your plan is to succeed you must get away quickly I'm afraid.'

Bryce swallowed the last of the hot sweet tea. 'That's all right Mrs Hawley. You've done marvellously and we're very grateful.'

She waved that aside. 'Nonsense, Peter. Now listen.' She turned and strode over to one of the horses. 'I've filled these saddle bags with whatever I felt might be useful.' She slapped the leather with the palm of her hand. 'There's just one thing I would like you to do.'

'What's that, ma'am?' Harrison asked.

'When you've finished with the horses, could you just put a note with my name and address in one of these.' She smiled ruefully. 'I would like them back, especially this one.' She stroked the neck affectionately. 'His name's Bruce.'

Harrison took off his cap. 'Be my pleasure, Mrs Hawley.'

She nodded curtly as though embarrassed by her slight display of sentimentality. 'Thank you, Roy. Now,' she said energetically, 'you'd better be on your way before Tynan shows up.' She handed Harrison the reins. 'You take this one,' she said quietly.

He stuck his hat back on his head. 'Don't you worry, ma'am, I'll take good care of him.'

Their eyes met for the moment. He wanted to put his arms around her, but was daunted by her flinty spirit. Instead he stuck out his hand awkwardly. 'Thank you, ma'am.' Her hand almost disappeared into his. He squeezed it gently. 'You're a real lady.' He smiled, then led the horse out of the stable, pulling the oilskin over his head.

Bryce and Crawford each shook hands with her quickly, then took their horses and joined Harrison outside. They all mounted up while Mrs Hawley stood just inside the stable door, outlined by the dim light from within.

Harrison turned and raised his arm towards her. She waved back. Then he began to lead them out of the yard. Just before he reached the archway Mrs Hawley called out.

'Wait. Just a minute, I almost forgot.'

She ran out, ignoring the rain, towards Harrison. She stopped by his horse, whose flanks were gently steaming in the wet. She stared up at him, her grey hair plastered down over her face.

'I thought you might like these.'

She handed up to him a small packet of chewing-gum. 'I was going to give it to you once before, but I forgot.'

He glanced at the tiny packet, then leaned down from his horse and kissed the side of her face. It was wet and cold, but her eyes shone brightly.

'You'll be hearing from me, Mrs Hawley.'

She smiled, the rain streaming down her face. He straightened up, dug his heels gently into the horse's flanks and disappeared into the night.

Crawford and Bryce rode by. 'Goodbye,' Peter said softly.

She waved and they were gone.

Reed and Stanley were making slow progess beneath the gaunt, dripping branches of the wood. It was difficult in the darkness to move quickly. Gorse and brambles tore at their clothing, catching their arms and legs. Stanley was getting behind and Reed stopped to wait for him. He noticed he was limping badly.

'You all right?' he asked.

Stanley tried to wave him away, but the sergeant insisted on seeing the leg. Stanley halted reluctantly and stood unwillingly while Reed pulled up the leg of his trousers. It was soaked with blood and there was a deep six-inch gash in his thigh. He looked up at Stanley impatiently.

'When did this happen?'

'Me OK. I just catch my leg on barbed wire near the gate.'

Reed examined the wound. Blood was pouring from it continuously. 'It's a bad one, Stanley.'

The Pole tried to pull himself free. 'Let's go. I be all right, you see.'

Reed grabbed at him and held him still. 'Not until I bind this up. You lose more blood and we'll get nowhere.'

He tore a strip from the bottom of his shirt and twisted it round the gash, binding it as tightly as he could. Then he stood up.

'Now we can go, all right?'

Stanley nodded mutely, spraying rain from his soaked hair. They pushed on and gradually the trees thinned. Reed could just discern the outline of a wooden fence surrounding an open field. It was almost totally dark, just the merest shadow of light as the clouds drove across the sky briefly uncovering the moon. The sergeant helped Stanley over the wooden fence and they set off across the field. The grass was soft and yielding, their feet occasionally plopping as they sank into a boggy patch.

Reed stopped, holding Stanley's arm. He listened. He could have sworn he'd heard something. There it was again. Something pounding into the sodden grass. Hoofbeats? He was right. It was a horse galloping towards them. The moon shone fitfully for an instant and Reed saw the outline of the animal. It must have been nearly eighteen hands high.

All of Reed's fear of animals surfaced on that wild soaking field. He took to his heels and ran, Stanley limping desperately alongside him. Reed held out his arm, trying to help Stanley to move faster, but the Pole stumbled on a clod of earth and fell, clutching at Reed, pulling him down as well. The horse closed on them as the sergeant tried to help Stanley to his feet. Reed caught a momentary glimpse of the animal's wide staring eyes, then he hurled himself to one side as the horse galloped between them. It turned almost at once, rearing up on its hind legs as it smelt the blood from Stanley's wound. Its hooves thudded into the earth inches from Stanley's head and he rolled quickly away, trying to avoid their lethal stabbing.

Reed forgot his fear long enough to jerk his belt from around his waist and wield it at the head of the animal. The horse broke away, frightened by the flicking sting of the leather. Reed grabbed Stanley's jacket and hauled him to his feet, running for the edge of the field.

The officer braked quietly and swung off the bicycle, motioning the soldiers to do the same. He could hear the horse still neighing, frightened.

He laid his bike softly on to the grass verge, indicating that the others should do the same. He pulled a pistol from his holster and, keeping to the verge, moved quietly down the narrow lane. The soldiers followed.

Reed came to a wide five-barred gate and climbed up on to it, helping Stanley up beside him. Stanley cocked his uninjured leg over and sat astride it for a moment sucking in the air. A narrow beam of light switched on in the darkness, catching Stanley full in the face. The officer yelled a warning.

'Don't move.'

His voice was high, slightly edged with fear. Reed was transfixed. He sat on the gate, staring at the beam of light on Stanley's face. The Pole reached out in the dark and gave Reed a sharp push in the chest, sending him backwards off the gate into the field. He jumped down into the lane at the same moment, masking Reed's fall. He faced the beam of light blinking slightly.

The officer and his men moved slowly forwards.

'Who are you?' he said.

Stanley remembered not to smile. 'I am work finished. I go home.'

The officer cast the beam of light down Stanley's body until he reached his legs. The beam stopped when the officer saw the blood-soaked trousers. Stanley glanced down at it also, then grinned, exposing his golden giveaways.

'I am a butcher,' he said by way of explaining the gore. 'I work late.'

The officer signalled to two of his men, who stepped forward and grabbed Stanley's arms, propelling him back up the lane towards the bikes. Reed lay behind the hedge unmoving, listening to Stanley protesting his innocence all the way.

Tynan's car crunched swiftly down the drive and stopped in Hawley's courtyard. He switched off the headlights and remained seated in the car, contemplating the front of The Old Mill. Lights were on downstairs. He glanced at his watch. It was still before eleven. He waited. Nothing moved, though he didn't doubt that Mrs Hawley knew of his presence. He heard the lorry coming slowly up the drive and got out and walked over to the front door.

The headlights of the lorry beamed around the shrubbery, coming to a halt on the front of the house. The sergeant leapt from the front seat as the men began to spill out of the back. He got them lined up – there were six of them – and reported them all present and correct to Tynan. The Provost-Marshal acknowledged briefly and thumped the knocker on the door three times. He heard nothing for a moment and was about to repeat the procedure when the light above the porch was switched on and the door swung open. Mrs Hawley stood before him. Her face betrayed no surprise.

'I was expecting you,' she said disdainfully. 'I heard the alarm.'

'In that case I must ask if you will permit my men to search the premises. Some of the internees may be hiding here.'

Mrs Hawley glanced at the soldiers lined up behind Tynan.

'Just make sure they clean their feet and do no damage. Otherwise I shall hold you responsible.'

Tynan smiled thinly. The old lady was a pain, but he found it difficult not to admire her.

'Of course,' he said. He turned and called to the sergeant. 'Make sure of that.'

The sergeant saluted. 'I'll keep an eye on them, sir.'

Tynan walked down the steps and spoke quietly to him. 'I don't expect you'll find anything, Sergeant, but make sure you go through every room, including the roof.'

'Sir,' the sergeant replied.

Tynan indicated that he should proceed, and the men were fallen out and led into the house by Mrs Hawley. Tynan watched them go, then stood quietly in the courtyard, listening. The rain had eased off now and the grounds dripped uneasily as though waiting for the next downpour. Tynan walked slowly across the courtyard towards the archway leading to the stables. He paused again below it, listening. Still nothing. He crossed the cobblestones as quietly as he could and stopped beside the stable door. It was ajar and he took a small torch from his pocket and flicked it on. There was some straw lying on the ground and a few more pieces scattered over the cobbles. He pushed the stable door wide and stepped inside, feeling for the switch on the wall. He found it and turned it on. The stables were empty, more straw scattered haphazardly on the floor, but something else too. Tynan crouched down and looked more closely at the small puddles of water that had dripped from the airmen's sodden overcoats. There was mud from their boots. He stood up and walked over to the boxes where the animals were normally kept. He felt the straw with his hand. It was still warm. He repeated the procedure in all of the boxes. Only two others had been used recently. So, there were three. He walked back to the entrance and switched off the light. He didn't close the stable door. There was no point. His quarry had fled – he was not displeased . . .

The small stone cottage was quiet, empty. Reed squatted down in the covered porch so that he could not be seen from the lane and waited. The rain had stopped, but he was cold and soaking wet. He felt miserable and hungry. All the elation of their escape had gone. Now that he was by himself he wondered if he could go through with it. He thought longingly of his warm bed, dry clothes and food. God, how he longed for something to eat. He glanced at his watch. It was nearly midnight. He hoped she hadn't found someone else to spend the night with.

He tensed, listening. He could hear footsteps. He recognized them. They were unmistakable: the high heels clip-clopping on the road, tapping out their message. Rosie was on her way home.

He leaned back into the porchway. She pushed the squeaky iron gate open, fishing in her handbag for her key She'd almost got it in the lock before she saw him . Her eyes dilated and her mouth opened to scream. Reed clapped his hand over it, holding her tight.

'It's all right,' he whispered savagely in her ear. 'It's me, Sergeant Reed.'

He felt her relax and let her go. She gazed at him, still frightened.

'Mother of God,' she said. 'I really thought me end had come that time. What did you want to frighten me like that for?'

Reed shivered involuntarily. 'Could we go inside and I'll tell you all about it.'

She looked at him closely, seeing the sodden clothing and the mud for the first time. She turned and fumbled with the key, opening the door.

'Come inside will you before you catch your death of cold.'

The warm, stale air, smelling faintly of cooking, enveloped him as Rosie put her hand to the switch. He stopped her. 'Pull the curtains first. I don't want anyone to know I'm here.'

She looked at him quizzically. 'It never bothered you before, Sergeant. Getting fussy are we?'

He shook his head tiredly. 'No, no it's not that, Rosie. Just do as I ask, will you?'

A quick retort was on her lips, but she could see he was exhausted and said nothing, pulling the curtains over the windows until the small room was in darkness. Reed switched the light on. Rosie was shocked by his appearance. He was caked in mud and his trousers were in tatters, dried blood from bramble scratches stuck to his legs. She crossed the room and helped him out of his overcoat, then sat him down by the red embers of the peat fire, stoking it up again and holding a sheet of paper across it until it had drawn and was blazing warmly. Reed was happy just to sit and thaw out.

'I'll make you some tea,' Rosie said, moving into the kitchen, but leaving the door open so that she could see him. 'What happened?' she asked.

He gazed into the flickering flames. He was thinking about Stanley, how he had saved his bacon. 'There was a break tonight,' he said quietly. 'I'm trying to get to a safe house in Dublin.'

Rosie poured the boiling water from the kettle into the teapot. 'How many?'

302

He looked at her blankly. 'What?'

'How many broke out?' she repeated.

He turned back to the fire. 'All of us,' he said. 'We all got out.' He wondered whether Stanley was in bed or in the cooler. He grinned to himself. A lot would depend upon Stanley, who always loved a fight. If he'd decided to take on the Irish Army all by himself he'd almost certainly be in the cooler by now.

Rosie carried in a small tray and gave him a steaming cup of tea. She'd cut some chunks of brown bread and butter and liberally loaded them with home-made jam. She put the tray down beside him and bustled upstairs.

'Be back in a minute,' she called out.

Reed drank the tea gratefully and wolfed down the bread and jam. Rosie reappeared on the stairs in a white satin dressing-gown that she knew he liked. She carried a woollen blanket and wrapped it round his shoulders, then curled up on the mat in front of the fire and sipped her cup of tea, leaning against his legs.

Reed began to feel better almost at once, just as he knew she intended him to. He ran his fingers through her hair.

'You're a good girl, Rosie.'

It was her turn to stare into the flames. 'There's a few round here who would disagree with you on that, Sergeant.'

He pulled her head gently back so that he could see her face. 'It's not that sort of goodness I'm talking about, Rosie.'

A trace of a smile crossed her face. 'I know,' she said softly.

He leaned down and kissed her, holding her face between his hands. Her arm slid up between his legs and he eased himself out of the chair on to the floor beside her. Halfway through their lovemaking he paused for a moment. 'You really are good,' he said emphatically.

*     *     *

The morning was grey and a cold wind was gusting from the west, whipping up the last of the dead leaves and whirling them across the barrack square. By dawn Tynan had a dozen officers and their horses assembled, together with the local huntsman and his pack. While there were no cavalry units stationed on The Curragh, many officers had horses and were allowed to stable them in the barracks for a minimal charge per week.

Tynan was grateful, the only way to pursue and recapture the airmen was on horseback. But Captain Slye had watched the arrival of the huntsman and his pack with mounting anguish. He loathed the idea of pursuing escaped detainees with dogs, and the thought of using a pack filled him with despair. There was, so far as he knew, no precedent for doing so under international law; and as Liaison Officer it was his responsibility to see that such laws were administered correctly.

Tynan waited impatiently for the sky to lighten and, as soon as he was satisfied, ordered Harrison's bedding and clothing to be thrown to the hounds. They descended upon it, sniffing and tearing at it. Tynan was not sure who the other two airmen might be, but he was certain that the American, Harrison, would be on one of the Hawleys' animals. From the moment Harrison had been brought into his office three months before, perhaps even earlier, when he'd first heard of his attempted escape in the police car before his arrival at The Curragh, he had sensed that the American was significant. Quite how he had not been sure himself.

For nearly twenty years he had been imprisoning men. He knew how self-destructive that was, and he'd had plenty of time to analyse his own feelings about the Republican prisoners who endured his harsh regime in 'Tintown' on the other side of The Curragh. He knew of his guilt, and what he had inflicted upon himself by such examination. However, he was not addicted to self-pity, and he could also see his soldier's duty in keeping enemies of the state safely under lock and key. That they had been his comrades in war was a harsh fact of life he had to bear as stoically as he could. In a curious way he had tried to make amends for the strictness that he had to impose upon the Irishmen in 'Tintown' by endeavouring to apply more humanitarian rules in the RAF/Luftwaffe Camp on K Lines.

He realized now that the American, a man who had no need to be in the war, who was here only because he wanted to be here, was a catalyst. Towards him Tynan had for once reacted instinctively, finding in him something of himself. It was strange, but this time he didn't question or analyse. He needed this; he needed Harrison.

Someone was tugging at his sleeve. He turned impatiently to Slye.

'Yes, what is it, Captain?'

An excuse flew to Slye's lips. He could get out of this, back away before it was too late. He listened almost incredulously to what he was saying.

'I should like a word with you if I may, sir.'

Some of the other officers were watching curiously. Tynan studied him, slightly irritated by his dogged manner.

'There is no time for that. What is it?'

Slye was horrified. He could still get off the hook, but he seemed to be compelled to destroy himself completely.

'Sir,' he said. Was that really his voice? 'I . . . well, I really must protest at the use of dogs to hunt escaped detainees. I realize you only wish to recapture them, but I . . . I . . .' His voice seemed to echo, trail away down a long dark tunnel.

Tynan was staring at him. 'Yes, Captain?'

It all came out in a rush, his voice high-pitched, frightened. 'Well, I think it is barbarous to use animals to hunt men and I . . .' he stopped, aghast at what he had said

305

to a superior officer. He looked up almost comically at the Provost-Marshal, his mouth open. He swallowed hard and shut it, trying to return his steady gaze.

Most of the other officers had heard what the Liaison Officer had said. Tynan knew they were waiting for his response.

'Captain,' he said quietly, 'your fine feelings do you much credit, but you are not fully aware of the facts. As Liaison Officer you are quite right to state your opinion on this matter, but I must point out that these dogs will not be used to trap or hunt the fugitives. Several of the prisoners have escaped on horseback and the only way I can bring them back is by pursuing them in the same way. Now it is impossible for me to know which way they have gone unless I use dogs. Once I know where they are headed, or I have them in sight, the dogs will be removed.' He paused, gazing at the Captain, who seemed hypnotised by his words.

'Do I make myself clear, Captain Slye?' he said, not unkindly.

Slye swallowed again, his mouth opening and shutting soundlessly.

Tynan tried again. 'I have work to do here, Captain, and so do you. I suggest you get on with it.'

Slye seemed rooted for a moment. Then, hardly daring to believe his luck, he said, 'Yes sir, of course. I er . . . I do, I do have lots of things I can do. Thank you, sir.'

He saluted and Tynan returned it formally. Slye turned and marched away, his head up.

Tynan looked at the assembled officers. They were all standing around, trying not to display openly their interest in the Slye episode. He called sharply to his Executive Officer. 'Lieutenant Grant?'

The young officer hurried over and saluted. 'Sir.'

'Is everything prepared?'

'Yes, sir,' he answered. 'They've all been to the armoury and they're fully provisioned.'

Tynan nodded. 'Good. I'll take the rifle now, Grant.'

The Lieutenant took the sling from his shoulder and handed the rifle to Tynan, who examined it carefully. It was an Enfield .303 Sniper's rifle No. 3, Mark 1*T(A), that had originally been used extensively during the First World War. Since then it had been updated and fitted with an Aldis telescopic sight. Tynan checked the sight, then slung the rifle across his back together with the cartridge belt that Grant gave him.

He signalled to his men, 'Mount up,' he swung effortlessly into the saddle and nodded to the huntsman. The huntsman put the bugle to his lips and sounded the hunt, the clear tones echoing back from the flat red-brick walls around the barrack square. The hounds yapped and bayed, milling for a few moments around Harrison's clothing, then slowly they began to move off down the lane past K Lines.

Stanley stood behind the barbed wire with the other flyers who had been recaptured and watched the pack of hounds move past them towards the perimeter of the grassy plain. Tynan's horse pranced nervously by, but the Provost-Marshal looked neither right nor left, ignoring the hostility. Twelve horsemen followed, their officer's uniforms hidden beneath green oilskins.

Burroughs watched from the doorway of his hut. He was angry, knowing that the outcome of the talks between London and Dublin regarding their return to England would not be helped by this mass escape. Yet he did feel a certain reluctant admiration for the escapers. It had been well planned, though he had known nothing of it and of the thirty-six flyers in the camp only he had stayed behind. There were still ten, in addition to Bryce, Harrison and

Crawford, on the loose. Maybe they would get back – that was all that really mattered in the end, that the service had as many operational pilots as possible.

Stanley fingered the dried blood on the cuts on his forehead. The Irish soldiers had not taken kindly to his antics last night, but nor had they found Sergeant Reed. He called out after Tynan defiantly.

'You'll never catch them, you bastards. You'll never catch them.' Neither Tynan nor his officers bothered to turn around and look at him. He'd sworn at them in Polish, but the message was unmistakable.

The road though Dalkey was difficult to follow: narrow winding streets, small corner shops, lime-washed houses. It reminded Colonel Bryce of the coastal towns of Cornwall. Eventually he found Vico Road. It led steeply up the side of the cliff, and he stopped the car as arranged between Hawk Cliff and Black Castle. He got out, spreading his hands on the grey-stone wall that ran alongside the road bounding the cliff edge. Lower down was a cutting for the railway line that followed the coast back to Dublin. The view across Killiney Bay was magnificent, the bulbous stone heads of Bray point farther down the coast marching out into the white-flecked sea as if determined to drown. He stood enjoying the vantage point. Then he heard a car toiling up the hill. He turned and looked back down the road. A Vauxhall with a fluted bonnet and slightly knock-kneed front wheels emerged around the bend and pulled slowly in towards him. Bryce glanced at his watch. He was on time.

A heavy-set man about fifty years old climbed out of the

Vauxhall and slammed the door exasperatedly. 'Bloody old banger. Didn't think I was going to get here at all.'

Bryce smiled. Corrigan never altered. 'Well, you're on time for a change anyway.'

They shook hands warmly, glad to see each other again.

'How long is it now?' Corrigan asked.

Bryce raised his eyebrows. 'Before the war. Must have been the beginning of last year, when you warned me about the IRA getting active again in the UK.'

Corrigan eyed him speculatively. They'd known each other a lot longer than that. Corrigan and Bryce had once served together in the British Army during the First World War. Corrigan had left when it had ended to return to Ireland. Like many others, the trenches had removed his taste for war or army life. It was sadly ironic that he had come back to Ireland only to be immediately embroiled in its bitter bloodshed.

'And what brings you over here incognito this time?' Corrigan enquired. A cold wind blew sharply in off the sea and he made a grab for his hat before it was snatched from his head. 'Let's talk in the car. Your car,' he added pointedly, glaring at his offending vehicle.

They got themselves settled comfortably in the front seats and Bryce pulled a bar of chocolate from the glove compartment.

'Want some?' he asked.

Corrigan shook his head. 'I'm supposed to be on a diet. We have a new Minister and the new broom is demanding that all operatives in the service are fit. Mother of God, you'd think we were training to be Commandos or something.'

'How is the new Minister?' Bryce enquired. Corrigan chuckled. 'Oh he's all right, I suppose, but it'll take a while to run him in to our ways.' He shrugged his shoulders. 'Intelligence work goes on in much the same way no matter who's up top.' He widened his eyes, looking pointedly at Bryce, 'As I'm sure you are aware.'

'True,' Bryce said shortly. 'How much do you know about a man named James Driscoll?'

Corrigan stared out of the window over the sea trying to gauge his reply. 'A good deal,' he said non-committally.

Bryce unbent. 'We know he has been seeing the German Ambassador here. We also know that he had meetings with Liam Quinn down in Tralee and that the three of them, Quinn, Driscoll, the Ambassador and a German officer named Gehler have attended another meeting at Driscoll's house in Newbridge.'

Corrigan looked at him sharply. 'Gehler did you say?'

Bryce nodded. 'That's right, Oberleutnant Gehler. He was killed by another German named Halder two days ago.'

Corrigan sat thinking for a while. 'I heard about that. It tied in with something else we were concerned about.'

Bryce didn't question him. He knew Corrigan would tell him if he could. 'We'd picked up on Driscoll,' Corrigan said quietly, 'when he had the meeting with Quinn. We know he has been playing a double game, apparently publishing a pro-British newspaper yet working to get Ireland involved with Germany.'

Bryce looked at Corrigan directly. 'He's a very dangerous man, Noel.'

Corrigan didn't doubt the significance of Bryce's remark. 'How dangerous?'

'We've been increasingly concerned about the nature of the signals passing between the German Embassy in Dublin and their Foreign Office in Berlin. It seems there has been a gradual build-up towards some kind of action and now somebody else has come into the picture.'

Corrigan looked up enquiringly.

Bryce continued. 'An army man. We first spotted him

310

when he visited the German Embassy in mufti. Later we saw him again at the meeting in Driscoll's house.'

'Have you identified him yet?'

Bryce nodded. 'Last night, which is why I asked to see you. His name's Lynch, General Lynch. He commands the 2nd Spearhead Division facing the border to the North.'

Corrigan sat still, absorbing the implications. 'Does London know?'

Bryce shook his head. 'Not yet. I wanted to talk to you first.'

'Thanks,' Corrigan said. He was worried. He knew this was dynamite.

'Look, Noel,' Bryce said quietly, 'I don't have to tell you that if London gets this just the way it is, it could start a whole train of events. They could take the view that, in order to protect the border from a possible alliance between the Germans and the Irish military, together with elements of the IRA, a pre-emptive strike is necessary.'

'I realize that,' Corrigan said. 'We didn't know about Lynch.'

Bryce sat quietly for a moment. The wind had risen and grey clouds were scurrying across the bay. 'Let me deal with Driscoll,' he said.

Corrigan stared through the windscreen. 'How?'

'I'll make it look like an IRA job.' Bryce smiled sardonically. 'He's supposed to be pro-British.'

'And Lynch?'

'He's yours, and he's got to be taken out of the command structure immediately. If I can tell London that Driscoll is dealt with and Lynch neutralized they may be prepared to accept that political figures were not involved and that the danger has passed.'

Corrigan didn't mention Driscoll's meeting with the Minister. That was something that would have to be

311

handled very delicately. He made up his mind. 'All right. I think that's the best way. I'll see that you have proof of Lynch's removal, but I shall need twenty-four hours.'

Bryce considered that. 'It's all I can give you, Noel. I can't hold this back any longer.' He paused. 'And Driscoll?'

'You take care of him. We'll treat it as an IRA killing and it will be reported in the papers as such.'

'Good.'

They both sat quietly in the car watching the dark clouds piling up over Bray Head. Bryce broke off a piece of chocolate and put it in his mouth. He offered the bar to Corrigan again. This time he accepted.

'Thanks.' He chewed for a moment. 'Did you know there was a break last night from the internment camp?'

'No.' Bryce looked at him surprised. 'No, I didn't. I came straight out here this morning to see you.'

Corrigan smiled grimly. 'Yes. Seems all the RAF boys got out. They toppled the main gate off its hinges apparently.' He shook his head. 'God knows how they did that, but they did. Half the Army's out lookin' for them.'

Colonel Bryce listened to the wind whipping round the car. Christ, it was cold out there! He shivered. He hoped Peter would be all right.

They had managed to cross the two main roads, from Naas and Dublin, during the night, ascending south of the road that ran through the Wicklow Gap towards the Table Mountain. Harrison wanted to be well into the high ground by daylight, but it did not prove easy. Crossing the roads was simple; there was hardly any traffic. The main problem was the treacherous terrain. Without warning they would suddenly find themselves in bogland or swamp, the horses sinking up to their bellies in the soft porous surface. It was impossible in the dark to see what they were getting into and more than once they had to slide quickly from the saddle and physically pull the animal free.

Harrison was glad when the first grey light began to seep over the rim of the Wicklow Mountains. At least now he could see where they were going. Occasionally they would pass abandoned stone cottages, and as the light grew stronger he began to look for one where they could stop for some food.

Near a tributary to King's River he found an overgrown track leading up towards a stone bluff. He dismounted and examined the track more closely. It had not been used for months, possibly longer. He remounted and led Bryce and Crawford up the track. It began to climb around the edge of the stone bluff until they came to a clearing. The derelict building faced outwards over the bluff, set back just from the rim. It would do. Scrubland and stunted trees surrounded it on three sides and it would be easy to keep watch.

He showed Bryce and Crawford how to tether the horses. Neither had experience with animals and already they were moving stiffly. He pointed to a spot where the horses could feed. 'We'll tie them there. That way they get to eat too.' The horses always came first with Harrison, without them their position would be hopeless.

The building was falling apart. The roof had begun to come in at certain points. But the chimney stack was still intact and, once he had removed a rotting bird's nest from its top, they were able to light a fire. Harrison stationed Crawford to keep watch through the empty windows while he and Bryce warmed some food. Mrs Hawley had been thorough, not only were there cans of stewed meat and vegetables, but also small pans to heat them in. Bryce got some water from a stream that cascaded over the edge of the bluff. There was a brief moment of alarm until the tin opener was found. The small but vital instrument had not been forgotten. They heated the stew and a can of baked beans, which served to make a delicious thick soup. This, with some lumps of bread and washed down with hot tea, left them all feeling better. Bryce had seldom tasted anything so good.

'You know,' he said, between mouthfuls, 'we should do this more often.'

Harrison stood up and walked over to the glassless windows. He looked out over the stone bluff down the side of the mountain towards the reservoir at Blessington that he could just see reflecting the light in the distance.

Crawford looked at his watch. It was ten thirty-six A.M. 'Perhaps we ought to stay here until it's dark.' He looked to Bryce for support. 'If we're seen they may realize what our intentions are and seal off all the roads to the coast.'

Harrison continued to stare towards the valley. 'We go on,' he said. 'We can't afford to hang around. Tynan will be on our tails.'

Bryce protested. 'But how? He doesn't know we have horses – even if he did, he will think we would head for the North.'

Harrison turned and faced them, his face in shadow, outlined by the sky behind him. 'Tynan *will* find us if we sit still. He's a hunter – he won't assume anything. Believe me,' he added quietly, 'he's already on his way. The ground is too tricky to risk travelling only at night, and it will get worse the higher we go. Make no mistake about it, the terrain up there is going to be tough.' He threw the dregs of his tea on to the fire. 'Pack up the gear, Crawford, make sure it's clean.' He kicked the ashes of the fire apart so that they

314

could not burst into flame again, then walked outside to check the horses.

Crawford turned to Bryce. 'What do you think?'

Bryce swallowed the last of his tea. 'We do as he says,' he replied.

The terrain altered as they climbed out of the foothills. The ground grew firmer, less boggy, the ascent steeper. Harrison understood these conditions. He followed the natural contours of the mountain wherever he could, always climbing, heading east and south. Sometimes on the screes and rock-strewn slopes he would dismount and lead his horse, Crawford and Bryce did the same.

Bryce didn't know what was worse, sliding around in the saddle or forcing his aching limbs to walk. Keeping up with Harrison was a problem. He tried not to slow him down, but the American frequently had to stop and wait for him and Crawford.

They crested the rounded ridge between Turlough Hill and Table Mountain at mid-afternoon. By now visibility was deteriorating fast, but between the dark clouds that swept by almost over their heads they could occasionally see the grey misty horizon to the east that was the Irish Sea. The ridge was high and exposed and Harrison led them a short way down the easterly side to escape the main force of the wind, then turned southwards, skirting the Vale of Glendalough below him.

They crossed a narrow road east of Table Mountain that fed the occasional traveller through the mountains from the Glen of Imaal and began to climb the rocky slopes of Lugnaquilla. The short midwinter day was drawing in and as they climbed the grey cloud swept down, swirling insidiously between them. All they could see was the vague outline of the rider in front. The cold wind buffeted them and the animals as though it were trying to sweep them from the mountainside.

Slowly the three figures crept over the high rounded shoulder of Lugnaquilla, Harrison was thinking about finding somewhere to shelter for the night. It would not be easy in this barren terrain. As they came off the crest of the mountain they got beneath the cloud base again. In the valley below lights glimmered palely through the gathering darkness. To the south, about three hundred feet down the side of the mountain, he could just see a narrow sloping plateau, some scrub and stunted growth clinging to the minimal shelter it offered. He pointed, indicating the spot to Bryce and Crawford. They acknowledged his signal with considerable relief. They were exhausted and gave him no argument. Bryce was ready to stop almost anywhere, just so long as they stopped. Harrison leaned forward in the saddle and prodded his mount towards the plateau.

The hounds were streaming upwards, clambering easily through the soft spongy ground that slowed Tynan and his officers. The Provost-Marshal dismounted and led his horse around a particularly bad section, the other officers following his example. Tynan knew the area well. The hunt came this way sometimes, though it seldom reached far above the treeline. The fox didn't like to be caught in the open. Harrison appeared to be heading directly eastwards, but the high ground would be his objective. Up there he could dictate the moves, his only boundaries the range of mountains themselves.

Gradually they ascended higher, the horsemen stringing out in a long line. Some of the less experienced amongst them were already feeling the punishment, their appetite for the chase visibly diminishing. Tynan did not slacken the pace, he wanted to get as far as possible before the light disappeared. He knew Harrison would only stop when it was dark. The rifle banged naggingly on his back and from time to time he adjusted its position, but the movement was automatic and he hardly noticed it. His concentration on the terrain was total.

The hounds found the track leading up to the stone bluff late that afternoon. Tynan saw them disappear over a rise in the ground and heard their baying alter. The pitch was higher, more excited. He reached the ridge and looked down a short slope into what appeared to be a cutting lined with stubby trees and gorse. The dogs were racing up what had once been a track towards a high stone bluff. He turned and looked back down the side of the mountain. The huntsman and his officers were at least half a mile behind him. He spurred his horse down on to the track, pushing the stallion as fast as it would go towards the bluff after the dogs. The track wound its way upwards through the trees into a small clearing. The hounds were milling round the door to a derelict building, some of them trying to leap up at the empty windows. Tynan reined his stallion to a halt and pulled the rifle from his back, releasing the safety catch and working a cartridge from the magazine into the breech.

He dismounted, slipping the reins over a low branch, then moved forward cautiously towards the building. He knew the pilots were unarmed, but he kept the rifle at the ready. He reached the wall of the house, then slid along it until he was close to the door. The hounds were snapping and snarling, jumping up at it. Tynan kicked it open and leapt inside, slamming it shut again behind him before the dogs could follow. The building was empty, but the dead embers in the fireplace and the discarded cans told him they'd been here. He searched the derelict house thoroughly, but there was nothing else.

He went back outside and waited for the huntsman and his officers to arrive. They would have to stay here tonight. Instinct told him to press on. He could have managed the mountain at night. That was not the problem. But he needed the dogs until he was close enough to have them in his sights. Then it was between Harrison and himself. Meanwhile this derelict house would do and he could afford to wait.

The long, straight narrow road undulated over the gently contoured landscape. The battered Morris 8 was badly sprung and Reed had the feeling he used to get as a child on a roller coaster. Rosie was driving. She knew the route they were taking, which was somewhat erratic, keeping to the back roads as much as possible until they got into Dublin.

A dog emerged suddenly from a gate, snapping at the car and causing Rosie to swerve violently. 'Bloody animals,' she said.

The sergeant made no comment. He sensed that she was annoyed about something and it was probably to do with him.

'I really don't know why I'm doin' this at all,' she said suddenly. Still he did not respond and that made her more angry.

'You've got no right, you know, to come knockin' on my door in the middle of the night.' She considered that for a moment, then added as an afterthought, 'At least not to do this sort of thing.' She looked at him for some reaction and he felt obliged to say something.

'I know, Rosie. I do appreciate your help.'

'Appreciate it,' she said, her voice rising several decibels. 'You listen to me, Mr Reed, I may not be a staunch Republican

318

an' all that, but I am an Irishwoman and what the divil I'm doin' helpin' some idjit Englishman to get out of the country I don't know.' She paused to draw breath, ''Cept we've been tryin' to get you lot out of Ireland for years. Ah, it makes no sense at all, why we should want to keep you lot here in the first place.'

Reed kept his thoughts to himself. He knew she was only sounding off because she was nervous, and she was right. He had no right to expect her to help him. She could find herself in hot water if she were caught. He sat quietly, letting her rabbit on; she was entitled.

'Whereabouts in Dublin did you say this safe house was?' The question almost caught him by surprise. 'Near St Stephen's Green. I know the way once we get there.'

'You'd better,' she said sharply. 'I don't want to be cruisin' round the centre of Dublin with you as me passenger.'

There was an uneasy silence between them for a while. They began to pass through a more built-up area.

'What happened to Stanley, do you know?' Her voice was more conciliatory.

'I don't,' he said. 'Probably just taken back to the camp. He probably won't get any special punishment, seeing how everybody except Burroughs broke out, though they may suspend the parole for a while.'

'Mother of God,' she muttered to herself, realizing that her regular custom would be slashed in half.

Reed glanced at her. 'I'm sorry for putting you to all this trouble, Rosie. I know you don't have to do it.'

She stared implacably through the windscreen. 'You're damn right I don't have to. I must be bloody mad helpin' you to get out of the country when all I want is for you to stay.' She sniffed and a tear seeped out of the corner of her eye.

'Rosie,' he said concerned, 'don't cry.'

'I'm not cryin', you stupid man. Now give me your handkerchief and make yourself useful.'

He reached into his pocket and handed it to her. She blew upon it thunderously and poked it down the front of her dress between her ample breasts.

'Least I'll have somethin' of yours,' she said, mollified. They were nearing St Stephen's Green now and he kept his eye on the road. He directed her round the green then off to the east along Baggot Street and Merrion Road. He tried to look as inconspicuous as possible, sinking low into his seat, but he felt vulnerable although Rosie seemed to have settled down and was quite enjoying the trip.

'If I see Stanley is there anything you'd like me to pass on?' Reed shook his head. 'No, just thank him for me. Tell him if I make it back I'll be in touch as soon as I can.' He directed her off the main road down a wide leafy avenue and pointed to some large metal gates. Then shouted a warning to Rosie:

'Carry on; don't stop!'

He'd seen a car parked in the driveway containing three men in civilian clothes, but he knew they were police. Nine months in K Lines had developed his nose for the law impressively.

His warning had come too late. He stared out of the back window. The car had shot out of the drive and was accelerating down the road after them.

'Get your foot down, Rosie. They're after us.'

The old Morris leapt forward, skidding round a bend, heading back towards the centre of the city. Rosie knew the back streets well, but she was handicapped by the lack of real power in the old car. She managed to lose the policemen once, but someone else picked them up after they had crossed the river and were heading up North Strand. She cut off the main road again and twisted and turned her way through the narrow streets, trying to elude them. Reed clutched the door handle and just hung on for dear life, half the time they appeared to be going round corners at an angle of ninety degrees, his face closer to the road than to his feet.

Rosie took a left and a right; the police car stuck doggedly to them. She tried another left. Reed saw the blank wall at the end the same moment she did. Rosie braked, skidding the car to a halt. She leapt from the driving seat and began to run back up the road to the corner.

'I'll try to lead them off,' she screamed. 'Good luck.'

The sergeant stood rooted for a moment, her voice floating round his ears, unable to move. He wanted to call her back, but the words rose unformed to his lips and his mouth opened soundlessly. He could see her running away, then suddenly the police car burst around the corner and he found himself moving. He leapt a hedge and ran through a garden, up the side of the house and though a gate at the back. He was in an entry that gave access to the rear of two rows of terraced houses. He ran along it. He could hear the sound of several police cars converging on the area, their bells clanging noisily, locking him in. He didn't want to be locked in, not again. Fear pumped adrenalin and speeded his running. He came to the end of the entry. It was a dead end. High barbed railings blocked his path. He looked right and left. The gate in the fence to his right yielded to his touch. He opened it quietly and slipped into the backyard of the terraced house.

No one screamed or shouted. So far he hadn't been seen. He could hear police whistles blowing and voices shouting in the distance. Any minute now someone would be attracted and look out of a window. There was a shed in the yard. He tried the door. It was padlocked on the outside. Next to it was an outside lavatory. He opened the door and glanced inside. Nowhere to hide there. He was about to shut the door when he noticed that the wall dividing it from the toolshed ended just below the roof. There was a gap of about eighteen inches.

Quietly he shut the door behind him and climbed up on to the seat. He reached up. He was just able to get his fingers over the top of the wall. Reed pulled himself upwards, sliding his leg over, then squeezing himself slowly through the gap. He dropped down the other side on to the floor of the toolshed. It was dark, not much light got through the single dirty window. There was a workbench next to the wall beneath it and he slid himself into the gap under it and waited.

He heard them coming up the entry, searching yards and gardens. The back gate banged open and the padlock on the toolshed was rattled. He heard the footsteps go round to the lavatory and the door was opened. He tensed. It banged shut again and the dim light from the window above him was partially blocked as the Garda tried to see inside the toolshed.

Reed lay absolutely still, hardly daring to breathe. The Garda was little more than three inches from him. The heavy silence dragged on interminably, then he heard boots scrape on the surface of the yard. The shadow shifted then disappeared and he heard the back door bang shut as the Garda departed. He let out a long sigh of relief and glanced around the interior of the shed. He saw something and smiled quietly to himself. He had a chance.

By the time they had worked their way down the scree to the narrow plateau it was almost completely dark. Harrison dismounted and took the reins from Crawford and Bryce.

'Find some wood, Crawford. We'll risk a small fire behind those trees. It's as good a place as any we'll find tonight.' He tethered the horses securely while Bryce started to take some provisions from the saddle bags. 'I'll get these saddles off first,' Harrison said. 'Hang on a minute.'

After the horses had been dealt with they heated some food on a fire that Crawford had lit. They wrapped themselves in blankets and curled down as close to the flames as possible, consuming the food quickly. The trees cut down some of the wind, but it was still bitterly cold on the mountain. Crawford had found plenty of dead wood during his forage in the dark, most of it splintered and broken, which was curious. But he was grateful: it burnt easily. He'd formed a small pile of it close to the fire so that he could keep restoking it during the night.

Harrison pulled the blanket up over his head just leaving a space to breathe through. What little conversation there had been after their arrival had dried up. He knew they would be suffering. Horse riding could be a painful experience for those not used to it. This terrain was some of the toughest he'd encountered. The contrast between the soft boggy ground and these rocky loose screes was remarkable, and the swift and completely unpredictable changes in the weather made it very dangerous.

During the clearer patches he'd seen vertical crevices in the side of the mountain. There were deep ravines worn by the constant rains. If any of them stumbled into one of them when visibility was bad, that would be that. Nor could he afford to slow down. He sensed Tynan's presence, how close he might be. Whether he'd picked up their trail yet he could not be sure, but Tynan would be there sooner or later and he could not take any chances.

Bryce lay on his back. The sky was clear and the stars seemed unbelievably close in the inky blackness above him. He had the illusion he could almost reach up and pluck them from the sky. The wind sighed through the few stunted trees. Occasionally a loose rock or stone would shift and roll a few feet on the scree above them. Christ, what if there were a landslide! He pushed the unpleasant thought from his mind. Harrison had chosen this spot and the way he had led them across the mountain had filled him with confidence. The American knew mountains; if anyone could get them through he would.

He never knew how long he had been sleeping when the explosion woke him. He sat bolt upright, flinging the blanket from him. Earth was still falling to the ground around him. He heard something whistling, screaming through the air. The intensity of the sound increased, then the shell exploded away among the trees to his left. The blast flung him sideways. He felt a sharp pain in his leg.

Harrison unwrapped his arms from around his head and leapt to his feet, running over to Bryce. The horses were rearing and snorting with fear. He shouted to Crawford as he sprinted. 'Saddle up. Clear everything.' He reached Bryce and rolled him on to his back. He was gripping the calf of his leg with both hands, his face contorted with pain. Harrison pulled his bloody hands away from the wound and examined it as best he could in the darkness. It was impossible to tell how bad it was. He tore a strip from the blanket and tied it round the wound, then helped Bryce to pull his high leather boots up over it. He leaned down towards his pale bloodless face.

'Can you ride?'

'Yes, I think so. It's just my leg.' He clutched at Harrison. 'What is it, what's happening?'

'Shells. This must be a firing range.'

Bryce stared at him uncomprehendingly. 'A firing range?'

'Yes, for chrissake,' Harrison said savagely. 'You don't think they'd waste the bloody things on us.'

Harrison was incensed with himself. He should have

guessed when he saw the pile of splintered wood Crawford had placed near the fire. It had nagged away at the back of his mind but he had been too tired to work it out.

He started to help Bryce to his feet. Another shell came whistling in and he pushed him down, falling across him. It exploded high up on the mountain, the impact sending a shower of small rocks rolling down the scree, some of them bouncing heavily on to the plateau. He hauled Bryce up again and helped him across to the horses. Crawford had quickly saddled two of them and Harrison cinched up the third as swiftly as he could. Crawford mounted and Harrison helped Bryce into the saddle. He glanced back at the fire and yelled at Crawford. 'Did you get everything?' Crawford nodded, trying to keep his frightened horse under control. Harrison wasted no more time. He leapt up on to his horse and dug his heels into its flanks, pushing the animal towards the southern end of the plateau. The others followed in the darkness. There was no time for safety measures. Harrison kicked his spurs in hard, forcing the animal up the rocky slope above the plateau. The horse scrabbled for a foothold but kept going, its own fear giving strength to its limbs.

Another shell came whistling in from the valley below them. They leaned down over the necks of their animals. It seemed to hang in the sky for ever, suspended above them, choosing its spot to fall. It exploded on to the plateau behind them, uprooting a tree that crashed on their fire, scattering its embers.

The three horses strained and fought their way up the steep rocky slope, their eyes white, dilated by fear, foam flecking the sides of their mouths. The men clung to their backs, clinging for dear life until they finally reached the escarpment above the scree. Only then did the pain return to Bryce's leg . . .

\*　　\*　　\*

Tynan stood listening by the open door of the derelict building. Faintly the sounds of the explosions echoed across the side of the mountain, carried clearly on the still, cold air. The sounds faded after a while and were not repeated. He stood there for a while, his senses alert, instinct awakened. He turned back to go inside. One of the officers was sitting up looking at him.

'What was it, sir? Who's firing?'

Tynan stepped over a sleeping figure and made his way back towards his own blankets.

'It's the artillery range at Coolmoney on a night practice. Nothing to worry about. Go back to sleep.'

The young officer, reassured, rolled over on to his side. Tynan lay quietly on his back for a long time, thinking. He didn't like the explosions in the dark. There was no need for concern, but it had been unexpected, an element he had not taken into consideration and that worried him – was that really the reason? Instinct was trying to tell him something different. He hardly slept at all after that.

Driscoll was late. After checking the house, Colonel Bryce had waited for nearly three hours in the car. He'd parked well away from the entrance to his drive, but facing the direction he expected Driscoll to come. He drove a grey Bentley, which was sufficiently unusual for Bryce to be able to spot him before he reached the house.

Headlights illuminated the bend in the road and then a car appeared. It was the Bentley. Bryce slid down in his seat as it went by, then it slowed before turning up the drive. Driscoll was alone; there had been no passengers in the car. Bryce opened his door and slid out, shutting it quietly behind him. He'd used an old Ford Popular that he'd picked up unattended outside a pub in Cabinteely. He walked casually down the road, then ducked into the drive after making sure that no one had seen him. He worked his way through the shrubbery of the grounds until he was facing the house. Lights were on in the hall and the main bedroom upstairs. Colonel Bryce walked up to the front door and knocked twice. There was no movement, so he knocked again. This time he heard footsteps coming down the stairs and crossing the hall. He pulled the revolver from his pocket. The door opened and Driscoll, tying the belt of his dressing-gown, peered out at the shadowy figure.

'Yes, what is it?' he said irritably. Then he stopped as the light from the hall glinted briefly on the pistol.

'Inside,' Bryce said quietly, pushing the barrel of the pistol into Driscoll's soft stomach. The Irishman backed away, his eyes wide, staring. He tried to bluster.

'What's the meaning of this . . .'

Bryce cut him short, jabbing the pistol hard into his diaphragm, winding him.

'In there,' he said, pointing with the gun to the dining-room just off the hall. Driscoll was frightened, though he tried not to show it. He opened the door that Bryce had indicated and backed into the room. Bryce stopped in the doorway and switched on the lights.

'Now,' he said, 'pull those curtains, Driscoll, and don't do anything else. I am good with this thing.'

Driscoll didn't doubt it for an instant. The man had a dangerously calm and methodical manner that was utterly professional. He pulled the curtains as instructed, then Bryce came into the room closing the door behind him. Driscoll watched him coldly.

'Well, you have been busy, Mr Driscoll,' Bryce said. In a different context the comment would have been friendly, even warm, but there was no mistaking the menace behind the apparently harmless remark.

Driscoll said nothing.

Bryce signalled to him with the pistol. 'Sit down.'

Driscoll did so, uncomfortably, on one of the dining chairs.

'Yes, quite the little intermediary, aren't you?'

Driscoll felt the blood draining away from his face.

'Meetings with the German Ambassador,' Bryce continued, 'Oberleutnant Gehler, a certain Mr Quinn from Tralee, not to mention General Lynch.'

'I don't know what you are talking about . . .'

Driscoll stopped as Bryce crossed the room towards him. Bryce brought the pistol down sharply across Driscoll's face, splitting it open across his cheek, cutting it almost to the bone. Driscoll's hand flew to his face and he crouched in the chair, cowering away from Bryce.

'Don't lie to me, Driscoll. I know all about it. You just tell me in your own words about these meetings and who knows, perhaps we can come to an understanding.'

Driscoll grasped at the political context of the remark. Blood was spurting between his fingers and his face was numb, but negotiation was something he could understand. The man was English, perhaps reasoned argument could prevail.

'I . . . er,' he shook his head, trying to think, spraying his blood over the table. 'We met here, in my house. I . . . the Ambassador had asked me to . . . er, arrange it. He knew of my connections with the English scene through my newspapers and he suggested that I ought to meet all these people and perhaps discuss a way of approaching London . . .' He saw the look in the gunman's eye and pushed himself back in the chair. Bryce held the pistol directly beneath Driscoll's jaw, jabbing it into his soft double chin, gripping his hair in his hand and twisting it painfully.

328

'I told you I know why these meetings were held – I know what you have been trying to do. Now I want to know exactly what was said and the next time I hear a lie I shall kill you. Is that clear, Driscoll?'

His eye was closing and the pain in his cheek was almost unbearable, the barrel of the gun hard and cold sticking into his flesh. He nodded his understanding. The gun was removed. He stared up into the hard cold eyes and knew that this was his last chance. He groaned as loudly as he could, scraping his chair noisily on the wooden floor.

'I asked them to come here. It was my idea.' He paused, swallowing some of his blood that was seeping into the corner of his mouth as it trickled down his face. 'We talked about our mutual interests, that is, Germany's and Ireland's, how . . . how we might be able to form an alliance.' He stopped.

'Go on,' Bryce said softly.

'To form an alliance,' he repeated. 'To get Britain out of Ireland.'

Driscoll tried to look into his eyes, to leave the subject there and not continue, but he couldn't. He didn't want to die, nor could he risk a half truth. He gazed at his feet.

'We also,' he whispered, 'discussed the possibility of German forces . . .' He stopped. He could hear footsteps coming down the stairs. Thank God. He'd thought she was never going to come down to see what was wrong. She had been waiting for him in his bedroom, as she always did on Thursdays. He had been about to make love to her when he'd heard the knock on the door. He tensed in his chair.

Bryce backed to one side of the door. The footsteps were light, no shoes, probably a woman. How had he managed to miss her? He'd checked the house and it had seemed to be empty. She must have been upstairs. Jesus, why did Driscoll have to choose this day to have his fancy woman here?

Bryce could not afford to let her see him. It might break

329

the cover story and would destroy any future operations for him in Ireland. He kept his eye on Driscoll. The door was flung open angrily and the woman saw Driscoll's bloodied face. Driscoll half rose from the chair, staring at Bryce, who was hidden from the woman by the door. Bryce switched off the lights in the room. Driscoll made a stupid dash for the door, forgetting that the light from the hall outlined him perfectly. Bryce had no choice. He shot him twice through the heart. He fell headlong in front of the woman, dead before he hit the floor.

The woman screamed. Bryce shoved her sharply in the back and she fell sprawling across Driscoll's body. Before she could turn Bryce stepped quickly into the hall and shut the door, turning the key in the lock. The woman was screaming hysterically in the dark, trying to push herself away from the dead body, her hands and flimsy nightgown covered in Driscoll's warm sticky blood.

Bryce left the house through the front door and ran swiftly down the drive. He could still hear the woman's screams but so far no one had responded. The houses in this road were widely spaced, in their own grounds, but they must have heard the shots. He'd intended to use the silencer, but the woman had disturbed him, forced him to act quickly. He reached the end of the drive and glanced up and down the road. Still no one, he ran for the car and clambered inside. The engine started without trouble and he accelerated away. A couple of men appeared opposite Driscoll's house as he roared by. They would have a chance to see the Irish number plates, but Bryce cursed himself for not finding the woman. Driscoll had been about to tell him what the meeting had planned. Both Gehler and Driscoll were dead and he could do nothing about the German Ambassador. That left General Lynch in Irish hands. Perhaps Corrigan could get something out of him, but he doubted it. There only remained Quinn . . .

Bryce felt weak. He reached down to his leg, feeling for the wound close to the top of his boot. He tried to twist the makeshift bandage tighter but it slipped from his frozen fingers, wet with blood. He didn't know how long they had been riding since leaving the plateau. His mind refused to function properly. It seemed like an eternity; it might only have been a few minutes. The blackness of the night, the freezing damp mist that hung clammily around them, became inextricably mixed with his own personal nightmare of pain and fear of burning.

There would sometimes be moments of clarity. He would see the moving dark mass of the animal in front and hear the clink of its bridle. The only other sound that penetrated was the horses' hooves as they plodded slowly across the ridge of the mountain. He swayed drunkenly in the saddle and would have fallen if Crawford hadn't been watching him carefully. He spurred his horse alongside and grabbed his arm, holding him upright. Bryce groaned, his head lolling forward. Crawford reined in his horse and yelled to Harrison. The American pulled the head of the stallion round and walked his horse back towards them.

'How bad is he?'

Crawford slipped out of the saddle to support Bryce. 'Pretty bad. He's practically unconscious.'

'Don't let him fall,' Harrison ordered. 'He'll never get back.'

Crawford examined the wound in Bryce's leg. 'He's lost an awful lot of blood. We've got to do something.'

Bryce heard the voice. It seemed to come from a great distance. His head jerked up. He saw Harrison.

'Sorry, Roy. I never could ride horses.' He smiled painfully, then shook his head to clear it. 'Take me down to a farm somewhere, then you go on.'

'Can't do that – they'd know which way we were heading and that we're on horseback.'

Crawford looked up at Harrison's grim face. 'Maybe they already know that. Does it matter?'

'It matters,' Harrison said tersely. 'With a man like Tynan it matters.' He looked to the east. The sky was just beginning to lighten, a faint grey line breaking across the horizon, tinged with red. Soon it would be light and Tynan would be looking for them, but Bryce was sorely injured. He could not just let him bleed to death. Yet there was something else, too, something niggling away at the back of his mind that wouldn't go away. Didn't he feel just the slightest relief that they would be slowed down, that Tynan might draw closer, test his skills? He thrust the thought aside. There was no time for such self-examination. He had work to do. He leaned down close to Bryce.

'You came down somewhere in these mountains, didn't you?' Bryce gazed blankly at him. Harrison grabbed the front of his rain cape and slapped him hard across the face. 'Bryce,' he said sharply.

Crawford was appalled. 'What the bloody hell do you think you're doing?'

Harrison looked at him balefully. 'Shut up, Crawford.' The voice was low, without emphasis, yet Crawford felt a chill of apprehension. There was something implacable about Harrison that did not brook defiance.

He slapped Bryce again, harder, and saw a flash of recognition in his eyes. 'Peter,' he said urgently, 'where did you come down? The girl Nora. Where is she?'

Bryce swallowed, his eyes fastening on Harrison, trying to hold on to some lucidity. 'Nora,' he repeated . . .

'Yes.' Harrison shook him violently. 'Nora. Where is the farm?' Bryce clung to consciousness. 'Nora,' he breathed heavily. 'Nora is at Balycoyle.' His head lolled forward again.

Harrison held him against his shoulder. 'Check the map, Crawford. Find the route to Balycoyle. We'll take him .'ere.'

The incline was steep. Even the dogs were finding the going hard and treacherous. They dislodged some small stones that bounced down the boulder-strewn slope, peppering the horsemen toiling up behind them. One ricocheted viciously from a boulder, hitting a horse just below the eye. The animal reared up, snorting, frightened, and the officer, taken completely by surprise, was thrown. He crashed sickeningly back on to a wickedly sharp ridge of rock. Tynan heard his spine crack fifteen feet away. The officer didn't move. He was blessedly unconscious.

Two of the officers nearest to him dismounted, one of them rushing towards the injured man. Tynan could see the danger.

'Don't move him,' he called out. 'His back is broken.' He turned to his Lieutenant. 'Grant, you stay here with this man. Help him where you can. Take this.' He pulled a silver flask from his pocket. 'It may be useful. Tell the other officer to ride down to Coolmoney and get medical help. It's not too far.'

Grant looked up at the side of the mountain towering above. He was glad to be out of it. 'You going on, sir?'

Tynan stared at the crumpled figure lying awkwardly, misshapen upon the ground. He didn't answer Grant. Brutally he wheeled his horse, digging his spurs deep into his side. The animal surged up the incline, its hindquarters straining, pushing itself towards the dogs.

★ ★ ★

It was raining once more, pouring down relentlessly through the gaps in the trees. Harrison and Crawford rode on either side of Bryce, supporting him as best they could. Down here on the eastern slopes of the Wicklow Mountains they were at least spared the full force of the numbing wind. They continued their descent. Crawford was exhausted, cold, and every bone in his body seemed to have been reduced to one single consuming ache. The oilskin Mrs Hawley had provided kept out most of the wet; and although it still trickled in round the neck, he hardly noticed that now.

He didn't see the road and only became aware of it when he heard the horses' hooves clattering on its hard surface. Harrison reined his horse to a halt, grabbing the bridle of Bryce's mount. The rain spattered down on the narrow lane that dropped through the trees.

Bryce raised his head. He seemed to have rallied slightly. He looked up and down the lane. 'Farther down,' he said thickly. 'Small place on the right. There's a barn.'

Harrison decided to risk staying on the road. It could not be far, and Bryce needed the easier going. Away down to his left through the bare spiderlike branches of the trees he caught a glimpse of Glencree River. They continued downwards about a mile. Then, as the trees on the upward slope of the mountain to his right began to thin, he saw the farm. He brought the horses to a halt and dismounted. He looked up at Crawford.

'That's it; over there. Give me five minutes then ride into the yard openly with Bryce. There should only be two of them, the old man and Nora, but he's got a gun. I'll deal with him. OK?'

Crawford nodded exhaustedly, too tired to even consider the dangers. Harrison led his own horse away into the trees and tethered it out of sight of the farm. Then he began to circle away from the road. Crawford watched him disappear into the dripping trees, then pulled back his oilskin and looked at his watch. It was just after three o'clock. He waited seven minutes, just to be on the safe side, then grabbed the bridle of Bryce's horse and led the animal towards the farm. Immediately he got within sight of the gates at the entrance two terriers appeared in the yard, yapping furiously. The horses pricked up their ears and Crawford halted the animals just outside the gate and waited.

He saw some movement behind the curtains and the door was flung open. A medium-sized man emerged, carrying a rifle. It was Tracey. He stayed on the porch out of the rain and held the rifle loosely in the crook of his arm.

'What do you want?'

Crawford wiped away some of the rain from his face. 'I need help.' He saw someone move behind Tracey and Nora pushed past her father, shielding her face from the downpour, peering towards the horsemen. She recognized Bryce and, ignoring the restraining hand of her father, ran out towards him.

Tracey followed and stopped halfway across the yard, levelling the rifle at the two horsemen. Crawford saw Harrison emerge from behind the corner of the building. He moved quickly and quietly. His arm went around Tracey's neck and his left hand chopped down on his forearm. The rifle clattered to the ground and Harrison flung the older man aside while he was still off balance and picked it up. The dogs turned from the gate and ran towards him, snarling. He backed away, pointing the gun at them.

'Call them off,' he yelled.

Nora turned, saw her father lying on the ground and screamed at the dogs. They responded to her command and slunk back to her, growling, reluctant to give up the fight.

Bryce had heard her voice. He felt her arms around him, helping him from the saddle, easing him to the ground. He could put no weight on his injured leg and Crawford and Nora practically carried him into the farmhouse, while

Harrison led the horses into the yard, keeping the rifle on Tracey all the time. He shut the gate behind them, then took them to the barn where they were out of sight of the lane. He waved the rifle in the direction of the house. 'Inside,' he said.

Tracey eyed him balefully, then moved towards the farm. Harrison followed him in.

Nora had put Bryce into the armchair and was cutting away the soggy leg of his trousers. The wound was deep, about three inches long. She stood up and turned to Crawford. 'I shall have to stitch this.'

Crawford looked at Harrison incredulously, then back to the girl. 'But you're not qualified. You're not a doctor.'

Nora filled the kettle at the tap then took it to the range. 'I'm not a lot of things, but I run this farm and I have to do my best with the animals when they're sick.'

Crawford was about to protest again, but Harrison stopped him.

'Leave it to the girl. She's the only chance he's got. Now get something to tie him up with.' He indicated Tracey, who was standing sullenly by the table.

'No,' Nora said. 'That's not necessary. He won't do anything. I give you my word.' She gazed imploringly at her father. 'Da, you'll promise, won't you?'

Tracey viewed the flyers with ill-concealed contempt. 'Don't make any promises for me, girl, or ask me to promise anything to this lot. You're a stupid girl, Nora. You should never have got involved with that bloody Englishman in the first place.' He looked at Bryce, who was lying back in the armchair. 'I hope the bastard dies.'

Nora bit back the tears and turned to the range, waiting for the kettle to boil, not letting him see how much he had upset her. In this mood she knew her father would only regard it as weakness. The arrival of Bryce seemed to have split all the wounds open again.

Harrison nodded to Crawford. 'Find some rope.'

When Tracey had been securely tied to one of the chairs, Harrison gave the rifle to Crawford and went outside. He brought his own horse in from the woods and took it into the barn with the other animals. He unsaddled them and rubbed them down gently with some straw, feeding them some oats he found in a sack behind the door.

Crawford couldn't watch. Nora had bathed the wound, cleaning it thoroughly, and sterilised the needle and linen thread, the toughest she could find, in boiling water. Crawford had fed Bryce some whisky and was seated on the arm of the chair.

Nora looked up at him. 'You'll have to hold him still. If I can bring the wound together it will heal.' She touched Peter's hand. 'I've got to do this. It's the only way.'

He squeezed her hand lightly. 'It's all right. I can't feel anything anyway.' She was kneeling in front of him. He could see the strain, the tears behind the determined face she was presenting to him. 'Seems you are always patching me up. Do a good job and I might come back again.' He smiled encouragingly.

Nora looked at Crawford and nodded. He held Bryce by the shoulders and she removed the needle from the hot water, held the lips of the wound together with her left hand and inserted the needle into the flesh.

Harrison came in from the barn and saw what she was doing. He turned away in disgust, feeling sick. He picked up the rifle that Crawford had stood in the corner. It was an old World War One German Mauser. He checked the breech and the magazine. It worked efficiently. It would do . . .

Tynan studied the artillery range on the slopes of Lugnaquilla Mountain through his binoculars. The hounds were already chasing far out into the range area, crossing the shoulder of the mountain. Far below him in the valley he could just see the emplacements and buildings of Coolmoney. A young Lieutenant named Kennedy reined in alongside him, anxiously watching the dogs strung out over the range.

'We can't go in there, sir. That's the range the artillery from Coolmoney use. Fifteen men got killed when a mine blew up on that last year.'

Tynan didn't even bother to look at him. 'Can't we indeed.' He kicked his heels into his horse and galloped after the hounds.

Three other officers joined Kennedy to watch Tynan's progress across the mountainside. Kennedy felt a sudden surge of elation as he watched the single horseman's undeviating line. He turned to the other officers and shouted, 'Come on!' dug his heels into his horse and galloped off after the Provost-Marshal. The excitement communicated itself to the other men. One of them swept his cap from his head, uttered a wild rebel yell and set off in pursuit. A moment later and the others were following.

The dogs were streaming down the side of the rocky scree towards the plateau. Tynan heard their familiar baying sharpen to shrill barks as they reached it. They crowded round the camp site, all of them bunching, tearing at a piece of bloodstained cloth that Harrison had torn from Bryce's trouser leg.

Tynan negotiated the slope as quickly as he could, then leapt from his horse as he reached the plateau. He moved into the hounds, yelling and shouting, kicking them aside until he could grab the remains of the piece of cloth from one of the dogs. Blood was still on it, soaked in the saliva of the hounds, who were leaping about him barking excitedly. He threw the cloth at them and they began fighting among themselves again. He walked over to where the camp fire had been, the embers scattered by the shell fire and the fallen tree. The tree was splintered and marked. This was where they had spent at least some of last night. He looked at his watch, there was plenty of daylight. He had all of the afternoon and half the morning.

Kennedy and three other officers reached the plateau. Suddenly one of the dogs began baying at the edge of the woods, setting off in a southerly direction. The other dogs quickly picked up the scent and chased after him.

Tynan mounted and waved to Kennedy. He pointed back towards the shoulder of the mountain. 'Get that bloody huntsman up with us. He's supposed to be leading this pack, not trailing back there.'

Kennedy jerked his horse round and watched Tynan and the others set off after the hounds. He was disappointed. 'Shit!' he said eloquently, then galloped back to the huntsman as swiftly as he could.

Tynan was immediately behind the hounds now. He knew they were strictly forbidden to be here on the firing range and if they'd been spotted from Coolmoney the telephone lines would be getting fairly hot, but he cared nothing for that. They were getting closer and one of the flyers was injured. He hoped it wasn't Harrison; he wanted Harrison for himself.

The hounds stopped and began to mill about again. They'd reached the spot where Bryce had almost fallen from his horse. The dogs barked frantically for a few moments, muzzles to the ground, then set off in a completely new direction, heading diagonally away towards the ridge of the mountain, towards the north-east.

Tynan reached the spot and dismounted. He found some dark stains on the rocks, more blood. He gazed thoughtfully after the hounds, waiting for the huntsman to arrive. Clearly the injury was a bad one and whoever it was needed medical aid and help. Otherwise they would have continued south.

Kennedy rode up with the huntsman, who was breathing

heavily, his face red from exertion and the cold wind. Tynan pointed to the retreating hounds.

'Call them off. I want you to take them back.'

The huntsman stared at him stupidly. 'Back?' he repeated.

'Do it!' Tynan said savagely. 'Use that bloody horn of yours.'

The huntsman picked up the horn that was slung around his neck and rode off after the hounds. He put it to his lips and the sharp, high cadences echoed back off the side of the mountain. At first the hounds seemed unaware of it, then they began to move around uncertainly, torn between the desire to follow the scent and to obey the leader of the pack. First one, then another ran back towards the huntsman, who continued to blow his horn. He did not return to Tynan, who was standing watching him with a few of the officers. The huntsman was glad to be off the mountain and this wild dangerous chase.

Almost all of the officers had reached Tynan by now and were looking at him curiously, puzzled by the events. Tynan raised himself from his reverie and beckoned to Lieutenant Kennedy. The officer dismounted and Tynan led him away from the main group.

'I want you to go with the huntsman and his pack down to Coolmoney and take the rest of the officers with you. You'll be able to arrange transportation there to get you back to The Curragh.'

Kennedy looked at him in dismay. 'But you're not giving up now, sir. They can't be far ahead.'

Tynan studied the young eager face in front of him. He could see the excitement of the manhunt had got into his blood.

'No. I'm not giving up, Kennedy, but you and the other officers are.' Kennedy was about to protest, but Tynan cut him off. 'I know where they have gone.'

'But sir.'

'That's an order, Kennedy.' He paused, appreciating the officer's enthusiasm. 'Flank out round the side of the valley,' he said. 'Get the dogs and yourself off this range as quickly as you can. You should be down there in a couple of hours. When you do, check that Grant made arrangements for the injured man. Is that understood?'

Kennedy nodded glumly, then pulled himself together. 'Yes sir,' he said smartly, then saluted.

Tynan returned the salute. 'Off you go then.'

He watched Kennedy mount and give the others their instructions. Kennedy rode over to Tynan and saluted once more. 'Good luck, sir.'

Tynan acknowledged it. 'Thank you, Kennedy.'

The officers departed, riding quickly after the huntsman and his hounds. Tynan pulled the rifle from his back and checked the gun and its telescopic sight. He pointed it towards the ridge of the mountain and pulled it quickly up to his shoulder, peering through the sight. The two hairlines crossed, bisecting the ridge. He lowered it slowly, then slung it across his back.

He walked over to his horse and mounted, moving off at a steady trot. He'd be at the farm by midnight.

The overalls fitted and Reed did not feel out of place in the dingy crowded streets, though he still found it difficult to get used to the idea of no blackout. There were a few shops still open, but he was dubious about the risk of going in to buy something. He kept walking, heading north and east. Eventually he would find what he was looking for.

A kid about seven years old passed him going in the

opposite direction. He was clutching a greasy bag of chips, sucking them noisily into his mouth, savouring the vinegar. Reed was so hungry he was almost tempted to snatch them from the boy.

He saw the shop, or rather, first, he smelt it. The delicious aroma of fried fish and chips wafted down on the breeze and his mouth watered in anticipation. His nose led him unerringly to the spot. He stood outside for a moment. The big flat windows were steamed up inside, but through the door he could see the dark vats of bubbling fat and a short dumpy woman with her sleeves rolled up dipping fillets of raw fish into batter and expertly flipping them into the boiling fat.

The sergeant could resist no longer. He slid into the narrow shop and stood in the queue behind a woman who was trying unsuccessfully to control two small boys. They were nagging her about what they wanted in high-pitched voices. She had evidently decided to ignore them and stared indifferently into the cold dark street. The boys then disagreed amongst themselves and began to wrestle with each other. The woman did nothing for a moment. Then, as they got within range, she casually reached out and belted each one of them sharply around the head. They reeled away astonished, too surprised to wail, and remained silent for all of ten seconds. Eventually it was her turn. She was served and left, feeding the hungry mouths on the spot with bags of chips.

The woman behind the counter filled the chip baskets with freshly-fried chips which she scooped out of the steaming fat, ladling them into the compartment between the vats. She then turned to Reed.

'Yes,' she said shortly.

Reed affected the most dreadful imitation of an Irish accent.

342

'Oi'll be havin',' he said, 'a piece of that there cod and six pennorth of chips if ya don't moind.'

The woman surveyed him coolly for a moment, then ran her tongue around her teeth contemplatively and turned back to the fryer. She filled a bag to overflowing with chips and wrapped a piece of golden fried cod in some newspaper. Then she faced him again.

'Will ya be wantin',' she said, in an equally atrocious accent, 'will ya be wantin' them wrapped up well for the boat back to England?'

Reed was totally abashed, and a sickly grin spread across his face. 'No,' he said in his normal voice. 'I'll just take them as they are.'

The woman nodded, satisfied, and sprayed the fish and chips liberally with salt and vinegar. She wrapped them together in another sheet of newspaper and handed them to Reed.

'That'll be one and a penny,' she said.

Reed gave her the money and started towards the door of the shop.

'Hope you have a decent sailing,' the woman shouted after him, 'and don't meet any of those bloody U-boats.'

Reed grinned. 'Thanks,' he said. 'I'll keep my fingers crossed.'

The woman nodded in a friendly fashion and turned back to her steaming, bubbling fryer. Reed tasted a chip. It was perfection.

He leaned over the stone parapet of the bridge and peered down into the darkness. The railway lines were just visible, glistening faintly in the lights from the main road. He crossed the bridge a little more, trying to see what bordered the track. From the side he was able to see a steep grassy embankment, the top of which was bordered by some

343

trees that separated a long garden from the cutting. A high wall protected the privacy of the garden from the road. He studied it carefully. Occasionally some traffic went by and he tried to make himself as inconspicuous as possible.

If he climbed up on to the parapet on the side of the bridge he could just about leap to the top of the embankment. It was a risk and he would have to choose the right moment, but he had little choice. He needed this railway line and he had no stomach for tramping further through the streets to find another easier bridge that crossed it. He leaned against the parapet, watching the traffic. Farther up the road there were a number of shops, but they were closed now and, apart from the occasional car, it was a quiet stretch of road. Two cars passed. He looked right and left; there was nothing else. He took the long-handled tool he'd stolen from the shed and flung it on to the embankment, then clambered up on to the narrow parapet, trying not to look at the black void below him. Jesus, he never had liked heights. How ludicrous that was suddenly struck him as he stood teetering on this narrow strip of granite, with a railway line some forty feet below him. Why in God's name had he joined the Air Force?

He gritted his teeth, fastened his eyes on the embankment in front of him. Then Reed jumped as his foot slipped on the edge of the parapet, a hot rush of fear pouring through him. He could not regain his balance. All his lift had to come from the one foot still on the parapet. He stretched forward, realizing he was not going to make the top of the embankment, and crashed into the almost vertical grassy bank, his hands clawing at the top as he managed to dig his fingers into the soft grass. He lay winded, half on, half off the embankment, then slowly he pulled himself up over the edge. He got painfully to his feet and staggered to the trees,

344

picking up the tool and sliding the handle into the long pocket of his overalls. He sat down behind a tree, resting his back against the trunk, and drew in great lungfuls of the cold night air, his hot breath causing little patches of grey steam in the darkness.

He looked at his hands. They were shaking. Dear God, that had been close – two bloody hairy for comfort. He turned round and looked back at the bridge. No one. It seemed his ridiculous behaviour had not been noticed. Now he had to wait. He looked at his watch: nearly ten P.M. If he was on the right line, the Dublin/Belfast train would soon come along this track.

Well, he thought, so far so good. At least he'd got this far. His plan was working. When he'd seen the overalls in the toolshed he'd remembered a story an old Irishman had told him in the bar of a pub in Newbridge one night. It had worked for his son, he'd said, in Spain during the Civil War. It was a good story and whether it was true or not didn't matter. Reed didn't have much choice.

He wondered how Rosie had made out. Even if she got away they would be able to trace the car. Knowing Rosie, and her connections, the number of eminent local people who could be embarrassed by anything she cared to say in public, the Garda would probably forget it. The social infrastructure around Newbridge was very tight and well-protected. He smiled to himself. Rosie would probably enjoy it all immensely. Her fame would spread still farther and her talents be more widely appreciated.

He heard the sound of an engine and crawled quickly to the top of the embankment. He listened. Yes, it was coming from the direction of the city. The huffing and puffing grew steadily louder. Then the steam engine burst from under the bridge in a cloud of black smoke. It thundered by and Reed glimpsed briefly the hunched, bent figure of the fireman reflected in the glow of the furnace as he shovelled coal into its hungry burning mouth.

The smoke cleared and he peered anxiously at the carriages as they clicked noisily by, the lights from the steamed-up windows tracing a pattern on the embankment below him. There it was in black and white on a long board just above the windows: 'Dublin–Belfast'. He'd found the right line. He sighed with relief. Bloody hell, maybe he could do it. He waited until the track had ceased to hum, then slid on his backside down the steep slope, his feet crashing into the stone shingle at the bottom. He looked up and down the line – nothing.

He pulled the long-handled hammer from the pocket of his overall and tapped the rail experimentally a couple of times, the way he had seen railway tappers do occasionally in stations. The rail responded with a deep melodic ringing tone. It sounded good, no doubt the way it should. Not that he gave a damn whether the rail was in good order or not, but it was a long way to Belfast and he intended to tap his way the entire distance as professionally as he could.

He stepped into the middle of the track. He'd have to keep his eyes and ears open, no point in getting run down at this stage. What a bloody irony that would be. He could see it on his report now: 'run over by a train while tapping his way out of Ireland'. He smiled grimly to himself. The CO would have some fun with that. He started to walk, stepping from one sleeper to the next, heading northwards – heading home. He began to whistle tunelessly, gradually disappearing into the night up the Dublin–Belfast railway track. Reed was on his way.

Tynan didn't feel the rain. Instinctively his body guided the horse when it had to. Most of the time the animal found its own way, down over War Hill and the Wilderness Trek, close to the waterfall at Powerscourt. Tynan intended to approach Tracey's farmhouse from the lower slopes, the opposite direction from which pursuit might be expected. Logically they should not anticipate that he would have discovered their escape had been on horseback, nor that the hunt had been so swiftly organized. But Harrison would know, because Harrison, like himself, understood.

He reached the lane that ran up towards the farm, but did not ride on it. He circled back on to the lower slopes of Tonduff and approached the farm from the south. When he saw the lights glittering faintly through the trees he dismounted and led his horse deep into the wood. Before he tethered the animal, he pulled the Enfield from his back, then crouched, running silently on the soft wet undergrowth until he had the farm in sight again. He began to circle it, looking for the right vantage point.

Nora drained the potatoes, adding a little butter, then pulled the boiled ham from the large pot on the range. She looked at Peter, who was sitting in the armchair watching her. He stood up and limped across the room. Harrison, who was cleaning the rifle, was relieved to see that he could move with ease. Bryce joined Nora.

'Can I slice that up for you?'

She glanced diffidently at her father, still bound in the chair. There was no expression on his face but his eyes were angry, bitter.

'You shouldn't have tried to walk yet,' she said.

'I feel better. I've been asleep most of the evening. Besides, I wanted to talk to you.'

She smiled shyly, very aware of the others in the room, and handed him a carving knife.

'Here, you take this; and mind you don't cut your finger off. It's sharp.'

Carefully he sliced the ham and placed the pieces on the five plates Nora had warmed. She drained the cabbage and stirred the parsley sauce. Bryce enjoyed carving the meat. It was something he had occasionally done for his mother when his father was away from home. For the first time he noticed there were five portions and glanced round at Tracey. Nora caught his look.

'He must eat,' she said. 'He's had nothing since lunch.'

Bryce looked enquiringly at Harrison. 'What do we do about him?'

Crawford, who had been fiddling with the radio trying to get an English station, turned round suddenly. 'We can't free him. You saw his attitude when we arrived. He'd have used that rifle.'

Bryce continued to stare at Harrison. 'Well?'

The American shrugged. 'It's up to him.' He turned to Nora. 'Will your daddy stay calm, or cause trouble?'

Nora was angry. She spooned some potatoes on to a plate, then added the cabbage. She picked up the plate and took it across to the table, putting it down in front of her father. 'I don't know,' she said, glaring at Harrison. 'I don't know if he'll cause any trouble. But if he doesn't get to eat his dinner, none of you get any.' She tossed her head, flicking some hair from her face, and stood facing Harrison with her hands on her hips.

He raised his eyebrows and looked at Bryce, who smiled, enjoying her defiance. It was his turn to shrug eloquently.

Harrison looked at the older man. 'Listen, Tracey, we're all hungry. If I loosen you, will you promise me no trouble?'

Tracey stared at him, his eyes venomous. 'I'll promise you nothin'!'

Nora's patience snapped and she directed her anger at him. 'Listen Da, I've just spent nearly an hour and a half preparin' this food and I'm not havin' it all spoiled cos of you. Now you'll sit there and eat your dinner just like everybody else.' She leaned down, wagging her finger under his nose. 'Otherwise,' she continued, 'I'll tip this whole plate of meat and potatoes over your head.'

She marched back to the range and proceeded to put the remaining plates of meat round the kitchen table, which she had already laid. Then she turned to the others, who had watched her preparations silently. 'Well,' she said irritably, 'what are you waiting for? Sit down.'

Bryce moved first, limping across the room. Nora helped him to sit down and the others joined him at the table. Crawford reached out to help himself to the cabbage.

'Wait!' Nora said sharply. She looked at Harrison and held out her hand. 'Give me the knife.'

He looked at her speculatively, weighing the odds. Then he pulled a penknife from his pocket, opened it and handed it to her. She took it from him and walked behind the chair her father was sitting in. Quickly she cut the ropes binding his wrists, then handed the penknife back to Harrison without comment. She went back to her father, who was rubbing his wrists. She leaned down towards him. 'Are you all right, Da?'

He didn't look at her. 'Leave me,' he said bitterly. 'Go look after your man over there.'

Nora flushed and bit her lip, fighting back the tears. Instinctively she knew that her father's vindictiveness was born out of shame, that she, a slip of a girl, should be seeming to fight his battles for him. It was also something of a bravado display for the other men, but its spitefulness hurt her deeply. She turned away and crossed to the kitchen range, her back to the men at the table. Bryce made a move to follow her, but Harrison shook his head. He knew that if Bryce tried to comfort the girl Tracey would react.

Harrison picked up his knife and fork and began to eat, the others slowly followed suit. Nora composed herself and returned to the table with the thickened sauce and sat down opposite Bryce. He smiled at her, trying to see into her eyes. She looked at him across the table. It was an intensely private moment, a moment of deep understanding and passion. Nora lowered her head and ate her food.

Harrison ate automatically. The ham was good, but there were other things on his mind. He kept a wary eye on Tracey. His feet were still tied to the chair and he could not cause much trouble even if he decided to try and use the knife he was eating with.

No, there was something else that prickled his scalp, made him uneasy. He didn't try to analyse it; it was atavistic, almost primitive and he'd felt it before. He glanced towards the kitchen window. At that precise moment it shattered, bursting inward, showering the floor with glass, the bullet lodged in the wall opposite. A fraction of a second later he heard the rifle shot. Harrison rolled to the floor, yelling to the others.

'Down, get down!'

There was a moment of frozen horror before the others reacted. Harrison grabbed Tracey and toppled him over in the chair, pulling him down beside him. Then he crawled to the wall and sat there quietly for a moment. He saw the rifle resting where he had left it, leaning against his chair. He tensed, then sprang upward, leaping across the room, grabbing the rifle as he rolled back on to the floor, removing

350

himself from the line of fire. The momentum carried him to the opposite wall. He slid along it to the window, then eased himself up and peered through a chink in the curtain. He could see nothing; it was dark and black outside, no trace of moonlight.

Another shot crashed through the window, the bullet thudding into almost exactly the same spot as the first. Harrison recoiled against the wall. Tynan could have killed him, but he hadn't. Tynan's voiced echoed hollowly from outside in the trees.

'Didn't think I'd let you get away, did you, Harrison?'

Crawford stared at the American, his eyes wide. 'It's Tynan,' he said incredulously.

Bryce put his arm around Nora protectively. 'How the hell did he know we were here?'

Harrison didn't answer. He waved them to be silent, prepared himself, then leapt up on one knee and fired off six quick rounds, the shots almost blended together, the noise in the confined space of the room shattering. The acrid smell of gunpowder caused Nora to cough. It was silent, no response from outside, then Tynan's voice again, slightly mocking.

'That's right, Harrison, only me. Not bad odds would you say?'

Bryce looked at Harrison puzzled. 'What does he mean?'

Harrison ignored him. He looked at Tracey. 'The ammunition. Where is it?'

Tracey didn't answer at once, then he jerked his head at Nora. 'You'd better ask her,' he said contemptuously.

Harrison turned to her.

'I'll get it,' she said.

Bryce held on to her. 'You stay here, tell me.'

Nora was about to protest, but she could see his determination. 'In the hall,' she said. 'There's a small dresser; there's a box in the drawer.'

Bryce crawled through the arch under the beading into the hall.

Crawford banged his fist on to the floor and swore. He looked at Harrison.

'Do you believe him? Is he the only one out there?'

Harrison nodded. 'Yeah, I believe him.'

'Then it's three against one. We could kill him.'

Harrison almost smiled. He lifted the rifle and offered it to Crawford. 'Do you want to try?'

Bryce crawled back into the room and gave Harrison the box of ammunition.

Harrison quickly reloaded.

Bryce watched him contemplatively. 'He must have thought I would come back.'

'Maybe,' Harrison said. He glanced at Nora. 'Do you have any transportation?'

She looked quickly at Bryce. 'Just the lorry.'

'We need a diversion,' Harrison said. 'Can you drive?'

Bryce stared at him incredulously. 'I don't believe this. You're not going to involve her.'

Harrison turned on him, snarling. 'She's already involved, for chrissake.' He pointed out of the window. 'Why do you think he's out there?'

Bryce didn't answer.

Harrison gripped him by the jacket, pulling him close. 'Because he knew that when someone was injured, we would come here – we had nowhere else to go. Now,' he said very quietly, 'she's our only chance of getting out of here and you are going to make that clear.'

Bryce stared into Harrison's cold eyes. He removed his hand from his jacket. 'I don't know if it's worth that price.' He turned away from the American and crawled across the room to Nora, leaning his back against the wall.

She gripped his arm urgently. 'Peter, I don't mind.'

352

He closed his eyes. She shook him. 'Listen to me. I want you to escape. I want you to go back to England.'

He was surprised; he looked at her puzzled. 'Why? I won't see you.' He grasped her arms. 'Nora, I love you. It doesn't matter about getting back any more. If I stay here I can continue to see you. We could find a place. We'd be together, don't you understand?'

Nora looked at him with an intensity of emotion that he found impossible to resist. He put his arms around her, holding her tightly, oblivious to the others in the room. He kissed her hair.

Nora knew what she had to do. She pushed him tenderly away. 'Look, Peter, this is only the beginning for us.' She put her hand to his unshaven cheek. 'Do you believe me?'

He gripped her hand. 'I believe you.'

'Then believe this, darling. I could not live here in Ireland with you.' He glanced at Tracey. 'Oh, it's not him,' she said impatiently. 'I don't care what he thinks, or anyone else for that matter.' She pulled him close. 'It's what you'll think, Peter. Suppose,' she continued, 'the American and Crawford got back and you're still here. I'd know that you stayed because of me. I'd see it in your eyes. I know that you'd regret it, maybe not today, maybe not tomorrow, but soon and for the rest of your life . . .'

He tried to protest.

'I know I would,' she said firmly. She looked at his face, seeing his anguish, knowing she had spoken the truth. 'Let me drive the lorry away.'

He shook his head. 'No, it's too dangerous; he might kill you.'

She looked at her father, who had crawled over near the fireplace. She turned back to Peter. 'If I drive that lorry . . .' She put her finger to his lips to prevent his interrupting. '. . . if I drive that lorry away from here, I shall not come back.' He did not understand. She smiled. 'Peter, listen to me. It's dark out there. I can go through the hall window and drive off before he even knows there is a lorry.' She rushed on. 'I meant what I said. I won't come back here ever. I can drive straight down to Dun Laoghaire and get the boat from there first thing in the morning to England.' She stopped for a moment and held his hand tightly. 'Don't you see, when you get back I'll be there waiting for you.'

He looked at her, remembering the first time he'd seen her in the wood, leaning over him when he'd recovered consciousness. Her eyes now were the same: compassionate, tender. He realized for the first time just how much he loved her.

'Do you have money?' he asked.

She nodded. 'Yes, upstairs. It's mine, it was my mother's.'

He made up his mind. 'Contact my mother when you get to England.' He pulled a pencil and a scrap of paper from his tunic pocket and scribbled down the address. 'You'll find her here.' He smiled at Nora. 'Tell her what's happened and give her this,' he pulled a signet ring from his finger. 'She'll look after you.' He paused. 'She's a nice old girl and I think you'll like her.'

Harrison had seen enough. He slid over to the table, grabbed two big plates of food and handed them to Bryce and Nora.

'OK. Eat this.'

Bryce looked at the food. 'What for?'

Harrison grinned. 'Listen, nobody does anything until our bellies are full.'

He glanced at Crawford. 'That goes for you too.'

Harrison picked up a fork and began to eat. 'Besides, I hate to see good food go to waste.'

\*　　\*　　\*

354

Harrison slipped inside the barn and stood by the door, his back to the wall, listening. No sound broke the stillness of the night, but Tynan was out there. He could feel his presence. He didn't know whether the diversion was going to work. Knowing Tynan, he doubted it. There was a growing inevitability about Tynan's pursuit, and a wriggling germ of knowledge at the back of Harrison's mind that told him the hunt would not end here. But he had to try and divert Tynan away from them, if not for himself, at least for the others.

Quietly, methodically, he saddled the three horses, then bound their hooves with the loose strips of material Nora had given him. He crossed the barn and stood by the door, opening it fractionally. Nothing moved. It was unnaturally quiet. He slid outside and along the wooden wall of the barn until he was as close to the house as he could get. He ran, a dark shadow flitting silently across the yard. The door to the outhouse off the kitchen was unlocked. He slipped inside. Bryce gripped his arm.

'You OK?' he whispered.

'Yeah, fine. Lock the door.'

Bryce did so and they crossed the room and went into the kitchen. The others were waiting. Harrison took the rifle from Crawford.

'Horses are saddled. We walk them until I tell you to mount up. Got that?'

Bryce and Crawford indicated their assent.

Harrison turned to Nora. 'OK. It's your turn now.'

She glanced at her father. He'd been pulled up on the seat again and his wrists bound. 'You won't harm him?'

'He stays here,' Harrison replied.

Crawford grabbed the American by the arm. 'We can't just leave him here. All he's got to do is tell whoever comes through that door and our escape route is known.'

Harrison shook his arm free and pushed Crawford away. 'Keep your hands off me, Crawford,' he said quietly, the threat barely concealed. Nora realized the danger to her father if the quarrelling developed any further. She crossed the room and knelt down in front of him. He stared sullenly at the floor, avoiding her eyes.

'Listen to me, Da. I'm going to England. I know what you think of Peter, but there's nothing here for me now.' She gripped his hard horny hand. 'He's my man, Da. He's the man I want. Please don't spoil it for me.'

His expression didn't alter and her voice hardened. 'If you try to stop us, prevent Peter and the others from getting away by informing the Garda, then they'll be all over this place, Da. They'll want to know where I am.' She paused, looking round the room at Crawford and Harrison, realizing she must convince them. She turned back to her father. 'Then there's the arms, Da. Suppose they found them. You would be finished, in prison – that's if you were lucky enough to get to prison.'

The threat was there, unspoken yet implicit. Tracey looked at her this time, searching her face, seeing only her implacable determination. He glanced round at the others, who were watching, then turned to Harrison. He cleared his throat. 'You have my word. I'll say nothin'.' He paused, then looked at Bryce. 'But you better not just be stringing her along. You look after her or one day I'll be on your doorstep.'

Bryce nodded gravely. 'I'll look after her, Tracey.'

Harrison picked up the rifle. 'OK. Let's go.'

'I'll be all right,' Nora whispered to her father. She kissed him lightly on the cheek then stood up.

Harrison took her by the arm and led her towards the beaded curtain. 'Try to make as little noise as possible. We won't move until we hear the engines start up. Once you are started, move out fast. After that I don't care how much noise you make. Remember we are all supposed to be in that truck.' He looked into her eyes. They were unafraid. He put his hand on her slim shoulder. 'Good luck.' She watched him cross the room back to Bryce.

'It's up to you,' Harrison said quietly.

Bryce didn't acknowledge the remark. He made his way awkwardly to Nora and led her through the beaded curtain into the hallway. He held her tightly for a moment, then gently pushed her away.

'Now listen carefully, Nora. What you are doing is no game. If you get away safely and reach England it may not be possible for you to come back for years. Are you sure you want to go through with it?' She gripped his shoulders. 'Of course I do, Peter, I love you . . .'

'I love you too, my darling, but this is a big decision and you are very young. You may change your mind.'

She kissed him, holding him tight, trying to make him feel her love, her total commitment. 'I shall never change my mind about you,' she whispered in his ear. 'Never.'

In the semi-darkness of the hall he could see her eyes glistening. He kissed her once more, then went over to the window and looked outside. He could just see the dim shape of the lorry parked opposite the front door. Nora grabbed her coat from the peg in the hall, knotted a scarf under her chin and picked up her bag then crossed to his side. He took her hand.

'If there is only Tynan out there, then he will be positioned to cover the side door and this one. He won't be able to see this window. Keep down. Take as much time as you need to get into the lorry, but be sure to get in from this side, away from the woods. OK?'

She nodded. 'Yes, I'll be all right.'

He had a sudden thought. 'Have you got the keys?'

She waved them under his nose. 'Stop worrying, Peter. Now you get back with the others and be ready to go when I leave.'

He knelt down by the sash window and helped her to slowly inch it up. She kissed him once then slid quietly over the sill into the yard. He held on to her hand until she slipped from his grasp. He watched her movement silently, the tension making him sweat.

Nora reached the corner of the narrow porch and looked up towards the woods to her left. She hesitated a moment, then ran for the side of the lorry, waiting for the bullet to strike her. The sixteen yards seemed to widen, stretching endlessly, she reached out, straining to get to its cover. She collided into the side of the lorry and sat down abruptly on the cobbles of the yard.

She could hardly believe it. She was alive, unhurt. She lifted herself up and slowly gripped the handle to the cab. It squeaked fractionally, then opened. She clambered quickly inside. The familiar smell of leather and farm produce assailed her nostrils. She inserted the key into the ignition and gave the accelerator a few pumps. 'Please,' she whispered to herself, 'please start.' She turned the key. The sound of the starter whined, growled, causing the chickens in the roost to cackle, then it engaged. She pumped more petrol in, pushed the gear into first and released the clutch. The lorry jerked forward, the wheels skidding momentarily on the moisture of the yard. Nora moved through into second and the lorry shot towards the gate – my God! It was still locked, she clenched her eyes shut for an instant as the vehicle crashed through it, splintering the wood, tossing it aside. Then she turned the wheel frantically. The lorry bounced off the grassy embankment bordering the lane then trundled off down it. The lights flicked on, then disappeared as the lorry descended the hill towards Powerscourt.

Gradually the sound of its engine faded. The wood remained silent.

They left Tracey still tied to the chair near the kitchen range. He would be able to work his way across to the table and make use of the knives to cut himself loose eventually. What he did after that was in the lap of the gods, though Bryce could not see him risking the arms he had stashed in the barn by exposing them. He knew Nora meant what she said, and so did Tracey.

Harrison made sure that no light from the kitchen escaped through into the outhouse, then he edged the door open slightly.

'I'll go first,' he whispered to Bryce. 'Crawford, you help him over to the barn as soon as I've got there.' He scanned the deep shadows of the yard carefully. He could see nothing, not that he expected to, even if Tynan was still out there. He slipped through the door and ran across the short space to the barn, flattening himself against the wall. He slid along it and through the half-opened door. He waited. Moments later Crawford and Bryce joined him. The horses moved restlessly, aware of their presence. Harrison took the reins of his horse and Crawford and Bryce did the same, following Harrison towards the door of the barn. The muffled hooves made very little noise. Harrison looked behind him at the others; they were ready, just waiting for him.

He opened the barn door fully and led his horse out into the yard. He turned left away from the lane across a field, skirting the trees that ran up the lower slopes of Tonduff. The horses made no sound on the soft spongy turf. Harrison stopped and listened intently. All he could hear was the animals' breathing; no sound disturbed the woods to his right.

'OK. We mount up now,' he whispered to Bryce. He helped him into the saddle as gently as he could. He did not want the carefully bound wound to break open. Bryce took the reins from him. 'You OK?' Harrison asked.

Bryce nodded. 'I'm fine.'

Crawford had already mounted and Harrison swung into the saddle and led them up towards the crest and War Hill.

Tynan waited until the last sound of the departing horsemen had faded, then gently he dug his heels into the flanks of the horse and emerged from the edge of the woods. It had worked; he had flushed them out. Now the hunt could begin again in earnest, three men pursued by one until the kill was executed. It was perfect, just the way he wanted it . . .

The telephone call had come late, but it was the one he had been waiting for. Gehler's death had been a blow. He of all the people at the meeting had given him the most confidence. When, later, he'd had the opportunity to get to know Gehler better, they had discovered much in common.

Gehler's earlier struggles in Austria to found the National Socialist Movement and his imprisonment after the death of Dollfuss, the Austrian Chancellor, appealed to Quinn; their struggles had been similar in some ways and it seemed an alliance would suit them both. Like Quinn, Gehler had never really trusted Driscoll. He was too much of a political animal, an opportunist. Lynch might prove extremely useful militarily, but he had been Quinn's natural enemy for too long for it to be easily forgotten. The last time he had spoken to Gehler had been to set up a rendezvous for his messenger.

Now that Gehler was dead that rendezvous had assumed much greater significance. He needed to know how and why Gehler had been killed. Whatever the circumstances, his death could have far-reaching effects. Gehler had spoken more than once of his close relationship with Hitler.

The telephone call had revealed the plan for the escape from K Lines. When news reached him of its success Quinn activated the agreed arrangement. He left almost at once.

The boarding hall at Dun Laoghaire was cold and crowded and Colonel Bryce glanced at his watch for the third time. Corrigan was late. Bryce was anxious to get on the ship into the warmth of the smoke room. Ireland seemed particularly unwelcome on this cold, bleak morning; or perhaps it was his abhorrence of last night's events that made him want to be away from it all, back where he felt more at home, more secure. He was too old for this sort of thing.

He saw the tall, heavy figure of Corrigan pushing his way through the crowds to his position near the newspaper seller. He raised an arm and Corrigan nodded, seeing him.

'Sorry I'm late,' he said a little breathlessly, 'but we ran into problems with Lynch.'

The two men began to walk slowly through the hall towards the pier.

'What sort of problems?' Bryce enquired.

'Had trouble removing him,' Corrigan said shortly.

Bryce decided to tread as delicately as he could. 'Really,' he commented.

Corrigan smiled, recognizing the deliberate diplomacy. 'Yes,' he said. 'Nothing the department couldn't handle; mostly political.'

Bryce raised an eyebrow.

'He had friends in high places,' Corrigan explained. 'However, he can't cause any more problems. I hear your job went well.'

'Not as well as I'd have liked,' Bryce said. 'I was interrupted and had to finish it too early.'

It was Corrigan's turn to tread carefully. 'Yes,' he said. 'I heard about the woman.'

Bryce stopped as they reached the pier, gazing out over the grey choppy water, the gulls squawking noisily, looking for any titbits thrown over the side.

'Something was planned, Corrigan, something big. Driscoll was going to tell me about it when I had to kill him.'

The Irishman rubbed his hands together. 'God, it's cold this morning.' He looked at Bryce, who was staring contemplatively at the ferry. The hull was beginning to rust badly in several places.

'We must have knocked it on the head. Driscoll is dead; so is Gehler. Lynch you don't have to worry about; we've had him taken out of the command structure. As of now he is on enforced leave of absence. If and when he is allowed back it will be in a position where he can cause no harm. That leaves Hemmrich, the German Ambassador, and he is effectively isolated.'

'Maybe,' Bryce said. 'Maybe you're right, Noel, but I don't like loose ends.'

'You mean Quinn?'

'Yes Quinn. He caused us more damage than any of the others. I can't prove it, but I'm pretty sure he was responsible for the two crashes on Mount Brandon.'

Corrigan put a hand on his shoulder. 'Don't worry too much. We'll be keeping a close eye on his activities. Now you'd better go or you'll miss your boat.'

Bryce turned and looked at him, smiling. 'Thanks Noel.

Sorry my work spilled over on to your patch. We'll keep you informed of any further developments.'

They walked together down the pier towards the gangway into the ferry. Bryce noticed the sign saying 'British Servicemen only'. He smiled. 'I didn't think we were allowed in Ireland in uniform?'

'You're not.' Corrigan looked at the sign. 'That's just there to facilitate the quick despatch of British Servicemen in mufti. A lot of Irishmen have joined the British Army. Officially it doesn't exist.'

'A bit like me,' Bryce said dryly.

'A bit like you,' Corrigan agreed.

They shook hands. 'I'll be in touch, Noel. Try and get to London some time.'

'I will, but not while the bloody Germans are dropping their bombs.'

They parted company, Corrigan walking back down the pier, Bryce finding himself a comfortable seat in the warmest part of the ship.

He saw the pretty dark-haired young girl staring out of the window at the distant shape of the Wicklow Mountains as they pulled clear of the Irish coast. He wondered why she didn't have any luggage, but it slipped from his mind as he relaxed drowsily with his second glass of whisky.

Nora couldn't sleep, although her eyes felt sore and tired. She watched the mountains fade into the horizon until she could see them no longer. Only then did she leave the window and find herself a seat.

The middle-aged man opposite was fast asleep, the small glass still clenched in his hand. Nora leaned over and took it from his grasp, then put it on the narrow table between them. She closed her eyes. Dear God, please let him get safely away, please.

The weather had gradually deteriorated, with cloud masses wrapping themselves round the mountain tops and boiling down the steep rocky slopes like grey treacle sliding down the side of a suet pudding. In the weird half light progress was slow, but Harrison had no intention of sacrificing the high ground so long as he could continue south. Bryce was cold, but although his injured leg was stiff it had not reopened. Nora had done a good job. He wondered where she was, whether she'd managed to board the boat all right. He had to get back now. He couldn't stay in Ireland without her. In a way that was good. The temptation to stay here with her, passively accept his internment and not face combat, had always been there, lurking at the back of his mind, chipping away at his resolve to escape. He turned suddenly and looked back past Crawford, who was following him. The visibility was poor, not more than a hundred yards, but it cleared momentarily and just for an instant he could see right along the ridge they were traversing. Climbing the side of a gully he thought he saw the wraithlike figure of a horseman; then the mists decended again, rolling up around the figure like huge bundles of cotton wool, and he was gone.

Bryce faced front again, he could feel the cold sweat breaking out on his face and under his arms. Was it Tynan, or was it just his imagination, another product of his own nightmare? He didn't know; he couldn't be sure. He stared at the mane of his horse, concentrating his attention on something that was real, touching it with his hand. It was as soft as silk, yet freezingly cold. He shivered, trying to shake off the fear that tormented him, patting the neck of the animal, stroking it. He found it strangely comforting and began to feel better.

By early afternoon they were descending to cross the road in the Vale of Glendalough. They emerged from beneath the cloud base and almost at once it began to rain, or, rather, it began to rain alongside them. Harrison had seen the phenomenon before in Wyoming, but it was completely new to Bryce and Crawford. The downpour was falling in a solid sheet almost alongside them, yet not touching them at all. The boundary line of the rainfall swept down the side of the mountain into the Vale and up the other side. The leaden blanket hung there, the ground below it shining and wet, while the other side of the rigid line remained untouched, dry. Then the wind caught it. Grey tendrils suddenly flicked out, advancing like an army down the mountain, and they too were engulfed, rain bouncing off their rubber oilskins and peaked caps.

They crossed the road by mid-afternoon and climbed up the edge of Mullacour. While the going was heavy, the rain had driven the mist away and Harrison was relieved: at least he could see where he was leading these inexperienced horsemen. From time to time he would glance behind to check that they were OK, and he also took the opportunity to scan the terrain. It was empty, desolate, no sign of life. They hadn't even seen a car on the road. Maybe Tynan had gone after the truck. But Harrison didn't believe it, not inside, not in his gut. The old twist of fear still nagged and warned.

They entered a tall dripping pine forest and Harrison found a trail that made the going easier. There were places they could have stopped and used as a camp site but Harrison wanted to push on as far as he could while there was still daylight. The winter day was short and it would be dark by five o'clock. The pines thinned out gradually and they emerged on a high cleft of the mountain overlooking the valley of Glenmalure. Below them in the upper reaches of the valley Harrison could see some buildings. He shielded his eyes and stared at them closely. They were built of granite stone from the mountain and there was a courtyard or square in front. Even from this distance he could see they were empty and crumbling. Harrison pointed and began to lead them down. The others were wet and tired, grateful that the day was nearly over, that they could remove their aching backsides from the creaking saddles. Slowly, wearily the three horsemen descended from the mountain to the grey stone line of buildings. The horses finally clattered into the square, the noise of their hooves magnified by the confines of the buildings. It was only then that Harrison realized that it had once been an army barracks.

He reined to a stop, and it was quiet again, just the soft patter of rain hissing on to the broken flags of the courtyard. Bryce looked round him at the glassless empty sockets of the windows. They were like blank eyes gazing curiously from the past.

Harrison dismounted. 'Come on,' he said. 'Let's find some cover and heat some food.'

The rusty pot-bellied stove in the middle of the long room glowed red in the darkness. The three men crouched around it, glad of its warmth, their oddly distorted shadows leaping up and down the crumbling walls. Harrison had a pot on top of the stove, heating some more of the canned stew, while Crawford was studying the map with the aid of a torch.

Harrison stirred the stew. It smelt delicious. 'Can you see the Blackstairs Mountains south of us?' he asked.

Crawford didn't look up. 'Yes.'

'We'll cross the road while it's dark and move up into them tomorrow.'

Bryce saw something white lying on the floor near the wall. 'What then?' he asked, picking it up.

366

Harrison continued to stir, mixing in a can of beans. 'After that the high ground peters out, so we move cross country. Hit the coast somewhere south of Wexford.'

Bryce was staring at the yellowing pages of the calendar he had picked up. 'Nineteen seventeen,' he said.

Crawford looked up from his map. 'What?'

'The date on this,' Bryce said, 'nineteen seventeen.' They fell silent, affected by the emptiness, the desolation of the barracks, just the sound of Harrison's spoon grating against the metal pan.

Bryce tore his eyes from the flickering shadows beyond the pool of red light glowing from the stove. 'Christ, this place gives me the shivers.'

'You'd be colder out there,' Harrison said laconically.

Bryce glanced at him irritated. 'I didn't mean that.'

Harrison smiled . . . 'I know.'

A door suddenly banged in the wind, the noise loud, echoing through the empty building. They all sat perfectly still, listening. There was nothing else, just the occasional creak of timber, wind sighing through an empty window.

'Do you think we lost him?' Bryce said suddenly.

Crawford folded the map and tucked it into his pocket. 'Must have done, otherwise we would have seen him.'

Harrison proceeded to serve the food, doling out three portions on the metal plates. 'He's out there.' He offered the food to Crawford, who was staring at him.

'Have you seen him?' he asked.

Harrison shook his head. 'No – take the food.'

Crawford accepted it. 'Then how?'

'I know Tynan.' Harrison gave Bryce the other portion, then put a pan of water on the stove and stirred in some condensed milk. The others watched him silently, not touching their food, absorbing the implications of his remark. Harrison waved a bag of loose tea. 'Anyone for tea?' he asked.

Nobody responded. Harrison took his plate of food. 'Come on, eat up, if he is out there he won't try anything tonight.'

Crawford stared into the red-hot stove. 'How can you be sure?'

Harrison chewed on the meat, not answering immediately. He swallowed it, then looked at Crawford and Bryce.

'He wants the chase,' he said slowly, 'to see how far we can get before he decides to make the kill.' Harrison continued to eat. The others listened to the night and bunched closer to the stove.

It was still dark when they broke camp next morning and mounted up in the barracks square. Bryce was glad to be out of the place. He hadn't slept well, too many extraneous noises had him wide awake and listening, wondering whether Tynan would try to jump them in the dark. The place was haunted and it was not just his overwrought imagination – he could feel the presence of the long-since-departed British soldiers who had once stood perilous guard at the end of this lonely valley, waiting to be shot at from the unfriendly mountains surrounding them.

They clattered out of the square just as the faintest glimmer of light was beginning to break over the ridge to the east. The light increased quickly, and the morning dawned fine and dry. They made good progress through some heavy timbered country before reaching the first road. Harrison led them down the steeply-wooded slope, the horses slithering much of the way on their haunches, the riders straining backward in the saddle, hauling on the reins to keep the animal's head high and preserve their balance. When the ground levelled out at the bottom Harrison dismounted and indicated the others should do the same. They led the horses quietly through the undergrowth bordering the road and stopped out of sight behind some bushes. Harrison held up his hand for silence and, faintly at first, growing stronger, they heard the sound of a car approaching. It trundled by, an old Ford not going anywhere too fast, a farmer out early on his way to market. Gradually it faded out of hearing.

'OK,' Harrison said. 'We lead the horses to the other side.' He looked at Bryce and Crawford for confirmation. They indicated their understanding.

Bryce was happy to be out of the saddle for as long as possible; already his lower regions ached abominably. Harrison took the reins of his horse and led it towards the road. Bryce and Crawford followed. Nothing disturbed the peace of the valley except the sounds of their own progress and they quickly mounted up again on the other side and began the long haul back to the high ground.

They continued to make excellent progress throughout the morning, crossing a number of roads, using the same procedure as before, and always heading south. Occasionally they would have to detour away from buildings or isolated cottages, but for the most part there was little to disturb them and their spirits rose the farther they went without a sign of pursuit. By afternoon they had crossed the river Slaney at the southernmost point of the Wicklow Mountains and climbed into the Blackstairs. The sun had now crossed its winter zenith and poured its light directly into their eyes as they continued south. Harrison felt good. Their progress had been spectacular after the delays and extreme conditions they had suffered since their escape from The Curragh two days before. Was it only two days? It felt like an age since he had crossed that compound wondering whether his big talk about lifting the heavy gate clear of its hinges would work. But they'd done it and the horses were standing up well to the mountains.

There remained Tynan. He'd checked the terrain behind them from time to time, but if Tynan was back there he was well back and out of sight. The clear visibility would undoubtedly hamper him and keep him at arm's length. Harrison didn't believe that he would let them go, but if he intended to make his move in the mountains, he would have to do it soon.

He heard the bolt of a rifle click as a round was moved into the breech. His hand flew to the rolled oilskin behind the saddle where he had put the weapon he'd taken from Tracey at the farm.

'It's not there,' Crawford said.

Harrison automatically reined in his horse and looked behind him. Bryce also had stopped and was staring incredulously at Crawford. The young fair-haired pilot was pointing the rifle directly at them, his finger curled around the trigger. He held the gun as if he knew how to use it.

'I took it last night,' he said. 'After you went to sleep.' A faint smile played around his lips. 'That's a piece of wood rolled up in your oilskin. I was glad it didn't rain today.'

'Put the bloody thing down, Crawford,' Bryce said, 'and stop playing silly buggers.'

Crawford's smile evaporated and he lifted the rifle menacingly at Bryce's chest. 'Don't patronise me, Bryce, otherwise I'll have to use this thing on you and that would be a pity after coming this far.'

Harrison slowly edged his horse round with his knees, keeping his hands well in sight. 'What's this all about, Crawford? Why the gun?'

The barrel swung unerringly on to his chest and Harrison stopped the horse.

'That's better,' Crawford said. 'Now no more questions.' He jerked the rifle towards the west. 'We go that way.'

Harrison swore. 'You're crazy! We need to head south and east to make the coast.'

Crawford's voice hardened. 'We're not going to the coast. Now move.'

Harrison looked at Bryce. 'Ah shit!' he said expressively. He jerked savagely at the reins of his horse and moved off in the direction Crawford had indicated. Bryce followed and Crawford closed up behind, keeping the rifle trained on the two men in front. Slowly they headed towards the setting sun.

Tynan lowered his binoculars, staring out over the escarpment of the mountain below him at the three tiny specks traversing the ridge. He pulled his rifle from his back and checked the breech and telescopic sight, training it on the last of the three riders. Satisfied, he slung it back over his shoulder and dug his heels into his horse, moving down the rock-strewn slope after the flyers.

The sun had just dipped below the crest of the mountains, casting giant shadows across the lake towards the far slope. The water, already cut off from the light, was leaden, almost black. Harrison had stopped his animal when he saw the lake far below, surrounded on three sides by the mountains. It was about two miles long, possibly a mile wide at its widest point, with an island in the middle on which stood a small stone cottage, smoke curling slowly up from the chimney in the still cold air. A tiny car was parked incongruously by the shore of the lake.

Harrison looked back at Crawford. The rifle was still trained on him. 'Is that where we are going?'

Crawford did not reply. He jerked the rifle at Harrison, indicating that he should continue. The American turned resignedly, urging his horse down towards the lake.

Quinn emerged from the cottage and trained his binoculars on the three horsemen. He was able to distinguish the RAF caps they were wearing. He concentrated on the last rider and saw the rifle aimed at the two men in front. He smiled.

Crawford had done well. He looked up at the ridge. The sun had gone. It would be dark before Crawford reached the jetty and that would give Bryce a chance to make a break. It was going to be tight and Crawford would need help.

He went back into the cottage, picking up a hand gun and sticking it into the waistband of his trousers, raced back out again and ran down to the small wooden pier, untying the rowing boat and pulling as quickly as he could for the shore. The water was like black plate glass, but in spite of the chill he was soon sweating with the exertion, his breath hanging like steam in front of him on the cold winter air. He glanced behind him a couple of times, making adjustments, trying to steer as direct a course for the other jetty as he could. By the time he'd reached it the riders were closer, but only just visible as the light faded from the mountain valley. He slung the rope painter round a short wooden post and then ran for the shore, dragging the pistol from his waistband. The turf was wet and spongy and his shoes and trouser legs were soon soaked, but he kept going, the horsemen were only a couple of hundred yards away by now.

Harrison could see him coming. He cursed silently under his breath, realizing that his chance had gone. There was still enough light for Crawford to see him clearly, and it would be suicide to try and make a run for it now.

'Try it if you want to, Harrison,' Crawford called out. 'I don't need you. You're just so much excess weight.' It was as if he had been reading Harrison's thoughts.

Harrison could almost feel the rifle trained on his back. His muscles tensed, waiting for the bone-crushing impact of a bullet. He rode carefully and made no sudden moves.

Quinn reached them, holding the pistol on Harrison, pressing it into his thigh on the bone. He strode alongside the horse, not looking at Crawford. 'OK. You cover Bryce. I've got this one. The boat's by the pier.'

They squelched over the last few hundred yards. Bryce felt

372

sick, totally nonplussed by the events of the last couple of hours. He couldn't fathom why Crawford was doing this. It made no sense, yet clearly it had been well planned. This rendezvous was no accident, but who the other man was he had no idea except that he seemed to be Irish.

They were forced to dismount when they reached the shoreline and Crawford used the straps on the oilskins to tie their hands. Then they were marched up the pier and bundled into the rowing boat. Bryce sat slumped in the stern, Harrison alongside him where Crawford could cover them with the rifle while the Irishman rowed. It was almost completely dark now and Bryce was exhausted. It was eerie, the boat gurgling forward into the blackness, the only light a pinprick flickering through the cottage window, the only sound the water beneath the boards and the oars slapping into the lake. They seemed suspended, drifting aimlessly through the black void, unreal. Bryce felt sure he would wake up at any moment and find it was only a bad dream.

The bottom of the boat scraped the shingle of the shoreline and ground to a halt. Quinn leapt from the boat and dragged it a little way up the shore.

'All right,' he said to Crawford. 'Bring them ashore now.'

Bryce stumbled out of the boat, finding it difficult to keep his balance with his hands tied behind his back; Harrison followed, wondering whether there was still a chance for a break in the darkness, but immediately found a gun jammed into his ribs.

'That way,' Quinn said, indicating the light from the cottage.

It was a fire. The warmth from the single downstairs room of the cottage enveloped them as Quinn kicked open the door and shoved Harrison inside. Quinn waited until Bryce and Crawford had followed, then he struck a match and lit an oil lamp, adjusting the wick after he had replaced its glass chimney.

Quinn picked up some thin strong ropes lying over a chair and threw them at Crawford.

'Tie him up,' he said, indicating Bryce. He pushed Harrison down on to the floor and began securing his arms and legs. Harrison studied his face curiously.

'I guess you were expecting us,' he said dryly.

Quinn tightened the ropes, cutting them cruelly into Harrison's wrists. He smiled, 'You might say that.' He looked across at Bryce to see that he was effectively tied up. 'Any trouble?' he asked Crawford.

The pilot straightened up, stretching himself. 'No, not once we got away from the farm.'

'The farm?' Quinn repeated tonelessly.

Crawford glanced at Bryce. 'We had to take him there. He was injured on a firing range. He knew the girl. It was where he was picked up originally.'

Quinn crossed the room and took a kettle from the fire, filling it with water from a bucket standing near the table. 'What happened? Was she alone?'

'No. She lived with her father, a man called Tracey.'

Quinn had his back to Crawford. He did not react. 'Tracey?' he said.

'Yes. We left him tied up. The girl got away in a lorry to create a diversion.' Crawford paused. 'We were followed from the camp by Tynan, the Provost-Marshal.'

'Just Tynan?' Quinn asked quietly.

'Yes, he must have been on horseback too. Otherwise he would never have found us.'

Quinn placed the kettle on the fire and turned to face Crawford. 'Any sign of him since?'

'No, nothing, not since he shot at us at the farm. I think we lost him.'

Quinn crossed to the window and pulled the curtain, then shot the iron bolt across the door. The others watched him silently. He glanced at Crawford. 'No point in taking any

374

chances.' He masked the cold anger he felt inside. Tracey had said nothing about the Englishman's stay at the farm. Clearly something had developed between Nora and Bryce, which was why the old man had been frightened to tell him. More importantly, meetings had taken place there. How much of that had leaked out because of the girl? He would have to pay a visit on Tracey.

The kettle began to boil and he poured the hot water into the tea pot he had prepared and stirred it vigorously. Crawford crossed the room and warmed his hands in front of the fire.

'You're sure about Tynan?' Quinn asked.

Crawford nodded. 'Certain.' He said emphatically, 'No one has seen him since the farm.'

Quinn poured some tea into a china mug and added a spoonful of condensed sweetened milk. He gave it to Crawford and studied him thoughtfully while he drank. 'You told me Gehler had been killed when you telephoned. How?' He kept his voice low.

Crawford glanced at Bryce and Harrison. They were far enough away not to hear. 'I couldn't say much. There wasn't time.'

Quinn nodded understandingly. Crawford continued quietly.

'One of our men killed him, a gunner named Halder. He has confessed to Von Bernstorff and will face a court martial, though apparently it is a formality.'

'Why?'

'Gehler was trying to eliminate him. I know Gehler was concerned about Halder. He couldn't trust him, which was why he gave me a message for you.'

Quinn looked at him sharply. 'Go on.'

Crawford swallowed some of the tea. 'I wasn't the only double agent in K Lines. The British had planted a man in our camp, a Lieutenant Bech. Gehler discovered his

375

existence and had to kill him; unfortunately Halder was a witness.'

Quinn didn't look at Crawford. He watched the two airmen in the corner. The pieces were beginning to fall into place, but Crawford had saved the most vital information till last.

'Before Bech died he told Oberleutnant Gehler that the Irish Government had been negotiating with London.'

Quinn focused on him unblinkingly.

'Apparently the RAF members of the camp,' Crawford continued 'are to be removed from K Lines and placed in another camp at Gormanstown. In fact, the pilots will be transferred to the North; only the other personnel will stay in Ireland. The Oberleutnant instructed me to tell you this directly. He said he could no longer trust Driscoll in view of this information, nor would he risk it through the normal diplomatic channels. He said it was vital.'

Slowly Quinn poured himself some tea, not wanting to reveal his excitement. It was more than vital. It could be the final key. Once Berlin knew of the Irish Government's duplicity they would have the excuse they needed to set the operation in motion. He knew that Gehler had been a personal favourite of the Führer's. Would he not be furious that he had died in Ireland? Killed trying to get the information back to him.

There was also the matter of Driscoll. Had he tried to dupe them all? Did he know of the Irish Government's negotiations with London? He had plenty of ammunition to stir Berlin into action. Perhaps he ought to return with Crawford. He looked at him over the rim of his cup. He was waiting for his reaction. 'The plane will be here at first light. I am to send a signal at midnight to indicate that you have reached the rendezvous with Bryce. Where will he go?'

'To Colditz. We already have several important members of the British establishment in the Prominenten there, and are holding them as hostages. That's why we need Bryce, to use as a lever on his father in MI9. It was Gehler who made the connection, through you, I believe?'

Quinn nodded. 'Yes. He saw the photograph of Colonel Bryce that I took at Mount Brandon.' He looked across at Crawford. 'That's when you were brought in.'

Crawford smiled. 'Gehler had connections in high places. Apparently my orders came right from the top. The Führer insisted that Gehler's idea must be acted upon. The only way to get Bryce out of Ireland and into Germany was by having someone infiltrate the Allied Camp – that was my job. The Luftwaffe dropped me at night by parachute. I was picked up next day and taken to The Curragh. I made contact with Gehler soon after my arrival. The rest you know.'

Quinn made no comment, but the confirmation of Gehler's importance was good news.

Crawford glanced at the two prisoners. 'At dawn you say?'

'That's right. You'd better get some sleep. I'll keep an eye on these. There's a bed upstairs.'

Crawford yawned. 'Is there any food? I've had nothing since this morning.'

'Yes, in the cupboard. Help yourself.'

Crawford pulled out some bread and jam and wolfed it down. Quinn made more tea, thickening it with teaspoonfuls of sweetened milk. He took a mug across the room and offered it to Bryce. 'You'd better drink this.'

Bryce raised his eyebrows. 'Easier said than done.'

Quinn held the mug up to his lips. 'I'll loosen your hands later so that you can eat. Drink this now.'

Bryce swallowed some of the deliciously hot sweet tea, then thanked his captor. 'What's happening?' he asked. 'Where are you taking us?'

Quinn ignored him and turned to Harrison. 'You want some?'

The American was glad to accept. He drank the rest of the tea but asked no questions. He watched the Irishman cutting some bread, his face expressionless.

Bryce leaned across. 'What do you think?' he whispered urgently. 'What's going on?'

Harrison would have shrugged his shoulders if he hadn't been so tightly tied.

'I don't know; could be IRA. Maybe they intend to hold us as hostages, exchange us for some of their prisoners. But you won't get anything out of the Irishman.'

Crawford finished eating and stretched. 'I'll have a lie down now. Will you be all right?'

Quinn glanced at him. 'Yes, get some sleep. I'll call you later.'

Crawford wearily climbed the narrow staircase in the corner of the room while Quinn spread some jam on the bread, then went across to Bryce and released his hands, keeping the pistol on him all the time. He gave him the bread and jam, which he was able to grip awkwardly and hold to his mouth; his fingers were still numb. Quinn repeated the procedure with Harrison after Bryce had finished and was tied again. He was too experienced a hand to allow either of them the chance to get the jump on him. Then he went back to the fire and sat down on a chair, watching them contemplatively. The importance of Gehler could not be minimized, but his death could work in their favour if it helped to put pressure on Berlin to act quickly, initiate Operation Osprey and bring in a German Task Force through Bantry Bay. The meeting at Driscoll's house had been productive in a number of ways, as indeed had the one immediately afterwards between himself and Gehler. Both of them had seen the necessity for positive action. Gehler's recognition of the connection between Colonel Bryce and the pilot in the Allied Camp was valuable. Quinn had known nothing about the Prominenten, but he could see the advantages of having Bryce taken to Germany in case Colonel Bryce became a danger to the operation. The arrangement to have Crawford planted had been made through the German Embassy. Thank God he had been infiltrated. Without him Quinn would still be in the dark as to why Gehler had died and, more importantly, the negotiations between Dublin and London would have remained a secret. Tomorrow he would fly back to Germany. This time he had all the ammunition he needed to precipitate a German reaction.

It was going to be a long hard night, and Quinn did not trouble to wake Crawford. If the Provost-Marshal was out there somewhere then his only hope was to surprise them while they were asleep. Quinn did not feel like entrusting their safety to Crawford, who was exhausted. He gave the two pilots a blanket each and some cushions. Their hands were tied in front of them so they could stretch out on the floor and rest. He stayed alert, sitting in the chair by the fire, the rifle on the crook of his arm, the pistol in his waistband. Whenever he began to feel sleepy he would get up and, keeping well clear of the two men on the floor, go to the door and breathe in some of the cold night air.

Harrison pretended to sleep, watching the Irishman, hoping he might doze or make a mistake. He never did; the IRA leader had been too long involved in terrorist activity to allow himself to be overpowered by a man bound hand and foot. Close to midnight he went to the food cupboard and pulled out a suitcase from the bottom. Harrison saw him open it and put the headphones on. It was a battery-operated short-wave transmitter. Quinn tapped out the coded Morse signal to the *Abwehr* in Berlin, informing them that they were ready for pick-up. Berlin confirmed the rendezvous, then signed off.

Although Harrison could not hear the signal he had learnt one thing: the Irishman was in close liaison with the Nazis. The set was German.

Quinn went back to the door afterwards, always keeping the two flyers in sight. The full moon shone palely over the lake, flattening the outline of the landscape, somehow reducing the perspective, making it appear smaller. The bare trees were etched starkly against the mountainside like needles in a pin cushion. Only his car stood ridiculously out of place by the far shore.

Nothing moved, not even the water reflecting the orb of the moon. He shivered and shut the door, bolting it, then moving back to his chair. He didn't want to leave Ireland. His place was here. But if he could somehow reach Hitler, tell him of Gehler's death and Dublin's treachery, then that was where he could do the most good for his divided country. So that was where he would go.

An hour before first light he woke Crawford and got Harrison and Bryce into the chairs, tying only their feet this time. Breakfast was simple, rudimentary, exactly as before. Bread, butter, jam and hot tea. Even so it tasted good to Bryce, who was ravenous. In spite of the rough floor he had slept. Nor was he as stiff as on previous days. Perhaps he was getting used to it, his body hardening.

Crawford moved away from the two prisoners and spoke quietly to Quinn. 'Did you confirm the rendezvous?'

'Yes, they should be here at first light. We're lucky the weather is good.'

Crawford gripped his arm. 'Thank you for letting me sleep.'

Quinn smiled. 'I don't think I could have woken you anyway. You were dead to the world.' He looked at the two airmen and gave Crawford the rifle. 'Keep an eye on them, especially the American. I'm going outside.'

He walked down to the shore where the rowing boat was

beached and dragged it round to the short jetty. He didn't want any delays once the plane arrived. The sky behind the mountains to the east was already taking shape, a grey light spreading down their slopes. He stopped and watched the rim of the sun slowly poke itself above the uppermost ridge. It was breathtaking, the light constantly changing, growing stronger, turning the vegetation from grey to blue and purple.

Imperceptibly the rising and falling intonation of the aircraft's engines penetrated his consciousness. He shaded his eyes. At first he could see nothing, but gradually the sound grew louder, more insistent, and then he saw the black shadow cross the mountains from the south. He ran to the cottage, crashing back the door, levelling the pistol at the two flyers. 'It's here,' he said to Crawford. 'Release their legs. I'll cover them.'

Crawford handed him the rifle and took the breadknife from the board, slicing through the ropes. Bryce rubbed his ankles and looked at Harrison. They'd both recognized the distinctive sound of German aero engines.

Crawford took the rifle back from the Irishman and Quinn pulled the suitcase containing the radio from the cupboard. He jerked the pistol, indicating the door. 'Outside,' he said.

Harrison stood up stiffly and stretched, feeling pins and needles in his legs. He walked to the door, then outside. At no point did either Crawford or the Irishman fail to have him covered. If he was going to get any opportunity to make a break, someone would have to slip up. The odds against that seemed pretty high.

The plane was circling the lake now and Harrison had identified it. It was a German long-range patrol flying boat, the BV 138, its distinctive high twin tailplanes and German swastikas already visible.

Quinn kept the American under the gun, lugging the

suitcase in his other hand. When they reached the jetty he dumped it in the prow of the boat and ordered Bryce and Harrison to sit in the stern as before.

Crawford was elated, his face shining with excitement. 'You will come with me as far as the plane. I won't be able to row and cover them at the same time.'

Quinn looked at him steadily. 'I'm coming back to Germany with you.'

Crawford was delighted. 'I'm glad,' he said simply. 'Perhaps together we can convince the High Command.'

Quinn smiled at the young man's enthusiasm. 'Get in the boat. Make sure you can always see both of them. This is the trickiest part of the operation.'

The seaplane's engines changed note, throttling back ready for landing. They stopped, watching it touch down. The slim straight lines of the BV 138 hovered briefly above the smooth surface of the lake then settled, the floats cleaving into the water, the engines throwing up a fine white spray. It slowed, then taxied close to the island, halting about two hundred yards way. Through the high perspex canopy above the nose they could see the outline of the pilot. He slid back the window and waved.

Quinn motioned Crawford into the boat, keeping his pistol on the two flyers. Harrison and Bryce exchanged a look, but said nothing. There was nothing to say. It was clear what the intention was and neither of them could see a way to avoid it without committing suicide.

Crawford got down into the prow of the rowing boat and levelled the rifle at them, then Quinn jammed the pistol into his trousers and clambered in himself, throwing the painter into the boat ahead of him, making sure he never masked Crawford's view of the two men. He picked up the oars and pushed off from the jetty, rowing steadily towards the German seaplane.

*    *    *

Tynan had chosen his spot well, intending to pick up his target within a radius of one to two hundred yards of the island. His view could only be obscured in one direction; if they decided to leave the island on the far side, away from the jetty. He regarded that as extremely unlikely, and even so they would come within range once they rowed out of the island's cover.

His position was behind a low ridge, his range about six hundred yards. He had built a small nest of rocks and was lying on his oilskins, the butt of the Mark 1*T(A) tucked securely into his shoulder. The Aldis telescopic sight gave him a perfect target, and the straight-pull Mauser action was very fast, enabling him to get off a round a second. Tynan's angle to the rowing boat was approximately 45 degrees as the hairlines on the sight slowly focused on the man's back.

The two engines of the seaplane were idling gently. The pilot wanted to be away as quickly as he could. His navigator had opened up the hatch behind him and the men in the boat were closing fast. The engine coughed, its pitch altering momentarily.

Crawford glanced behind him, checking their distance and direction. The bullet crashed through the side of his ribcage, puncturing his heart and lungs, its force propelling him over the side of the boat into the lake, carrying the rifle with him.

The second shot hit Quinn square in the back as he strained forward with the oars, rupturing the tissue and causing a massive high-pressure wave through his body. The bullet smashed through the sternum in his chest and thudded weakly into the wood of the boat between Bryce and Harrison. Quinn pitched forward. Only then did the reverberations of the two shots reach them across the lake. Harrison caught Quinn's body as he slumped on to him, blood spattering him from the massive exit wound in his chest.

The German pilot in the seaplane froze for a moment, then screamed a warning to his navigator behind him as he thrust the throttles up and forward. Tynan quickly adjusted his aim. This would be the difficult target. Surprise had gone and already the engines and the floats were throwing up huge amounts of spray as the flying boat surged forward powerfully through the calm waters of the lake. As in most seaplanes, and the BV 138 was no exception, the pilot's cockpit was high above the surface to give him clear visibility, the tall square perspex canopy looking oddly like a greenhouse perched behind the turned-up nose of the fuselage. The pilot's silhouette was perfectly framed, and Tynan fired four more shots in quick succession, aiming as low as possible.

The flying boat was just lifting clear of the lake, the gap between the hull and the surface widening as the bullets penetrated the cockpit. One hit the control column; the pilot instinctively adjusted. The second missed everything, splintering the perspex again as it went out the other side. The third smashed the femur bone in the pilot's thigh and the fourth entered the pilot's body at the hip, severing the femoral artery, rupturing the soft tissue and flesh between his legs and the lower abdomen.

The shock was enormous, although the pilot didn't lose consciousness immediately, clutching the control column in a tight grasp. His body was totally numb below the waist and he could make no adjustments to the rudder bars. He hauled back on the control column, lifting the flying boat higher. He could feel his consciousness slipping from him. The plane veered slightly to port. He tried to compensate, his brain sending signals to his legs which refused to function. The port wing of the plane dipped back towards the lake, skimming just above it. The aircraft stalled, slipped, the wing buried itself in the water and, almost in slow motion, the seaplane began to spin across the surface like a giant catherine wheel, gradually disintegrating. The wings snapped; the engine mountings ripped loose, propellers still whirling, giving them lift, carrying them forward. The tail section detached from the main fuselage as it finally buried itself into the lake, the engines flailing into the water in a hissing cloud of spray some distance ahead.

Nothing remained on the surface but a few sticks of wreckage and an ever-widening pool of oil. The sounds faded, echoing back from the mountains until it was silent again, unnaturally still and calm.

Bryce could not move his eyes from the oilslick. He stared at it fascinated as it slowly spread green and brown, flattening the water, removing the last ripple. Harrison pushed Quinn's body from him, easing him back into the prow of the boat, his blood covering the front of his tunic. He checked the pulse in his neck, knowing him to be dead; but it was automatic, a gesture. He closed his eyes with the palm of his hand, then pulled the two oars that were trailing in the water high into the boat.

Bryce was still staring transfixed at the surface of the lake. Harrison gripped his arm and shook him. 'Come on,' he said. 'Tynan's still out there. We must move.'

Bryce looked at him blankly. He was in shock, but Harrison had no time for niceties. He backhanded him across the face. 'Come on,' he repeated. 'Snap out of it.' He hit him again and Bryce held up his hand weakly to protect himself. Once more the American slapped him hard. This time it had the desired effect. Bryce swore and grabbed his hand tightly.

'Leave me,' he said viciously, his voice harsh, strained.

Slowly Harrison pulled his hand down, releasing his own. 'That's better. Now listen. Tynan's out there watching us this very minute. If he wanted to kill us now he could, don't you see?'

Bryce kept his eyes away from Harrison, trying not to look

at the blood all over his tunic. 'See what?' he said.

Harrison realized what a sickening mess he was in and began to splash water from the lake on to his tunic, wiping some of the blood away.

'Tynan's not finished with us yet. That's why he only killed Crawford and the Irishman.'

Bryce scanned the shoreline, trying to see Tynan. 'He's mad.' He looked at Harrison. 'He must be mad.' He saw the excitement in the American's face, the blood still staining his jacket, and slowly he began to fully comprehend. 'You wanted this!'

Harrison didn't look at him.

'You wanted it as much as he did. This is some kind of game for you, isn't it, with our lives at stake.'

Harrison said nothing. He continued to clean his jacket.

Bryce looked at Quinn's dead body in the prow of the boat, horrified. 'Jesus Christ,' he whispered, half to himself, 'and I thought we were just trying to escape.'

Harrison grabbed at the front of Bryce's tunic, lifting him almost off the seat, his face distorted by anger. 'Listen, Bryce, I've had enough of your bellyachin'. Without you I could have been out of this country by now, in the clear. All this,' he waved an arm at the lake and the oil slick, 'was because of you, because of your connections . . . The Germans wanted you, not me, do you understand?'

Bryce did not react. He knew the American was right. He gazed down at the bottom of the boat.

Harrison let go of him, the anger draining away. 'Look,' he said, 'we still have a chance. Tynan's giving us one.' He looked at the shore, trying to spot some telltale gleam, but there was nothing, just the ridiculous car. He clambered into the stern and found the car keys in Quinn's jacket pocket. He held them under Bryce's face in the palm of his hand, closing them in his fist. He grinned triumphantly at Bryce. 'Come on, Peter, look what I've found.'

Bryce looked up, infected by his enthusiasm. 'How far is it, do you think?'

'I don't know, but we're going to head directly east. The coast can't be be more than twenty miles.'

Bryce sat down on the rowing seat beside him and grabbed an oar. 'OK,' he said. 'Let's go.' He paused, glancing at Harrison beside him. 'Ready?'

The American nodded. The two oars went in together. Swiftly the little boat began to slip through the water towards the shore.

Tynan reloaded the rifle and watched their progress. He took no pleasure in the killing. The only satisfaction he felt was in his marksmanship, and that he would now be more severely tested by Harrison. While it had become clear through Crawford's behaviour and the rendezvous with the flying boat that he must be German, the downing of the plane and the elimination of Crawford and the other man had not been a political act. Tynan, like Harrison and Bryce, knew nothing of Quinn's hopes of bringing German forces into Ireland to free the North from British rule. He had destroyed Operation Osprey, eliminating the possibility of a German occupation by denying Hitler knowledge of the negotiations between Dublin and London. But he had done it unwittingly, obeying only his instinct, the challenge that he needed from Harrison. It was a monumental irony of which he was entirely ignorant.

Bryce and Harrison leapt from the boat and ran towards the car, Harrison jumping in the driving seat and inserting the keys into the ignition. He stopped. Bryce was still standing outside, by the bonnet, looking down at the front wheels.

'What's the matter?' Harrison asked.

Bryce looked up at him, then kicked the wheel angrily. 'They're flat,' he said. 'The bastard's let them down.'

Harrison rested his head on his hands in dismay. He could feel the hope draining from his body. But it didn't make sense. Why would Tynan remove all possibility of escape if he wanted the pursuit to continue? The horses! He lifted his head. Bryce was running across the turf towards the two animals, who were grazing some three or four hundred yards away. He yanked open the door of the car and ran after him. Tynan would have little chance of keeping up with them in a car, so he had sabotaged it during the night. As Harrison drew closer, catching up on Bryce, who could not move quickly, he could see that the animals had been ground-tethered and that they were still saddled, the oilskins rolled up neatly again. He stopped dead in his tracks.

Bryce joined him breathing heavily. 'What is it?'

Harrison looked back towards the boat. It was just beginning to drift slowly out into the lake. 'The gun,' he said, 'The Irishman's gun. We need it.' He turned and started to run back to the boat. Bryce screamed after him. 'No! It's no good, Roy; he'll kill you.'

The bullet ricocheted off a rock close to his feet. Harrison weaved, another hit the ground immediately in front of him. He stopped, his chest heaving, drawing in the cold air. Three more bullets thudded in a line, barring his path. He looked up to the ridge behind which Tynan was sheltering. There was a madness in Harrison's eyes, a savage intensity. He crouched ready to run, knowing he had no chance; but the ferocity of his rage blanked out any sense of risk or calculation.

Tynan knew he would have to kill him; he could see his body tensing in the hairlines of his sight, his finger tightened round the trigger, ready to fire.

The whole weight of Bryce's body crashed into Harrison, crushing him to the ground. The American struggled madly at first, but Bryce hung on, pinning him to the earth, holding him down.

'It's no good, Roy,' he screamed in his ear. 'Let's use the horses. You can't beat him this way.'

Harrison began to calm down. The madness left him.

Bryce was exhausted, sweat pouring down his face, he could not have held on to him for a moment longer. He stared down at Harrison's face. 'Let's try the horses, Roy. We can do it.'

The American shook his head in disgust. 'Shit, I almost got myself killed.' He clenched his eyes shut, composing himself. 'All right, Peter, you can climb off now.'

Bryce rolled off him and the American sprang up, helping him to his feet. They both looked up at the ridge, knowing Tynan was there, watching. They turned silently and made their way to the horses. Harrison helped Bryce to mount. He looked up at him. 'How's the leg?'

Bryce grinned. 'Fine. How's the temper?'

Harrison returned the smile and swung into the saddle. 'Getting better all the time.' He dug his heels into the horse and set off at a steady gallop.

The two horsemen quickly reached the lower slopes to the east and began to climb the last range between them and the Irish Sea.

Tynan waited until they were mere specks. Then, slinging the rifle round on to his back, he mounted his horse and followed.

Harrison pushed his animal brutally up the steep gradient of the mountain. It had been well rested and grazed, but the loose shale gave little foothold. The American dismounted and led him over the scree, Bryce following close behind. Harrison glanced up ahead of them, the ridge was appreciably closer. Soon the loose stones gave way to firmer footing and they remounted, pressing upwards as fast as they could. The last few hundred yards to the ridge evened out and Harrison galloped his animal to the top, Bryce alongside him. They reined to a halt and looked back. Tynan was already halfway up the side of the ridge, pushing towards them relentlessly, looking neither up at them nor behind, keeping his eyes firmly on the terrain in front.

They turned to see what lay ahead. Far below was a winding road half hidden by pine and scrub. More importantly, gleaming like silver silk about fifteen miles distant, but looking incredibly close, was the Irish Sea. Their first target was at last in sight. Bryce and Harrison exchanged a look, then together they spurred their horses down the incline towards the road.

Harrison glanced at his watch. It was nearly nine A.M. They had been waiting almost five minutes.

Bryce looked at him anxiously. 'We can't stay here any longer. Let's go; try to reach the coast on the horses.'

Harrison checked the road again. Still no sign of a car. He looked at the mountain behind them. Tynan had disappeared. He could be approaching the road, closing on them even now. He was about to push on when he heard something. He held up his hand. 'Wait.'

They listened. It was a car. They heard it shift noisily through the gears as it neared them from the west. It wheezed around a bend, the headlights still blazing, doing all of twenty-five miles an hour. It was a huge old Humber, at least ten years old, built like a battleship, great chromium bumpers protruding ostentatiously in front. Harrison waited until it was about fifty yards away, then spurred his horse out, blocking the oncoming car.

The vehicle's brakes jammed on, squealing, causing Harrison's mount to rear up, startled. The American controlled the animal easily and the car came to a halt with twenty feet to spare. Harrison rode to one side of the vehicle, Bryce ran to the other. There were two people inside, a man and a woman, both elderly. The driver sat frozen in his seat, his face drained of blood.

'All right, get out.' Harrison ordered.

The old man didn't move, and for one horrible moment Harrison thought he was going to have a heart attack, but his wife leaned over and touched his arm. 'It's all right, Paeder. I think we'll be doin' as the man says.'

Her husband glanced at her dazedly, then automatically he climbed stiffly out and, ignoring both Harrison and Bryce, went slowly round to the other side of the car and opened the door for his wife. He helped her from her seat and they both stood by the side of the road holding hands.

Harrison was rapidly scribbling a note to Mrs Hawley and tucking it into his horse's saddle bag.

Bryce tried to explain to the elderly couple, apologizing for having to take their car. They did not answer, their dignified silence making him feel even worse.

Harrison got the engine started and looked for Bryce. 'Come on,' he yelled angrily. 'Get your arse in here for chrissake. They'll be all right.'

Bryce glanced once more at the old couple, then jumped in the passenger seat. Harrison accelerated the ancient vehicle away as fast as he could. He looked in the rearview mirror; the couple hadn't moved.

Slowly the car gained some momentum until they were doing nearly fifty, but the speedometer wouldn't inch a millimetre above that. He concentrated on the driving, pushing the car as hard as he could. 'Keep your eyes open, Peter. Let me know if you see anything.'

Bryce looked round anxiously. 'Wouldn't we have been better going directly across country? I don't like being tied to a road.'

'No,' Harrison said shortly, 'not with him on our tails. He knows this country, I don't. On horseback we didn't have a chance – that's why he forced us to use the horses in the first place.'

The car bounced crazily over a pot-hole, swerving to the

391

side of the road. Bryce yelled a warning and Harrison straightened her out. 'Jesus Christ,' he swore vehemently, 'if we ever get out of this bloody country, first thing I'm gonna do is send them a bucket of tar.'

He swerved the old Humber to miss another one, but didn't slow down. Tynan was deadlier than any pot-hole.

He lowered the glasses and scanned the terrain in front of the car. The road twisted and turned its way down on to the green plain between the mountains and the sea. There was one place where he might make an interception if he could reach it in time. He spurred the horse ruthlessly, forcing the tired animal to gallop. He moved directly off the ridge, down to a narrow valley between the hills.

Harrison craned his head forward, trying to see the mountain. 'Any sign of him?'

Bryce looked at him anxiously. 'Keep your eyes on the road, for God's sake.'

They had almost reached the plain now. The road twisted between some hills. Bryce saw the white flash of Tynan's horse as he breasted the hill to their left, then the rifle jerking up to his shoulder. He screamed a warning to Harrison and they both ducked instinctively. A bullet smashed through the side window behind them, another thudded into the bodywork of the heavy car and suddenly they were both glad of the protection it offered.

Tynan got off one more round before the car disappeared behind the hill. Now all that lay between the flyers and the coast was the plain. He pushed the animal hard. He knew where the road might be blocked if he could reach a telephone, but telephones were not in plentiful supply. Harrison was proving his resourcefulness, but there was some way to go yet.

He saw the big house set back from the road, a long drive

leading to the front door. The telegraph poles were clearly visible and he forced his tired mount as fast as he could.

The house looked empty, the impression confirmed when no one answered his repeated bangings on the front door. He wasted no more time and broke a large window at the front, forcing an entry. He found the old-fashioned black phone and separate receiver in the hall. Quickly he was passed through to the Garda station near a road bridge that crossed the Carrock River. He identified himself and issued a string of orders, then slammed the earpiece back on to the hook and ran back to his horse.

Bryce and Harrison had seen nothing of Tynan since the shooting. There was little traffic on the road and they were making good time, always heading in an easterly direction. They had lost sight of the coast and neither of them knew exactly where they were, but as long as they stuck to this route they were bound to reach it soon.

'Do you think we've lost him?' Bryce asked.

Harrison glanced in the rearview mirror. 'Don't count on it.'

They passed an old man driving a pony and trap. He stared curiously at the shattered windows of the Humber.

Bryce could feel his leg throbbing. He slid his hand down over the bandages. They were wet: the wound had opened again. It was hardly surprising. He looked at Harrison. 'Have you thought about what we do when we get there?'

Harrison continued to stare grimly through the wind-screen. 'We steal a boat. What else?' He wasn't thinking any farther ahead than the next bend in the road. He did not expect Tynan to give them a free run to the coast. Certainly, if he were in Tynan's shoes, he knew what he'd be doing. But Harrison had made his mind up too – nothing was going to stop him. The road ran into a shallow valley alongside a river in the lee of a hill. He tensed. This would be as good a spot as any. The car rounded a bend and immediately in front of them was a narrow bridge crossing the river which snaked below it.

Harrison and Bryce saw the roadblock simultaneously. The two police cars drawn across the middle of the bridge, bonnet to bonnet, not an inch to spare on either side. Harrison pressed his foot hard down on the accelerator, pushing it right to the floor. The old Humber picked up speed. A policeman leapt from one of the cars on the bridge and raced towards the far side. Three others waved ineffectually before taking aim with their Webley revolvers.

Harrison shouted a warning to Bryce, who ducked down and braced himself for the impact, then gripped the wheel and aimed the long bonnet of the powerful car directly for the small space between the two vehicles blocking the bridge. The heavy chromium bumpers struck first, crumpling the mudguards of the police cars, then flattening into the front of the Humber as the heavy old car ploughed through the gap widening before it.

Metal shrieked and tore as the police cars were bundled like old barrels before the Humber's solid frame. They toppled backwards into the wooden stanchions of the bridge, splintering through them and falling slowly, twisting in mid air like clumsy ducks before crumpling into the river below.

The Humber continued inexorably, boring across the bridge like a tank, Bryce and Harrison hooting and cheering like maniacs. The Garda continued to fire hopelessly after the retreating vehicle, but at that range the bullets simply bounced off the solid steel structure. Soon the old car was gone, the sound of its engine throbbing into the distance.

Tynan surveyed the carnage of the bridge from the hill above the river. The road was now totally blocked by a minor traffic build-up of horses, carts, policemen and excited spectators craning their necks and peering at the two

394

crushed police cars lying in the shallow water below them. Of the Humber there was no sign and Tynan realized they had got through. He forded the river a mile or so below the bridge and headed directly for the coast at a point close to the mouth of the bay that he could see glinting between the trees to his right. His horse was moving only on instinct now and Tynan didn't push him. It would have achieved nothing; the animal was almost spent.

The odds were about even. Harrison had done remarkably well, nullifying Tynan's advantage, his knowledge of the terrain, by commandeering the car. He'd been lucky that it had proved to be such a powerful one, but there was nothing lucky in the courage he had demonstrated in forcing a passage through the roadblock.

On the flat stretches the game, sturdy animal managed a weary canter. Tynan felt no tiredness himself, though he had not slept properly for more than thirty-six hours. He was alert, his senses finely tuned, every instinct awake, knowing that soon, one way or the other, it would be decided.

The big car skidded to a halt near the long wooden jetty as Harrison jammed on the brakes. A number of yachts were moored out in the bay, their rigs jiggling and bobbing gently against the masts as the wind drifted across the water. The bay was deserted in this dead of winter, and it was a curious lonely sound, like skeletons in a cupboard knocking to come out.

He ran along the jetty looking for something suitable. He knew nothing about boats, but he was good with engines. Any reasonably-sized engined craft would get them across the seventy-odd miles of sea that separated Ireland from Wales at this point, provided they didn't run into bad weather. That was something they would have to risk.

Most of the anchored vessels were yachts. The two motor craft he'd seen were large, powerful and very locked up.

He'd almost reached the end of the jetty when he spotted it, riding at the end of a painter ten feet away. It was a small open-topped vessel with an auxiliary engine, probably used for ferrying people out to the yachts. Harrison hauled it in and leapt on to the duckboards. Swiftly he searched for the starter to the engine, found it and jerked it out. The engine coughed once, then died. He tried again and got the same negative result.

Bryce limped as quickly as he could up the jetty, favouring his injured leg. The blood was seeping down into his boot. He ignored it. All that mattered was getting the boat to start. He drew level and looked down at Harrison, who was still searching for something.

'Having trouble?'

'Can't find the choke.'

Bryce held out his hand. 'Help me down.'

Harrison grabbed his arm and assisted him into the boat. He saw the bloodstain down the side of his trousers for the first time. 'Your wound. It's re-opened.'

Bryce shook his head. 'Forget it. If we can get this thing moving I can stop the bleeding. Now look for some fuel. Try beneath the bench seats.'

Bryce leaned down and found the choke, which was partly obscured by the wooden struts bracing the hull. He fed some juice into the engine and gave the starter a good long pull. This time it coughed twice, then roared into life.

Harrison yelled with excitement, brandishing two cans of petrol he had pulled from beneath the bench seats.

'Jesus, we've made it.' He put down the cans and grabbed Bryce. They hugged and pummelled each other in a moment of supreme exultation, laughing like schoolkids as they suddenly believed for the first time that they would be able to get back.

Bryce tried to break himself clear from Harrison's bearlike hug. 'Cast off, you mad bugger, and let's be on our way before somebody stops us.'

Harrison laughed uproariously and grabbed the ropes, flinging them into the prow. Bryce fed more petrol into the engine and, using the tiller, guided the small boat through the tinkling anchored cluster of yachts towards the entrance of the bay.

The horse was foaming at the mouth, white flecks around its bridle dripping to the ground. Tynan pushed the animal up the last slope of the headland. It almost staggered as it crested the top. The cliff dropped sheer away below him into the narrow inlet that joined the bay to the Irish Sea.

He looked back to the harbour. He could see the open boat chugging slowly towards the inlet. He pulled the rifle from his back and worked the action, forcing a round into the breech. He raised the rifle to his shoulder and levelled it at Bryce. He would kill Harrison last. He brought the sights into focus, the twin hairlines crossing exactly on the Englishman's chest.

Harrison stood up and gazed back at the jetty and the shore. It was empty, no sign of Tynan, not even an irate boat owner. He grinned. 'I think we beat the bastard.'

Bryce didn't reply. He was looking past him up at the point above the inlet. Harrison turned and followed his gaze.

The horse stood mute and stationary, its head hanging down, spent, the reins trailing to the ground. Tynan sat motionless in the saddle, the rifle to his shoulder, aimed unerringly at them. There was no escape, no cover. He had them at his mercy, the way he had always intended.

Harrison said nothing. Slowly he released his pent-up breath. The elation poured from him like air from a pricked balloon. Bryce stared up at the solitary menacing figure. He looked at Harrison.

'Do we go back?'

Harrison did not turn or look away, keeping his eyes always on Tynan.

'Not me.' He spoke without expression, without bravado, a simple statement of fact.

They both knew it was hopeless. They gazed up at Tynan as the boat gradually drew level, side by side, facing him.

Harrison cleared his throat, and then, almost inaudibly, he began to sing:

'Hitler has only got one ball,'

Bryce glanced at him, then picked up the mocking parody.

'Rommel has two, but very small,'

Then loudly in unison they sang:

'Himmler has something similar,

But poor old Goebbels has no balls at all . . .'

It was defiant, but it was something else too. It stated something, that they were soldiers, just as he was. That it might not be his war, but it was theirs. They repeated the familiar words, the song gathering momentum, swelling, resounding in the space between the cliff walls hurling their defiance.

The challenge thundered in Tynan's ears like a trumpet blast. His finger tightened slowly round the trigger, squeezing it gently. The bullet exploded from the barrel at a velocity of 2,440 feet per second and slammed between the tiny gap separating the two men, thudding into the boat's gunnel behind them, the crack of the single shot reverberating from the cliff walls.

Bryce and Harrison glanced at each other, then at the splintered wood behind them. They knew that Tynan had spared them, that he too had made his point. They continued to sing in unison, looking up at him:

'Hitler has only got one ball . . .'

The silly, sad song grew in intensity as the boat chugged quietly through the inlet and out to the sea beyond, their voices slowly fading as the distance grew.

Tynan lowered the rifle to his side and watched them go. He hadn't needed the killing and he didn't feel as though he had lost.

# Notes

# NOTES

Eire was neutral during the whole of World War II, but was at various times extremely vulnerable to invasion from either the Allies or Germany.

The Irish Prime Minister, the Taoiseach, Eamon De Valera, felt it necessary, therefore, to demonstrate his complete impartiality by interning all combative belligerents, from either side, who fell into his hands. Thus was set up the internment camp on K Lines, close to the Irish Military Barracks on The Curragh.

Luftwaffe and RAF were interned in the same camp, separated only by barbed wire and a corrugated-iron fence. During the period between the summer of 1940 and the latter half of 1943 there were approximately 30–40 Allies interned and a somewhat higher number of German aviators. Nowhere else in World War II did the two belligerents find themselves prisoners of war together.

There was a very civilized parole system that allowed the prisoners to visit local areas during the day, provided they came back at night. They signed a Parole Book to this effect, and a code of honour prevented them from trying to escape while on parole. However, there was one notable exception, an American. He broke parole, escaped and was returned by the British. That much is true. It is also true that a number of aircraft crashed on Mount Brandon in County Kerry. On 27 July 1943, a BOAC civilian flying boat, en route from South Africa, took off from Lisbon in Portugal at 9.30 P.M. local time. On board were eighteen passengers and crew of seven. When it arrived over Foynes, about fifty-five miles north of Mount Brandon as the crow flies, it began a wide circular holding pattern, as it could not land in the dark. Shortly afterwards, in the early hours of the morning, it crashed on the mountain and, according to the *Kerryman* of Saturday, 31 July 1943, ten were killed, nine passengers and one member of the crew. Fifteen survivors were taken to St Catherine's Hospital in Tralee. Subsequently six of the bodies were taken north to the border and handed over to the British authorities. Four were buried together in a local churchyard. The headstone simply lists their names. Later, when the war was over, two smaller headstones were erected on either side of the main tombstone giving more details of two of those buried there. It became clear that they were both members of the British armed forces, a Colonel and an RAF Group Captain.

The main tombstone is wrong in two respects. The plane was not a Sunderland. It was a civilian Sandringham, flying from one neutral country to another, and the date of the crash was 28 July, not the 29th. Some months later, one of the bodies was exhumed and buried in Cork as he was a Jew. The name, however, has not been removed from the stone.

Twenty-five days after the Sandringham crashed, on 22 August 1943, little more than a mile from the original crash site, an RAF Sunderland came down on the mountain at night. There were at least two survivors. The RAF Sunderland was the wartime version of the civilian Sandringham. It was an amazing coincidence.

Almost four months later to the day, on 20 December 1943, an RAF Wellington crashed, again at night, within two hundred yards of the Sunderland. All members of the crew were killed. And there is one further coincidence. Three years earlier, on 20 August 1940, a Luftwaffe four-engined Condor of KG 40, out of Bordeaux, crash-landed approximately a mile and a half away on the slopes of the mountain. No one was killed, and one of the officers subsequently became the Luftwaffe Commandant of the German section of the Internment Camp on The Curragh. I think it is worth pointing out that no planes had crashed on Mount Brandon before World War II, or have done since.

The story I have woven into this factual background is, of

course, fiction, and no similarity to anyone living or dead exists, or is intended.

I first heard about the internment camp when I was attending the Cork Film Festival in the summer of 1979. The festival is helped enormously by generous volunteer work, and one of the volunteer drivers asked me about my first book, *KG 200*. I told him something of the background to the story and he remarked that there had been something similar to that in Ireland during the 'Emergency'.

I asked, 'The Emergency?'

'Yes,' he said, 'World War II!'

He was right. That was the official classification of World War II in neutral Eire during the period 1939 to 1945.

Intrigued, I began my research at once, and it has continued on and off for more than two years. Initially I found it difficult to get to the roots of the truth, but then Gay Byrne was kind enough to invite me on to his 'Late, Late, Show', and before I had parted company with the television cameras there were dozens of phone calls responding to my appeal for information. The floodgates opened. The next four months were a haze of phone calls, personal interviews, letters, and communication in general as I religiously answered every letter and call, following up every lead. By the time that initial phase was over I had enough material for several books. It took my wife, Carole, and myself more than a month to cross-index and file. I was surrounded by an abundance of information.

Clearly a book cannot have a hundred leading characters, a hundred different stories. As with all my novels thus far, I now had to free my imagination from the weight of this material and weave from it a good story that was honest, authentic, giving the reader a handful of believable characters and events.

For those whose interest goes deeper, there follows some of the documentation and information that I gathered in the course of my research. I have spoken to many people who are involved in the actual events, depicted fictionally, in this book. Some held responsible positions, some were merely there. All have been extremely helpful, a few were fascinating. I could have listened for hours, I sometimes did. I have not revealed their confidences, nor in these notes have I speculated upon the events they were involved in. I think truth needs no embellishment here.

*Report in the* Völkischer Beobachter, *11 June 1939*

'The events of the last night, the most extensive to date of the Irish attacks on English soil, suggest an operation which was intended to be a demonstration. It is the obvious presumption that this operation was the IRA's answer to the arrest of Sean Russell, whom the English press describe as the leader of the IRA, which has not been proved. As the London newspapers have reported, under banner headlines, Russell, who was on a lecture tour of the USA, was taken into custody in Detroit before the arrival of King George VI and Queen Elizabeth, and this was allegedly done at the request of Scotland Yard. This incident immediately aroused enormous indignation among the ten million Irish–Americans. This culminated in a protest by the seventy-six American members of Congress who were of Irish descent, who demanded an explanation from Roosevelt about the "Russell Case", failing which they would not participate in the Congress reception for the King of England.'

Information from Enno Stephan, *Geheimauftrag Irland* (Gerhard Stalling Verlag, Hamburg, 1961, p 34)

From:
*German Consul–General*, Genoa.
*Despatched at 2.50 P.M. on 24 January 1940*
To:
*Foreign Office*, Berlin.
*Received at 4.55 P.M., same day*

'John McCarthy, the ambassador of the Irish movement who has arrived from New York today, asked whether the German Government would be prepared to provide transport to Ireland for Sean Russell, Chief of Staff of the IRA, who unknown to the American Government is still in New York. If this is possible he will make his way here by a new direct line from New York under an alias and be identified by McCarthy, who leaves by sea today for Naples. Would be grateful for a decision on his return from there on Saturday, 27 January.'

                                   (signed) Schmid

*Entry in German War Diary of Abwehr 11, 30 January 1940*

'The Director [Canaris] approves in principle that the request of the Irish leader Russell, addressed to Abwehr 11 via the Consul–General, Genoa, for establishing liaison should be investigated.'

*Entry in German War Diary of Abwehr 11, 3 May 1940*

'Sean Russell, former adjutant to the IRA leader arrived in Berlin from Genoa this evening in company with interpreter Fromme of Referat 1, West. At Foreign Office request, this office assuming responsibility for looking after and accommodating him in a weekend cottage near Berlin as a preliminary to the possibility of his employment in the political field. Dr Veesenmayer, representative of the Foreign Office in this matter, requested interpreter Fromme be placed at his disposal, both to ensure collaboration with Abwehr 11 and in the interests of Russell. Abwehr 11 agreed to this proposal.'

Information from Enno Stephan, op. cit.

*Urgent, Top Secret: Telegram No 190*
From:
*Under Secretary of State Woermann, Foreign Office,* Berlin.
*15 June 1940*
To:
*German Ambassador,* Dublin.

'The Irish Government must be clear that the war between Germany and England is entering a decisive phase. Germany is conscious that in the war, which has been forced upon it by England, measures are necessary which are harmful to Irish interests. For this reason the German Government regards it as important once more to inform the Irish Government that the war is against England alone. The German Government believes that Ireland, for whom England is the historical enemy, appreciates that the outcome of the war will be of decisive importance for the Irish people and for the final attainment of Irish national aspirations. In these circumstances the German Government believes that it will be able to count on the Irish Government's most sympathetic understanding despite Irish neutrality even if Ireland should be affected in some degree by German measures.'

Information from: Enno Stephan, op. cit.

'After the indefinite postponement of Operation Sea Lion, the German plan to invade England in the fall of 1940, Hitler thought for a while that some sort of foothold in Ireland might help German raiders trying to hit the northwest ports of Britain. If Ireland could be occupied, it might also be possible to cut England's Atlantic lifeline and shorten the war.'

Information from Peter Fleming, *Invasion 1940* (Hart Davis, 1957)

*Top Secret: Telegram No 422*
From:
*Foreign Minister von Ribbentrop,* Berlin.
*5 December 1940*
To:
*German Ambassador,* Dublin.

'At the next opportunity of conversation with De Valera I would like you again to discuss the possibility of British intervention in Ireland.'

In this telegram Ribbentrop suggested that Hempel could proceed somewhat on the following lines: He could say that he had a message from Germany that the German Government would naturally be interested in strengthening Ireland's power of resistance in the event of a British attack. At the conclusion of the French campaign large quantities of British weapons had fallen into Germany's hands. He, Hempel, regarded it as not improbable that his Government would be ready and able to place at the Irish Government's disposal without charge considerable quantities of weapons of the same type and calibre as were in use in the Irish Army.

Details about available arms would be sent to him as soon as De Valera indicated any interest in the matter. Naturally special steps would have to be taken to conceal delivery of arms. Cargo shops could head out from France into the Atlantic and then appear from the west, camouflaged as transports from the USA, and proceed to Ireland under the Irish flag on the normal shipping routes. Details would be discussed with the Irish Government as convenient. He could, however, discuss the matter now if De Valera showed any interest.

Ribbentrop ended his message on an optimistic note: 'Looked at technically, we have no doubt that the shipment of arms could be carried out in a way which would not compromise Ireland's neutrality.'

*Urgent and Top Secret Telegram No 825*, from Dublin, dated 17 December, contained Ireland's decision. It was negative. Information from: Enno Stephan, op. cit.

From:
*Winston Churchill, 10 Downing Street, Whitehall*
*8 December 1940*
To:
*The President of the USA*

'My dear Mr President,
   ... 'We should also need the good offices of the United States and the whole influence of its Government, continually exerted, to procure for Great Britain the necessary facilities upon the southern and western shores of Eire for our flotillas, and, still more important, for our aircraft, working to the westward into the Atlantic. If it were proclaimed an American interest that the resistance of Great Britain should be prolonged and the Atlantic route kept open for the important

armaments now being prepared for Great Britain in North America, the Irish in the United States might be willing to point out to the Government of Eire the dangers which its present policy is creating for the United States itself.

'His Majesty's Government would of course take the most effective measures beforehand to protect Ireland if Irish action exposed it to German attack. It is not possible for us to compel the people of Northern Ireland against their will to leave the United Kingdom and join Southern Ireland. But I do not doubt that if the Government of Eire would show its solidarity with the democracies of the English-speaking world at this crisis a Council for Defence of all Ireland could be set up out of which the unity of the island would probably in some form or other emerge after the war.'

From Winston Churchill, *The Second World War*, vol II (Cassell, 1949).

Both the following pieces of information are from *The Shamrock and the Swastika* by Carolle J. Carter (Pacific Books, Palo Alto, California, 1977). First piece is from Notes, p 261. Second piece is on p 166. The original sources are printed below.

'Actually, General O'Duffy [see below] had already put Goertz (*Abwehr* agent) in touch with MacNeill. One of the few Army officers who supported Collins and Griffith, MacNeill joined Fianna Fail before De Valera's accession to power. He was one of three or four generals who worried Irish Intelligence because they were unpredictable, emotional and strongly anti-British. Very bright in some ways, MacNeill lacked judgement and common sense, and Intelligence warned him to be more discreet.

'He held the second highest position in the army and might have received top command if Ireland had entered the war. As it was, from 1941 to 1946 he commanded the 2nd (Spearhead) Division, whose chief duty was to watch the British in the North and to resist them if they invaded the South. Until such an event occurred, he was ordered not to spy upon them or to interfere with them in any way.

'In December 1940, MacNeill mentioned to Thomsen (German Legation, Dublin) that he regretted that Germany had no military attaché in Dublin, which would permit him to contact the Legation in a more circumspect fashion, although he realized that appointing one during wartime would raise problems.'

Information from: Germany, Auswärtiges Amt. Records of the German Foreign Office received by the Department of State, Washington DC (microfilm): T-120, Reel 89, frames 100464, 100647, Documents of 26 December 1940, 19 February 1941; Oliver Macdonagh, *Ireland* (Prentice Hall, 1968); *Irish Times*, 3 April 1953: confidential government source.

'General O'Duffy (former IRA member, former Chief Commissioner of the Civic Guard, leader of the National Guard) sat in on some of MacNeill's talks with Thomsen (German Legation). They discussed Irish military plans and the possibility of German aid to Ireland.[1] According to MacNeill, the Irish Army expected the British to attack in spring 1941, in one of three possible ways.

1. Occupation of Lough Swilly, defence against which was useless;
2. Occupation of Lough Swilly and of airports, especially Ryanna (Shannon) and Foynes, simultaneously with an attack from the sea on Shannon–Munding;
3. Both (1) and (2) above, plus Cork, Wexford, Dublin and eventually Berehaven. MacNeill wanted to know whether the Germans could drop confiscated English anti-tank cannon and Vickers heavy machine guns by parachute, and if so, when

---

[1] Information from: Germany, AA, Reel 402, from 307547, Document of 7 December 1940.

they could be ready. Only as a second choice did he suggest sea delivery, because no Irish ships would be available.'[1]

In February 1941 Wendell Willkie (who had opposed Roosevelt in the Presidential Election of November 1940) visited Dublin. He had what he described as a brutally frank discussion with De Valera. He told the *Taoiseach* that the Irish were making fools of themselves by thinking that they could remain neutral. Hitler would attack them whenever it suited him, he contended, so Ireland might as well join the British at once and give them the ports.

Information from T. Ryle Dwyer, *Irish Neutrality and the USA* (Gill & Macmillan, Dublin, 1977).

'At the Totenkopf (Death's Head) Barracks in Berlin-Oranienburg a rival kind of troop to the Brandenburg was established. It was designated as No. 1 SS Special Service Troop. It comprised about a hundred volunteers, mainly experienced men from the ranks of very varied SS troop sections. My [Helmut Clissmann's] job was to test the suitability of these men and to give them instruction based on local knowledge about Anglo-Saxon manners and habits. In order to preserve secrecy about the Irish plan, a rumour was planted among this troop that they had been selected for a raid on the Suez Canal.

'The SS volunteers were given elaborate training in captured English weapons and in sabotage . . .'
Quote from Helmut Clissmann in Enno Stephan, op. cit.

---

[1]  Ibid. Reel 89, frame 100458, Document of 6 December 1940.

From:
*John D. Kearney, High Commissioner for Canada in Ireland*,
Dublin.
*24 February 1942*
To:
*The Secretary of State for External Affairs*, Ottawa.
*Confidential No 39*

'Sir,

'I have the honour to now report to you with regard to the recent attempted break by the Allies interned at The Curragh Camp in Ireland.

'I am leaving for London tomorrow and instead of mailing this depatch from Dublin, I am taking advantage of my presence there to have it sent to you through the facilities afforded by the High Commissioner in London ... I did not like to mention in my telegram that our internees have been instructed by the Air Ministry to do all they can to escape, but, without using violence, and without breaking parole.

'One thing which gave us here a good deal of concern in connection with the recent attempted break was the fact that our boys apparently while out on parole profited by the occasion to procure and smuggle into the camp, material which could aid them in their escape. When the internees are out on parole they are under obligation not only to make no attempt to escape, but also not to do anything to further a contemplated escape ...

'If our men escape by dishonouring their parole they are immediately sent back by the Royal Air Force authorities to The Curragh. You will notice by the enclosed list that there is an American interned at The Curragh. Recently, after signing the parole-book he asked for permission to return for his

412

gloves. He later reported to the Royal Air Force Office in Belfast. His contention was that by returning for his gloves he had been relieved of his parole undertaking; but because of protests from the Irish authorities, he was sent back to The Curragh Camp . . .

'The boys did not report the attempted break until their parole was cancelled, which was on Thursday, February 12th . . .

'I was glad to be able to cable you today that the Irish authorities are restoring parole, at least on a limited scale . . .

'I should like to add a word about the German internees at the Camp. They are in a camp just alongside the Allies and it does not seem to be as heavily wired. Of course the inducement for them to escape is not as great as for our boys because it is much more difficult for them to return to their units . . . The enemy internees have, I understand, organized educational classes and have a self-imposed daily routine. The only escape, or attempted escape, by the Germans insofar as I have been able to ascertain, is one that occurred a few days ago when nine of them were being let out on parole. Through hurrying the parole officer, or by some other ruse, only eight of them signed the parole register. The ninth German is still at large. On the whole, the Germans seem to have settled down for the duration of the war.

'Our boys, rightly or wrongly, feel that if they organize classes it might be interpreted as acquiescence of their lot, whereas they want it known that they are doing all they can to rejoin their units. . . .'

*From a document made available from a private source*

*US Military Assessment of the Republic of Ireland, March 1942 by Lieutenant-Colonel John Reynold*

Lt.-Col. Reynold 'formed a very favourable impression of the character and ability of the officers and the excellent discipline and quality of the troops.' He was convinced the Irish Army would fight bravely and its high command would welcome Allied assistance if Eire faced a German invasion. But they lacked 'all equipment necessary to an efficient modern fighting force' and 'bravely as it would resist, the Eire Army would be brushed aside by the sort of invasion that fell on Crete'.

'The conquest of Ireland would involve such rich rewards that the Germans might well gamble on their audacity and ingenuity to overcome the very real hazards of the venture,' the report concluded.

The American military officer who drafted the report had made a thorough study of the State and its people, as well as the army and the LDF ('very raw' and 'poorly equipped') and he found a situation bordering on disaffection. 'Under such conditions the ranks of the disaffected will swell and become receptive to the sort of propaganda spread by German agents. This fact bears on the strength of a defence force which may encounter *attack* and *obstruction* from the *Irish* as well as the Germans.'

The model was Crete. The previous May, 18,000 battle-hardened German troops avoided the British Navy by landing from the air and in a week overwhelmed the island's 36,000 defenders. Would a similar battle plan succeed in Ireland?

The German forces were then deep in Russia, but Grey (American Ambassador to Ireland) thought Hitler might seize Ireland to force British surrender. De Valera partly agreed.

From 'Neutrality Under Fire' by Sean Cronin, a four-part series in the *Irish Times*, beginning Monday, 30 August 1982. Sean Cronin is a Washington Correspondent.

From:
*John Kearney, High Commissioner for Canada in Ireland,* Dublin.
*31 August 1942*
To:
*The Secretary of State for External Affairs,* Ottawa.
*Confidential No 224*

'Sir,
  'I have the honour to refer to my telegrams No 58 of August 21st and No 65 of August 31st.
  'The following are the details in connection with the successful escape from The Curragh Internment Camp, Co. Kildare . . .
  'On the evening of August 17th, a national of the United States of America, attached to the Royal Air Force, and . . . of the Royal Canadian Air Force, were going out to a party. The American, who had his bicycle with him, reached the first gate. He stooped down to adjust his bicycle clips and said – "All right, you go ahead, I won't be a minute." (Only one officer is allowed to go through this gate at a time.) No sooner had the sentry opened the gate for . . . than . . . threw his bicycle between the gate and the gate-post, thus preventing the gate from closing, and they both then overpowered the sentry. Immediately a party of about thirteen or fourteen internees rushed through the first gate and with two iron bars, which they had dismantled from the shower-bath, lifted the second gate clear off its hinges. This unexpected manoeuvre took the sentry, who was posted at the second gate, by surprise, and the gate fell on top of him. The internees had

then a third and outer ring of barbed wire to clear. It was not very high, and nine of them managed to scramble over it with no worse damages than torn clothes and a few slight scratches. The others attempting to escape were captured before they could surmount the third ring of barbed wire, but nine, four of whom were Canadians, managed to escape . . .'

*From a document made available from a private source*

Veesenmayer accompanied Helmut Clissman to Spain twice. He was given additional tasks on these trips so that no one would suspect his real purpose. From what Kerney (Irish Ambassador to Spain) had said, he had concluded that De Valera would strongly resist any attempt at invasion and that he would ask Germany for help if the invader were England or the United States. In the event of invasion, he said, Kerney felt that De Valera and the IRA would automatically close ranks. Kerney said he did not believe De Valera would go to extremes to maintain his policy of neutrality. Rather, he would declare war on the Allies the moment the chance of liberating Northern Ireland appeared. If the Germans chose to assist him, they would first try to deny any interest in Ireland and declare that their troops would stay only long enough to wage the collective struggle against the Allies.

Information from Carolle J. Carter, op. cit.